THE HYBRID CURE

A YOUNG ADULT DYSTOPIAN NOVEL

THE KASEATH CHRONICLES
BOOK 1

JACKIE MCCARTHY

CURLING TEA PRESS

CHAPTER 1

TODAY WAS race day and by the odds in Pocks' playbook, my sister and I were on the losing end.

The peak of Trash Mountain spread way below me, into a vast valley of flattened, picked-over garbage: jagged pieces of broken plastic in faded browns and blues, wads of rusted metal, general sludge and rotting food.

The evening sun, made golden by the smog of burning hearths over the shacks, hung low above the horizon. My sunburnt skin itched, especially in that small patch on my upper right arm, between the interlocking orange scales that I tried so hard to hide. Pulling the sleeve of my t-shirt to cover them, I shielded my eyes—flecked with the same orange as my scales—against the sunlight.

On both my flanks, rubbish towered at least twice my height. Vertigo sensations spun the ground. The stacks teetered up here. The wind brushed against my cheeks, bringing a stench of decay. Rubbish spires threatened to collapse at any moment and they might take me with them. I planted my feet into the packed trash beneath me.

I motioned to my teammate—my sister Imogen, pasty and frail at eight years old, like an elderly lady being sucked inside her very bones. She touched the dirty scarf wrapped around her nose and mouth, stained with the deep blue sweat of the plague, thick as sap, pushing painfully from her pores when she exerted herself.

"Hey, Limpet," I said.

"Are you sure we're ready for this?" she asked.

"What have we got to lose?"

She returned a pained glance with our mother's brown eyes —not flecked with luminous orange, as mine were.

The self-proclaimed king of the kids, Shifty Pocks, stood on a mound with the other Northies kids. His long leather coat was pocked with bullet holes from the guy who'd worn it previously. His cheeks were rutted with deep wrinkles, even though he was in his thirties. His greasy hair was pulled into a ponytail around the shaved sides and base of his skull.

Pocks didn't just rule the kids, he oversaw the entire population of Northies, along with his band of heavies. Pocks controlled the rations, the black market, and wasn't shy of underhand tactics to keep us in check.

"Welcome, you Northies rats, to London's tenth annual Mech Car Championships!" Pocks boomed. "Both teams step forward."

Imogen and I revealed our position to Pocks and the spectating kids below. The kids shouted and jeered; the gist being Imogen and I were toast. On the far side of the gully, our opponents—a mean boy and a scraggly girl—stepped into view.

Pocks held the mech car aloft, turning the small robotic car so we could see. It was the length of my forearm, its wheels the size of my hands. If it had been less beaten up, its metal would have caught the sun.

"The first team to hit the button here wins." He smacked the roof of the car with the flat of his hand. The car lit up like a disco ball.

Kids cheered, their eyes greedy at the thought of the prize.

"The winner today moves onto the next round. They'll compete for the best prize—one shiny Tin! Which is more bling than any of you have seen in your sorry, trashy lives."

His audience drew in closer, paying attention. This was the good bit.

It was a slim possibility in a game we'd never won. If we made the last round, we'd win something impossibly valuable— a single Tin, a piece of gold film, shiny and life-changing. That Tin could set our family up on the black market for months, keeping us in meat or fresh vegetables or whatever you wanted. You could buy hard-to-come-by items on the black market.

Rumour had it, you could buy a cure for the plague, if you had enough Tins. Now that would be something. I glanced at Imogen, who leaned against her wall of junk, her gaze at the ground. I caught her eye and nodded encouragement. She straightened and gave me a thumbs up.

"Play fair, play dirty, I don't care," Pocks continued. "The team that wins the final gets the ultimate prize. So, here goes everything!"

Pocks placed the car onto the ground, and the rubber wheels settled into the sludge. He stepped back, producing a remote from the pocket of his long coat, extending the collapsible metal aerial.

Pocks lifted his free arm up high above his head, then let it drop.

The kids squealed and jostled for elbow space as the car sped off, flinging mud from its wheels as it disappeared behind a trash spire to my right.

I waited, senses alert, concentrating on the mech car's tinny whine. I cocked my ear to the valley below, turning the ball in my hands, tossing it to test the weight. It was a small wad of rubber bands twisted together to make an uneven, erratic ball.

Ready to launch below. My tactic was to hit the car's roof with the balls from our high position. We had better visibility, and Imogen wasn't up for chasing the car.

Imogen stood behind me, on the other side of a trash spire. She tugged at the scarf so it didn't ride so far up her nose, obscuring her vision. I flicked my head and pointed to the top of one of our opponents' greasy heads, visible below the next rise of rubbish. The girl was younger than me but stronger and known for her dirty tactics.

"Cover her," I mouthed, but Imogen frowned. I was a fair shot, but my sister sucked at this game. We never cleared the first round.

Imogen heaved for breath, her thin body rocking as she stepped out into the open, doubling over. That asthmatic gasp of the plague. Her eyes were full of fear, wondering if she'd draw breath again.

I faltered and waited for her to recover. I almost jogged to her, giving up my position. But it was the best position, the high ground. Always go to the high ground.

She motioned she was okay, and I turned my attention back to the game.

The boy opponent was the fastest, scooting behind an ageing trash mound.

Just then, the girl opponent ran out on the path, trailing the robotic mech car that raced away from us, its wheels kicking up and jolting over the rough surface. It bounced along, just out of her reach.

A few kids booed as the wily boy slipped into a fresh position. The other team presented stronger competition for the next round. I reminded myself that the game was still young; they hadn't won yet.

I tossed my rubber ball in my hand, testing its weight,

fingers closing over the twist of each band. Squinting in concentration, I raised my arm.

And then I let the ball fly.

It hurtled towards the car, arced downwards, then the uneven weight pulled it to the side.

The rubber grazed the rear wheel of the mech car, then skittered away.

"Yes!" I shouted, jumping up, giving away my position.

I ducked as half a shoe whizzed over my head. I gave the evil eye to the girl, who grinned from each side of her grubby face, sweat frizzing her greasy hair.

"Dirty tactics!" I yelled.

"The wheels don't count," she replied, ducking as I feigned throwing the ball at her noggin.

The car struggled to regain traction. Its wheels spun underneath it, caught on a soft piece of plastic wedged deep into the ground, and sped off away from us, shooting along the path of twisted rubbish.

"Crap!" I swore, motioning to Imogen.

She launched her own rubber band ball, but she was a lousy throw, and her ball wasn't as aerodynamic as mine. It pulled to the left, where the bands bulged. The ball dribbled down the mountain, nestling a few metres away. I ducked out of my hiding place, grabbed the ball, and crouched. Another ball skimmed my shoulder, bouncing on the rubble wall, falling at my feet.

Two fresh rounds of ammunition!

The onlooking kids were ecstatic—this was a serious upset. The crowd shifted to our side and hope propelled me into another gully. I could see better from here.

The mech car flipped across a chunk of metal, got air, and landed in a rut. It stuck in the hole, its back wheels spinning in the air.

This was my chance.

I popped up over the lip of the debris and threw the ball. It missed, bouncing into the bowels of Trash Mountain, to be scavenged another day.

Our opponents had lost sight of the mech car. This was our chance to win the game.

"Come on, Ofelia!" Imogen yelled, but stopped when a wheezing fit overtook her. I was torn between helping her and the game.

She doubled over, and for a moment, my concentration lagged. A shadow crossed my face. I dove in front of Imogen before the missile hit her—a quarter of a tennis ball, ripped apart by a dog's teeth. The soft, frayed insides smacked my cheek and dropped like a dead thing to my feet. Stunned, I rolled to crouching and pressed flat against the opposite wall of debris, out of harm's way.

I'd take a bullet for my sister any day.

Imogen caught her breath and waved to the car.

I stood up, ducking and weaving as the girl threw things at my head; a crushed can, a bucket missing its bottom, and a rotting apple core. Rancid apple juice landed in my open mouth. I retched, swallowing trash droplets.

I wiped the smelly splashes on the sleeve of my t-shirt. Raised my arm behind me. Flung the rubber ball into the air with everything I had. Way, way over to where the car sat, its wheels spinning in the hole.

The ball arced up, straight through the flight path of passing seagulls. They cawed and flew away.

Then the ball plummeted.

It landed plumb on top of the car! The entire roof lit up as the lights flashed red on the display.

"Knocked for six!" I yelled, leaping from my hiding place and pumping my fist in the air.

I couldn't believe it. Game finished. We'd won.

The girl and Imogen jumped up. I couldn't resist hurling the rotting apple core her way, and there was a satisfying wet sound as it smacked the rear of her neck.

"Game over!" she protested, a sore loser. "You can't do that!"

"Sorry," I said, trying not to be too smug.

My sister and I navigated the slopes to the pathway below, avoiding an electronic motherboard, a couch cushion with the stuffing spewing out of a slit and an ancient electric heater. I draped my arm over her shoulders.

On the way, I pocketed two of the rubber balls that we'd made. I searched for the third, but my attention returned to Pocks, who was uncharacteristically jovial.

"I didn't think you two had it in you!" he said, clapping Imogen on the shoulder roughly, as if greeting a man his size. Imogen's eyes widened in shock. I stepped in front to deflect attention.

Hang on, Limpet, I've got you.

The boy ran towards us, holding onto the mech car.

Pocks held out his hand and said, "Pay up, my friend."

The boy placed the car into Pocks' outstretched hand. The sides of Pocks' mouth twitched. He lifted the car high, the spectating kids ecstatic, thinking they had a better chance to knock Imogen and me out than our opponents.

Pocks—always theatrical—reached into the chassis of the car and pulled out a small, smooth green rubber ball. Unlike the ones I had made with the ancient stretched rubber bands twisted together, this ball was smooth, spherical and aerodynamic. We'd have every advantage in the next round. I've got to admit, my heart was pumping as if I had sprinted all the way home.

Pocks presented the ball to me.

I took it gracefully, with a bow and everything. The girl winced, and the boy looked like I'd run over his pet dog. I lifted my fist in the air, as Pocks had done—and my arms poked out further from my t-shirt than usual. The hole in my shirt sleeve exposed a small glimpse of the rash of scales on my bicep. The orange-brown patch of interlocking scales faded into normal skin further towards my elbow. I rarely flashed my rash around, or brought attention to the fact that I was a freak.

Pocks handed me the ball with a smirk, and a flicker passed over his face. Had he noticed my rash? Did it gross him out?

No, that wasn't it. I pulled on my sleeve, pocketing our winnings. Pocks' grin disappeared, and in its place was what— surprise? No, he could have just won the mech car game himself, by his expression.

"We have an upset!" Pocks boomed out, and everyone hushed. "A brand-new team won the first round. Give it up for plague girl and lizard freak!"

What the actual heck?

What did he call us? Heat rose towards my neck, my knees trembled. I clasped my hands to stop them from shaking.

The kids laughed like it was the funniest thing they'd ever heard.

We'd never live that down. We just wanted to fit in, like everyone else. Nobody respects the freak show sisters.

Angry red crept up from my pinkish cheeks into my fore-head as Pocks scrutinised me. I forced an expression of disdain, as if I didn't care. But it was humiliating. Poor Imogen—she'd live with *that* for the rest of her life.

Imogen's gaze fell to the ground, her lip trembling under-neath the scarf. My angry flush grew.

The other kids jeered that they'd crush us in the next game. But they kept a safe distance from plague girl and lizard freak.

"To the winners!" Pocks yelled, holding my fist in the air. Our opponent reached out to touch the ball, but I was careful to keep a firm grip. She eyed my prize like it was a jackpot of Tins. Which I guess it could be. The first step towards the first Tin.

Imogen's eyes shone in the sunlight, her forehead prickling with the dark blue sweat, the colour of a deep ocean in that documentary I'd watched at school. Her forehead flushed with humiliation, along with the fever.

I waited for Pocks, who held that weird expression. He gripped me so hard, white indents formed where his fingers dug. He let go of my fist and inclined his chin, dismissing us.

"C'mon, Imogen," I said, rubbing at the part where Pocks had my fist. He was always so rough, and his sudden interest had me worried.

I grabbed my goody bag of scavenged trash, which I'd stashed to one side. It only held a single rusting can top—the only thing I'd been able to scavenge before the game—but the bag was strong hessian, and we'd need it again tomorrow.

"We let you win," the boy jeered, holding up a fistful of coins. "Who is stupid enough to bet on you two?"

"We're that stupid," said our friend, Mouse Run, a runty, tough girl of twelve, whose fuzzy, matted dreadlocks resembled a hat. She held her own fistful of black-market coins.

"Yeah, they were a sure thing," our other friend, Aze, said. She was lithe, two years older than Mouse Run, with white teeth flashing in a midnight grin. She insisted on wearing a bright red eye patch, even though she had two perfectly working eyes.

They were my best friends. We'd do anything for each other.

Had the other team let us win? Did we have a chance for the final prize?

At least we'd made Aze and Mousie happy, as they weighed the coins in their hands.

"Let's go home," I said, and Imogen, Mousie and Aze followed me up the winding ridges of Trash Mountain, until we hit the middle path that swung to ground level. To the level of the shacks.

"We'll come with you," Mouse Run said.

"Make sure you get home safe," Aze said, eying Pocks, who noted our every move.

"You mean you'll jump us first," I said, grinning.

"I can take you home," Pocks said, sidling up beside me. His shadow passed over my sun-warmed skin, and I rubbed at the rash on my arm beneath my t-shirt.

"That's okay, we can manage." I forced the alarm from my voice.

"We haven't been introduced," Pocks said, waving us ahead.

I did not enjoy this one bit. Until this point, Pocks ignored me and Imogen, which was preferable. What did he want now?

"I'm Ofelia," I mumbled.

"And who's this?"

"My sister," I said, meeting his gaze.

"You don't look too flash, little sister," Pocks said, but the corners of his mouth curled up. He thought it was funny.

"We're fine, thank you," I said, grabbing Imogen's hand and pulling us away.

"Suit yourself," Pocks shouted after us, stroking his greasy ponytail. I glanced over my shoulder as Pocks flicked his head at a raggedy kid, his informant. Her eyes zeroed in on me.

We'd have to lose her before we got home.

CHAPTER 2

THE STORM HAD PASSED through earlier in the day—hot, wet and angry, making the roads slippery. Rutted lanes wove through a metal maze of tin shacks. The shacks were single storey, in disrepair, the metal sheets jagged and discoloured. Inside each one, a family slept on the floor, nudging the hearth.

Two men patched a leaking shack roof, rearranging overlapping metal sheets. The uneven road steamed in the heat. Imogen and I split up from Mousie and Aze. We navigated through the familiar streets, a reflection in the wet metal sheets following us.

Pocks' little informer, KitKat.

We had to lose her.

An old lady, wrapped in a threadbare shawl, pushed a wobbly cart filled with dented vegetables. I vaulted out of the cart's path as the hardened wooden wheel crunched into the mud, clipping my toes. We passed two naked toddlers fighting over a piece of wood they'd found in a ditch. One man missing a leg swung by on a padded crutch.

Imogen and I slipped into a throng of workers returning from their day up the hill. Pocks took the workers' handmade goods and organic food and sold it to the swanky suburbs. The swanky folk weren't privy to the filthy brown river sludge that watered them.

My nose crinkled at the stench of unwashed humans and metallic blood from the nearby butcher. KitKat's head bobbed into view between the crowd's shoulders. I hauled on Imogen's arm, but she struggled to keep pace.

"Why are you tugging? I'm tired!" she said, stopping on the road.

"It's one of Pocks' rats," I whispered.

Imogen caught sight of KitKat and stopped resisting. We dodged through the maze, feigning right but going left. Stopped next to the black market meat stall, its ruddy-pink wares hanging on a hook, an emaciated dog licking at a pool of blood at our feet.

KitKat passed, eyes darting every which way. We peeked out from behind the sinewy flesh of a skinned rabbit.

"We lost her." I nudged Imogen into the road.

"Let's go home," she said.

Other Northies residents avoided us, because of Imogen's stained face scarf. They averted their gaze, as if that rendered them immune to her sickness. The beaded sweat exited her pores like dark-veined, shimmering blue blood. The sweat stained her face scarf the deep cyan of printer's ink.

I squeezed Imogen's hand as we arrived at our familiar shack—numberless, nameless, similar to the others squashed in beside each other. The one difference was the vivid green shoots of the herbs growing in the window gap, seeking the sun.

We slipped inside into the sudden cool darkness. Mum turned as we let the sunlight in and shuffled so we could fit. She squatted on the floor, stirring a banged-up pot over the fire. I closed the door to be sure we lost Pocks' little informer, waiting for my eyes to adjust.

We eased off our sneakers and left them by the door. My bare feet sank into the coarse woven matting on the floor.

"Hi, kids," Mum said, wrapping Imogen in a hug.

"Hi Mum," Imogen replied.

I grunted a greeting, eyes on the floor.

Mum's hair was dusted with grey at the temples, like caught flour, tied in a messy ponytail with a too-stretched elastic. Her face was hard, similar to other Northies dwellers. But I envied her soft brown irises. Normal brown beneath thick, calm lashes. She could sort out almost any problem.

I wished my eyes were the same as my mother's.

The fire at the hearth crackled, smoke whirling to escape out of the metal window kept ajar. My useless stepfather, Roland, slept in his bedroll, covered by a thinning blanket, out to the world. Shelves hung on the far wall, holding our possessions—pots and bowls, cooking utensils, a sack of blackened potatoes, glass jars filled with dry herbs and salt. Our 10-litre water container sat by the door, a small plastic jug floating on the oily film on the surface. The regulation TV lurked in the corner, its power cord running up to the ceiling and disappearing through a small gap.

Mum had decorated our shack with woven blankets in colourful fabric, pinned to the walls like the tapestries in fairy-tale castles. Blue and white thread dominated one blanket, with two white blobs in the centre, Imogen's eyes submerged in a sea of her own blue plague-sweat. Losing her to the deep murkiness.

Imogen sat next to Mum and pulled off her scarf, resting it on the shelf behind her. Mum, Roland and I had survived the plague a while back. Imogen was the unlucky twenty per cent who didn't recover, but she wasn't a danger to our family—now we had immunity.

My heart still fluttered at my chest, knocking a tune on my

ribs. My cheeks flushed from the hunt, but the danger had passed, for now. The heat of adrenalin from the chase pumped through my veins.

"See what we won today?" I pulled out my prize, the smooth turquoise rubber ball, spinning it around in my hand. Painting a pattern in my dirt-streaked, sweaty palm.

"Where did you find that?" Mum's lips pressed together.

"Let's just say we're one step closer to a Tin." I winked at Imogen.

"This is your job." Mum's tone hardened, and she poked at the hessian bag with her big toe. "And it's your job to keep your sister safe, not to risk both your lives!"

"But—"

Mum grabbed the bag and shook out the rusting can top, which rolled and stopped shy of the hearth.

"But we can buy whatever we need with a Tin." My lower lip jutted out. Mum should thank me. Why did she always criticise? My hope seeped deep through the holes in our rattan floor-mats, into the earth below, where I couldn't reach it.

"The black market only brings trouble," Mum said. "We don't want trouble."

Imogen's gaze bounced from me to our mother, and she shrank into herself. I felt as mad as Pocks being insulted by a Northies kid. The feeling wound up into my throat, this choking, writhing animal, the familiar memory of the times Mum had judged me before. It was so unfair; I was sick of it. She squashed the thrill of the win, the kids' envy, even Pocks' attention...

"I trust you to look after your sister." Mum gripped my shoulders.

"What do you think I'm doing?" I blurted out, stuffing the ball into my jeans pocket. "You think we'll help Imogen by collecting worthless trash all day?"

Mum kept her voice even when she replied, removing Imogen's scarf from the shelf and replacing it with a clean one. "Dinner's nearly ready."

"Yes, soggy black potato soup. Same as always," I said. "You're looking after us fine."

"You're lucky we're eating at all."

I stomped over to Roland's sleeping lump, but he barely stirred as I huffed into place in my bedroll. He lay on one side, his hairy forearm dangling behind his hip, his relaxed fingers resting on the floor. A repaired hole in his t-shirt sleeve swelled a cotton zipper.

As I pretended to read a torn biology textbook, tears surged behind my eyelids. I blinked to ward them off, not keen on conceding another fight. Oh, to be an adult. I'd no longer be an 'in-betweener', not-quite-sixteen-year-old, unable to make a living. As soon as I could contribute money to the household, they'd have to respect me.

We crammed in so close on our bedrolls that Roland's arm hairs irritated my leg. The text was blurry through my brimming tears as I flipped pages detailing animals long extinct. I knew the text by heart, had mourned the tiger, the blue whale and the snowy owl.

Why had I expected her to be proud of me?

There was a cure—I'd overheard KitKat talking to her friends. Her aunt knew of a healer who only traded in Tins.

Roland stirred, his ribcage rising and sinking with the deep breaths of sleep. He shifted his bony elbow to rest on my leg. I pulled away in sharp anger, my cheeks hot, lip trembling.

Why had Mum shacked up with Roland? He'd never earn a promotion or more shifts. Mum already worked around the clock to pay Pocks' guys for the rent. Rent was exorbitant and controlled by Pocks. If you didn't pay, you didn't have a house or access to rations. Most paid. But it meant that our family would never leave.

My sister would die here.

I had a step-sister, once. Maybe I still did.

My mind flashed back to the toppling trash. The sun scorched as always, but I hid beneath my scavenger bag. A coward. Jagged trash pressed into my back as I peered through the gap. My heart had never beaten in such panic. I'd hidden there, under the bag, scanning the men in black, the lady in the baseball cap. Watching them snatch my sister while I froze in the searing daylight.

Demi was out there, but Mum changed the subject whenever it was raised. What mother let her step-daughter go, as if she was already dead?

I shot a flint-hard stare at Mum as she stirred dinner. Hurt flickered behind her expression, but instead of apologising to me—which she should have done—she turned to Imogen.

"Feeling better?" Mum kissed the crown of her head.

Imogen drew in a deep breath and wheezed. The lungful of air caught, as if solid. Mum patted Imogen's back until the congestion subsided.

Mum shot me a disappointed stare, and I shrugged in return. Disappointment was worse than anger.

I'm working on it, I thought.

We had to win the mech car final—I couldn't lose another sister.

Imogen sat taller, peering into the saucepan. She passed for a normal kid, without her stained scarf hiding her innocent face. Weak and skinny and struggling for breath. But I'd take it.

Mum noticed Imogen staring at the pot.

"Compliments of the chef." Mum forced a smile, stirring watery lumps. The saying was from Before. It made the food taste better, or maybe it was the herbs. But everyone's stomach growled at those words. Even my belly forgot its anger as hunger pulled. Black potato soup was better than no soup, and the fragrant herbs were delicious.

A spurt of saliva responded, hurting the inside of my mouth. I wiped my nose with my t-shirt, not keen to miss dinner because of our spat. And anyway, it was government-mandated TV time.

The ancient, chipped TV sat in the corner, a crack running across the flatscreen. My elongated reflection caught in the smudged monitor in my periphery, over the textbook.

I differed from the other kids—from everyone else in the world. It was no fun having this skin condition. Patches covered my bicep, and almost my entire stomach, in tiny, interlocking, reptilian-like scales. They were more pronounced in sunlight, so I sought the shade. There was no shade on Trash Mountain and no hiding my affliction. I wanted to blend in, like other kids. Standing out was difficult.

I'd take the scales over the plague any day. I rubbed my stomach, re-shelved the textbook, and approached the TV. At first, I saw the reflection of Northies kids laughing at us. Lizard freak and plague girl.

I pressed my thumb on the grubby power button, and the distorted picture flickered. A second later the sound blared—so loud!

Roland shifted on his bedroll. He lifted his head, snorted, and fell asleep again. He was perfect for the night shift, sleeping through daytime disturbances, like someone nothing bad ever happened to.

"It's okay. He needs to eat before work." Mum shrugged.

"Dad!" Imogen shouted.

Roland bolted upright with a bewildered expression, his dark brown hair flat against his temple.

"Wha—?" He pretended not to know where he was,

peering each way. As if we weren't sitting right there, an arm's length away.

I snorted before I could stop myself—it *was* pretty funny—but transformed back into petulant teenager before anyone noticed.

Imogen and Mum giggled.

"Oh, thank goodness!" He focussed on his family sitting around the fire. "You mean I'm not the Leader of the Known World, and I haven't lost you to the Emperor of the Aliens?"

"You're such an embarrassment!" Imogen said, but she didn't mind. I grabbed chipped bowls from the rickety shelf above my head.

"Morning, girls." He mashed sleep from his eye sockets, shuffled over on his haunches, and kissed Mum's cheek.

"Your morning, our night." Mum allowed his peck to graze her cheek but didn't return the affection.

Roland ruffled Imogen's hair, then mine. It was a habit that irritated me. I wasn't a kid anymore, but I was lucky. Roland was the most boring guy I knew, but he was decent. We could do worse. Plenty of other kids who picked over Trash Mountain sported bruises, or exposed ribs from lack of nutrition.

We gathered at the hearth with our bowls.

"Are you starting early again?" Mum asked, trying to sound casual. She served the soup, giving an extra potato to Imogen.

"Have to, I'm afraid," Roland replied, slurping straight from the bowl. He rubbed at the rash on his chin, below his beard. It was the wispy beard of a teenager, not an adult. As if he hadn't grown it in yet.

"Are you getting paid for the extra hours?" Mum avoided his eyes.

"I tried raising it with Ian…"

Mum's lips pressed together, a thin line of disapproval, but she said nothing. Did I mention that my step-dad was a colossal wimp? He'd do anything to avoid a confrontation. The shifting keys hanging from his pocket glinted in the fire. I'd wondered about the keyring—a chipped four-leaf clover. Roland said it brought luck.

We were still waiting.

"So tell us about the launch pad," Imogen said.

"I don't know," Roland replied. "I only clean the junkyard."

"Yeah," Imogen prodded. "But tell us."

He took the hint, grinning like a kid riding in a car, on the freeways we saw on TV.

"Oh, it's not that special—only a hundred-million Tins worth of sophisticated equipment, sitting on a tonne of fuel so potent you'd go belly-up at a mere whiff."

"Have you been to the ship?" Imogen prodded.

"Not close enough to touch it, but everyone seems very busy and important."

"Why are they here, the aliens?" I asked.

Roland scratched his chin. "They've been in Earth's orbit for decades. Maybe they're waiting for us to make contact?"

"Haven't they already visited, and they brought the plague with them?"

"That's the official story," Mum said.

Roland patted Imogen's shoulder before turning back to his soup. "I think you're getting better."

It was hopeful. But it wasn't the truth.

"Hey, there's your rocket ship on the news." Imogen pointed to the television. I twisted dials and whacked the box until the sound burst through. We leaned in to watch the coverage.

Comically tiny on our small screen was a shot of the spaceship at the nearby launch pad. It was an ageing rocket built decades ago. Fuel cells connected to the tip of the reusable rocket. It appeared ready to launch.

19

There was a picture of our pale leader of the remaining countries, Gill Pollins, wearing a charcoal suit and red tie. Pollins claimed to be humanity's last hope, having pulled us back from extinction, to navigate us past the dark decades in the Before. He'd promised a cure, so we all voted for him, and then he voted special powers for himself, which sparked World War III. We won the key battle, but the war wasn't quite over.

The countries that didn't join the Alliance of Remaining Countries were wiped off the map. We lost touch with the entire southern hemisphere. Pollins didn't relinquish his power after the war—in fact, he took over all the countries in the Alliance, as their Prime Minister. He didn't even bother with the farce of a political party. He was in total control, keeping us up to date via the government-mandated television, standard issue for each Northies dwelling. My mother grew up in the Before. She didn't talk about it, didn't like to open old wounds. I wondered what had been so bad, and it only fed my curiosity.

Everyone in our neighbourhood had their own theories. One said Pollins could be an alien himself, in human clothing. Others thought the alien craft was a hoax. But the plague? That part was too real. It couldn't be a lie. The only real question was how to cure my sister, to make her well.

In the grainy image on the television, Pollins planted his feet on the viewing platform, pointing things out for the camera. Several specialists hovered nearby, wearing hard hats— as if that could protect them if the fuel cells exploded and took out the surrounding shacks with them.

"That bucket-of-bolts spaceship will never fly," I said.

The volume cut out altogether, and the picture wobbled with static. We groaned, and I smacked the box with the flat of my hand. No dice.

Roland grinned, and began narrating, as if he was the news-caster himself.

"'Project TinFoil' is underway! Top scientists and military personnel prepare for the most important space mission in the history of Earth."

The grainy view switched to the reporter and Mr Pollins, standing in a room with several flags. They represented the remaining countries of human civilisation, which Pollins led, unopposed. Roland continued.

"Our venerated Mr Pollins has inspected the shuttle, and has endorsed the mission, scheduled for one month from never."

The view turned to a shot from within the International Space Station, the periphery dominated by Earth. Our floating disc was so serene from that impossible angle.

The picture crackled and glitched. Once the image returned, a smooth alien vessel sat within Earth's orbit. The massive ship was coated in glinting silver. Even from this distance, it dwarfed the International Space Station. Best guesses put the ship at a kilometre wide.

It would have been inspiring, if it wasn't such a frightening sight.

"Blah blah, aliens, blah," Roland said, pointing at the television.

Imogen laughed, but fear nudged at my belly. I wondered if they had already landed on Earth, like Pollins said. Was it my imagination, or was the alien ship's orbit closer than the last newscast?

The reporter interviewed a woman in a white lab coat, her hair blow-dried and smooth. She was older than Mum, in her mid-forties. She wore flattering makeup and well-fitting clothes below her coat, and stood in front of a glass door. The door led into a research lab, with benches and glass-fronted freezers in the background.

Her eyes were familiar, as if I'd seen them before in a dream.

"Stop—turn it up!" Mum said.

Surprised by Mum's sudden interest, I nudged the volume knob. After a couple more whacks, the sound burst out.

"Doctor Figg," the real newscaster said. "What's the progress with finding the plague cure?"

"We are wrapping up the final stages of a prototype cure here in my lab at the Elditch Research Facility," Figg replied, but her smile stopped below the ridges of her cheekbones.

"A cure for the plague?" I said, my eyes shifting to Imogen. She was listening with desperate hope, and Mum also leaned into the newscast.

Static overcame the image and the sound warped. I thumped the top of the box, but a grainy sandstorm replaced the broadcast. The closing credit sequence played through the static. I switched off the TV.

There was something odd about that doctor. An old memory tugged just beyond reach.

"I think I know that woman..." I said, half to myself.

"I do too." Mum peered at the screen. "From... Before."

"No way!" Imogen said. Mum never spoke of Before. "What did she do back then?"

"Nothing good," Mum said. She was never this serious and had forgotten that she was mad at me. A queasiness churned in my stomach and it wasn't the potatoes.

Mum asked, "Wait—you weren't born in the Before. How can you know that woman?"

"I can't place it, but I've seen her. Somewhere in Northies."

Mum stared at Imogen and me.

"If you see that woman," Mum said, "run in the opposite direction."

Mum was missing the point. Imogen's cure was already there in that doctor's lab.

CHAPTER 3

ROLAND RETURNED from his shift the next morning, as the sunrise broke the night. He brought the early morning air in with him, and I shivered as I left my bedroll and tiptoed around Imogen. I nodded a casual 'hello' to Roland. He put his finger to his lips and pulled something from behind his back.

In his hands sat two white eggs, their perfect shells luminous in the dim light, and his grin matched mine. This time, my reaction was genuine. I appreciated that he sometimes took care of us.

He set to making breakfast, scooping water from our container into a pot and putting it to boil.

Imogen and Mum woke to the sound of boiling water, and Imogen's eyes followed every movement as Roland eased the eggs around the pot. The shells clinked into each other, a hypnotic dance of pure white amongst the brownish water bubbles.

Mum changed for work. I cut slices of stale bread, and halved each egg, distributing the glistening whites and glorious, semi-hard yolk to each plate. Half an egg each.

I savoured the delicious fat of the firm yolk, turning it in my mouth, then tasting the sweet slipperiness of the white flesh. We sat eating a breakfast made for champions.

"We'll find twice as much treasure in the trash today," I said, and winked at Imogen.

"Two cans instead of one?" Mum said, a slight bitterness at the edge.

I ignored her jibe as we licked our lips and dislodged bread seeds from our teeth.

Roland reached for our plates and washed up, which was our permission to leave. I snatched my scavenger bag and motioned Imogen out of the shack, leaving Roland to finish up and catch some zzz's.

Mum popped out, shouting, "Ofelia, look after your sister!" She headed towards the best shack in Northies, up on the hill where Shifty Pocks lived. He controlled the neighbourhood by assigning the food and water rations. Sure, you could choose not to abide by his rules, but you wouldn't survive long. Mum worked in his garden, sometimes slipping vegetables into a fold in her work dress, to sneak them home for our dinner. The consequences of being discovered were deadly. Nobody crossed Pocks and got away with their hands still attached to their arms. Or, rather, their coat without bullet holes.

Imogen pulled at her scarf as we turned along the dirt road through the shacks, our bodies jostling in the crowd, everyone heading out to their day. We were used to the smell of unwashed bodies and rancid clothes. Too-thin frames passed with stiff, greasy hair. Their grim faces said it—they just hoped to survive another day.

The streets weren't slick with overnight rain, so scavenging would be more bearable. Dry air replaced the humidity of yesterday, thick with the dust of the moving foot traffic.

Shading my face from the slanting sun, I saw seagulls circling up ahead. The peaks of Trash Mountain spiked upwards, conical spires over the roofs of the last row of shacks. I crouched to Imogen's eye-level.

"Hey, Limpet, if you're not well, you can always stay home today."

"You say that every day."

"Yeah, but you know I mean it, right? I can manage on my own."

Imogen kicked at the dusty road with the big toe of her scraggly sneaker.

"Okay, come on," I said, draping my arm around her shoulders. I had to duck—she had stopped growing when she contracted the plague. She was also behind the older kids academically. At least we'd managed a few years' worth of school before they'd closed it—Imogen hadn't learned to read, had never sat in a classroom.

I handed Imogen my hessian bag, and we rounded on Trash Mountain, which loomed higher than the buildings of the launch pad beside it. Other kids with ratty bags picked over the pile, seeking their own treasures to sell. I nodded to Mousie and Aze, who worked the gully deeper into the trash piles.

There was no mech car game today—we'd have to wait until next week—so it was a regular scavenging day.

"Let's set up over here." I pulled Imogen to a quieter corner near the fence. She pressed her face to the wire, marking hexagonal shapes against her scarf-covered cheeks. She stared at the vehicles, warehouses, and the control tower, barely visible over the roof of the warehouse nearby. The buildings obscured the spaceship from this angle. Were the aliens here to hurt or help us?

Nobody knew, but I hoped they were benevolent.

Hope was everything for two Northies kids. This year was my last chance to qualify for the mech car games. Once I hit sixteen, I'd have to get a menial job paying less-than-enough to keep us in not-nearly-enough. I wouldn't have time for this junk heap.

A wheezing fit convulsed Imogen's thin frame.

"It will be okay. Let it pass. Don't stress yourself," I crooned, pointing to a piece of paper wafting in the breeze, half stuck underneath a rubber tyre. "Ready for a lesson?"

Imogen retrieved the paper and handed it to me. It was an ancient newspaper clipping from a decade ago. I wondered how it had survived this long. I read the torn scrap, which only had partial stories on the front, the body copy illegible. But a headline read:

Too late for plague cure?

Thankfully, Imogen couldn't read well. I scrunched the paper into my scavenger bag.

"Wait—I want to learn!" Imogen reached for the paper.

"Nice find, Limpet," I said. "You'll hit the scoreboard today."

Imogen's expression soured as I climbed to my vantage point from yesterday. Who would protect her when I found a job? The scales on my upper arm itched as I bent to pick up my broken broom handle, which I'd sharpened at one end. I passed the broom to Imogen. She jabbed it into the ground, dislodging fragments of disintegrating plastic. At least she didn't have to dig through the debris with her hands.

There was dangerous stuff in this junk pile—an infected cut could be deadly, and Imogen was already sick. She stabbed at soft plastics that broke free and disintegrated like colourful confetti dust. A slab of rubber popped out of the wall of trash, flapping in newfound freedom. I helped Imogen to pull it free. She grinned as I allowed her to add it to her bag.

Next, we found a metal ring pull—a real find, as it was still intact. I added the jagged crushed soda can to my haul. But we had to sift carefully through the bags of waste and putrid offcuts of rancid food. I found a couple of shrivelled carrots with their tops gone bad—we could cut off those parts. I added them to my bag, too.

Today was a decent haul. Maybe Mum would appreciate our efforts.

Aze worked on the peak to our right, moving objects, standing up again. She fancied herself as a pirate on the high seas, instead of a trash-sifter. Her family migrated from an island many generations past. That was why she wore her ridiculous eye patch, like the plumage of a red tropical bird against her ochre skin. I guess we all had our ways of coping. I waved, and she lifted her chin in silent reply.

Mouse Run searched in a gully in the shade. My friends both looked up, catching my eye.

Who could resist showing off? I pulled the prize rubber ball out of my jeans pocket, playing catch with myself. My head followed the turquoise flash arcing up and back into my palm.

Mousie and Aze grinned, but then KitKat—Pocks' informant—popped up from a ridge, scowling. She was the next-oldest kid picking over Trash Mountain.

KitKat glared at my sister, and I shivered as if plunged into a northern winter. I'd have to have a word with Mousie and Aze—someone needed to watch Imogen after I left.

KitKat lost interest, and I slipped the ball into my sock and pulled my flared jeans leg over the top. It would be safe there while I worked, and if KitKat jumped me later, maybe she wouldn't find the ball. I was used to being jumped and could handle myself, but Imogen was an easy target.

My arm itched out here in the sun. I rested a hand over the patches of scales hidden beneath the long sleeves of my t-shirt. The discomfort passed, and I picked at a cardboard lump, flattened into mashed sheets with the pounding rain of yesterday morning. I ripped a solid piece, but it crumbled in my fingertips.

Once Imogen and the other kids became engrossed in their work, and KitKat moved to another trench, I headed to the fence, edging along, pretending to pick at the edges of trash. I approached the locked mesh gate at the road into the yard.

Trucks and vans passed through this checkpoint, and I'd seen the snatcher's van in there too, every Friday. The guarded entrance to Northies sat a kilometre away. Plenty had tried to leave and ended up riddled with bullets.

Imogen squatted nearby on her haunches, mashing the pile with her broom handle. Seagulls fought overhead, feathers rippling on the updrafts. They cawed and screeched, dive-bombing one another as they found food or pieces of plastic in the debris. A gull with grey feathers bent its head, watching from the side of its beak, beady-eyed.

If they stopped squabbling amongst themselves, there would be food enough for all.

I sidled next to the gate, looping my fingers through the wire. An overhang of barbed wire stretched 2 metres tall in either direction. There was no means to climb it—plenty had tried—and I scrutinised the silver metal gate.

The gate towered, overhung with barbed wire twisted a metre thick. The bottom of the gate sagged in the middle. A thick chain was lashed around the handholds, fitted with a chunky padlock. As I rattled the mesh, the padlock hardly budged.

Pallets of plastic-wrapped supplies, heavy military boxes, an idle forklift and several stacked shipping containers scattered the yard. Behind that, a warehouse stood, flanked by a sentry box manned by a guard. The yard ended at the warehouse. A roller door led to the launch site, the only other Northies exit.

A growling engine approached the road, menacing and out of place.

That meant—

Oh no, where was Imogen?

My chest constricted as if enormous steel hands squeezed my ribcage.

I took a deep, painful breath and leaped up the stack towards my sister, scattering debris with each footfall. Reaching the crest of the first level, I spied her, digging a hole with the broom handle.

"Snatchers!" I yelled.

Imogen's attention yanked to me and I wolf-whistled to the other kids.

The Northies kids scattered.

I was the closest to the dark, windowless van when it stopped. Two bulky men dressed in black leaped out, followed by Pocks and a lady in a baseball cap and reflective sunglasses.

She was the snatcher who'd taken Demi. She was even worse than Pocks.

Imogen clambered uphill and disappeared over the crest. One young child ran the wrong way in panic.

I whipped my attention towards the van.

The man in black raised his tranquilliser gun.

The tranq gun was pointed at my head, with the kid at my back. This was it for both of us.

I rooted to the spot, unable to move.

The dart left the barrel.

Then time went still. Frozen in a moment.

A green haze sprang up in front of me, as if I peered through a glass bottle.

Pocks, mouth wide, was immobilised mid-step. His men beside him froze, too.

The lady, mid-air in a leap, zoned in on the kid behind me. The tranquilliser dart almost touched me. Hovering there, mid-air, hanging as its point pierced the other side of the green glass.

Everyone else froze in time and space, gravity suspended. The seagulls paused mid-squawk. I lifted my hands and waved them about. The frozen time hadn't caught me, just everyone else. I could move in this weird, stopped time. Was this my suspended moment before death? That one elongated second, that flash of life?

But it didn't last long. There was no moment to think. In the next split-second, everything moved.

The scene was normal—the green hues gone, the shouting and danger real again. The frozen movie resumed. An unharmed kid bolted away.

The snatcher lady landed and propelled herself towards me. Henchmen advanced as the dart dropped to the ground at my feet.

What had just happened? Why hadn't the dart hit me? But the danger was still real; I couldn't dissect events right now.

Sprinting in the opposite direction, towards Imogen, one thought played in my mind.

I had to save her.

Pocks pointed towards my sister and bellowed at his henchmen. He strode up the ridge, and the lady followed, keeping to the road. The henchman who had shot at me reloaded his tranquilliser gun. The other one shouldered his own gun and followed Pocks up the pile.

Pocks flexed his neck as he spotted me. His snarl returned, that upturned lip. His eye glinted as if reflecting a shiny Tin.

31

I scampered up the mountain, the thin, flexible soles of my sneakers gripping the uneven surface better than the henchmen's thick-soled boots. I was nimble from years of practice and reached the top before the henchmen scaled it themselves. Debris toppled under their heavy weight, the rubble collapsing like sand with each step.

I followed Imogen's path as one of the henchmen fired a dart. Before it hit, I jumped, landing with a heavy thump that knocked the breath from my chest. My legs buzzed with pain, pooling at the backs of my knees. I shook myself as Pocks crested the peak. He pointed at me.

I scrambled to my feet and ran in a zigzag between the mounds, to prevent a clear shot, nimble on my home turf.

I dove into a drainpipe, my shoulders narrowly fitting, wriggling on my elbows and knees. The metal scraped the skin on my knees as I scurried away from Pocks, and the henchmen, and the lady who had taken my other sister. I couldn't save Demi, but I could save Imogen. I hoped she was in front of me —it was the only place the snatchers couldn't follow.

A henchman's shouts echoed in the pipe as he yelled at his mates.

"She went in here."

"Forget her, we can't fit through," the other henchman said, and I imagined him flexing his biceps to prove his point.

"There—there's another one!"

"Grab her!"

Oh, no—could it be Imogen? My heart twanged a painful beat.

I shuffled my body in the cramped space and searched between my ankles to the light shining at the end of the tunnel. Just in time to watch a scuffle. The men in black overpowered a kid with long hair, who fell limp. The sharp light haloed the kid's face, so I couldn't make out her features.

"Imogen?" I whispered, scrambling up the pipe, until Pocks' voice echoed from the other end.

"She'll do," he said.

Another silhouette filled the end of the pipe—the lady snatcher. This was the closest encounter we'd had. She removed her reflective sunglasses to better peer into the gloom, and I saw her eyes.

I knew those eyes. They belonged to the doctor on the TV. The doctor and snatcher were the same person. I hadn't recognised her in her baseball cap and sunglasses.

This woman had the plague cure—she could help Imogen!

But she was also a snatcher of the worst kind. I shuffled my bottom along the pipe, but it was too cramped.

There was no chance of defeating them. Our best chance was to hide, and I hoped Imogen had done the same. Pocks was too strong, and his henchmen close. How could I help Imogen if they snatched me? But what if they already had her? Nothing would stop me from helping her. Another shadow passed the lip of the pipe, and I held my breath until they moved on. Leaving my hiding place now was too risky. It was selfish, but I hoped they'd snatched another kid. Any other kid.

Please, not Imogen.

"Let's go." A henchman dislodged trash underfoot as he carried the unlucky captive girl to the black van.

The lady slipped her sunglasses on and stood. Then sunlight returned to the pipe as she strode away.

We would never see that girl again. Demi's image flashed in my mind's eye—her surprise as the snatchers grabbed her. Her limp arm hanging as they carried her away. It was too painful—I couldn't think of that possibility now.

I had to make sure they hadn't kidnapped Imogen.

I poked my head out of the pipe, but the snatchers had gone.

CHAPTER 4

SLUDGE SQUISHED through my fingers as I clambered through the slimy pipe, hoping to heck that they hadn't captured Imogen. Two kids argued up ahead. I listened for Imogen's voice in the echo, but the chatter was deep, not breathless. A couple of pre-adolescent boys.

Sunlight flashed in between the moving bodies up ahead. I grabbed the roof of the rusting metal pipe and swung my legs out, landing on my feet. My eyes adjusted to the sudden glare. Two kids, hands resting on hips, scoped out their escape route. They nodded to me.

No adults had pursued us through the pipe. A childish head disappeared down the gully of trash. Seagulls screeched above—a shadow passed between me and the relentless sun.

The kids signalled, holding the thumb of one hand to the side. It was the unspoken sign of the Northies rats—run from danger, as fast as you can. Every kid for themselves. We scattered in different directions.

I didn't ask them about Imogen, preferring to keep our hiding place secret, so I waited until they bobbed out of view. I snuck around a ridge. Trash Mountain was as big as an entire suburb, the pipe only intersected it. This older section was well picked over. I jogged along the packed path to the grey building crumbling into the debris.

Garbage spilled out of the walls of the building itself. It had once been a bookstore, destroyed by fire long ago. The ceiling had caved in, the corners sheltering from the rain and sun. Bricks crumbled at the edges, as if scrubbed with caustic sandpaper around scrawls of fading graffiti.

I glanced behind to make sure the kids hadn't followed. I was alone with the wind ruffling the stench of old trash.

The sagging doorframe stood there, without its supporting walls, a portal to another dimension. I ducked beneath it into the bookstore.

It was cooler inside, shaded by the single wall that hadn't collapsed. I stuck to the shadow, approaching the corner piled with rubble. A decaying wooden crate shifted, its clunk echoing off stone.

"Imogen?" I called out, my voice cracking.

"In here," came a muffled reply.

Relief rushed over me, and my shoulders dropped as the tension left. I headed to the little cubby hole we'd constructed behind the crate. She snuggled there, like a frightened nocturnal animal.

I hugged and squeezed my little sister so hard that she had a wheezing fit. She fought for breath and I let go.

"Sorry, Imogen," I said. "I thought they had you."

My eyes fell to the floor so she couldn't see my worry.

"Not yet." She smiled bravely. "That was close, though."

Blue-black sweat oozed painfully from her pores, like small beetles backing out of her skin, their shells shiny. Like they had burrowed in and were now seeping out, forming navy teardrops on her cheeks. I used her scarf to wipe the plague sweat from around the racing vein pulsating in her temple.

"Yeah, too close." I remembered the dart shooting towards

me, but frozen in time. Why hadn't it hit me? I should have been out cold. And what was that green glass? It was like a force field...

"Can we stay here, Ofelia?" Imogen asked.

"Sure, little one."

"I'm not little anymore," she said, but wheezed again. It sounded dry, as if hairs scraped her neck and she was out of air.

I laid the blue sweat-stained scarf over my lap and rubbed her back. When her wheezing stopped, she asked, "Teach me to read?"

I play-punched her shoulder and lifted the crate that hid our hidey-hole, so we could do what we did best—picking through the garbage, looking for treasure. I discovered a book on earth sciences, its edges burnt, the pictures torn out. Imogen uncovered a shabby postcard of our city from Before. We settled in our haven, resting on toppled cladding, to examine our finds.

Imogen turned the postcard over, scrawled in decorative font, the caption's colours faded from age.

London, by night.

It was a sight to behold—the inviting wrought-iron streetlights cast a soft, yellow halo on the cobbled streets. The laneways were uncrowded. Relaxed tourists ambled along, their only job to take in the view. The buildings towered, built in white stone with grey tiled roofs. A clean, well-dressed couple held hands, their backs to us, their faces turned to each other.

The caption read:

"Wish I was there too," Imogen said.

"Yeah, anywhere *but* here," I said.

"Did the city ever look that way?"

"Maybe it still does."

"You mean out of Northies?"

"Sure."

The thought just occurred to me. We only saw beyond our neighbourhood on TV; curated images that our leader, Gill Pollins, wanted his subjects to see after the plague nearly wiped humans out, spreading from the melting Siberian tundra. Pollins asserted emergency power and declared that the aliens would give us the plague cure. But that was before I was born.

We knew Pollins kept things from us, because sometimes, defectors were forced into Northies from outside as punishment. They weren't supposed to talk, but some did. They told us stories of the swanky suburbs where they lived, and the freedoms and wealth they had. Defectors didn't last long. Pocks tolerated residents as long as they conformed. People from outside weren't used to taking orders, or to the meagre rations.

We were still without the aliens' cure. Pollins had not kept his promise. But had the snatcher, Dr Figg, given us hope—did we need the aliens' cooperation now? Was the space mission needed?

I guess even the leader of the remaining countries needed a Plan B.

Imogen studied the picture on the postcard. Her finger traced the grey roofs, the wide streets, ending in the cheerful couple.

I waited until she'd absorbed the image.

"I will make you better," I said.

Imogen touched the scaly part of my arm, through my t-shirt, which didn't itch here in the shade.

"Demi wasn't your fault," she said.

My throat closed, as if I was the one with the plague, unable to breathe. She'd said the words I dreaded, that I couldn't face.

"I'll make you well again, Imogen." I leaned in and whispered, "I'll get you your cure."

A plan formulated. I had to escape Northies and find the Elditch Research Facility. And my best chance of leaving was getting into that yard. Maybe I could hide out in the van, hitch a ride to Dr Figg's workplace. Slip by unnoticed, grab the cure and return, saving my little sister. I might have to break a few rules to enact my plan. I'm sure Roland would understand.

The van entered the junkyard each Friday. Tomorrow was Friday. This was my best chance.

My sister and I hid in the bookstore until we were ready to head home. We took the longer route to avoid being followed. Other kids had picked over our hidey-hole, losing interest once they had ripped the pictures out of each book. The younger kids couldn't read. They didn't have an almost-sixteen-year-old sister to teach them.

The sun set as we reached home. Roland paced outside our shack, wearing his brown janitor's uniform. When he saw us, he grabbed Imogen, checking for injuries.

"We're okay," I said.

Roland held his arms wide for a hug. I ignored him and slipped inside through the metal door.

Mum paced inside and hadn't started dinner yet. I guess in case she had to search for us. Roland and Imogen ducked into the shack.

"Ofelia, where have you two been?" Mum said, winding her arms around Imogen and I. She accidentally tugged at my hair and my eyes watered as strands threatened to pull free from the roots.

"Ouch! Mum!" I said.

"I heard about the snatchers, I thought—" Mum let go and I rubbed at my scalp.

Roland allowed her to nestle into his shoulder, and they leaned into each other. Mum held the soup ladle, as if forgetting what it was for. Then she sank to the floor, the skirt of her uniform ballooning at her legs. She reminded me of a broken ballerina, her collarbones protruding, her limbs as delicate. As if we'd placed her on a stage, ready for the swelling music.

Roland stepped over to the fireplace.

"I'll start dinner." He eased the soup ladle out of Mum's hands. She blinked, uncertain.

"You won't have time to eat before work," Mum said, smoothing her skirt, theatrics gone, her usual pragmatism returning.

"I'll call in sick," Roland said.

At that moment, I respected him, even if I didn't love him as my own father. He wouldn't be paid for a sick day. Things would be tight, but family was important.

He grabbed matches from the shelf and lit the kindling on the hearth. The flames warmed my cheeks as the atmosphere cooled.

An urge overtook me, and I stood and hugged him, awkwardly, to everyone's shock. Once I'd committed to the hug, I couldn't pull back. Roland and I paused, arms locked around each other.

Mum stared as if I was growing a second head. I overcame my surprise and pulled out of the hug. He left his hand on my shoulder, the steady warmth radiating into my skin. He felt strong. That wasn't how I saw him. His expression had... hope?

I felt Roland and I had healed our entire family in that one moment.

"Thanks, Roland," I said.

His demeanour softened, grew more relaxed.

Roland's keys hung from his belt, within reach, this clinking temptation. They bunched on a ring with that ancient symbol—a four-leaf clover. The green had chipped off, revealing tarnished silver.

Before he noticed, I unhooked his keys and pocketed them.

I covered it up by pressing my cheek into his shirt. He smelt of bleach and diesel fuel. I'd return the keys before he left for work tomorrow night. Nobody had to find out.

"You can always call me Dad, you know," he said.

"It's okay," I said, concentrating on holding the keys so they didn't clink. "You're a nice guy, but you're not my dad."

He removed his warm handprint. Pain flitted over his face, and I realised my gaffe.

"Well, you're a kind of dad, just not—sorry," I mumbled, not knowing what else to say. I was too hard on the guy. He was the only father I had known. I didn't even know who my real dad was. Mum refused to talk about him.

Roland and I avoided each other's eyes, waiting for the awkwardness to pass. Then Mum did something unexpected. She leaned in and touched my shoulder with her finger.

"Thanks, love," she said. "Thanks for looking after your sister."

I know Mum didn't mean it that way, but I felt the familiar guilt scratching away, like fingernails on the inside of my ear. The discomfort of remorse.

Demi was my sister, too.

CHAPTER 5

THE FOLLOWING morning I ladled leftovers—watery soup—into chipped bowls for breakfast. At least it was hot, and Mum had sifted a handful of rice into the pot, which gave it a thickened glugginess. I stifled the fire and waited until the embers smouldered and the smoke became a finger seeking our tin sheet window. I pushed the front door ajar to let in the light. Roland joined me at the hearth before the others woke.

"How's it going?" he whispered.

Even a whisper amplified inside the tin-sheeted shack, so that everyone heard. I didn't know if Mum and Imogen were asleep or dozing.

"Good thanks," I replied, handing him breakfast.

"Mmm, oh my gosh, what a feast!" he said, with too much enthusiasm, and I chuckled despite myself. He called them 'dad jokes', which meant they weren't funny. But I guess sometimes they were. At least it broke the tension.

"Sorry, no eggs today," he said.

"That's okay."

"So, um, Ofelia," he began. He stopped, cleared his throat. Uh-oh. What was coming next?

"I ah..." he continued. "I understand if you don't want to call me Dad. It was stupid of me to suggest it."

"Oh," I said, relieved. "Well, I'm sorry too. I kinda wish you were my dad sometimes."

I'd never seen Roland grin so much, showing off his yellowing teeth, his stupid haircut bobbing as he fell over himself to hug me.

Apparently, hugging was a thing now.

Imogen stirred, had a whooping fit, sat up with her face flushed and red. Wet hair stuck to her forehead—was she running a fever? She grew sicker with each passing day.

My stomach dropped at thoughts of today's mission. Would I succeed?

"You two are cute," Mum said, her eyes flitting from me to Roland, still deep in our hug.

I pulled away like Roland was on fire and I'd just realised he was giving me third-degree burns. Roland handed Mum a bowl as she joined him at the hearth.

I shuffled to Imogen's bedroll and handed her a steaming bowl, lifting the spoon as if to feed her, but she pushed it aside.

"I'll do it," she said, grabbing the spoon from me.

Mum placed her bowl on the shack floor and rested her hand against Imogen's forehead.

"Sweetie, you're hot." Mum's eyebrows knit together with concern.

"I'm okay," Imogen said, shoving a whole spoonful of small, black-skinned potato into her mouth to make her point. But the potato was too big, her cheeks bulging. Her eyes grew wide, realising her mouthful was more than she could chew. I giggled despite myself.

Mum shook her head, returning to her food.

"You girls should stay indoors today," she said. "Besides, pickings are slim. It might be time to change territories."

"We can't change territories," Imogen said. "It doesn't work that way."

"There are politics at the junk pile?" Roland asked.

"Yeah, we have ranking officials and everything." Imogen couldn't keep a straight face.

I ran my prize ball between my fingers; the rubber was cool and smooth. Mum frowned, so I tucked the ball into my sock. Leaving it in the shack wasn't possible, and I'd be stupid to flash it around Trash Mountain.

"I don't think you should go." Mum rested a hand over Imogen's elbow as I pulled my saggy ankle sock up to hide the ball.

"I'll look out for her," I said.

Mum struggled with a thought.

"Do that then," she said, pivoting to grab her uniform.

"I always look out for her," I said, as Imogen and I stacked breakfast bowls and headed out into glaring full sunshine.

We traipsed through the ramshackle rows, watching the day's activities unfold. The down-and-outers going to low-paying jobs. The beggars setting up on the corners. Those lucky enough to have food scoffing it at their hearths, their backs concealing what they had. Tin-sheet doors banged open and slammed shut. Echoes up the streets embedded with discarded food wrappers picked over by unsupervised kids.

My heart beat faster than usual, a low thrumming in my chest. My face flushed too—like Imogen's—but from excitement. I clasped the keys in my jean shorts pocket, feeling powerful for a change.

"You can scope out fresh territory today," I said.

"I'm sticking with you," Imogen ended in a whine.

"It's faster if we split up."

"So you don't want me around?"

"Of course I do," I said, pushing her playfully. "How could you think that? It's *all* I want."

I brought the glint of Roland's keys out of my pocket. Enough for Imogen to see the four-leaf clover—without advertising it.

"I'm definitely sticking with you," she said, her tone brighter than I'd heard in weeks. My plan of reverse psychology had backfired.

"It's too dangerous. Work on the mountain, I'll check things out."

"Whatever you say," she said.

Imogen used her broken broom handle as a walking stick, thwacking it into the dirt as we went. Little divots left in our wake, like a trail of breadcrumbs. If they really were breadcrumbs, some poor soul would eat them and we'd lose our way back.

Most days we took a short-cut through the abandoned shacks, straight to the heart of Trash Mountain. But this time we hugged the road. Imogen raised an eyebrow at me, but followed. The dirt trail led to the gate from yesterday, into the launch pad yard, where Roland worked.

Aze and Mouse Run dug far off in their section, holding their finds to the sun. I held Imogen back and said, "Wait for me here. I have to speak to Aze and Mousie."

Imogen kicked at a metal pipe sticking up from the ground, but stayed put.

I joined my friends, who were deep in scavenging mode and didn't see me approach. The van arrived about this time. I'd have to be quick.

"Hey, Ofelia," Mousie began, wiping dirt across her brow with the back of her hand. "Thanks to you, we had meat last night. We bought a whole rabbit! You should come over for dinner."

"Yeah, we bought a winter blanket," Aze said. "You've saved our skins..."

"You're welcome," I replied, with other things on my mind. "I have a favour to ask."

"Sure," Aze said, and Mousie nodded. We drew in closer.

"I'm about to try something a little nuts," I said, clocking their worried reactions. "You know the lady snatcher from yesterday?"

They nodded with serious expressions.

"Well, she's also that doctor on the news, you know, the virologist. She has the plague cure."

I let the information sink in.

"So what? Wasn't it in that research facility or something?" Aze asked, flipping up her pirate patch.

"Exactly," I said. "I'm going to get it, for Imogen."

"How will you leave Northies?" Mousie asked.

"In the lady snatcher's van. I bet she'll drive straight back to her lab."

"There's no way that will work!" Aze's eyes widened.

"They'll find you and kill you," Mousie said, slamming her fist into her open palm to make her point.

"Not if I hide in the van. There's plenty of room, and it's full of sacks and old junk. I'll hide until the coast is clear, then break inside."

"Here's hoping they give you a nice funeral," Aze said, flipping her eye patch down.

"It will work. It has to," I said, glancing back at Imogen, who wheezed and bent to catch her breath. "Imogen can't stay out in this junk pile. She's not getting better. She's running out of time."

Mouse Run and Aze couldn't argue with that logic, but they still didn't seem convinced.

"Let me worry about the van," I said, leaning in so nobody

overheard us. "I need your help. Will you keep Imogen safe while I'm gone? She needs to stay home, rather than out here in the elements. The scraps we find out here aren't worth risking her health. And can you keep her away from the other kids, especially KitKat?"

Aze frowned, and Mousie put her hand to her cheek. They processed what I was asking them to do.

"Can we talk you out of this?" Aze asked. "What about the mech games?"

"Realistically, we won't make it any further," I said.

My friends' gazes fell to the trash floor.

"If I don't do this, Imogen will die." My voice broke as I watched Imogen running her fingers into the dust beside the fence. I could do this, right?

"We're honoured to look after your sister," Mousie said, nudging Aze.

"Yeah, if you've decided..." she said.

"Thanks, guys. I have to go. The van will arrive soon."

"What should we do?" Aze said, glancing at Imogen.

"Distract Imogen while I go into the junkyard. Wait until I'm gone and tell her my plan. I don't want her thinking I've abandoned her."

"Sure," Mousie said, patting my back like it was the next round of mech cars. "Good luck."

"Thanks." My heart felt too large for my chest cavity and quickened its beat.

"Come here..." Aze said, hugging me, and Mousie joined in. Would I see them again?

I let go of my two best friends and joined Imogen by the gate, nodding towards the junkyard.

"I'm going in alone, you know, scope things out. Then I'll give you the signal that the coast is clear. Wait with Mousie and Aze, so I know you're safe."

"What do you think is in there?" Imogen gazed through the fence.

"Something better than Tins," I said.

"There's nothing better than Tins."

"Do you think the swanky suburbs bother with Tins? They have the best life. Their life is the postcard you found."

"That postcard's ancient. That place doesn't exist anymore."

"I'm going to find out," I replied, my chest fluttering as Mousie and Aze joined us. They retreated behind a cement pillar, hidden from the road.

"I want to come with you!" Imogen whined.

"Stay with Mousie and Aze," I said.

I pushed the first key into the padlock. It didn't turn, so I tried the next, and the next. I couldn't tell one key from the other. Imogen, our lookout, leaned her back on the fence as I worked.

I inserted the last key, and the metal padlock opened with a satisfying click. A thrill passed through my fingers as I eased the lock free from the chain.

Imogen's gaze darted to the road.

Unwinding the clanging chain—it was heavy to lift—I coiled it on the ground, a thick snake ready to pounce.

I caught Imogen's eye and pushed the gate open.

The three of them hung behind the pylon, out of sight as I slipped into the yard.

Winding the chains up again, I eased the padlock over to keep them bound. But I left the lock ajar, in case I needed to escape in a hurry.

My heartbeat thumped so loud I was sure the whole neighbourhood could hear. Adrenalin shook my hands.

I bent low and crossed the yard, hiding behind the closest shipping container. I peeked out and scanned for patrols. Over by the roller door to the warehouse, a guard in his sentry box played cards. A television blared with the usual news programs and ads for things we would never afford.

The container door was locked and none of the keys fitted. I would have to hide elsewhere.

Imogen twirled her finger around the wire fence, her eyes locked on my position as I moved to the pallets piled high with drums.

The guard stood up, running his eyes over the junkyard. A gaggle of seagulls lifted into the air, squabbling and pecking at each other. He checked out his window, shaking his head at the birds. He stretched, killing time, then turned up the TV and bent back to his card game.

One nearby cylindrical drum rested on an empty, picked-over pallet. The drum sat on four feet, lying lengthways, rather than upright. And it had a hinged lid, like the makeshift barbecues in the meat shops.

The guard lost his game, throwing his cards on the counter with disgust. But he wasn't that interested in the yard.

Imogen pushed through the gate, and I motioned for her to get back, but she didn't listen.

"I want to see..." she said.

I put a finger to my lips. "You have to go back!"

"What's in there?" Imogen asked.

"Imogen, go back, now!" I said, pointing to the gate. But she crept closer to the drum.

"Let me stay for a minute," she said.

"You're not risking your life for this."

"I know you just want to protect me, but you don't have to. Don't leave me behind."

My mind flashed to Demi, and how I'd abandoned her. I realised Imogen wouldn't let me enact my mission on my own, and returned my attention to the drum.

"Help me with this," I said.

We heaved, lifting the lid of the drum, inches at a time. If we moved faster, the hinges squeaked. Cracking it open enough to peer inside, something reflected the golden sunlight.

Imogen sucked in a breath, almost dropping the lid in surprise.

We had found the ultimate treasure. I had to take a moment. Imogen patted my arm so hard I thought she'd bruise me.

"It's... it's..." She couldn't speak.

"I know!" I replied.

Inside was the biggest stash of Tins I had witnessed in one place. They weren't flat, as we knew them—the Tins wrapped around a solid bar shape the length of my hand. The wrappers glinted in the sun, and my instincts screamed to shove them in every imaginable pocket and run.

We'd be the richest kids in the entire neighbourhood! The Tins would keep our family alive for many years and cure Imogen for ten lifetimes! Did I need the van after all?

The security guard spoke into the phone, his conversation muted. Monitoring the guard, I shoved bars into my scavenger bag. Imogen filled hers as well.

The growl of an engine approached. The same van from yesterday. It grumbled via the road towards the gate. The snatchers had returned, right on cue.

The vehicle swerved to a stop behind the gate. There was no time to escape.

"Quick, get in." I linked my fingers to help Imogen into the drum. Tins took up half of the space, which left room to wriggle in beside Imogen. We pulled our scavenger bags over us.

My heart tickled my throat, and I stifled the urge to cough. We couldn't be caught in here. Scavenging trash was one thing, but stealing Tins from a locked launch pad yard? Pocks would blast bullet holes through us both.

How could I be so stupid? I'd put Imogen in danger, too.

"Idiot!" I whispered to myself, but Imogen swatted my arm as if to say 'shut up'.

Just before I lowered the lid, the gate opened, and the van sidled into the yard, its tyres crunching to a stop a mere metre in front of our pallet. And, slipping from the rear cab, were Pocks, his henchmen, and the lady snatcher, Dr Figg.

Pocks' fingers smoothed out his greasy rat's tail. His eyes drew everything in, smacking his lips as if breaking a fast.

I snapped the lid to, and we cowered in panicked darkness.

CHAPTER 6

IMOGEN and I huddled in the drum as the occupants of the van approached, their voices raised in argument. Their inaudible conversation grew more animated until they stood right by our drum.

Figg's words stopped my heart.

"Find out why the gate was unlocked."

My arm twitched and rustled the foil Tins beneath me. Imogen and I held our breath as the voices moved further away, towards the warehouse. A small hole near my head allowed a skewer of light into the drum. I eased my eye to see through, but we faced the front gate, obscuring the view of the rear.

The adults argued with the guard. Maybe Figg was blaming him for leaving the gate unlocked? Then the mechanical roller door clanged as it lifted. Footsteps strode through. The door closed behind them, and the yard was quiet, save for squawking seagulls and the clinking chain. The guard turned the television up in his sentry box.

I wriggled to ease the pressure on the elbow that was stuck underneath me. My attention reverted to the Tins. I picked up a bar and sniffed it. The scent was strange—it was food, because my stomach growled in response. But I couldn't place the sweet, fatty aroma.

We waited for a few minutes, to be sure, before my sister whispered, "Can we try one?"

I shifted my weight again and the foil bar wrappers crinkled. It was tempting.

I picked up a bar from the edge and eased open the wrapper's corner, careful to keep the Tin itself intact. The brown insides appeared, the scent of sugar and fat overwhelming my tastebuds. I nibbled, closing my eyes.

I had never tasted chocolate.

It softened in my warm mouth, tingling as my taste receptors perked right up. I rolled the morsel around my tongue, melting and delicious. My entire jaw ached. It was a disappointment once the bite slid from my throat into my empty belly.

I opened my eyes to Imogen's hopeful expression.

"Okay," I said. "You've got to try these bad boys."

I peeled the foil free carefully, keeping the Tins wrapper intact, and passed it to my sister. She examined the bar in the light shining in from the hole. I nodded that it was okay.

We chomped together. My tastebuds shuddered and saliva rushed to my mouth. So rich-tasting, and sweet, and goddamn delicious. I crunched on the puffed rice embedded in the chocolate for a flavour explosion—the saccharine sugar, the velvety cocoa. The eternal food of heaven.

I sucked in a deep, satisfied breath, and chomped the block into mush. Imogen savoured her treat, producing little 'mmm' noises.

I fought my instinct to wolf the whole thing. This was what eating should be!

We sat licking the spaces in our teeth and picking crispy

rice grains out of our molars. We'd grown up knowing not to waste the food we came by.

Imogen was silent after our feast, and I knew what she wanted to ask.

"One more?" I prodded.

"Yes, please," she gushed.

"Okay, but remember, we haven't eaten much in a while. We don't want to be sick."

We should have eaten two bars each and stopped. But we had never seen so much high-calorie food. Who could dream of such a stash? We were trapped here, and another wouldn't hurt, surely? Nobody knew, except us.

Chocolate, in that moment of discovery, was a new type of packaged happiness.

Imogen forgot her wheeze. It was Christmas, with actual presents melting underneath our body heat.

We had three bars each before the nausea hit. It was from overeating, something I hadn't experienced before, but I'd heard a kid saying his grandma had it when she was young. Chocolate stuck in my throat, as if the bars lined up—end to end—from my belly to my teeth. My brain told me to eat more, but my stomach rebelled with a winding ache. Imogen squirmed.

"I don't feel so great," she said.

"Me either. Let's hang here for a while."

As we sat in the pounding heat in the plastic drum, I wanted to lean out of our barrel and hurl chunks, but that might reveal our position. I'd kill for a mouthful of water. Instead, I lay on my back, breathing in, trying not to make any sudden moves, the ache swirling in my abdomen. A unique sensation to hunger, and just as unpleasant.

I burped and tasted sugar and fat, burning and acidic. To

distract myself from being sick, I wondered out loud, "How will we sneak them home?"

"We have our bags..." Imogen replied.

"Yeah, but they can't be full. It'd be suspicious."

"We'd be jumped for sure."

"Come here." Nausea hit as the chocolate pooled in my stomach.

Imogen snuggled closer, and I rested my arm underneath her head, forming a pillow. We lay for a while.

"Will the Tins last?" Imogen asked.

"I wouldn't worry, Limpet."

Imogen turned towards me.

"Do you think people will survive?"

"What?" Her questions caught me off guard.

"Humans. The aliens. The plague. Sometimes I don't think we'll make it."

"We'd better concentrate on surviving this yard."

"No." Imogen propped herself up to face me. "Will humans survive? They say the aliens have the plague cure, and they're not sharing it."

"We might not need the aliens. The doctor can help you. That's why I'm here."

"Huh?"

I moved closer.

"We've discovered the biggest stash of Tins known to Northies, as in—ever! And they're wrapped around *actual* chocolate. This is literally the best day of our lives—we have food, *and* Tins!"

Imogen didn't reply, so I continued.

"You can't die," I said. "We have enough Tins to buy the black market cure. It helped KitKat's mum, right?"

"That's a rumour..."

"It's not a rumour!" I snapped, then sucked in my breath. "Sorry, that sounded harsh. I'll make you well, I mean it."

Imogen waited a breath or two.

"I'm not Demi," she said.

A ball of fire built in my chest, as if I'd explode bubbling chocolate bars through our hiding place. We hadn't spoken properly about Demi. I always changed the subject. But it felt right at this moment.

"I did nothing." A sigh heaved from deep inside me, from an old festering wound. "I just lay there. I didn't help her."

"You were too far away. And Aze said there were four snatchers with tranq darts."

I met her gaze, compassion misting my eyes.

"They won't hurt you," I said. "I will find your cure."

Figg, Pocks, and his henchmen remained beyond the warehouse for a few minutes. We had to grab as many Tins as possible. Just as I opened the lid, the guard's heavy boots clumped on the dusty ground. He headed our way, jangling the keys on his belt and turning over boxes in the yard.

Looking for us.

He poked at the debris, upending a box and shifting our packing crate. I watched his progress through the slitted hole in the barrel.

Imogen and I couldn't risk moving now. But my legs cramped, I needed the bathroom, and I was thirsty as heck. Those chocolate bars were sugary and rich. Imogen and I weren't used to it. My insides ached, wrung dry, and my head pounded as if someone drummed sticks against my skull. They were a decent percussionist.

At least my stomach had stopped growling.

Could we escape the yard, with more Tins than a lowly Northies kid had ever seen in the entire history of Northies?

I thought of the bullet holes in Pocks' jacket—Pocks, his henchmen, and the doctor snatcher meant the most serious business there was, and this guard answered to them. Respect that, or you were dead.

I shifted my weight from one elbow to the other, stretching my twinging leg. We banged into each other's bony frames, and I grazed my forehead against the top of the barrel.

"Okay, shove as many bars as you can carry into your bag," I whispered.

We stuffed her bag to a third full. I pressed my finger to my lips, and we listened out for the guard. His whistle had moved off towards the gate. I hoped that Mousie and Aze were making themselves scarce.

"Maybe double that." Was I being greedy? No, I told myself, I was keeping my promise to Imogen. I was saving her and more than just our family.

I jiggled the bag, weighing our haul.

"More?" Imogen asked.

I shrugged, and we wriggled our bums, revealing more bars, stuffing Imogen's bag to the halfway mark. Any fuller, and we risked raising suspicion. The leftover bars justified a return trip.

I placed a hand on Imogen's shoulder. We waited until the guard covered the whole yard and sauntered past, returning to the sentry box.

The guard snapped off the television and his stool squeaked as he sat.

We cracked the lid open a hand-width, adjusting to the harsh light of the midday sun. The over-exposed, too white sunlight blinded me. My scaly skin itched when the light made contact through my t-shirt hole. We sat under the raised lid for a few more seconds. I motioned for Imogen to stay and crawled out of the barrel, pressing my feet onto the wooden pallet like a stray cat easing past a piping-hot roof. Dropping my full weight to the pallet, I froze, alert to movement.

The guard leaned into his chair, his cap over his eyes, not chasing the employee of the month award. I flinched as the chain around the gate clinked in the wind. The scent shifted— from cocoa and sugar to the wood shavings on the ground beside the pallet.

"Stay where you are, until I give the signal," I said to Imogen.

I kept low and dashed to the forklift. Pausing for a few minutes, I peered from behind the forklift cab, watching for movement. The windows were head height, smudged with handprints. It was several metres from here to the fence.

I signalled Imogen to the gate. She crawled out of the barrel. The guard at the sentry box stood.

He turned our way, and I waved my hand low to the ground, gesturing for Imogen to stay put. The guard spoke on the phone, raising the roller door to the warehouse.

The retracting door clanged a terrible warning. We had to leave.

The door lifted to waist height, revealing four pairs of adult legs. Two dressed in black, one in jeans, and the fourth wearing a filthy, bullet-pocked long coat.

"Stay put!" I whispered, and waited while Imogen closed the lid, her expression the most scared I'd ever seen her. She stifled a wheezing fit, heaving breath into her lungs.

I shouldn't have brought her in here.

Swallowing bile, I felt ready to throw up. My pounding head wasn't helping. I needed to concentrate...

The four adults approached the black van, which was parked between us and the gate. They walked past the pallet with the barrel, and Imogen whooped in an asthmatic breath that echoed in the open yard.

"What the hell?" one henchman said. "Hey, there's someone there."

"Who?" The woman strode to his side.

The snatchers would find Imogen.

What other choice did I have?

I leaped from my hiding place and waved my arms.

"Hey, losers!" I shouted. The adults snapped their eyes at me. I flung my bag of Tins at them, and they threw their arms up to protect themselves from my 'missile'.

"Go, Imogen!" I yelled.

Imogen shoved off the pallet and bolted, quick as a dart shot from a tranq gun. She was off, clutching her scavenger sack. One henchman moved towards her, and the other scouted me.

"Come and get me, you greasy cowards!" I yelled.

The henchman had reached Imogen, but Figg's attention was laser-focussed on me.

Why did none of them care about the Tins falling from my threadbare hessian sack? Imogen gripped her bag as she ran.

She reached the gate and yanked to loosen the chains. She slipped her body through; the sack snagging on the wrong side of the gate. The gap was wider than her body, but not wide enough for her bulging scavenger bag full of Tins. Mousie and Aze tried to pull Imogen to safety.

Imogen tugged the bag, but before she could wedge it through, the henchman grabbed her arm.

"Leave her alone!" I yelled.

Mousie and Aze kept pulling Imogen.

"Drop your bag!" Aze yelled to Imogen, not realising what was inside.

The other henchman raised his tranquilliser gun. He fired before I could duck. I squinted as the missile shot my way.

Time froze, as it had in my last encounter with the snatchers.

Green glass appeared, everything wavy on the other side. The woman froze in time, observing me. The henchman closest to me was mid-stride, his face twisted in hate. Pocks leaned against the van, picking at his teeth with a knife, eyeing the chocolate Tins scattered in the dirt.

And right in front of me, positioned behind the glass, the dart hung, frozen there in time, its point touching the green force field. That's what it must be. A force field protecting me. But how?

Before I could react, the glass disappeared. The dart dropped to the dust. Time restarted.

The henchman stuffed his dart gun into the holster on his belt and leaped forward, grabbing a fistful of my hair. He yanked, and I cried out. He was way too strong for me.

I couldn't wriggle loose. My hands held his, trying to take my weight. The henchman had a powerful grip on me. Strong enough to pull my hair free and my whole scalp with it.

He shoved me closer to the doctor. She crouched to my height.

"Careful, please," she said, and the henchman relaxed his grip, but didn't let go.

Pocks shook his head with his usual evil smirk. I had monumentally improved his day.

Figg removed her sunglasses and pushed the peak of her cap up, so I examined the faint lines of her forehead, her unnerving stare. She pulled me so close I smelled her minty breath. She was the woman from Mum's warning.

"It's her," Figg said, wonder tinging her expression.

"Told ya," Pocks said with a magnanimous smirk.

"How did you find her?"

"I have my ways," Pocks said, bending to pick up the sack full of chocolate bar Tins that I'd thrown at the henchmen. He packed all of the bars back into the plastic drum.

The second henchman gripped Imogen, his large hand wrapped around her upper arm. She had slipped halfway through the gate and wouldn't let go of her scavenger bag.

She squirmed, but couldn't escape.

"Leave her alone—take me instead!" I struggled against my henchman. But his muscles hardly bulged as I fought to break free. He was not on a diet of black-potato soup.

"So you volunteer?" Figg asked.

"Yes, take me, leave her alone," I said, wriggling out of the henchman's sweaty grasp.

"We have our next willing test subject." Figg smiled, nodding to the man holding Imogen.

He released Imogen, but the Tin bars were too bulky. She had to drop the bag as she wriggled through. Mousie and Aze pulled her to the safe side of the gate, hugging her.

Imogen was crying; the tears dirty tracks on her face. She wasn't upset about leaving the Tins—her eyes searched for me. My friends remained defiant, but their eyes flashed with fear. Figg's attention returned to me.

"Get in." Figg inclined her head at the van.

"I'll wait until my friends are safe," I said. "Then I'll go with you."

"Go on, get outta here!" Pocks barked.

My friends flanked Imogen and their sandshoes slapped the dirt as they retreated through the maze of shacks.

The henchman grabbed me again.

"Back off," I said, wrenching my arm free. Roland's keys fell out of my jeans pocket, jangling as they slapped on the ground.

I tried to grab them, but the henchman kicked my arm out of the way.

"Please, is that a way to treat our guest?" Figg said. "After you."

She waved me forward, and I stepped closer to the van, my heart squeezing in my chest.

Pocks jumped in the back, pushing me in beside him. One henchman joined us as Pocks bound my hands with rope. The coarse fibres glinted in the sun before the doors shut us into darkness. The van rocked as it backed out of the yard, through the gates, to the sound of crunching gravel of the pitted road beyond. Terror overcame me in the dark as the van jolted over a pothole, and I almost bit my tongue. My heart raced until I hyperventilated. This could only end badly for me and everyone I knew.

CHAPTER 7

My sit bones bounced on the bench as the van lurched on the uneven road. The impact of my butt on the metal seat hurt with each jolt.

My henchman was better-fed and had thicker padding. He sat beside me with a vice-grip around my arms, near my shoulders. Pocks sat on the bench opposite, keeping tabs on me. I stared at Pocks first. His eyes were deep receding pits. In this poor lighting, his face was shadowed over, eyeless, and creepy.

The sinister blacked-out windows added to my fear. It clambered up my ribcage like a feral animal, making it difficult to breathe.

I held onto that last image—the Tins scattering in the dirt, Imogen sprinting from the yard to safety. Mousie and Aze taking care of her. The residual echo of their sneakers in my ears. Shouting men, frozen time. Had I imagined it?

The jaunt into the junkyard had put our family at risk. Imogen had to make it home—Mousie and Aze would protect her. Imogen could alert Mum and Roland and they would hide out.

And anyway, it sounded like Dr Figg was more interested

in me than in Imogen. I didn't know why, but I could use that to my advantage.

We drove far from everyone I knew, and I wondered, now that it was real, how I was going to break into Figg's lab. I hadn't planned on having to escape two beefed-up grunts, Pocks and the lady snatcher. How would I get away?

It was stuffy in the van, which reeked of bleach so strong my eyes itched. Sweat dripped along my temple and I was close to puking. I hadn't travelled in a vehicle before and I regretted stuffing my face with chocolate. The swerving motion sent saliva coursing along the rear of my throat, faster than I could swallow.

"I'm going to be sick," I said, concentrating on the dim ground.

"We're not falling for—"

"BLEAGH!"

I vomited between my legs, spitting the last onto the metal floor. The stench was acrid. Pocks lifted his feet when a trickle shot under his seat. His snarl was pure hatred.

He banged his fist against the driver's cab and the divider between the cab and our section of the van sliced open. I squinted against the glare of bright light filtering through.

"Problem?" Dr Figg held the divider open.

"The kid threw up everywhere," Pocks grunted.

"We're not stopping," Figg replied. "I'm sorry, it's not much further."

She slid the divider shut again, and we returned to the gloom.

"Hey, it stinks in here!" Pocks yelled.

No response. The wheels sped over the bumps, and I swallowed my nausea.

We slowed, then stopped—we must be at the checkpoint out of Northies. I'd never been this far out before, although I'd heard stories. The checkpoint was to keep us gutter folk away from the swanky suburbs. I'd only passed this checkpoint via images on our wonky, tiny television.

We waited for a few more minutes as a rusty gate swung on its hinges. We eased through, and the gate slammed as we left my home turf.

A better road smoothed out the ride. None of Northies' roads were wide enough for vehicles at this speed. We glided so effortlessly I wondered if we were hovering above the ground. It didn't ease my nausea, though.

We drove for what felt like an hour, but maybe only ten minutes passed—feeling sick distorted my perception of time, dragging out the minutes. How would I find my way back without seeing the passing landmarks? I lost count of the turns and bends.

A drilling sensation started behind my ears. Thrumming. Pulsing.

I closed my eyes to preserve my energy.

The tyres squeaked as the driver brought us to a stop and yanked the handbrake. He left the engine running. I opened my eyes, alert to every sound. Figg spoke to someone outside, but their conversation was too muffled to hear over the engine. A keypad beeped, and we drove on. Another checkpoint?

Figg slid the divider open, glancing from me to Pocks.

"All good back there?" she asked.

"Nope," Pocks grunted.

The divider closed, and we eased through what must have been a security gate. Our driver navigated a twisted, turning route. We sloped down a ramp—I slipped off the seat with the unexpected movement—but my trusty henchman grabbed me, gripping tighter.

Tyres squealed beneath us. The van grew cooler. So we were underground somewhere—but where? We circled more ramps further into the guts of the building. Then the van halted and the driver cut the engine.

"Get up," Pocks said, and the henchman pulled me to my feet. I tried to avoid the mess on the floor, but he dragged my sneakers right through. Pocks flung open the doors, and I squinted at the dull fluorescent lights in the grey car park. It had an aroma of stale petrol and burnt rubber.

No other vehicles were parked on this floor. The closest painted numbers on the concrete columns dividing the car park said 'F10'. But before I noticed much more, Pocks pushed me in front. The other henchman exited the driver's cab and joined his mate. They pulled me towards the industrial elevator doors, scratched and paint-flaked. The sign next to the call buttons read 'Car Park Level F—Elditch Research Facility'.

So I'd thought right—Figg had taken me straight to her lab. Maybe I could slip away and locate the cure? Somehow, I didn't think they were taking me on the behind-the-scenes tour.

We piled into the lift. Rough hands pushed my head to face the corner while Figg swiped her card on the inner panel. I knew by the 'beep' that she must have punched in a floor number.

My first lift ride. It might have been fun if I wasn't ascending to danger. The mechanics groaned and swayed as we travelled upwards, my stomach lurching with anxiety. Who knew what happened to the kids they snatched?

Minor details could prove helpful later, but as if Pocks could read my mind, he pulled a rank-smelling hood over my head, throwing me into darkness. Tiny pinpricks of light pierced the line of stitching in front of my eyes. The coarse fabric scratched at my face, reeking of fearful sweat, dialling up my terror.

The doors opened, and the henchmen shoved me along a hall with smooth flooring. My sneakers echoed as they clipped the hard surface. The ball I'd won in the mech car games dug into my ankle, tucked into my sock, reminding me of what I was fighting to return to.

Kids' shouts echoed in another room, but the words themselves were inaudible. Something hard thwacked on a flat surface. The shouting stopped.

It was too sinister for a research facility. Was it a hospital? The air reeked of the same disinfectant that infused Roland's work uniform, but this building didn't seem to hold sick people. Doctors cared for people in the hospital. At least, that's what the television portrayed. Northies folk couldn't afford the trip to verify.

The light above me flickered through the hood—and the henchman twisted my arm until we stopped. Another beep, and a lock slid open. A door clanged. Someone pushed me inside a small space and the air closed around me. Pocks whipped off my hood and untied the rope binding my hands. I pivoted in time to see his smirk as he slammed the door. The electronic lock beeped.

"I'll be back soon." Figg bent to peer through a flap in the metal door. "Just try to rest until then."

"Wait—let me out!"

Their heavy-booted footsteps echoed as they strode along the hall.

They had locked me in a cell for one, and desperation descended into my guts as their footfalls exited the wing. I felt tiny, like a small bird fallen from the nest. Alone and vulnerable on the ground, far from safety.

I shook my head and breathed in, turning my attention to my cell. What did I have to work with?

A grungy steel toilet sat in one corner, with a washbasin and a bedroll on the floor covered by a ratty blanket and limp pillow. Set into the wall, over the sink, was a blistered mirror. A single light bulb glowed in the ceiling above me, with a metal cage around it, to prevent anyone breaking the globe. Creases of mould lined each corner where the walls and flooring met. Paint flaked and bubbled on the walls. The floor was scuffed bald in several places from prior inmates' boots, revealing smooth concrete.

At least it was a step up from my shack in one way—it had indoor plumbing.

The cell door handle didn't budge; the thin peephole into the corridor was wedged shut. I pulled at the metal flap with the dying hope of a cornered animal. My fingernail split as I tried to pull it open, and I tore off the broken part of the nail. Blood swelled, and I sucked my finger at the exposed tender part.

I kicked the door, but only stubbed a toe on the thick, solid metal. By the dents in the peeling paint, prior prisoners had tried that tactic many times.

What was the punishment for breaking into a locked yard and stealing a massive haul of valuable black-market currency? How long would Pocks keep me? Could I be here for life? And what did it mean to volunteer for Figg's experiments? That sounded worse.

The smell of sick had seeped right into my skin, so I slipped off my shoes, finding the rubber ball that I'd tucked into my sock earlier that day, running it around in my fingertips, noticing the slight dimpling as I squeezed. My thoughts snagged as I pictured Imogen, her terror as she bolted from the junkyard.

Pocks may find out where we lived and snatch Imogen too.

I crumbled under the weight of that thought, giving in to hopelessness. How easy to let go, forget the people I loved, to assume I was already dead.

I scowled at my reflection in the black-spotted, smudged

mirror. Sucking in a breath of the stale, recirculating air, I steadied my hands on the small basin, wiping my thoughts clean. I had to stay calm and save Imogen.

Concentrate on getting that cure, however long it takes.

I washed the soles of my sneakers under the tap, wiping my sickly footprints with wet hands. My cell smelt less of sick and more of the disinfectant from the hall. Guilt descended as I wasted water, but the stench had to go. I scrubbed my hands and rubbed the sweaty hood feeling from my cheeks.

I drank from the tap, relishing the cool water slipping down my throat. Life itself. It was less brown than the murky rations in our 10-litre bucket in our shack.

There's nothing to do in jail, so I paced. Movement helped —bouncing the rubber ball against the wall, catching it with soft hands. I allowed my thoughts to clear with the methodical movement. All that remained was this soft 'clunk' as the rubber met the smooth concrete, the dimpled pressure as I caught it.

I thought back to the yard, when everyone else froze in time. Had it just been my imagination? It seemed too real.

What had Figg said before they'd shoved me in the windowless van?

She'd said not to worry about Imogen. She wanted me.

But why?

Whatever the reason, it had seemed as if Pocks listened to Figg. She was higher up the food chain. Maybe even Pocks took his orders from her?

The ball ricocheted off my hand, skidding into the corner, underneath the toilet.

I sighed and retrieved the ball, tucking it back into my sock. Maybe this was it for me.

If I believed Imogen was safe, I wouldn't mind dying in this place. My mind wandered to the fire eating into my flesh on the funeral pyre, the scorching flames lapping my skin, my ashes scattered by my mother from the top of Trash Mountain. I imagined my powdery essence floating on the wind, carrying into every corner of the shacks, becoming one with my home. Mum fighting tears, leaning into Roland's supportive shoulder...

What was I thinking?

Stay sharp, find a way out, and locate Figg's lab.

Eventually, someone would have to pay me a visit and open the cell door. I calmed myself with deep breaths and closed my eyes to awaken my other senses.

As soon as I closed my eyes, she appeared.

The most terrible day of my life was when I'd first seen Figg. Snatchers had descended out of nowhere—we hadn't even heard their van. We were working a normal day on Trash Mountain and Demi was showing off, true to form.

"I've found more cans than you," Demi said, with a smirk that hurt to remember.

"So what?" I replied. "Nobody cares."

"Dad cares," she said. "That's cause I'm his favourite. You don't even have a dad."

"Do so!" A rush of anger shot up my arms. I pushed her before my thoughts caught up, and she landed on the floor of trash.

She cut her leg on a protruding shard of twisted metal. Even I drew in a breath.

"What the heck?" she'd yelled. "I could get sick."

"Sorry," I said, my eyes watering, my throat tightening. I couldn't meet Demi's stare, too ashamed of myself.

"We can't afford a doctor!" she said.

"I said I was sorry."

"It's your fault if I die!"

The next moment, the snatchers descended. Demi and I scattered in opposite directions. I hid in a hole in the trash, pulling my scavenger bag over me. I'd watched through a tear in the bag—I'd just laid there—when the tranquilliser dart hit her. As the henchman picked up her limp body, her dark hair over her face, her arm swung as if attached to a corpse.

The black van had approached from a stealthy angle. And, standing by the open door to the passenger seat, in her baseball cap and dark glasses, was Doctor Figg.

Figg took Demi.

The breath knocked out of me with realisation.

Figg had taken my sister *exactly here, to this very building!*

It was obvious, right? It felt so logical it had to be true.

Finding Demi would make up for hiding instead of fighting the snatchers. This time, I would overpower our enemies and keep my family safe.

The last thing she said to me was, "It's your fault if I die." Her words had stayed with me ever since, on rotation in my nightmares, catching me in my waking hours, too.

My mission was growing in scope by the second. Now I had two sisters to save.

The flap in the door scraped open and a thick, hairy hand pushed through a plastic moulded tray. This must be dinner. I was famished after throwing up the chocolate bars, and my stomach had the all-too-familiar growling edge to it. Did I prefer queasiness to hunger? Maybe queasiness. Hunger was too familiar.

"Hello? Can I leave now, please?" I asked, peering into the corridor. The owner of the hairy hand was dressed in orderly whites. But the light was dim and flickered, and I lost sight of him as he shoved a tray into a nearby cell.

Onto the next phase—refuelling to keep my energy high. Escape would be easier on a full stomach.

They had sectioned the food off in parts, and a metal mug filled with muddy, steaming liquid sat on one edge. The food looked foreign—there was a rich-smelling sauce on one lumpy section. A healthy clump of white rice nestled beside cooked carrots and peas.

Although I didn't recognise the saucy lumps, their scent pulled a rousing growl from my belly as saliva reached my tongue.

I poked at the meal and sniffed. It smelt good. The unfamiliar scent reminded me of hiding from KitKat in Northies. It smelt of the butcher's—red things hanging from sharp hooks—pigeons plucked of feathers, or a small skinned rabbit. And beside the butcher was a counter selling warm stew.

The chunks in my dinner were meat! I couldn't recall the taste. But I placed the smell, mingling with the shack's swirling smoke.

Lifting the tray so the liquid didn't leak, I squatted over my mattress, rolling backwards to sit.

The plastic spork was smooth and flimsy—not much use as a weapon. It bent as I scooped up the first mouthful of stew, taking small bites so I didn't overdo things and throw up again. The meat was gristly but delicious; little shreds stuck in my teeth. The gravy sauce was thick and fragrant and the grey-white rice filled me up so I couldn't finish. But who knew when my next meal would arrive? Nothing had changed there, so I savoured every grain, sharpening my mind.

Once I finished the food and licked my tray clean, I sipped the brown liquid from the cup. The bitter flavour was black tea.

Mum made it for us on special occasions. I pictured her standing over the hearth, angling her hip out to avoid the fire, steeping the leaves in the boiling water. She'd pour the celebratory drink into steaming mugs on our birthday or holidays. It was an art, slurping the tea while it was still hot but wouldn't burn your tongue. We'd pick out the leaves and re-use them, each brew weaker than the last.

Poor Mum. I pictured her wringing her hands by our hearth. She couldn't lose another daughter, and Imogen wouldn't survive losing me. Mousie and Aze couldn't be with her around the clock.

Every second that passed put my family in more danger.

I placed the tray on the flap, keeping my unfinished mug of tea. A red pinpoint of light reflected on the walls of the hallway opposite my cell. It bounced from the electronic lock on my door.

Sipping my tea, I savoured the memories it evoked. I pictured Mum brushing Imogen's hair, and Roland telling dad jokes, and Imogen's flushed face.

I stared through the finger of steam rising from my mug. This brew tasted bitter and strong, not weak tea, on its second or third steep. When I'd finished the tea, I was thirsty, so I filled my mug with water from the tap and used the indoor plumbing —which flushed and everything. I bounced the mug in my palm. It might be useful later. The thick, hairy hand returned to collect the empty food tray.

"Hi again, sir." I kept my voice reasonable. "I'd like to see the doctor, please?"

The hand grunted and shut the flap in reply.

The lights in the cell dimmed and other trays scraped; flaps clanged as they locked in place. My fellow inmates settled in for the night. Prickles slid over my scales, my eyes adjusting to the gloom.

My stomach ached, growling as it digested the unfamiliar food. I rubbed the bruises on my arms from where Pocks' henchmen had grabbed me. As I crouched, my hips hurt from bouncing on the steel bench. My whole body throbbed as if they had run me over multiple times.

As the unfamiliar echoing sounds settled, I felt even more alone. The walls of my cell, bubbled and uneven, had been plastered with concrete and a lazy paint job. Subtle depressions formed over the paint and, if I glazed my vision, unfocussed just right, faces formed—a fierce dog with snapping jaws. Or was it a bear? And then, was it Demi with her streak of bleached hair?

They'd trapped me in this concrete bunker. Unlike the patchwork lattice of the metal sheets of home, the cell was solid, smooth, intact. Back home, while I waited for sleep to take me, I followed the path of a rogue star peeking between a mislaid tin sheet. Here it was darker than a coffin, the sky lost. They'd buried me in a grave, sinking into the earth, lost to everyone in this impenetrable jail. Had the sky ceased to be? Nobody would find me in the bowels of this solid building.

I'd already disappeared.

I forced myself to think of other things; I would revisit my escape plan in the morning. For now, the lead crate of exhaustion settled over me. Escape seemed elusive. Things were usually better in the morning.

But as soon as I closed my eyes, she appeared.

Two images froze in my mind—Demi's defiant stance on Trash Mountain, and Imogen, her face a rivulet of tears as she watched Figg take me away. I had to reunite with my family.

CHAPTER 8

THE DRIPPING TAP WOKE ME, a foreign sound indicating opulence. Not wanting to waste water, I placed my mug in the sink to catch each precious drop. Then I paced.

The claustrophobic air was rank, pent up between these four walls. The fluorescent lights hummed with low-frequency energy. Kids' voices pleaded, whined, and then adults shouted, telling them to be quiet or to behave. Metal doors banged, cacophonous and desperate, and I couldn't concentrate on one thought before the next interruption.

My head pounded with the overbearing smell of disinfectant. My veins felt spent, as if I'd run a marathon, and the after-effects of adrenalin were stale.

Concentrate on getting the cure.

First, I had to escape the cell. Second, I had to spring Demi. Third, I had to locate Figg's lab and grab the cure.

What did I have to work with?

I examined the bedroll, tossing the blankets aside. They didn't seem helpful.

Turning the mug over, I wondered if I could use it as a weapon. Just in case, I tucked it next to the bedroll, within reach.

Remaking the bed, I lay under the blanket, calmer now after resting and eating. In fact, my stomach didn't growl now, but the food stuck to my insides, my body not used to digesting such a heavy meal.

Piece by painful piece, I reconstructed memories of Demi, so I'd recognise her when I found her. My mind's image was fuzzy—a year was an eternity and we couldn't afford photographs. The worst thing would be forgetting her.

As time passed, I worried that her memory would become a spire of trash, and every day we'd chip away a fresh layer. Flakes of her face carried on the wind.

I was ashamed to admit I might not recognise her now.

She had dark hair, the same as Roland's. Her bleached streak would have grown out by now. Her mouth was Mum's. She had freckles over the bridge of her nose. And brown eyes. Perfect, non-flecked, crinkled in a joke. She might be taller than me—but that wasn't hard. I was runty for an almost-sixteen-year-old. She had this brashness. You noticed her when she was around, and she dragged her feet when she walked, like you were lucky she'd put in the effort to move at all. Her bravado got her captured.

No—*I* was at fault. I should have saved her, should have fought instead of hiding. A coward in the trash.

"Aaaargh!" I said in frustration. "Shut up, mind!"

But my voice echoed against the painted concrete walls. Just another scared kid in hell.

After an hour of racing thoughts, I grew tired, rolling onto my side. My breathing slowed, and I fell into a light sleep.

And then I dreamt.

My thoughts quietened, and the shouting in the other cells stopped. Tuning into a different frequency, I floated high above the room, clearing the building, then rose into the sky, until the tiled roof of the research facility was a dot all that way below me. I floated further, past the thin skin of Earth's atmosphere, into outer space, then into a spacecraft. My view transformed into the crescent of Earth in the porthole, luminous with swirling misty clouds, blue oceans, and brown land masses.

I floated in the spaceship, peering through the glass portal towards the Earth glowing in the vast blackness of space. I wore a space suit without the helmet. The air I breathed was stale, manufactured and recycled. White wires and panelling covered the insides of the spacecraft, and I peered along a hallway. My toes fitted beneath two steel plates welded to the floor, so I stood still. Earth rotated upside-down—or did the spacecraft rotate? The horizon of Earth steadied to its upright position.

Calm settled on my shoulders, the sensation of warm water seeping into the rest of my body, spreading out into my fingertips and toes. My whole being relaxed.

Earth's glow lit my face, our planet the only colour in the deep darkness of space. A sound vibrated in the small bones deep inside my ears. I couldn't make out the origin of the noise, murmured words, although I was alone in the spacecraft.

I twisted to each side, seeing no one else. The cramped aisle of the spaceship was ghostly, empty of other passengers.

I concentrated on the voice.

The frequency was low and pleasant, with a feminine lilt. Like a gentle bass guitar. Sensation started in my ears, vibrating through my body, the timbre like a song sung in another language. Reverb became a part of me. The bass bounced, prickling my neck hairs with energy.

The noise wasn't frightening or invasive. I relaxed for a few minutes. And then unfamiliar words formed.

The accented words were disjointed and deep. A phrase

repeated, a radio transmission? The same insistent message, but without pleading. A distress call, but calmer than that—as if the speaker expected someone to discover their message.

The sound swam in my head as I concentrated, trying to understand.

And then—my ear attuned, I could follow.

"I am here," the voice said. "Do not come for me."

My veins shot fear into my feet as I jolted awake, returning to the dull light of the cell, the shapes in the paint, disinfectant in my nostrils, the dripping tap as foreign as the voice I'd just heard. Was the voice female? Such a strange accent—I couldn't place it. Definitely not from Northies. Foreign languages were banned and English was the official language of the remaining countries.

The blanket twisted around my legs, the nightmare paralysing. I was terrified to move in case the image returned. I waited until the shaky feeling left my legs and my breathing normalised.

It was just a hyper-realistic nightmare. Everything seemed more intense, like I couldn't trust reality.

"Don't freak out," I told myself, my voice small, uncertain.

Slipping on my shoes, I tucked the ball inside my sock, went to the sink and drank more water, then splashed my face. I replaced my mug in the sink, under the nozzle, to catch each precious drop. It was the first night, and I was already used to indoor plumbing. I took water for granted when it was literally on tap.

I couldn't stand sitting, and so I paced.

As I slowed my breathing, I fought to keep that image of Demi, trace her clenched jawline, the hardness in her heavy brown eyes. She could glare as much as she wanted, if she'd just reveal her location.

Then, the shock of sound reached me, my pupils widened

and at first I thought it was Demi, whispering to me from another cell. I recognised the voice from my dream, but the sound was internal. It buzzed percussion in the connecting tissues deep in my skull.

"I am here. Do not come for me."

I stood bolt upright and scanned my surroundings. Nobody here. The words had whispered a direct connection with my brain.

It didn't sound like Demi's voice, as I remembered it. This voice had the deep resonance of someone fully grown. It had to be one of Figg's tests, right? Or a fellow cellmate?

"Who's there, please?" I said. "This is not funny."

"I am here. Do not come for me."

"Is that you, Demi?"

The message repeated as I shuffled around the room, lifting my ears to locate the source. The tone wasn't louder through the flap into the corridor. Where was the sound's origin?

I stood still and closed my eyelids, capturing the tone, the frequency, and the accent. Blocking out the other senses, I concentrated only on the sound.

The loop repeated at the same interval of 10 seconds. The foreign accent was difficult to follow. And the frequency had that same bass quality, that low, resonant tone.

"Where are you?" I asked.

"I am here. Do not come for me."

The reverb was inside my skull; it was consistent wherever I stood. It didn't grow louder or softer as I moved. It never faltered. Monotonous and annoying, dropping madness on my forehead, a single dribble at a time...

I huffed into the bed, determined not to let the distraction get to me. But the voice deadened other sounds. I stayed with it until the words became nonsensical with repetition.

Iyameredonotcomeformeee.

I pushed the humming mantra to the edge of my mind, laying my own concerns on top so I could hear my own plans.

I have to break free, I thought.

The looping stopped. Gone, as before, like a muted television. My senses returned.

Help me find Demi, I thought, pleased that I could concentrate.

"Who is Demi?" the voice in my head asked.

Holy crap. Could they hear me?

Fear overtook my body, a swiping hand from above flushing me with adrenalin. It was as if my breath squeezed, wringing me dry, and I was tipping off the surface of the floor. Up was down. Down was up. And I... heard voices that could talk back?

Had I imagined the words? The noises, the tests, the food and Figg's interest in me—this was a nightmare. I'd wake up soon, in the shack, listening to Roland's dad jokes, and Imogen's racking whoops, and Mum's spoon nicking the pot as she stirred our breakfast filled with the fresh-grown herbs, the smoke from the hearth swirling on its journey out the window. Surrounded by the shouts and commotions of home.

I'd wake to normal life soon, right?

"Who is Demi?" the voice repeated, and I knew I wasn't asleep.

The light was too harsh, the smell of disinfectant too over-powering, the chill of the air vent on my skin too real. I was awake, and the tone in my skull was talking to me.

"She's my sister," I said.

"Who is Demi?"

"I just said —" I stopped, considering an idea. I could only hear the words inside my head. Maybe I had to reply there too? I concentrated inwards.

She's my sister, I thought.

At first, there was no reply. But then the command came to me.

"Use the cup," they said.

My heart raced. Was this happening?

What cup?

No acknowledgement. The sound receded.

What do you mean? I thought. Then, in frustration, I yelled out, "What stupid cup, you stupid voice?"

Yeah, real smooth, playing it cool.

Then the voice said, "She is here."

The lights flickered; the voice trailed off with a lingering echo.

A security panel beeped, and the door opened.

Doctor Figg stood with two members of staff.

The male orderlies in starchy white uniforms flanked the cell door, one wearing a scowl and the other an expression of supreme boredom. Scowly held a nightstick at his side, and Bored picked at a hangnail, keeping a casual eye on me.

They could have played on the national football team for the Remaining Countries World Cup and taken home the trophy. Scowly's muscular shoulders draped like a sack across the back of his neck. Bored was pudgier, but he could wrestle a small army and win on sheer bodyweight. Both men were bursting out of their hospital whites.

Figg hovered over their shoulder, immaculate and presentation-ready. The doctor fit for television, rather than the doctor-in-hiding, whose hobbies included snatching children.

I chalked up the creepy voice to Figg conducting her first test on me. She was trying to get me to divulge information about Demi.

"A bit unnecessary?" I said, turning my eyes towards Scowly's nightstick.

"Don't give me a reason to use it," Scowly grumbled,

shoving the stick into a link in his belt with an aggressive flourish.

"Now, let's treat our guest with respect, please," Figg said, squeezing between the orderlies, her face fresh, anticipating great things. She took an electronic device from the pocket of her coat and her straightened hair dipped to the side as she bent towards me.

"How did you sleep?" she asked.

"Like you care," I spat back, hugging my arms to my body and backing away.

"I care more about you than you realise," Figg said pleasantly, holding up the device so I could see. "It's just to take your temperature."

My body tensed, but I allowed her to stick the thermometer into my ear, mimicking the echoing sound of the rumbling van on the road against my eardrum. Figg removed the device, and the sound returned to normal—clanging doors, scuffed boots, distant sobbing. You know, the things that gave you hope to keep on living.

Figg read the electronic display. "You're a little higher than I'd like."

"Probably because of the kidnapping..."

"You volunteered, as I recall?" She smiled, but it didn't reach her eyes, a repeat of her television appearance. My mother said this lady was dangerous, and I believed it too.

"What do you want from me?" I demanded, observing her pocketing the plastic cover of the thermometer and leaving her hand there, as if I'd reach into her pocket and steal it.

"I've been searching for you," she said. "For a long time."

"That makes no sense," I said.

"You're a very special girl."

I snorted a laugh. It caught me as much by surprise as it did Figg. Was she kidding? This time crinkles reached her eyes in genuine amusement. She shifted her stance, one foot towards me, angling out. The doctor clasped her hands in front of her, as if she was approaching a delightful problem, or explaining the universe to a toddler.

"You are extraordinary, Ofelia," she said.

"Lady, you're delusional." I studied the stark shadow beneath the blistered, blurred mirror where it met the wall.

"You'll come to see," she replied. "We'll run tests, analyse your blood. You shouldn't worry. We'll be gentle."

"As gentle as Pocks' henchmen?"

"Mr... ah... Pocks is no longer in this facility."

Figg tilted her head with wonder.

She creeped me out. I'd take Pocks and his pitted, shadowy face over this lady any day. Pocks made his rules clear. I had no clue what Figg wanted from me. What if I couldn't give her what she needed?

"You remind me of her," Figg said.

"Who?" I said.

"Your sister." She sniffed, as if warding off emotion, and slipped her hand back into her pocket, tapping the temperature device on her coat.

"Don't you dare talk about my sister," I said, stalling for time. Which sister was she talking about?

"Demi, her name was, if I'm right?"

"Where is she now?"

"She's not here, if that's what you're wondering." Figg bent down to move a hair from my eyes. I flinched as her nail moved across my forehead. "It doesn't matter, because I've finally found you."

"You didn't even know me before today," I said, pulling away. Her gesture didn't seem threatening. It felt like she was talking to her niece or something.

"You're the special one, Ofelia." Her crow's feet crinkled.

Was she for real? Who did she think I was?

"Let me save you the trouble. I'm just your regular street rat lizard freak!"

"Well, let's find out, shall we?" Figg said, stepping aside and waving to the corridor.

"After you, kid." Scowly stood aside to let me pass.

CHAPTER 9

I PEEKED out into the grey, antiseptic-like hallway as Scowly moved to make room. Figg and Bored fell in beside me. Doors to the other cells lined the corridor, the space between each door matching the width of my cell. As we passed, I snuck glances at the occupants through the open food tray flaps. There were two kids in a cell, my age or younger. Their face masks were in much better shape than Imogen's, in pale hospital blues.

I didn't recognise the kids. The first pair scoffed their food —so they must have been Northies kids from the other section. Only the hungry ate like that, shovelling food as if it would disappear. Others sat on their bedrolls, poking forks at their trays as if they'd been here a while.

I scanned each cell but didn't see Demi.

The last open flap in the row revealed Pocks' little informer, KitKat, scoffing food into her greedy mouth.

My heart skipped—that confirmed my theory. All the kids came here. That meant Demi, too!

"Hey KitKat—" I said, taking a nightstick between my shoulder blades for the trouble. The sharp impact stung, forcing the air out of my lungs. I coughed and gasped for breath, the air seeming to be a solid thing lodging in my wind-pipe. I checked for Figg's reaction, but she hadn't seen the blow.

While I recovered, I paused by KitKat's cell.

She turned her head and recognised me, setting her tray on the floor and running to the cell door.

"You've got her now!" she pleaded. "Let me go!"

"Where's Demi?" I yelled.

Bored slammed the flap shut and shoved me along the hall. There was no mistaking KitKat's muffled voice.

"It's not fair! You said I'd go home!"

"Have you seen—" I said.

Scowly shoved my head towards the front.

"Careful, you oaf," Figg said to the orderly, who scowled at me. Then he noticed Figg's combative expression. He scowled less.

"Thanks for the apology." My sarcasm waned as he reached for his nightstick.

My mind whirred with this development. Did KitKat give me up? But then, why had they taken her captive too? And could Pocks' little informant help me find Demi? Even better, KitKat couldn't spy on my family if she was in here. Maybe Imogen and my parents could avoid detection until Pocks grew tired of searching?

I had to focus, find the lab. Demi could wait if she'd survived here this long. I'd have to improvise with whatever opportunities arrived next.

They led me to a shower block—an entire white-tiled room, with water just for bathing! My first ever shower.

My day was about to get better. Infinitely better. Like, the dreams that angels had on vacation on their sixteenth birthdays.

Figg pointed to the soap and shampoo nestled in a

dispenser in the wall, leaving a clean bra, underwear and folded hospital gown on a bench away from the nozzle. She closed the door behind her, leaving me alone in the bathroom.

We had a communal bath at home; our family used it once a month. The last person in had the honour of bathing in everyone else's grime. A pang shot through me as I realised Roland always volunteered to bathe last.

This bathroom was devoid of windows or any other ways of escaping, so I undressed, tossing my clothes onto the bench outside the shower curtain. I tucked the rubber ball underneath the hospital gown. A flake of dirt fell from the underside of my leg as I stepped into the shower. I twisted the taps and water shot out. The solid dirt shard melted with the water sifting into the drain.

I stepped beneath the jet of water, warm and steaming. It rushed over my scalp, the hair wetting of monsoon season. Warm, clean water coursed over my shoulders, separating me from the layers of Northies muck. As I scrubbed the soap, fragrant lather appeared, and I popped the white bubbles with my finger. My skin glowed as the unclean layers washed away. The lather from the shampoo was a delight, and my tangled light brown hair smoothed out as I wrung it free from the suds. I smelt like pristine pine needles on a serene mountain top, free from the worries of the world below, bursting with new life.

Now I understood the crisp, clean feeling of regular suburbs folk.

An orderly tapped the door, and I twisted the taps closed. My skin softened as I rubbed dry with a towel, being careful of the tender hexagonal scales on my stomach and bicep. They stung if I rubbed too vigorously. I dressed in the underwear, bra and gown.

A steamed mirror was set into the wall above the bench. My reflection was so clean I could pass for someone from the swanky suburbs. I ran my fingers through my wet, luxurious hair, feeling like a million Tins.

Figg was treating me well, although the orderlies could be better trained. But she didn't want me hurt. For the moment, I was her prize guinea pig, washed and fed and ready for her initiation.

But an initiation into what?

A nightstick clonked on the door.

"Hurry in there," Scowly grunted.

"Almost ready," I replied.

A dilemma presented itself as I donned the gown—the rubber ball. I assumed I wasn't wearing my ratty shoes and socks to whatever they had in store for me. I'd have to hide the ball, but the gown didn't have any pockets, and it gaped at my bum. The turquoise soft rubber felt as warm as Imogen's hand. It was my only and most important possession.

With nowhere else to stash it, I tucked it into the waistband of my underwear, but it bulged at my hip. I gathered the gown, to hide the protrusion, as if too modest to let it gape. I favoured that side as I walked, so the fabric hung loose over the lump.

Rehearsing the walk, I carried my gown just so, until my gait appeared natural. Another nightstick rap interrupted my routine. I had to confront Figg, and stepped into the hallway.

"What about my clothes?" I asked.

"Leave them. We'll need you upstairs." Figg spoke as if she was showing a fresh recruit around one of those corporate offices in the city proper.

"What's upstairs?" I asked casually.

"You'll see," Scowly grunted.

"Charming," I said.

Figg approved of my appearance with an almost-imperceptible nod and nudged my shoulder towards the lift.

Pushed off-balance, my wet soles slipped and the ball-bulge

became apparent, but my companions were concentrating on the opening lift doors and didn't notice.

We stepped into the lift, and I checked my reflection in the mirror at the back. My wet tangle of hair dripped onto the floor. I felt fresh and invigorated. Who was I if I wasn't a Northies rat? My eyes were less orange today, here in the gloom, almost brown in this light—like Mum's, whose fleckless irises I'd always envied.

The lift arrived on level four, presenting us with a hallway with a whole new vibe. No more prison feeling; this was a fancy hospital.

For a start, the walls were painted yellow—and not a dirty pumpkin, but a cheerful tone that suburbs people painted a baby's bedroom. I'd seen similar scenes in children's books I'd swiped from our derelict bookstore early on. The doctors up here wore blue paper outers over regular clothes, clean white face masks and surgical caps. Most peered through oversized protective glasses.

A nurse stood up from her chair next to the lift, handing us disposable face masks. I donned the mask, as did Figg and the two orderlies. Figg signed a form on an iScreen, which the nurse then checked, and waved us into the ward.

Everyone on the ward, bar none, wore masks. So, the plague had penetrated beyond Northies. Maybe beyond the fence wasn't as pristine as the swanky suburbs defectors portrayed?

An orderly, dressed in navy blue patterned with stars and planets, pushed a kid in a wheelchair. Everyone stared at me, Figg, and the burly orderlies as we passed, as if I was a criminal. Maybe because Bored had a crunching grip of my elbow, to prevent escape. Nobody else in the ward wore the gaping hospital gowns; they wore normal clothes that weren't in need of mending.

Each room contained six curtained beds housing kids with plaster casts on their legs or tubes attached to their noses. Others appeared weak and emaciated, with patchy hair.

The ages ranged from toddler up to my age, around sixteen. They played with toys on their beds. A few kids were in poor physical shape, but they seemed content.

The kids' parents spoke to doctors and monitored their offspring.

Something occurred to me: the toys were clean and unbroken. Their colours were fresh. These toys hadn't been handed down for generations. The dolls still had their eyes and hair attached. It was creepy.

In the next dayroom, a massive, colourful television transfixed a bunch of tweens, following the characters on the screen. How rich were these kids? I hadn't seen a real-life video game before. One boy jeered as his character dispatched the other in a boxing match, and the kid who lost started crying.

"You cheated!" he whined.

These patients hadn't travelled from Northies. Their demeanour made me feel out of place—I couldn't navigate a video game if my very escape depended on it. I'd only ever played the mech cars that Pocks ran on Trash Mountain. There was nothing virtual about those games.

Why did Figg bring me here?

We pushed into another corridor.

As we walked, I searched for any sign of Figg's lab, but this didn't seem like the right floor. Figg's lab had a glass-fronted door on the news segment on television, and these doors were painted solid.

We pushed through the first solid door. A huge white machine sat, hollow in the middle, a bed extending from inside. The medical machine looked threatening. I wondered if it was for torture? Would it kill me in a horrible, painful way? It wasn't logical to make me shower first. I backed up, bumping against the pudgy stomach of Bored.

"In you go," he said, standing his ground. It was pudgy man or death-by-machine.

"Don't be scared," Figg said, "it won't hurt you. Have you heard of X-rays?"

"Yes."

"Well, it's similar, only more powerful. It will give us a magnificent view of you."

"Can't you see me from here?" I asked.

"It looks inside of you," Figg said. Her genuine smile was back. Maybe she cared about me?

At least if she thought I was special, maybe she wouldn't hurt me?

"Okay, I guess, since I don't have a choice," I said.

A nurse with protective, clear glasses entered, placing a plastic bowl on the bed. She patted for me to sit and pulled out the biggest needle I'd ever seen.

"Um, *do* I have a choice?" I asked, eyeing the needle.

The nurse smiled underneath her mask. "I'm only taking blood, so we can run tests. We need to figure out why you're sick, sweetie."

"I'm not your sweetie, and you're not sticking me with that needle!"

Her expression read as if I'd told a bad-taste joke. Figg leaned in to whisper into the nurse's ear, who left, leaving her container of pointy objects.

Figg snapped on disposable gloves, plucked from a dispenser on the wall. This was worse, way worse.

"I can take your blood myself," Figg said, as Scowly gripped my shoulders and Bored seized my wrists.

I struggled, never taking my eye off the needle that Figg was preparing, but the orderlies were too strong and restrained me.

"Little prick," Figg said, jabbing the needle into my skin until dark blood spurted into the vial. It didn't hurt too much, but it was still a shock. I squirmed as she filled the first vial, then attached another, and another. I wriggled until she finished.

"Press here," she said.

I held the cotton bud to my arm as she withdrew the needle and marked the stickers on each vial of blood. I counted ten vials—was that too much? Would I die from blood loss?

Figg placed the vials in the plastic container. Bored took the container to another room. When he returned, Figg instructed me to lie on my back on the extended bed, and then shift backwards. I didn't enjoy where this was going, but I followed her instructions to keep Scowly's hand off his nightstick.

I realised my gown bunched on the wrong side and the waistband of my undies was showing.

"What's this?" Figg frowned, pointing to the protrusion at my hip.

I sighed and fished the prize ball from my waistband, slapping it into her outstretched palm. She examined it with a concentrated frown, then handed it to Bored, who bounced it on the floor.

Bounce. Bounce. Bounce.

Those orderlies sure knew how to get a rise out of me, but despite myself, I couldn't help but watch the smooth ball arc off the polished, flat floor. Such controlled conditions didn't exist in the mech car game.

Figg shot an impatient, eyebrow-raised challenge, and Bored shrugged and pocketed the ball.

"Hey, give that back!" I demanded. "Dr Figg, please?"

"We'll give it back to you after the tests, if you behave for us."

Bored had confiscated my last connection to home and now I was about to be ray-gunned to death in this creepy, massive machine.

Figg asked me to scoot up so my head was near the circular opening. Was this my inevitable ending? A control panel sat behind a glass window. I'd have to get past the orderlies to reach the door.

"You won't feel a thing," she said.

"Will it kill me quickly?" I asked in a small voice.

A puffed laugh escaped as she replied, "No, it won't kill you. You won't notice the test. Trust me, you're fine."

"What do I have to do?"

"Lie as still as you can. We'll talk to you from this microphone." Figg pointed to a small circle of tiny holes in the cylinder's top. "Please, just follow our instructions."

Scowly and Bored passed straps around my body, hands and feet, to restrain me.

"It's just so you don't fall off," Figg said, patting me on the head.

I mean, really? Her condescending gesture made me even madder.

"I'm pretty sure I won't fall off a flat bed," I said, but Figg didn't react.

They left and watched from behind the glass wall as the bed rolled into the machine, the enormous opening passing overhead, until the huge, curving white cavity surrounded me. It was cramped and noisy, with ominous, mechanical knocking sounds, and I worried that I'd disintegrate into powder. The knocking grew louder. The vibrations echoed throughout my chest as I resisted the panic escalating in my mind.

Apart from the buzzing noise, nothing else happened. No other bodily sensations or pain followed. I stopped struggling after a while; it wasted my energy.

"Take a deep breath and hold it for us," Figg said, through the speaker above me.

"If I do, can I return to my cell?" I shot back.

"The longer you struggle, the longer we'll keep you in there."

I didn't believe her, but I was out of choices. If all I had to do was breathe and stay still, I'd cooperate.

I pretended to be hiding in the pipe at the trash pile, frozen, while the snatchers searched for us. The machine was loud and frightening at first, and I resented the claustrophobic space. As the minutes passed, it was just boring.

After an age, the bed slid out from inside the cylinder. Figg and her friends in white returned.

"This will go by faster if you follow instructions," Figg said, shaking her head at me, her amusement lingering in the corner of her pursed mouth.

Scowly and Bored untied me, and I sat up, rubbing my wrists.

Before I could swipe Figg's smug face, Bored restrained my arms, pinning them behind my back. He dragged me to the corridor, and I scanned for Figg's lab. Nothing resembled the image on the television news segment.

Figg took me to another room with an X-ray machine.

A technician handed me a strange oversized vest. I almost dropped it as she handed it to me. It was so heavy.

"That will protect you from the X-rays," she said. "Just stand still. Easy, right?"

I nodded, and she helped me put the vest on, so that it covered my torso and my upper legs. She directed me to stand in front of the arm of a machine, which she pointed at my neck and head. Then she left the room.

Wait—Scowly and Bored had disappeared, too. They

lingered some distance from the X-rays. I was alone in the room, there was nothing stopping me from escaping!

I edged towards the door and reached for the handle. The machine beeped, remaining in position. I threw off the heavy vest and pushed the door, but it was locked. I moved to the alcove where the technician sat. She glanced up, not expecting to see me.

"So that's why it failed," she said. "You need to stay still."

I ignored her, pushing through into the corridor, right where Scowly and Bored leaned against the wall.

"Hey." Scowly grabbed me before I could make a dash for it. I wriggled, but he was stronger. They forced me back into the room with the X-ray machine.

"We'll tell Dr Figg, unless you cooperate," Bored said, annoyed he had to do actual work.

I allowed the technician to take pictures of every part of my body as I stood at various angles. The tests themselves might not kill me. It might be best to cooperate.

Figg returned, and she seemed satisfied with me as she held films to the X-ray light box. It was pretty cool, seeing my bones and soft parts in the film. My ploy to cooperate worked, because Scowly relaxed and wasn't so quick to grab me. Could I slip away if I waited for my moment?

Figg, the orderlies, and I headed for a vacant room. The doctor waved at the chair in the corner. I sat.

She played it cool, trying not to treat me like a barrel-full of Tins. I knew what the results would show—a complete waste of everyone's time. There was nothing special about me.

"Are we done?" I asked, as I retied my hospital gown to reduce the gaping. The scales on my upper arm transfixed Figg.

"I just want to look."

I held still as she examined my scaly patches, pressing with her fingers at the edges. She lingered at the scales surrounding my stomach.

Another doctor arrived, pale beneath his mask, as if he rarely saw sunlight, more used to the night shift. His suit pants stuck out from the bottom of his blue paper outers. His manner suggested he didn't waste time. I wondered if he was more senior than Figg.

"Let me go, please," I said, but his expression didn't change. It was as if I hadn't spoken.

"Take your gown off, please," he said, washing his hands in a basin in the corner.

"They took me against my will," I said. His expression didn't change—so he was in on Figg's experiments then?

"Do as I ask, please," he said. There was zero room for disobedience in his tone.

I untied the gown and stood in my bra and underwear, feeling exposed and uncomfortable. The doctor sat me on a bed. He snapped on blue rubber gloves and prodded my skin, both where the scales were, and where the normal skin grew.

Figg leaned in with a tube of cream and squeezed the ointment onto a fresh white cloth. She rubbed the ointment onto my scales.

"This will numb the area," Figg said, nodding to the doctor.

He brushed at his fringe with a gloved finger and picked up a scalpel. Its blade flashed in the overhead lighting as he examined the steel.

"Ah, what the actual—" I said, pulling away.

"Over here," he said, and Scowly and Bored grabbed me.

The doctor brought the scalpel closer. This was it—he was going to cut me!

"Get off me!" I said. "Help! Help me! Doctor Figg!"

I wriggled against the vice-gripped orderlies. The doctor

brought the scalpel closer. Bored and Scowly struggled as I concentrated all my strength into breaking free.

"Stay still please, Ofelia," Figg said, her brow crinkling with concern.

"This won't hurt much," the male doctor said.

"Much???" I squirmed desperately.

But the orderlies' joint strength forced my arm out straight, exposing my orange scales.

The blade hovered; cool steel pressed against my arm. The doctor made a swift incision. I threw my weight backwards, away from this sadistic man as the shock burst through my nerves.

"What the hell, man?" I yelled. Blood trickled through his gloved fingers.

"Sorry... I just want a sample," he said.

He held up the scalpel, peering at the bloody scale he'd removed.

And then something spectacular happened.

The scrapings on his scalpel disintegrated into ash, reminding me of our hearth at home. The ash stuck to the blade. In the next instant, the bloody ash disappeared, the edge of his scalpel clean, as if he hadn't cut me.

If Figg's face was ecstatic before, now she bordered on manic.

"See, Sebastian?" she said, taking his scalpel and holding it to the light. "This is what I was saying."

I snatched my hand away from my arm, where he'd cut into my flesh.

The blood had gone, and my scales healed. There was no trace of the incision. It didn't even hurt anymore. The scale had regrown in the same position.

"What the heck is happening?" I asked.

Sebastian's eyes were almost as wide as Figg's.

"This is it!" He snapped off his gloves and threw them into a nearby garbage can. "We've only got two days, though, to prove what she is. They're pulling the plug otherwise..."

"She'll be ready." Figg's eyes flashed over to me, as proud as if I was her daughter taking out a national piano recital. "She has to be."

"Ready for what?" I yelled, confusion overwhelming me. "What should I be prepared for?"

Figg leaned in. "To fulfil your purpose, Ofelia."

"What does that even mean?" I asked.

"Let's find out!"

CHAPTER 10

FIGG ACCOMPANIED me to the much less cheery basement, to grey, desperate walls. Ushered into my claustrophobic cell, returning to punishment. The door slammed, the echo rolling through the corridor like a retreating, scurrying dog. Figg's eyes crinkled in apology as she crouched to talk to me through the flap.

"I'm sorry you have to be here," she said, and I hated to admit it, but she sounded sincere. "It's just until the test results come through, for everyone's safety."

I snorted a laugh.

"I'm not a rabid dog," I said.

"No, you're not," Figg replied. "You're the most special patient I have ever worked with. You'll see that I'm trying to help."

"Help who?"

"Everyone, Ofelia. Think of it. A cure for the plague..."

"But you already have the cure," I said. "Why do you need me?"

"Your sister was full of questions too," Figg whispered, studying my face, lingering over my eyes. Her expression glistened with emotion. "You're so alike."

"Where are you keeping her?" I asked.

A flit of pain covered Figg's face, but she recovered with a bright smile. "Don't worry about that now. Just rest, Ofelia. We have work to do. The most important work anyone could do."

"What work? What are you talking about?"

"We think your genes are extra special, a real breakthrough."

"Special, yeah right. More like a freak..."

"You're not a freak, Ofelia. You're the best chance we have."

"Where are you keeping Demi?"

"I can't tell you now. It's not the right time."

"I'm not doing anything else for you until you take me to Demi."

"Please, Ofelia, I promise to take you when the time is right. Why can't you trust me?"

"Trust you?" I scoffed. "Are you kidding? Anyone who fraternises with Pocks has to be shady."

Figg's hurt expression seemed genuine. "I'm doing everything I can to keep you safe. Just sleep, if you can. We have a big day tomorrow."

The white of her lab coat obscured the view, and her high heels clipped along the hallway. She believed what she was saying. But why?

Someone had folded clothes on top of my bed—a clean, flower-printed t-shirt in pastel colours, a pair of dark, flared jeans and white socks. I didn't fancy hanging out in a hospital gown. If I was going to find Demi and Figg's lab, I needed outside clothes.

Lab rat. Northies rat. Lizard freak.

Why couldn't I be someone else, someone extraordinary, someone with genuine power? Figg had the power, hiding me in a concrete bunker. She controlled my future. At least

Northies wasn't locked down; I could roam wherever I wanted there. I longed for the freedom of Trash Mountain, laying an arm over Imogen's shoulders as we roamed the steaming streets.

But no, I was stuck in kiddie prison.

I left the gown folded on the open flap and sat on my bed, now dressed. My toes played with the edge of the mattress; the sensation as the sock ends rolled around scrunched toes, the warmth of the cotton. Socks without holes, t-shirts fully ravelled, jeans sans rip. I was a traitor, gussied up and working for evil.

My next move was unformulated as a distorted vision of Demi surfaced. Her hair could be longer, touching her shoulders. She may have grown a couple of centimetres taller. Would she recognise me?

I turned her in my mind as I would a three-course meal, savouring each flavour. Poking first at the sharp ridge of her cheekbones, moving to her dimpled chin, remembering that dark flash of smile when she was about to break the rules, which happened often. Her hair with the bleached stripe hung limp, her arm swinging as they carried her away...

My hands sought the scaled part of my arm, rough beneath my touch. I lifted my shirt and examined the rash of scales, an orange paintbrush over my belly. The scales had faded, maybe because I'd been away from sunlight. They had an orange-brown tinge at the edges, and each scale was the size of the fingernail on my pinkie finger. I checked the arm that the doctor had cut into, and it was fine, as if I hadn't had a scale extracted only moments earlier.

My stomach growled, now accustomed to being fed.

Focus. Food later. Escape now.

I drank from the tap because I could, marvelling that clean water was available anytime, wishing Imogen could experience this. An image came to me; Mum hauling our single bucket of water rations from the communal pump back to our shack. She would tiptoe to stop the drips from overflowing as she bent to the weight of the bucket. That bucket lasted us a week. Pocks mandated the rations. It was how he controlled every family in Northies.

A pang shot up my side at the thought of Pocks' greasy ponytail bobbing through the door to our shack... please let my family be okay.

I paused by the sink, catching my blurred reflection, steadying both hands against the basin. The metal mug's dull surface reflected the bare light bulb. A theory occurred to me. Did the voice mean this cup?

They must have.

I dumped the rest of the liquid into the sink, the light flashing in the metal finish. What was special about it?

I banged the mug on the door hinge, using it as a hammer. Bang. Bang. Bang. My forehead sported sweat beads and my hands rubbed raw, but the hinge was solid, used to similar abuse.

Next, I pried with the mug's handle to jimmy the lock open. But the metal was too thick, and the handle didn't slip between the fingernail-wide gap between the hinge and the greasy metal door.

I heaved and pulled, knowing it was useless, until my muscles gave out. My arms ached, shooting pain. I felt weak. As I squatted on my haunches and caught my breath, I flexed my shaking arms, drawing strength.

Impatient to escape the cell, anger rose until I couldn't stand it anymore.

I ran straight forward, flinging the mug as if I was clocking the roof in the mech car game.

Something weird happened.

The mug bounced off and arced towards me. I flung my

forearms up to protect against the missile, but instead of hitting me, everything froze, as it had in the junkyard.

The green glass-like force field returned, and the mug hung in the air, suspended, touching the shield in front of my body.

I unfurled my arms. The cup held steady in its gravity-defying position.

I could see through the layer protecting me, but everything distorted with the green hue of a waterfall. Except frozen solid, and stopping time.

Or had *I* stopped time?

How cool was that? But, as I lost concentration, life resumed. The mug smacked into the force field, clattering to the ground. It rolled into the corner.

The shield vanished.

What the actual heck?

My scales sizzled with latent heat as I placed my palms over my stomach.

With the force field gone, and the cup resting in a slight groove on the cement floor, I moved to the mirror. I peered at my scales in my reflection. They were more pronounced. Strange, their colour had been subdued moments ago. My back-lit irises alarmed me—the orange flecks were iridescent, as if someone had shone a powerful LED light behind the orange specks. I blinked, and the glowing flickered.

What was happening to me?

I felt drained of energy. My scales were hot to the touch, my eyes bright as a nightclub dance floor. After creating a *freaking force field*!

Pretty cool for little old me.

I trained my laser eyes on the rivets in the door. But that didn't cause a ripple. I'm ashamed to say that I even rubbed my scaled arms on the hinge, as if they could eat through a half-metre-thick chunk of metal, like acid. It was worth a try, right?

Nope—still trapped.

I swiped the cup and studied it. The metal wound into a square handle, secured with two tiny screws. I slotted my chewed fingernail into the groove, twisting like a screwdriver, but the screws were glued in place.

Could the mug be the key? What was I missing?

My gaze fell to the dripping tap in the corner, and a solution came to me. I filled the mug to the brim until it dribbled over the sides. Carried it as if it was our week's worth of rations. Clocked the path to the door, confirming my trajectory.

I sprinted towards the door and hurled the brimming cup, every muscle taut.

The mug ricocheted with a splash.

Before the water could hit me, the green protection appeared.

Time froze.

Both the water and the cup poised mid-hurtle.

I held the force field open longer, by thinking of nothing else. I moved behind the glass-like exterior, eyeing the scene from every angle. The shield moved with me. Everything waited, frozen, until I was ready. This was freakin' awesome!

Before I could congratulate myself too much, and lose concentration, I returned to my original position, and resumed time—more intuitively, rather than with an obvious command. But it worked.

The messy spray bounced off, and the mug clattered to the floor, spinning near the pool of liquid.

The water sped with such power that liquid shot into the doorframe. Electricity flashed as the metal cup and fluid connected with the power source of the lock.

A colossal electrical jolt threw me into the wall behind me. I sat in a crumpled heap, dazed from the blow, the scent of singed hair in my nostrils.

As I found my feet, my entire body ached. I checked my reflection in the mirror—complete with glowing eyes and slightly smoking hair—but I was unhurt.

I bent to the tray flap; the red sensor light no longer bounced off the opposite wall. My neighbour's sensor dot shone, as usual, on the wall further along the hallway.

Had I shorted the electronic lock?

I heaved at the metal mechanism on my side, and it budged! The lock shifted from 'engaged' to 'open', but with a crunching squeal of metal on metal. I paused, waiting for the heavy boots of the orderlies. But the hall was subdued in its nightly ritual.

I placed the mug on the basin and sopped up the water puddle with my blanket. Squeezing the blanket into the sink, I remade my soggy bed. I checked through the flap. Roaming staff were elsewhere, so I pushed the door ajar.

I poked a tentative head out into the empty hallway. I was out! Escape. Freedom.

A flickering globe in the overhead lights lent a sinister beat in the hallway. The air felt cooler out here, well-circulated, less stale. Before they discovered me, I had to find Demi and spring us both. Then she could help me find Figg's lab. Demi had to be in a nearby cell.

The cells led off the main corridor. The door to the next wing was in front, the orderly's station behind. Two orderlies chatted, their backs to me.

Scowly cornered a female orderly and his face cracked in a creepy grin, becoming a charming version of himself. He laughed as he struck up a conversation. It was obvious she thought little of him, but he was oblivious.

He lay the smooth rubber ball on the desk, within the orderly's reach.

"Look after this?" he said, leaning in.

He handed it over like a prize dinner proffered in front of a beggar.

"Um, okay," she said.

She deposited it beside the computer monitor at the orderly's station, her body language showing she had no interest in the guy.

While Scowly flirted, I hugged the grungy-painted walls, scooting to the first cell. Peeking through the flap, I identified the occupants as two boys around ten years old, both wearing masks. I recognised the boy with the scar on his cheek.

Panic shot into my chest as he turned and noticed me!

"Hey, you!" he yelled.

"Shhh..." I put my fingers to my lips.

"How'd you get out? Hey, someone's out!"

Eager faces crowded at the row of doors, peering out into the corridor. They spotted me. That started a cacophony of kids, yelling to be set free. It wasn't fair; they wanted to be rescued too.

Yep, they called Northies their home.

"Hey, stop that racket," Scowly barked, swivelling his head to the corridor. He saw me frozen like a rabbit in a spotlight. "Not you again!"

My heart hurt the back of my ribs from beating so fast. I took a breath. Scowly's boots clattered as I backed up against the wall. There was nowhere to go.

Disappointment dropped as Scowly tackled me, slamming my shoulders to the ground. I struggled against the pressure of the gigantic man as he gripped both my wrists in one hand. His other hand drove my ankles to the floor. He slapped plastic restraints around my wrists so I couldn't move. I tried to make a force field, to stop time again, but couldn't produce a single electrical fizz.

"Are you done fighting?" Scowly demanded, pressing the end of his nightstick into the small of my back.

"Yes," I replied. This was not a winning position. Pain shot through my arms, twisted behind me.

"Good girl." Scowly popped me up on my knees, and then he grabbed me under the arms and carried me to my room.

The kids whistled and shouted as he carried me. This was the best show they'd seen for a while, and I had to assume their only escape attempt. Unless they could create time-stopping force fields too?

We reached my cell, finding the door ajar. Scowly pushed me inside, blocking the exit with his muscled frame.

He grabbed a walkie-talkie from his hip and spoke into it.

"Doctor Figg? You'll want to see this."

CHAPTER 11

FIGG CAME STRAIGHT from her lair and I was in trouble-land. She examined the cell door, paying close attention to the water-damaged sensor before surveying every inch of my room.

The orderlies turned their backs while she made me strip to my underwear and bra, touching my stomach scales and examining my pupils. She huffed, as if I hadn't returned the results she was after. Then she told me to dress myself and demanded the orderlies take me to a fresh cell.

"How did you do it?" Figg asked as they pushed past.

"Do what?" I asked.

Scowly gripped my upper arm like he was kneading dough. I cringed and pulled away.

"Don't hurt her!" Figg said. "She's the missing link."

"I'm the what, now?" I asked.

Scowly lost his scowl for a brief second. Figg wanted me treated well, which gave me hope. I could use that to gain an advantage.

She marched me to another cell, and the orderlies threw me inside and locked the door. Figg bent at the waist to speak through the tray flap.

"Stay put. It's for your own safety as much as ours."

There was that safety speech again. Did they know about the force field?

"If you didn't lock me up, I wouldn't have to escape," I said.

"Please, Ofelia? Try to help me out here," Figg said, as if reprimanding her misbehaving niece. She clicked the flap shut and threw the bolt on the other side, and the electronic lock beeped as she swiped her card.

This cell was identical to my old digs. Except that it had a working door lock.

And... a cellmate?

Two bedrolls lay on the floor, one with folded blankets sitting on top of the rubber mattress. The other contained a girl a couple of years younger than me. Her crinkled black hair splayed across her pillow. She had a smooth, russet-brown complexion, unlike my trademark pinkish-red sunburnt skin.

She reminded me of a woodland fairy from that book I'd swiped from the derelict bookshop, with a delicate, pointed face. But a harassed woodland fairy, beaten down by life. Optimism glinted behind her guarded stare, as if she expected to wake up, as if not believing her situation was real.

She gripped the blanket so that her knuckles bulged. She didn't wear a face mask, so I assumed she was immune, same as me.

I smiled at the kid and stuck out my hand in greeting.

"I'm Ofelia."

Her eyes widened, accentuating long black lashes. A spark of jealousy hit my stomach. I felt ratty by comparison—even in this place, with her hair frizzed and tense facial muscles attempting to hide her reactions. "It's okay, I won't hurt you," I said, dropping my hand. "What's your name?"

"I'm Maya," she whispered. Her posh accent had a musical lilt.

"Good to know you, Maya. Wish we were someplace else, though."

My roomie stifled a smile. It was a start.

"Are you from around here?" I asked, although it was improbable. Her skin was unblemished, her nails cut short, not bitten and dirty. She wore well-fitting jeans and a swirling-print blouse.

"I don't really know where here is." Her eyes averted, acknowledging a truth.

"I don't recognise you," I tried again, "so you could be from, you know, the other part."

"Other part of what?" she asked.

"Never mind." I settled myself on my bedroll. We sat facing each other, two alley cats eyeing unfamiliar territory. Maya was way curious, but played it cool. Her focal point travelled up from the floor, to my bedroll, to my knees. Her deep eyes flicked to my face to see if I noticed. I focussed on a spot on the wall behind her, trying not to freak her out by staring.

"What do you do for fun?" I changed tack, lightening the mood.

"Fun?" she asked, making eye contact. "There's no fun in here. They take you, and then you die."

"Well, I'm sure we can change that. They take us, we have fun, and *then* we die."

She raised one perfect brow like I'd sprouted a turnip out of my eyeball. I tilted my head towards her picked-over dinner.

"Do you mind?" I asked.

She shrugged, pushing the food closer to me. I snatched the tray and wolfed her leftovers.

"How can you eat that stuff? It's days old and gross," she said.

I pointed to the tray with my wooden fork. "It's a five-star hotel in here. Free food, soft bed, a solid roof keeping us dry."

"What would you know about a five-star hotel?"

"Nothing, I guess. My mum used to say it." My heart fluttered as I mentioned Mum.

Maya watched me shovelling down her room-temperature meal. I was conscious to finish before she changed her mind.

She lay on her side in her bedroll, her knees bent and nose crinkling as she brought the blanket up to cover her shoulders.

"Where are *you* from?" I rested my fork on the side. "I mean, for real?"

"Our family is from Goa."

"Where's that?"

"It's part of India. Although I guess the country doesn't exist anymore..."

"What happened to it?"

"Same as here. They amalgamated the remaining countries. Things were bad, so my family left..." She trailed off. But her confidence with me was growing; she maintained eye contact.

"So, where do you live now?" I prodded, attempting not to seem too eager. This was the most interesting conversation I'd had in ages. The curated view I'd watched on state television told an incomplete story.

"We live in Cookham East now," Maya said.

"Never heard of it."

"Because you've never been outside of Northies?" She wasn't trying to insult me. It was a truth.

"How'd ya figure me for a Northies rat?" I grinned, scooping up the last of the gravy with my knife. But then something occurred to me. "Why is Figg snatching in the swanky suburbs?"

"Swanky...?"

"I assumed they only snatched kids from our neighbourhood, cause nobody could complain. We're expendable and

Pocks can stop a revolt. But kids from the suburbs? It makes no sense."

"Kids go missing every day. They tell our parents we're taken to the United Nations Youth Council to work important jobs."

"You're what—twelve in the shade?" I asked. "You work at the UN?"

"I'm fourteen, and I guess we thought we were special."

"Trust the suburbs to think they're better than us," I scoffed.

"We *are* better than you." She folded her arms, warming to the subject. "What do you do all day?"

"Scavenge trash." I licked a dribble of gravy off the knife.

"You don't attend school?"

"They shut the school years ago."

"So you're better than me, and you collect trash for a living?"

"I didn't say we were better. We're more your equals."

Maya shook her head. "Well, it doesn't matter. We're both equally dead now."

I snorted a laugh. "That was sharp! You're funny."

She allowed herself a smirk, but then her serious expression returned. She wanted to ask something. Her mouth opened and closed, her attention fixed on me.

"What is it?" I placed the licked knife on my tray.

"What's up with your eyes?" she asked.

I shrugged. "Don't worry. I'm not contagious."

"But, they're orange..."

"Meet the lizard freak!" I tried to make light of it. But inside, I wasn't feeling crash hot—I felt isolated, as if nobody knew how I felt. I was unlike any other I knew. And this feeling intensified as I sat in front of someone I wanted to impress. I mean, Maya lived in the suburbs—I had so many questions about that exotic realm of endless resources.

"I didn't mean—" Maya said.

"It's okay," I replied. "I'm used to it. No big deal."

But despite my bravado, I was the lowest of the low, even in prison. I hadn't lived in an actual house, dreaming of a job at the United Nations. Unlike Maya, my plans for the future were basic—secure a low-paying job, keep Pocks' men at bay, cure my sister. If I had different parents, maybe I wouldn't be the freakazoid circus act.

I returned Maya's tray to the flap and lay on the thin mattress, with my roommate scrutinising me. But I didn't mind. I was cultivating an ally. Once she trusted me, we would help each other escape.

After dinner, my cellmate left me to my thoughts. Sure, she was a snooty suburbs kid, but maybe that wasn't her fault. Two heads would be sharper than my stubborn noggin alone.

"I don't think you're a freak," Maya said, breaking an uncomfortable silence.

I grinned back, as if I'd come to the same conclusion. "It's okay, Maya, really."

"No, it's not. I've seen some freaks in here, that's for sure. And none of them are kids."

I scooted closer. "What do you know about Dr Figg?"

"Nothing good," Maya said. "I wish there was a way out."

"There just might be. I escaped before," I replied. "It's why they put me in here."

"How did you escape?"

"It's a long and crazy story."

"We have time," Maya said, irony tinging her words.

"Do you have a mug from dinner?"

"They took it away right after I'd finished the water."

"Let's see what we have." I stood up and assessed the room.

I couldn't pry the embedded mirror from the wall. But with Maya's help, I might reach the light cage. If I could bust the globe, maybe I could use the shards as a weapon next time the guards paid us a visit?

"Hey, help me here," I said, and Maya clambered from her bedroll.

"How?"

"Interlock your fingers like this, I'll use you as a step." I showed her. Maya did as I instructed, and I rested one hand on her shoulder, the other ready to reach. "Okay, now when I say, push me up towards the ceiling."

I shifted my weight onto Maya's interlocked fingers.

"Go!"

Maya lifted with all her strength, and I jumped into the air, but missed the light cage by a good half metre. We tried again, and this time my fingertips brushed the cage. But my fingers were too large to fit through the wire. We abandoned the attempt, and Maya and I rested after the exertion, lost in our own thoughts.

I asked a casual question during the lull of her reminiscing.

"You haven't met a girl in here called Demi?" I averted my eyes to the wall. Paint cracked in the shape of a bear's head, complete with snapping jaws. Had I revealed too much? Her answer was too important.

"No, sorry," Maya said. "How did you know her?"

"It doesn't matter. I'm not even sure she's here."

My stomach felt like it had dropped through the basement floor. Maybe Maya hadn't been here long. I changed the subject, asking about school, which Maya said she missed.

As Maya told me about her entrance exam, the voice returned.

"I am here. Do not come for me."

Okay, okay. I won't come for you, I thought, then turned to Maya.

"Hey, can you hear that?" I asked.

She met my gaze. "Hear what?"

"Did it work?" the voice said.

"Right there," I said to Maya. "Can you hear her?"

She shook her head and sat back on her bedroll, studying me.

"Just me, then," I said.

"Whatever." Maya made a point of getting comfortable for this evening's entertainment—me. She propped her back against the wall, casually glancing in my direction.

The voice said, "You are closer."

Well, that's something? I thought, confused. *Is this part of the tests?*

"No tests."

Who are you?

"Someone who can help you. I can help everyone."

I don't understand. What's your name?

"You can call me Trix."

I sat on my bedroll with my back leaning against the wall, crossing my legs. I got comfy before replying, and for better concentration.

Hi, Trix, I'm Ofelia. Am I losing the plot?

"It is my turn not to understand."

You're a voice in my head. That's not normal.

"Not normal for you, but normal for us."

Who's 'us'?

"You may not enjoy my answer."

Just say it.

I paused and waited for the reply. Maya observed my silent conversation, distrust brewing in her expression. I ignored her and allowed my lids to close, concentrating. The voice returned.

"We are the Kaseath."

What is that? I frowned.

"We are from far away."

The suburbs?

"We are not from Earth."

I sucked in my breath. Could it be true?

The aliens? You're joking.

There was silence for a while, and I worried I might have offended her. I brought my crossed knees in closer to my body.

Sorry, I guess we are alien to you, too, I thought. The anxious silence continued. Would Trix speak to me again?

What if she hurt me? Could the creature have four arms with sharp claws and breathe fire? Was this building to the ultimate human-alien showdown on national TV?

I hoped she hadn't heard those thoughts.

"I do not breathe fire," Trix said.

Crap, she'd heard, and I hit my knee with the heel of my hand in frustration. Maya crinkled her forehead at my reaction, unsettled by witnessing my silent discussion.

Trix had helped so far, suggesting how to use my power to escape. Could I trust her, or was she another of Figg's tests?

"You can trust me," Trix said. "The Kaseath cannot lie. All things are known to everyone."

Knowing what people think could be embarrassing.

"Why would that be embarrassing? It would just be the truth."

You could be lying now.

"I can assure you I am not lying."

Are you in the research facility, too?

"I am also a captive like you."

I uncrossed my legs, stretching them in front of me. I forced a stony face and thought, *Do you know how we can escape?*

The question hung in my mind, worried that she wouldn't answer.

"Yes," she said.

My breath caught in relief, and I stood up, moving into a two-step happy dance. My feet tapped, shifting my weight from side to side. I lifted my arms and pirouetted on one foot, stopping midway at Maya's concerned stare.

I stopped the dance. This was great! An ally in hell. Although Trix could set a trap; could I trust her? But I had to believe her good intentions. Time to move on to the serious part of the conversation.

Do you know where Dr Figg's lab is? I thought.

"I do not know the location of the doctor's lab," Trix replied.

Damn, but I guess it was worth a try.

Where can I find my sister?

"The one you call Demi is not here."

I know she is.

"So, the reason for your escape is to find your sister?"

Yes. And to find Dr Figg's lab.

"These are futile quests. I will not help you."

Why are they futile?

"Because it's not possible to save your sister. And finding the lab has a low chance of success."

Please, we have to try.

"Now is not the time."

So you really won't help me?

"We have more pressing worries."

I threw my hands into the air and paced the room, my happy dance forgotten. At least Maya was enjoying the show.

She snuggled further into her bedroll, and I couldn't tell if she was curious or totally freaked out.

"Um, what are you doing?" she asked.

"I'm angry as hell, so I'm pacing."

"Cool." She rolled over, her back to me.

Okay, freaked out then.

The anger was a flash that overcame me. Demi had to be here, and I could bring her home. I could atone for her being taken. She'd get over whatever they'd done to her in here. We'd go home to a normal life, bringing Imogen's cure with us.

I didn't expect an alien to understand that. How could I make them understand?

"I have to show you something," Trix said.

Okay. I stopped pacing.

"Lie still. Picture a large white box, and the box is empty. The empty box is your mind."

Oh, heck, this was frustrating. I made my bed and lay inside.

"Finally," Maya said. "Goodnight."

"Yeah, sure," I said, pulling up the blanket.

I closed my eyes. Blood-orange light filtered through my closed lids, swirling and jolting through purple veins. In the hallway, orderlies shouted and kids cried. I hardly noticed the stench of disinfectant now, as clattering echoes drifted further away from my waking concerns.

My mind went into overdrive, racing with questions. Who was this alien? Why could she communicate with me? Why couldn't Maya hear?

The government implied attempts to contact the Kaseath had failed. Not that we called them by that name. 'Aliens' was as far as we'd managed. Had Trix fabricated her story?

"Remember the empty box," Trix commanded.

I'm trying. It's hard.

I blocked out the echoed bangs and knocks, the far-off wailing children. The tap dripped in the corner and Maya's breathing whistled each time she inhaled. The electricity hummed in time to my heartbeat as I concentrated. My mind raced less, grew quiet despite the background noise. A heavy blanket of ease settled.

And then, as if I was dreaming, a movie played beneath my eyelids.

I was in space, hovering in the dream, observing from a bird's-eye view. Except this bird was a spaceship, and I was inside that spaceship.

The view out into space via the porthole revealed the iridescent planet's north crescent. The bottom slice was as black as the vacuum behind it. Cosmic radiation thrummed energy through my body. The Earth appeared peaceful from up here; blue oceans and green landmass and white clouds in great cumulous swirls. A precious planet.

Then I noticed the other spaceship. Not one of ours—way too massive, in gun-metal grey. It was sleek, larger than my world, the same alien ship I'd seen on the television. It moved closer to the Earth and hovered just beyond our outer orbit.

The veins of the lights on Earth thickened and joined in a single pulse. Clouds gathered, more massive, more often. Angular objects escaped our atmosphere: small ships floating out into orbit alongside tiny satellites. The shuttle building the International Space Station, sticking it together piece by piece.

The alien craft shifted, hovering closer in our orbit, amongst the satellites.

Earth continued to turn. The clouds formed massive storms, cyclones and typhoons, gorgeous swirls on an artist's canvas, stark white against the inky void of space, until the lights below and their connecting veins thinned out, growing smaller. The cities shrank, the strength of civilisation dimmed.

A shuttle descended from the alien mother ship into Earth's atmosphere, engulfed by the massive planet. The mother ship hung, resisting the gravitational pull of our planet, observing.

I shifted to my left, and someone stood beside me, floating in zero gravity, facing away, their feet wedged under a toe hold. Could it be Trix? The person's face bobbed into view—it was Dr Figg! Dressed in the same space suit I wore, also without a helmet. She greeted me as an old friend. Gratitude welled until my chest expanded with emotion.

She pointed to a computer panel on the spaceship's wall. I floated next to her, inputting figures, and she nodded approval.

Why was I helping Figg? She was the last person I'd cooperate with. But in the dream, our gestures spoke of partnership. She moved aside so I could see out of the porthole as if I was her equal, not her minion.

Before I could ask questions, a white object advanced in space, visible in one of the portal windows, propelled by an orange-yellow blast of fire.

The missile exited Earth's atmosphere, hurtling past us towards the alien spacecraft. Their ship remained in the missile's path. Right before the missile hit, a bright explosion of shock waves shattered the very vacuum of the universe. It vaporised me, along with Figg, and our ship disintegrated into the inky void of space, becoming cosmic dust...

The vision ceased. My consciousness returned to the cell, to the icy walls and electric hum of the light fixture.

What was that? I thought.

Trix's words formed inside my skull. "It is your history—Earth's history."

So we blew up your ship?

"That part has not happened yet."

Do the visions always come true?

"No, we can change our fate. Our future is determined by our present."

So, we might not nuke your ship after all?

"I hope not."

Why are you helping me?

"Because they do not understand me."

What do you mean?

"You are the only one so far."

Only one?

What did the vision signify? Was our future already written? Would we nuke the Kaseath? Trix sought freedom, too. Would she destroy humanity to get what she wanted?

I concentrated on my thoughts.

I don't have time to waste. Figg said we only had a couple of days. I have to find Demi and the cure in Figg's lab. She said I had to be ready... to die?

"None of the other test subjects survived the doctor's final test. You have been fast-tracked."

So, what now?

"You need to strengthen your abilities."

I frowned and sat up again, playing with the hem on my shirt.

What abilities are those?

"You know."

Tell me.

"You can stop things before they occur."

Like playing with time?

"That is one thing, yes."

I want to escape tonight, I thought.

"Not yet. You are so impatient and stubborn. Your whole species is the same."

Well, I am a teenager.

"Yes, you are not fully evolved."

Hey!

"Was that offensive?"

I'm evolved enough.

"That is enough for today. Thank you, Ofelia."

And the volume dulled, trailing in a thudding echo.

Strands of thoughts overtook others before I could finish the sentences in my mind. The information was overwhelming. Was it a future I couldn't change? Were we doomed? And why in hell's name had I helped Figg, of all people?

I struggled to stay cool in front of Maya, instead of freaking out at the virtual future-history lesson from an alien being who was talking into my skull. The vision was more animated than a dream.

Maya couldn't hear Trix, and I was sure she hadn't seen the vision, either, because she was still lying with her back to me.

I was losing it in here.

But—what if I wasn't?

Trix knew of my powers—I don't think I'd imagined those, either. Trix was my best bet to spring this place: a better chance than a sheltered rich kid. The longer I stayed, the further I stumbled from the cure and Demi. What if she was next to me and I couldn't reach her? Figg couldn't win, not after everything she'd done to my family.

The alien didn't understand. I had to make things right again. I felt close to Demi, but also distant. My vantage point felt as remote as that spaceship in the vision, observing from afar.

I didn't believe what Trix had said about Demi, that I couldn't save her. I had to break free from the cell and locate my sister.

This time, I would avoid being caught.

CHAPTER 12

THE SMELL OF ALMOST-BURNT TOAST, scrambled eggs and bacon floated towards us, pulling my stomach to the food flap as the orderlies scraped trays through to neighbouring cells. Scowly's hairy hand slipped in both trays, and I grabbed one. Using my powers made me wicked hungry.

I dug into the delicious, fresh meal.

"Mmmmm..." I groaned as the flavours of food-not-gone-bad hit my tastebuds. I said around my mouthful, "This meal is tasty."

Maya's eyebrows furrowed. "You're kidding, right?"

"Nope," I said. "We've got it made in here. Running water, flushing loo, fresh food with—get this—meat! This is better than the suburbs."

"You've clearly not been to the suburbs."

I shovelled a sporkful of bacon into my face, stopping mid-chew.

"Enlighten me."

"Well, for a start, we live in houses..."

"I'm impressed..."

"And our mums and dads have jobs, and drive cars, and the kids go to school."

"My mum and dad have jobs too," I scoffed, "and we have our own... um... shack. But we don't have cars or schools. Okay, four points for you, two for me."

"It's not a competition," Maya said.

"We'll see."

Maya grinned. "It's good to talk to you. It feels less, I don't know."

"Less hopeless?"

"I guess."

"Thanks, Maya," I replied, popping the last corner of toast into my mouth, licking the spork, and then my fingers, and swivelling to sit cross-legged on my bedroll.

I tried to picture a house in the suburbs, imagining four sturdy walls of brick and a tiled roof with a carpeted floor. A pieced-together image from a memory I had, from back when school was a thing. I'd learned to read in a book that had just this type of house drawn in a quaint, pastel-coloured cartoon style. How would the air flow through without the vents of overlapping tin sheets? No breeze could penetrate a building so solid. How lonely it would feel in there, without the sounds of your community wrapping around you. It would feel like a tomb, like this cell.

"Are you okay?" Maya asked

"I need to talk to someone else."

Maya raised her eyebrows, looking around our otherwise empty cell, then shrugged.

Hey, Trix, I thought.

Radio silence. I screwed up my face, concentrating beyond the walls that contained us. I visualised my mind travelling through the air vents and into the next ward.

"What are you doing?" Maya asked.

"Shush," I said, "I'm talking."

"Weird."

Maya's brow crinkled in concern, so I decided to clue her in.

"You really couldn't hear that voice?" I said.

"No, what can you hear?" Maya asked.

"I think I'm talking to an alien, or it could be one of Figg's tests. I'm not entirely sure."

"You're kidding, right?" Maya's eyebrows shot up into her fringe.

I grinned at her sheepishly, and she mouthed "wow".

"I've got to concentrate, okay?" I said, and Maya nodded.

Hey, where are you at? I thought.

Still no reply. I released a deep breath, clearing my mind.

Come on, you're out there somewhere.

"Better," Trix replied. "I need you focussed."

Way to leave a girl hanging.

"What are you hanging on?"

It's an expression—never mind.

"Have you considered our last conversation?"

I don't know if you're real, or I'm imagining it.

"I'm real."

A voice in my head would say that.

"But I showed you the visions."

I could have imagined it.

"It didn't feel real?"

Oh, it felt real, alright. But I have an over-active imagination.

"Please trust me."

I squeezed my eyelids closed tighter in frustration. Tensing, then relaxing, unclenching my facial muscles, feeling my cheeks grow heavy. Our conversation forced like a large item of trash being pushed through a tiny hole in my hessian bag.

So, what's up with you today? I thought after a while.

"Ofelia, I am sorry. I have been on your planet for a long time. I am tired."

Me too. Let's take our minds off things.

"I cannot hear you if you take your mind off this conversation."

It means distraction, not losing concentration.

"Distraction?"

Yeah, we explore an unrelated topic, and our minds focus elsewhere.

There was a pause. Trix was grumpy as my mate Scowly today.

What do you say? I persisted.

"I will try this method," Trix said.

Good. So, let me ask you about your home. Where do you live?

"I have shown you."

Yes, the ship. But where did you come from? Where is your planet?

"I have never been there."

Really?

This surprised me. What if I had lived aboard a spaceship all my life, only to be trapped on a foreign planet, never having known Earth, my true home?

What do you know about your planet?

"It is extremely hot. You would fry in a millisecond."

How did you travel here?

"Over many generations."

Are the other Kaseath like you? Are they good?

Trix hesitated before replying.

"We are neither good nor bad, as you define those terms. We believe in the balance of the universe. It is our only purpose."

Do you have family aboard your ship?

"Yes, all Kaseath are related."

Tell me about your people.

"We have more pressing priorities, Ofelia," Trix said.

The whole point is to distract us from those...

"Listen to me, please."

Facing reality was tough right now. But I had to help my family and free the kids. The burden might be halved with an alien on my side.

I'm listening.

"We are running out of chances to escape," she said.

What are you saying?

"They have fast-tracked you. Tomorrow is your ultimate test," Trix said.

What do you mean?

"Nobody returns from this test."

Wait—nobody?

"She is here."

There was a clanging outside my cell, and Trix's connection severed, as if removing her touch. Figg appeared at our cell door.

Maya scrambled back and her tray clattered to the floor, loud as a thousand metal roofs under pelting rain.

"Good morning, Ofelia. I hope you are well rested? It's time to go." Figg placed a folded hospital gown onto the tray flap, ignoring Maya.

"Aww, are you serious?" I grumbled.

I resigned myself to my new working day. Why had Trix said I was nearing my ultimate test? If nobody returned from that test, it mean that Figg killed them first. Did I have one day left alive?

There was a slight impatience to Figg's gaze, but she was trying to hide it. I wondered if her overly pleasant demeanour with me was a show, or genuine.

Playing the part, I took a bow. I felt fresh after a hot breakfast and a comfortable night's sleep. Fresh enough to pull off an escape before my imminent death.

The orderlies and Figg escorted me to the lifts. We rode to the first floor, two levels up from the basement cells. We emerged from the lifts onto a floor containing scientists and doctors in lab coats heading in and out of offices. Each office had a gold plaque with black lettering on a faux-wooden door, listing names and specialities. Professor E. Gambit, Epidemiologist, or Doctor G.G. Louse, Molecular Biology. I read each name, searching for Figg's name plate. We must be close to her lab.

A glass-fronted door beckoned at the end of the corridor. It was the only glass-fronted room I'd passed, resembling Figg's lab from the television broadcast. That must be it!

The room had a blue hue. A connecting room led into the lab. Beyond that, shelving, refrigerated cabinets and long silver benches. And, most promising, a security panel on the outside, a blinking red light in one corner. None of the other doors had security panels—that room held something extra special.

"Is the plague cure in there?" I asked as casually as I could.

Scowly bumped me with the butt of his nightstick. My head smarted like the blazes. Pain radiated from the centre of the blow, and I lost concentration. I squinted with the pain, warding off tears as we walked away from the most promising lead so far.

Had Scowly just confirmed my suspicions? Was that Figg's lab, and was the plague cure inside?

"Eyes front, please," he said, low enough for Figg not to hear.

Figg led me to an observation room with a brisk step. She took more blood and wired me up to more machines. She hadn't lied about the tests, which didn't hurt and were uncomfortable, but I had decided they wouldn't kill me, not just yet anyway. My body jerked in shock as the needle pierced my skin. Before each jab, Figg said, "Just a little prick," as if revealing a delicious snack. I wondered how she remained so upbeat with such terrible work.

She sounded apologetic, but her interest in me had stopped being novel and become annoying. I was her prize lab rat. She'd never let me go until she had what she wanted, or until the tests fried my senses.

Figg pressed her fingers to her temples, as if massaging a deep ache. The orderlies had stopped guarding me altogether and lounged in chairs, playing games on their phones.

"So why all these tests?" I asked as she slipped another vial of my dark-hued blood into a kidney-shaped plastic bowl.

"We have to confirm some things, genetically," Figg replied.

"What's with my genes?"

"I've been searching for this sequence for the last sixteen years."

"Why?"

"Because I created it."

"Huh?" That made no sense.

"That's enough for now, thank you, Ofelia," Figg said, with the unnatural smile that she used when she was on camera. So, she wanted me cooperative then.

"No, tell me about my genes," I said.

"We'll speak in the morning," Figg replied. "I really have to go now."

Figg motioned to the orderlies, and they accompanied me into the outer corridor, leaving the good doctor staring at a computer screen filled with a bunch of charts and figures.

Once we were out of Figg's earshot, I tried to scope out the lab I'd seen before, the one that resembled the lab on the television. But Scowly was rougher than usual, almost as if preempting my demise the next day, reducing me to a non-human. He grabbed my underarms, dragging me straight into the elevator at the opposite end to the lab. I craned my neck but couldn't see much more as the lift doors closed.

I'd discovered Figg's lab. Now I had to plan a break-in.

We arrived at the basement hall and Scowly deposited me in my cell, giving the stink eye to his companion.

"You gonna do actual work today?" Scowly sneered.

"What? You've got this runt covered..." Bored shrugged and slammed the door.

I rubbed the finger marks under each arm as the orderlies locked our cell. Concern crinkled Maya's brow, even if she didn't say anything out loud.

"I'm okay," I said. "Have you eaten yet?"

She pushed a tray towards me, filled with rice, meat chunks and vegetables in this delicious yellow sauce. The taste mingled in a sticky, sweet dream, with enough rice to feed my entire family for a week.

She observed me eating, and her nose crinkled as I took my first bite. I played into her disgust, making noises of pleasure with exaggerated chewing. She shifted uneasily.

"What, you don't like curry?" I asked.

"I wouldn't call that a curry."

"What would you call it?"

"Mass-produced prison slop."

"I don't mind it."

"Cause you don't know any better."

"And you do?"

A soft sigh escaped her lips. "All I can think about is the humann my Aajee makes."

"What's that?"

She smiled at the memory. "My grandmother's fish curry."

"Does your grandmother live with you?"

"Yes, I miss her."

"I don't have a grandmother. I don't even have a father."

"Of course you have a father somewhere."

"Well, obviously, but I don't know who he is."

I dug in, drained of energy from the tests and the vials of blood that Figg had taken. After I ate, Maya and I chatted, and I learned she had a younger sister, same as me. Her parents worked long hours, and her grandmother and aunt minded Maya and her sister after school.

The conversation lulled as I ate, relishing the sweet bite of the spices. Chatty staff passed outside our cell during shift change. My last evening had begun—Trix could help me with my powers. I'd spring my cell and break into Figg's lab.

A relaxed state overtook me as I sat next to my bedroll and waited for Maya to lie still. But she was alert—observing me. Novelty in a prison cell was savoured, lingered over. Recalled images were valuable for passing night hours, and I was the opening act.

She assessed me differently than Figg, though. Maya was curious in a casual way. Figg's interest in me bordered on obsession.

I ignored my cellmate and pressed both index fingers to my temples. This only worked if I concentrated and I needed Trix to help me break into the lab. My powers still felt weak; I'd be unable to ward off a muscular orderly with a baton.

I'm ready, I thought, planting my feet shoulder-width apart.

"Hello, Ofelia," Trix replied.

Tell me what to do.

"Concentrate," she said. "Regulate your breathing."

Sucking in a breath, my ribcage expanded. Recirculated air filled my lungs. I relaxed my neck and shook out the tension in my spine until my mind quietened.

Trix knew whether I followed her instructions. This invisible wire connected us in areas I couldn't name, that human words couldn't explain. We communicated by thought, but she sensed how I was. You know, in the parts that didn't speak. It was more than just muscles and nervous systems and those swirling bits of blood and electrical impulses I'd studied in school, when school existed in our neighbourhood.

"Now pick up your pillow," Trix said.

Got it. I found my feet, holding the pillow loose in one hand.

"Stand in front of the wall."

I stepped a pace away, facing the wall.

Maya sat taller, transfixed, observing as if I was the weirdest thing she'd encountered in her life.

"Enact the force field," Trix said.

I lobbed the pillow with both hands—and it ricocheted, a missile of sorts.

My force field caught before the pillow hit. The stupid shield didn't know the pillow couldn't hurt me, but it wasn't possible to stop time on my own. I could only prevent that soft bedding from flaying me alive—unable to attack, merely defend.

You've gotta wonder how smart this power was. Maintaining my focus, I let the pillow fall.

"Did you see that?" I asked Maya.

"Did I see you throw your pillow at the wall?"

"Yeah, but what happened afterwards?"

"Gravity happened. Now it's on the ground. It's kinda unsanitary."

"Okay, I'm figuring this out."

Maya sighed in an all-suffering way, fed up with my shenanigans. "You'll annoy the orderlies."

"That's a happy side-effect," I replied with a deferential dip of my head.

"My last cellmate was tidier."

"But way less fun."

An idea formed. "Punch me in the face," I said to Maya.

"What?" Maya said, as if doubting my sanity.

"I'm testing something."

"How stupid you can be?"

"Just stand here." I pointed to the floor.

"Will you let me sleep if I do this?"

"Sure."

Maya stood as I instructed and I moved to half a metre in front of her. Would the same thing happen with Maya's fist as happened with the pillow? Would I be able to enact the shield if someone attacked me from close range?

"Punch me as hard as you can."

Maya shrugged and lifted her right hand, bunching a fist. I breathed in and concentrated on Maya.

"Now!" I shouted.

Maya sprang forward, clocking me on the tip of my nose. Her fist connected, my nose bent backwards. Surprise registered in both of our expressions. My bent nose tingled and went numb. Maya's fist retracted, and my hands went to my face in shock.

Then the pain hit. The tingling turned to throbbing pain and when I drew my hands back, blood trickled into my palms.

"Oh no, I'm sorry, Ofelia," Maya said, "I didn't mean to punch you there!"

"It's okay..." I said, my voice muffled as I pinched the bridge of my nose to stop the bleeding.

"Are you all right?" Maya moved to look at my nose. "Let me see."

I washed the blood from my face in the sink. It mixed with the water into rose-coloured liquid, dribbling down the drain.

"Here, hold your head forward to stop the bleeding," Maya said with concern.

The bleeding stopped after a minute, and it felt like my nose was swelling and retracting, pulsing with the beat of engorged blood vessels.

"Why did you ask me to punch you?" Maya asked.

"It was an experiment," I replied.

Maya watched over me for the next half hour, but I felt okay. I grew used to my nose throbbing, and the pain subsided. My force field needed a missile of sorts, rather than close physical combat, to enact. I had concentrated hard before the punch, but it was too close and grounded. For whatever reason, my shield didn't work that way.

"Keep practising," Trix commanded. "We're running out of time."

Maya lost interest in my experiments, which was fair enough, as she was missing the most interesting bit: when time stopped. While she pretended to sleep, I practised. Others didn't notice the frozen time. My powers were undetectable. Only the reaction remained, the side-effect of my actions during the suspended time.

I tossed the pillow, freezing Maya mid exaggerated-snore. The force field went up. The pillow hung suspended in the air, grazing the shield.

This time, I concentrated on the green haze between me and the pillow. I reached out to touch the crackly barrier. My finger connected, shooting me with electrical jolts, but it didn't hurt to touch it. My fingertip didn't even turn red from the electrical heat. The shield felt powerful and solid. Nothing passed through.

The barrier was only as wide as my body and curved towards me at each end. Every time I invoked the force field, it

134

grew less translucent, the edges more curved. Either edge protected me from the right and left flank.

When I was ready, the pillow fell to the floor, and the green-hued barricade disappeared.

This was the longest I'd maintained my power, with the most control. But my powers were only useful for repelling an attack. I couldn't cause violence, only block. I'd been taught the defensive half of karate without ever learning to land my own blows.

"Hey Maya. Could we do another experiment?"

Maya sighed and propped up on one elbow. "You are a sucker for punishment."

"This one won't hurt," I replied. "At least it shouldn't."

"What do I have to do?"

"Throw the pillow at me, while I'm not looking."

Maya was about to crack a wise retort, but glanced at my swollen nose. She stood and bunched the flimsy pillow into a ball.

"Okay. But I'm not punching you again."

"Deal."

I faced the door, instructing Maya to stand behind me, holding the pillow.

"When I say so, throw it at me as hard as you can."

I relaxed, focussed my mind, and concentrated on nothing at all, allowing the dance of light behind my eyelids.

"Now!" I said.

I heard Maya bring the pillow up, then the 'oof' sound as she let fly. It grazed my shoulder, with a slight pressure, and then dropped to my ankles.

So, I had to face the missile. If someone attacked from behind, before I saw them—nada. This rendered escaping difficult. I'd be fine as long as a missile was fired at me. From in front. While I concentrated on nothing at all.

But the practice kept me occupied, so I persisted until my muscles twinged and my skull ached in time with the pulsing bare light bulb. It was like I formed the electrical current itself.

Time to move to the next phase. Squatting with my ear to the hinges, I assessed the echoed shouts. One of those kids might be Demi, although I hadn't recognised her voice. I had to stay hopeful.

The alien returned inside my head—we needed to have a serious discussion on boundaries.

"Boundaries to where?" she asked.

I'll explain another time.

"Are you ready to escape?"

I jumped from my squatted position, banging my elbow on the door.

"Ouch." I rubbed my funny bone where it tingle-hurt.

"Ofelia?" Trix said.

Yes. Hell, yes, I'm ready.

"Then follow my instructions," Trix said. "This is your last chance."

You're saying if I don't succeed tonight, I'm dead?

"Yes, Ofelia. I do not want that to happen."

Me either.

So, no pressure. If my plan to break into Figg's lab didn't work, she'd fry her prize lab rat into a pile of ash and bone.

I thought to Trix, *Time to get this escape party started.*

CHAPTER 13

I STOOD alert in the cell, waiting for Trix's signal. The space grew more claustrophobic than usual as I waited for freedom. Time to bust out, find Demi and break into the lab.

Maya observed me while the night shift staff settled into their routine.

I removed my sneaker, tossing it into the air, playing throw-and-catch with myself until lights out. Well, 'lights dimmed' was a more exact description. The room clicked into a fuzzy outline instead of a stark white prison cage. I crept to the door, dressed in the clothes that Figg had given me. Maya half smiled, acknowledging my own fears.

"Come with me," I offered.

"Um, no thanks. You know they'll catch you, right?"

"This is my last chance, before..."

"Before I get a new cellmate?" Maya said, cottoning on.

"So snoop around, have fun?"

She shook her head, scooting forward and grabbing me in a hug.

"It's your funeral..." I regretted my choice of words. Her expression grew pained, because it wasn't only a saying in here, it was a reality. So I softened and said, "I'll find you afterwards, okay?"

She nodded, hugging her knees, a terrified expression crinkling her forehead.

I pressed my ear against the metal slab. A television echoed far away, along with subdued sobbing.

Then—something loud and angry, nearby.

An orderly ran his nightstick along the wall, intimidating his inmates, scraping metal on concrete. An inmate howled as if racing the orderly's clanging stick to the end of the hall.

The nightstick collided with the last doorjamb.

"Sleep tight, rug rats," he called.

The wing door slammed, and the electrical lock caught. Maya's shoulders twitched.

Muffled crying floated from other nooks, and one poor soul called out for her mother. If my step-dad was typical, the night watch wasn't the crack team of the bunch, and that was worth betting my freedom on. I still wasn't confident in my powers, but I couldn't wait until they were slick and impenetrable.

They couldn't apprehend me again. Figg valued me, but was I expendable? I didn't want the same fate as Maya's other cellmates. My tummy jittered with nerves—everything hinged on my escape.

I tossed my shoe in my right hand, used to the heavy heel's sole. Pressed my chest against the door, glazing my focus and settling my mind.

I stepped backwards and hurled the shoe; the missile deflected, the moment froze.

My forearms rose to protect me, but my defences saved me from shoe-in-face. There was only space for the shoe and the force field itself. I was glad I'd practised my reactions as I edged the barricade forward.

As Trix had taught me, I concentrated, tipping the shield.

Each flank swivelled until it touched the metal door itself—carrying the electrical current into the hinge. Crackles of power surged through the element.

The sensor sparked, then fizzed and shorted out.

I'd disabled the lock with the shield.

Time resumed, the barrier disappeared, the shoe dropped to the ground.

Smoke twined from the hinges, and Maya sniffed. "Is that smoke?"

"Shhhh." I pressed a finger to my lips.

Her shocked expression spoke volumes. "You're causing trouble!"

The block was subdued—no shouting staff, no calling for backup—so I forced the mechanism open. The hinge creaked as I pushed the door ajar. Stronger light from the corridor filtered over the threshold. I poked out my head, checking for action—there was none.

"Come with me." I reached out my hand, but Maya didn't take it. She hugged herself, shaking, pretending not to comprehend what was happening.

The fried electrical lock stopped sizzling, leaving a burning smell in the air, fibre licked by fire. I slipped on my shoe and moved out into the hall, hoping I'd return for Maya before my escape.

I slowed the door's close into a subtle 'click'. The red sensor lights flicked back on, not permanently fried. There was little time.

The orderly on duty sat inside the nurses' station, lounging beside our cell. She rested a magazine on her portly middle, flicking through the articles. A television blared, shooting lights as the picture changed, green-hued, blue-hued.

She hadn't seen me. I ducked, hidden in the gloom. Her box illuminated a shopping mall in a TV drama, glowing stores filled with treasure. I wanted to see how life was in the swanky suburbs. Things were brighter on television. But I had no time for recreation.

I held my breath as the kaleidoscope of colours flickered with the soundtrack of the program.

Crouching low, I edged in the opposite direction to the nurses' station, easing my footfalls on the cool linoleum, pausing near the first cell.

Next problem—there were several rooms on this wing alone. Searching for Demi would be difficult. It was 'lights dimmed' and it was risky waking people. If they caused a fuss, they'd alert the staff. Maybe Trix was wrong, and she was in one of these cells. I had to try.

I approached the first flap, stealthy as a cat hunting insects at night. Pulled the stiff latch. As I tugged, the latch banged open.

So loud!

The occupants stirred. The kids were too big to be my sister. I moved to the next room. Inside, a boy scrunched into the foetal position, hugging his torso, while a girl slept—around Demi's age. I held my breath—was it her?

She pulled the blanket to her chin, obscuring her features. From this angle, her hair colour may be a deep chestnut, or a deeper black, like Demi's. She was the right height, straightening her folded knees. My ribcage ached with possibility.

"Demi?" I whispered.

She whipped her head towards me, her expression one of terrorised prisoner.

"Who's there?" she asked, grabbing a mask from the floor.

Her voice didn't resemble my sister's, and my stomach

dropped with disappointment. It was worth the risk to ask her, I decided.

"I'm looking for Demi," I said.

"She's not here."

"So you know her?"

"Yes, she was one of the lucky ones," the girl said. Hope surged through my chest; here was confirmation that Figg had brought Demi here.

"What does that mean?" I asked.

"It means she's not here now."

"Where is she?"

"I'm sorry, I don't know. I can't help you," she said, turning away. "Please go away. You're causing trouble."

"Where did you last see her?" I whispered. "I have to find her."

"I don't remember." The girl settled in her bed.

"Please? Where do the lucky ones go?"

She shuddered but didn't respond, so I hooked the cover into place.

I gathered myself before peering into the adjacent cell. Could they have taken Demi to another floor, away from the hellish cells? Was she living it up somewhere else in this building? My heart tap-danced against my ribs, fluttering clacks.

Shuddering lights of a soap opera hit the wall near the orderly's box. Other than the TV, and my hammering heart, all was quiet. My sister could be close.

I pulled the next tray open.

The sole occupant was awake. She paced, muttering to herself, and didn't see me at first. She didn't resemble Demi and was in a dishevelled state. The girl shoulder-charged the wall and screamed fit to wake our dead ancestors.

I stiffened and wondered what to do.

"It's okay. You're okay," I said, in my most reasonable tone.

"She's going to die soon!" she wailed.

"Quiet, or we're both toast."

"She's not getting out. She's never getting out!"

The orderly shifted in her seat, and the soft padding of the chair squeaked. There was nowhere to hide!

I clicked the flap shut, slipped off my shoe and ran the heel over the walls, mimicking the nightstick trick.

The girl clammed up. So the staff terrorised her, too. She apologised, repeating a familiar mantra.

"She's sorry, so very sorry. It won't happen again."

Poor thing, I couldn't leave her that way.

"Thank you. Now go to sleep," I said. Silence descended as the orderly settled in her chair. She had avoided doing any actual work—lazy staff boded well for my escape.

My attention returned to inspecting the next three rooms, eliminating the occupants.

I snuck closer to the fourth and final room.

"Ofelia?" a voice said, and my adrenalin spiked. Had Demi recognised me?

I swivelled to the last cell's occupants, approaching their tray flap. I almost didn't recognise her without her bright red pirate patch—it was Aze. Sidling next to her, hair matted, was Mouse Run.

"What are you guys doing here?" I asked, moving closer.

"Snatchers," Aze said, shrugging. She placed her ebony hand through the flap and I squeezed a reply.

"Are you hurt?" I said. They shook their heads.

"Did you have a shower?" Mousie observed. "You're so... clean..."

"Yeah, guess I'm the prize lab rat, hey?" I said, my mood slumping. "So who's looking after Imogen?"

Mousie's eyes fell to the floor. Aze kicked the wall with her big toe peeping through the gap in her sandals.

"Yeah, we're sorry about that, hey?" Aze said.

"They took so many this time. I don't know why..."

"Is she okay?" I dreaded the answer.

"Yes," Mousie said, her blue eyes still not meeting mine. "But Pocks is harassing everyone more than usual. I think he's looking for her."

Air escaped my lungs in a strangled way, and I stepped back from the cell. Pocks couldn't snatch Imogen and bring her to this place. How would she survive Figg's tests? My baby sister was already in poor health.

I gathered my nerve, so close to grabbing her cure. Pocks would eventually discover my family—where else would they go? The only escape was through the locked security gate, via Figg's van.

"Have you seen Demi in here?" I asked, grasping a slight chance.

"No, sorry. We haven't seen much of the block though..." Mousie replied.

"They might have transferred her or something," I said.

"So, how did you break out?" Aze asked.

"I'll tell you later. I have to get to the first floor, the cure's there. I've seen Figg's lab..."

"You've what?" Mousie said, meeting my worried gaze.

"I'm not sure how, but I'm breaking in, grabbing the cure. And then I'm busting us all out."

My friends' expressions were less enthusiastic than I'd hoped.

"That's great," Aze said, peering into the hall. "But it's dangerous, right? Won't they catch you?"

"I have my ways." I grinned. "Just be ready."

"Ready for what?"

"Ready for mayhem," I said.

My face brightened at the thought of setting anarchy alive

in this place, kids streaming from their cells as I held the cure to save my little sister.

Voices floated along the block—adult voices heading to the nurses' station. I flicked my eyes in that direction, and then to my friends. They mouthed 'good luck' and retreated into the darkness, two regular prisoners waiting for time-passing sleep.

I snuck forward, shoe at the ready. A printed sign read:

Fire stairs, emergency exit.

The orderly chose that moment to do the cursory hall check. Without getting out of her chair, she poked her head from the station, shining her flashlight along the hallway.

The beam of light flitted over my arm.

I flattened against the wall, feeling as conspicuous as a ten-foot tall fence with a target painted in my middle. The orderly was at the opposite end, but if she checked properly, I was a goner.

At that moment, the pacing inmate rambled and banged on her door.

"She's out!" the girl shrieked. "Take me with you!"

Oh crap.

The orderly started towards me, her torchlight dancing from one wall to the other, as if following an animal at night. She'd see me if she focussed her torch, if she did her job right.

I peered straight ahead, willing myself unseen. There was a useful power—invisibility.

Heavy tread scuffed the floor.

What could I do? The light swung around; the torch held loose in her hand as she advanced. Couldn't she see the beam flicking the edges of my toes, flitting over my terrified face? Her attention was on the prisoner.

She halted at the screaming girl's cell, opening the peephole. She shone the torch.

"Hey, stop that."

"She's escaping without me!" the girl said.

"You're not going anywhere. Now let these people sleep."

"That way! Over there!"

The girl laughed in this weird, strangled tone. The sound amplified the terror winding through me. Twining fear, a suffocating smoke.

The orderly swung her flashlight into the hall. She'd catch me for sure. But it was a lazy sweep. She'd checked these halls on hundreds of prior shifts, and nothing had ever happened. Except maybe this girl had lost it—that part was not new.

"Shut it or I'll alert the day shift," the orderly shouted.

"She's quiet now," the girl mumbled.

The tray flap banged, and the woman waddled back to her box.

A sigh expelled from the seat cushion as she settled her weight back in the chair.

I breathed out, my muscles taut.

Once the orderly returned to her TV show, I slipped off my sneaker. My pulse pounded in my ribs, rapid as a semi-automatic round of tranq darts. But I had to keep moving.

I heaved the shoe towards the door. Shifted the shield to short out the electronic lock. Slipped into the stairwell.

A dingy staircase led upwards, the handrail finished in scuffed wood. Bare branches shifted in the wind through a window above me, silhouetted by the darkening sky.

Actual sky! Freedom was moments away.

My feet tiptoed up the staircase, unsure of who else might be lurking. Windows set into each landing above revealed other buildings and a courtyard. Floodlights picked out each corner of the courtyard. Trying to be both quick and silent, I reached the ground level of the staircase.

I hadn't been able to locate Demi, but I intended to keep my promise to Imogen. I would find her cure. And then I'd bust all of us out of this prison.

CHAPTER 14

I CLIMBED THE INTERNAL STAIRWELL, stealthy as a burglar, to the first floor. My feet itched to find the lab and break in pronto, but I also had to avoid detection. I had the advantage of surprise—nobody knew I was out of my cell. Given the limitations of my powers, I couldn't overcome burly orderlies in a hand-to-hand skirmish. My still-smarting nose throbbed where Maya's experimental punch had landed.

At the first floor, I tried the handle, half expecting it to be locked. But it shifted, and I pushed the door ajar to glance through.

Rows of wooden doors with gold-and-black name plaques flanked the corridor like sentinels, hiding secrets within. The scent of hospital-grade disinfectant was more subtle on this floor.

Figg's glass-fronted lab sat at the opposite end of the hallway.

As I scoped out the area from my hiding place, staff in white coats swished past, unconcerned with their surroundings, heads bent to their iScreens. They couldn't be unproductive for even a second. I suppose creating the cure for the plague was top priority for the staff. And anyway, 'lights out' in the cells was early. But it meant I'd have to scout in plain sight of roaming workers.

Could I pretend to be a patient?

I took a deep breath, wiping the worry from my forehead. I'd have to act as if I belonged there. Like it's totally normal for a lizard freak Northies rat to roam the halls of unprecedented scientific achievements.

I pushed into the hall, my eyes averted. The door to the fire stairs clicked into place. A tall doctor passed and his sharp cologne tickled my nose hairs. He barely noticed me. A nurse bumped straight into me, too engrossed in her iScreen. She apologised and shifted at the last second, scrutinising me from an arm's length away. A frown followed.

"Are you lost, sweetie?" she asked.

I recognised the nurse who tried to take my blood during the first day of tests. I wanted to retort, "I'm not your sweetie," but she might have realised. My mind reached back, visualising the name plaques on the office doors.

"I'm looking for Professor Gambit, the epidemiologist?"

I was darn proud of myself in that moment for remembering that detail. The nurse's eyebrows twitched, perplexed by my grin.

"A few doors that way," she said, pointing away from Figg's lab.

She waited while I stood there and nodded, bathed in an aura of self-congratulations.

"Oh," I twigged. "Yes, I'll walk that way then."

I began my jaunt to the epidemiologist's room. A flash of recognition passed through the nurse's eyes. She knew me but couldn't remember where from. Her eyebrow tilted skywards. Before her memory returned, I knocked on the epidemiologist's door.

"Yes?" a gruff voice asked.

"Hmmm..." I said, watching the nurse frown as a new thought overtook her attention. She scurried away as if late for an appointment.

"Can I help you?" the gruff voice returned at the open door, revealing the grizzled academic in front of me, squinting over smudged glasses.

"Oh, sorry, I have the wrong office," I said.

"Damn kids..." he grumbled under his breath, closing the door in my face.

White coats swished, iScreens pinged and the foot traffic ignored me. Now I had to approach Figg's lab and enact my shield, disable the lock and slip inside, with no one noticing.

I pushed my hairball of hesitation aside and stepped along the hallway, the back of my throat dancing around like it was carnival time. I hesitated, scoping things out first.

The lab's glass door sat in backlit blue, the light from inside thrown against the opposite wall. I focussed on the security panel, and the sinister, red-blinking light. As I crept closer, the numbers on the keypad came into view. The keypad must need a code. There was a card tap point above the keypad. I just hoped my powers would work, that they could short the lock, same as in my cell. Although, I worried that the security here might be more robust.

Before I could investigate further, two young scientists exited the lab, the swish of the decontamination chamber smoke following them into the hall. I jumped back and pretended to study the wall—I was about as inconspicuous as if I waved a colourful flag whilst shouting through a loudspeaker, announcing just how badly I didn't fit into this scene. But the assistants didn't notice. They turned their backs, comparing figures on an iScreen.

"Figg will be devastated..." the first said.

"I just don't know what we're missing," the second said.

Dissipating smoke escaped as the lab door gaped open. This might be my chance! I leaped forward, but the door slammed shut before I could slip inside. The security panel beeped again as it armed. Both scientists headed towards the end of the wing. I couldn't believe they hadn't seen me. The research on their iScreens must have been compelling.

I checked either side for onlookers; the corridor was clear. I lifted my right foot up behind me and leaned down to slip off my sneaker. I held the shoe, standing flush against the lab's glass door, then took a half-metre step backwards and threw my shoe with all the strength I had.

My shield caught the shoe before it hit my face.

I observed the corridor in more detail in the frozen moment as my force field crackled with warmth and energy.

The lift light had just blinked onto the fourth floor, so I had time before it arrived. A doctor with a stethoscope wrapped around her neck was mid-turn from a connecting corridor.

Checking the end closest to me, the two retreating scientists froze in their conversation and didn't pose a threat. I could discount the remaining staff, having grabbed a quiet spot in the foot traffic. Nobody would notice me restarting time with a fried lock, and I could slip in undetected.

I focussed on the glass door. A decontamination chamber connected the lab. The security panel light had frozen into the red 'locked' position.

My shield hummed around me, lending warmth in that chilly corridor. But I couldn't hold it for much longer. I shifted one shield flank, and then the other, until it kissed the wall. I thrust into the side panel. The shield fizzled as it came in contact, but the light remained lit. Why hadn't my charge shorted the lock?

This was a different locking system to my cell. Frizzled

wiring scents didn't taint the air and the finger of smoke was missing. They'd protected the lock from electrical overload.

I leaned back and relaxed, re-pooling my energy into a second attempt. The shield rammed with everything I had, but the electricity rebounded on me with a green-tinted energy. The heat was intense and my muscles ached as the power threatened to arc back my way. I eased my efforts, regrouping, but my shield flickered and dissipated. Time resumed. The two scientists' voices echoed off the ceiling. The doctor's phone pinged as she rounded the corner. My skin prickled from the loss of the latent heat.

And then the worst possible thing happened.

The two chatting scientists ceased their conversation. They stood stock still, and in front of them, her face clouded with defeat, was Dr Figg herself!

"Please tell me it's not true," Figg said, touching the first scientist lightly on the arm.

"Ah, I'm sorry, Dr Figg." The scientist looked at the floor.

"We were about to..." the other said.

"This can't be happening..." Figg's shoulders slumped, and she put her index fingers to her forehead.

Both scientists scrambled to console her.

"It's still groundbreaking scientific work..."

"We were close this time..."

"But not close enough." Figg leaned against the wall, lifting her forehead to the ceiling, fighting emotion. Her forehead creased, and I saw a vulnerable side she hadn't shown me. Gone was the self-assured, respected and powerful doctor fit for television.

Was she talking about me—was I her failed experiment? But I couldn't stay to eavesdrop. They may return to the lab, and I was standing right by the door.

I slipped on my sneaker, turned and angled towards the fire stairs.

"The Phoenix Compound is ready," one scientist said.

Figg brightened.

"The Phoenix Compound is our last shot. We'll integrate the fresh DNA samples we've taken from Ofelia."

Wait—that's what they were using me for? They were adding my DNA—but why? Why would my DNA specifically help?

I realised why Figg was so interested in me—she believed I could help create a vaccine to the plague. But didn't they already have the cure in her lab? That's what she'd said on the news segment back in our shack. And what was this 'Phoenix Compound'?

I leaped into the fire stairwell just as Figg approached the lab, her heels clicking in a no-nonsense beat down the hall. Her research assistants scuffled after her, throwing concerned looks at each other. I risked holding the door open a crack and peeking out—I had to see how she passed the security panel.

She pulled a security pass from her hip and held it over the sensor. At the beep, she keyed in a four-digit passcode. My angle obscured the numbers, but I could follow each button press, memorising the pattern. Top right, middle centre, top left and bottom left. I repeated it in my mind as the glass door sluiced open and Figg and her hapless research assistants entered the decontamination pod. Germ-eradicating smoky air blasted them on each side.

I snuck back for a better vantage point. As I did, the inner lab door opened, the smoke blast dissipated, and they moved inside.

Running the keypad digits over in my mind, I left the stairwell. I stalled for time, pausing opposite and dropping to one knee to retie my shoelace. From my crouched position, I had an angled view into the lab. Figg faced a container secured with a touchpad. She bunched her hair into a ponytail and donned a blue paper cap, splash-proof glasses and a plastic face shield. She snapped on thick, long rubber gloves that stretched to her elbows.

Figg swiped her pass. The container door hissed open with a slight escape of steam, and she grabbed tongs lying on the bench. Reached in and grabbed a single test tube in the centre of the container, and removed it, taking great care.

The tube was bright yellow, the liquid thick. Figg placed it into a test tube rack while her research assistant locked the container.

I read the large sticker on the front of the box: 'Phoenix Compound'.

I had found Imogen's cure. But was it ready?

———————————

There was no point in infiltrating the lab with Figg inside. I'd wait until she left. I was conspicuous in the hallways, having retied my shoelaces so often I looked like a witless grifter. Backing into the fire stairwell, I cracked the door ajar to observe the surroundings.

But whatever Figg and her minions were doing in there, they weren't in a hurry. Every second I remained in the stairwell, I risked being caught. A few minutes passed, I guessed. The morning sun would soon rise, heralding breakfast-on-a-tray time, when Scowly and Bored would pronounce me missing from my cell.

Since my powers didn't work on this security system, I'd have to figure out a way to grab Figg's pass when she wasn't looking. She was taking me to the last test in the morning, so tonight was my only chance. If I didn't succeed, I was a 'dead lab rat running'. I had to believe that they would fix the cure. It was my only chance between now and my last morning on earth.

The lab door swished open, and I jerked to high alert. Figg and her helpers left. Figg armed the lock with a tap of her pass and strode towards the offices. They left the test tube in the lab, and Figg carried her iScreen with graphs and figures.

I counted a couple of seconds, then peered out. The tails of Figg's white coat swished into an office.

I exited the stairwell, darting towards the office. The name plaque read 'Dr Melina Figg, Chief Virologist'. How had I not noticed that the last time I was here?

The only logical step from here was to infiltrate Figg's office and nab her security pass. I didn't know how, since Figg carried her pass with her. I hesitated—could I do this? What if she caught me? But I needed that cure, and this was my best option so far. If Figg was killing me tomorrow anyway, there wasn't a choice.

Figg's office door had a round chrome handle, which I eased to the right. I nudged the door open a sliver, halting with every sense alert. Figg's conversation inside was low. She was busy bouncing ideas off her minions, but I couldn't make out the words. The tone indicated they had covered this ground before, and were hopefully revisiting each pre-formulated idea.

I yanked the door open, slipping inside. The door clicked closed behind me.

"What was that?" Figg asked, her weight shifting off the chair, her voice loud as a megaphone.

A small storage room led off to one side, and I dove in, hiding behind a stack of boxes marked 'patient files'. Figg flung the office door open, peering outside.

"That damn Johnson trying to steal my results," she said, scanning the corridor, then moving back to her desk. "I don't understand—I'm only trying to save the entire human race. I'm trying to do good, to save billions of lives..."

"Of course, Dr Figg," one minion quipped.

Figg grumbled more about her hapless colleagues, while I stuck a tentative nose out of the supply closet.

The two research assistants stood with their backs to me, in front of Figg, who sat at a large desk stacked with papers and folders.

I scanned the room. To the side of the desk was an over-sized armchair, although I couldn't imagine Figg inviting anyone to sit there. A set of bookshelves was embedded into one wall, and the other displayed several framed certificates: Figg's credentials.

There was a charging station on her desk for her iScreen and two translucent monitors which sprang into action, depicting complex results and a rotating, colourful three-dimensional blob that probably represented the virus itself.

It looked so innocuous there on the screen, a round green ball with cute-looking red suckers on the outside, like an inflated puffer-fish.

"Okay, let's get back to basics," Figg mused, moving closer to her screens, using her fingers to pinch focus in and back out again. "Our DNA vaccine needs to cross the cytoplasm and the nuclear membrane. But..."

"We've accounted for that in the physical method of delivery," the research assistant finished. "Do you think it could be the procedure itself?"

"I know how to give an intradermal injection," Figg said.

Figg and her assistants focussed their attention on the rotating chemical compound. My best chance to act was while they were distracted. I crept forward, ensuring my body was hidden from Figg by the bodies of the research assistants. If they moved, I'd be caught in Figg's office, up to no good.

"Could it be the introduced DNA itself?" one assistant asked, and I scooted further towards the desk while all three of them leaned towards the translucent monitor screen. I took the opportunity and slid beside the desk, so that the desk itself hid my body.

One research assistant looked behind her, sensing movement, and I held my breath.

"Ofelia's DNA is perfect." Pride broke Figg's voice on her last word. "Hers is the only DNA to integrate strands from both species."

Wait—both species? What the heck did that mean? What did she think I was? It made no sense. Although, I couldn't help feeling a little superior when Figg described my DNA as 'perfect'. At least my parents got one thing right.

"The Phoenix Compound has to work." The research assistant turned back to Figg.

"We have to believe the latest samples will be the answer." Figg crossed something off her list. "What dosage did we land on?"

"A 2 mg dose of DNA, spike antigen and signal peptide," her minion quipped.

"Then we're ready to integrate the latest samples," Figg said. "This is it!"

If they made changes tonight, could the cure work? I still needed Figg's pass to get into the lab.

Silence followed, as I imagined them poring over the molecular bubble on the screen. I peeked from behind the desk. Figg's white coat was within arm's reach. The coat shifted as she leaned forward, exposing a corner of her security pass.

The pass was hooked to a clip on her hip, revealing one corner with her picture, that immaculate, shiny hair.

I reached out, my hand inching closer to the pass. My fingers closed around the smooth plastic corner just as Figg stood back again. My fingers vice-gripped the pass. I wasn't letting go. But the pass was stuck, it wouldn't pull free.

"It's our last chance," she said. Did she mean me? Would my ultimate test reduce me to their molecular display? Then she said something that surprised me. "Our last chance to honour those children..."

The inflection in her tone cracked with emotion. Wait, so she cared about us now? Was she remorseful that she hurt us? This was no show for her junior staff. She believed it in her own warped way. The minions allowed their gazes to fall to their feet, and a few moments of silence passed. Figg sniffed, then blew her nose on a tissue. She shoved the tissue into her pocket on the far side of her lab coat.

Figg could be human, after all. I shook off the thought and pulled the pass—but it was attached to the lanyard clipped to her hip. The string pulled out, but the pass itself wouldn't detach. If I pulled any harder, Figg would feel it.

Figg turned. If she looked down, she would notice me, crouched there beside her desk with her pass in my fist. This would not work.

I eased the pass back to her clip, and it whipped out of reach.

Repositioning myself, I reached my right arm out towards the clip—maybe I could unhook the lanyard from her belt— just as she stood back, out of reach. She gathered her research off her desk and began handing them to her assistants.

"We'll know once the samples bond," Figg said. "It will be a long night."

I crab-walked behind the solid armchair, holding my breath, retreating from sight.

"We need the Phoenix Compound to be ready for tomorrow's tests. They must be conclusive," Figg said, "or the Prime

Minister will shut us down. All those lost lives, we have to make their sacrifice count."

"We understand," one research assistant said, putting a tender hand on Figg's arm.

"Let's save humanity," Figg said, with a smile, and her assistants nodded. I was intruding on a moment here.

As I crouched behind the armchair, the breath I was holding expanded like a bubble of gas, and my chest hurt as I held everything still. I swore Figg could hear my heartbeat pulsing in my ears like a drumbeat. Panic rose as I fought the urge to jump from my hiding spot and declare myself fit for execution.

Figg's minions followed her to the office door.

I willed my lungs to be silent as my breath escaped in short bursts. Figg and her scientists left the office, and a key scraped in the lock.

I huffed out and gasped for breath. I'd squandered my only chance. Of course, the pass had to be connected by a retractable string. How would I get the cure now?

I followed them to the door, but Figg had locked me in. Now I was trapped in Figg's office, and Imogen's cure was further away than it had ever been.

CHAPTER 15

I SEARCHED FIGG'S OFFICE, from the mess of papers scattered on her desk to the boxes of patient files in the storeroom. I lingered over one weathered box. Maybe it was used when Demi first arrived? But I couldn't search every file. I didn't like my chances of staying hidden if Figg returned to her office. I'd been exceptionally lucky not to be discovered already. Time to leave this office and steal her pass.

I tried my shield on the door, but it only opened with a key. There was no electrical current to short out. I ran my hands over the shelving for any tools or metal objects I could use to open Figg's office door. A paperclip rested on her desk.

Maybe I could pick the door lock? I inserted the straightened metal clip into the lock, my fingers closing over the flimsy tool. The paperclip scraped against the lock mechanism, but there was no give. I lost my grip on the other end, and it wedged inside.

I scanned the textbooks on the shelves, but advanced medical theory wouldn't release me from this bind. The desk drawers were locked.

Pulling up the blinds revealed a glass window that looked down to the courtyard below, the same scene I'd viewed from the stairwell. Except this was a higher vantage point—we were one floor off the ground. I tried the window, but it didn't budge. The window lock required a key, so I searched the desk. I lifted papers and moved folders, but suspected the key was in the locked desk drawers.

Giving up, I slumped into Figg's executive chair, my chest concave and shoulders rounded. Helplessness crept in, and I let my focus relax with the realisation that I was stuck here. As my eye line lowered, I noticed a small box stuck to the underside of the desk. Ah-ha! Wriggling my fingers over the box, I pushed a clasp, and the lid opened. A key was nestled inside.

The key matched the window lock, and I pushed open the window as wide as it would go, the light breeze shifting the sweat on my forehead. A thrill of relief passed through me. My body could fit through, but I was high off the ground.

I leaned out of the window, looking for padding on the ground. Shrubbery ran alongside the building—would it break my fall? My head spun as I regarded the gravel courtyard. The vertigo reminded me of teetering amongst the stacks on Trash Mountain.

The pattern of red brick that ran the length of the building may be useful as steps. Unsure if it would take my weight, I wobbled the nearest jutting brick embedded into the wall with my hand. It felt sturdy.

This was it—I could escape via the window, traverse the wall via the jutting bricks to the corner stairwell and drop down the drainpipe to the courtyard below.

I stepped up onto the desk, hanging onto the windowsill with a fierce grip. I bent my head to fit under the window, and swung my right leg out first, so that I straddled the windowsill itself. Holding onto the bottom of the window, I eased my left leg out, standing on the first brick. Then my right leg joined the other. I steadied my weight on the narrow brick.

160

The fresh air out here smelt sweet—a whiff of nearby pine trees after the metallic, chemical stench of the medical area. But the breeze caught me off-guard, and I wobbled on the windowsill as I grew used to its tug and pull.

I clung onto the brickwork and pushed the window closed.

The jutting bricks weren't as deep as I would like. I shifted my weight, holding firm. A pattern of bricks wove into the wall about head height, and I used them as handholds, scooting towards the fire stairs column, towards the drainpipe. The breeze blew my hair into my face, and I shook strands from my eyes, concentrating on placing my feet just so.

My foot slipped, sending a thrill of panic through my fingers.

I gripped the brick hand holds, waiting until my balance returned, then shuffled sideways until I came to the next office —dark and empty of workers. I moved past, sweat trickling down my temple.

Hot-footing it past the last office, I reached the drainpipe and wrapped my arms around the metal. I gripped the pipe with both arms, slipping to the next rivet about a metre down, and then the next. Vertigo returned as I glanced down. My controlled slide hit the ground too fast, and I fell into the shrubbery. It wasn't as soft as it looked from above, and I scratched my arm on the scraggly branches. I emerged from the bushes and studied the courtyard.

The building was four storeys high, with offices on the floor I'd just exited. The floor above held the hospital wards—I could see the runners for the privacy curtains surrounding each bed. And the fourth floor had white-blocked windows, so I couldn't see. What secrets hid there?

The archway was the only way out. It was tempting to escape this nightmare. Hadn't I been working towards free-dom? The archway beckoned me to follow the road to Imogen, to my family. I peered through into the darkness beyond, the rushing river gurgling in the distance. A shiver passed through me as I contemplated escape. I would have a head start, before the orderlies delivered one too many breakfast trays. But I had to obtain the cure. I couldn't leave when I was so close. And I couldn't abandon my friends, or Trix, or Demi.

I allowed myself one last yearning glance out of the archway. For now, I was heading back into captivity, back to my cell.

If I couldn't go to Figg, she would come to me. I had promises to keep.

The fire stairs from the courtyard were unlocked, and I let myself into the ground floor level, padding down to the basement. The stairwell was darker here, shrouded in shadow. I removed my shoe and enacted the force field, shorted the lock, and pushed through into the basement cell wing. The electrics weren't permanently fried, as they were when I'd used the mug full of water. I could pass undetected.

The wing was quiet; the inmates subdued tonight. I didn't fancy being noticed this time around, and so I scooted, treading silently.

Breakfast would soon be served. I had little time.

Mousie saw me and raised her eyebrows, giving me a questioning thumbs up and crooking her head to the side. I shook my head in reply and lifted my hands as if to say 'I tried'. Mousie smiled back in encouragement, but my attention turned to the orderlies, who chatted in chairs behind the nearby nurses' station.

I flattened against the wall and crept forward, taking advantage of their distraction. Their conversation revolved around the international rugby match. One had placed a bet on the long shot team, reminding me of my win on the mech cars. They didn't notice me bend low underneath the counter, scoot past and stand by my cell. I shorted the lock and entered the cell. The door clicked shut, and the lock armed. Our red light shone on the opposite wall through the tray flap.

Maya threw her arms around me in a gripping hug. Pine soap and musty knitted jumper filled my nostrils.

"I missed you too, Swanky," I replied, trying to pull out of the awkward hug. But Maya was strong.

"I didn't think you'd come back," she said, not letting go.

"Didn't I say I would?" I replied, patting her back.

She pulled out of the hug, tears clinging to her long black lashes. "But today's your last test. Nobody survives. Why did you come back?"

"I found Figg's lab. I'm breaking in."

"So break in. Why are you here?"

"I need her pass."

She shook her head. "But you'll be dead before then."

I hadn't realised just how badly I'd missed Maya. I drank her in, like a castaway rescued from the middle of a vast sea. Observing her worried eyes and furrowed brow. The distrust in the set of her shoulders. She seeded doubt on my plans, but I had to succeed.

There was a clanging outside my cell, and my cellmate sat back on her bedroll, hugging her knees.

"I'll have to grab Figg's pass when she returns. Then I'll slip away. Don't worry about me."

"Please don't die," she whispered.

Then I said, "I'll come back for you. I promised, and I will."

CHAPTER 16

THE ELECTRIC SENSOR BEEPED, the door unlocked and Figg stood there, tapping her hip with her finger, flanked by Scowly and Bored, the A-team orderlies.

"Let's go," she said, her face tense, motioning for me to stand.

"Where are we going?" I asked, shuffling against the wall.

"There's someone to see you."

"So show them in."

Figg dipped her head, as if negotiating with a toddler refusing bath time. She handed me a jacket and a pair of socks and hiking boots.

"Put them on, please," she asked.

"Why? Where are we going?" I asked.

"We want you to feel more comfortable for this next test. Would you prefer a hospital gown?"

"Definitely not," I said, grabbing the clothes.

The corduroy jacket pinched in at the waist. It was the nicest piece of clothing I'd ever seen. The high-top brown leather boots were well made, polished, the laces intact. I slipped my hand into the sock, expecting my finger to pop out at the inevitable hole in the toe. But the socks were brand new, hole-free.

I raised my eyebrows at Maya, but she gazed at the floor in fear. So Figg had hurt Maya, too. Maya reminded me of a fawn, ears twitching, ready to spring, taut and alert. Figg was her hunter, brandishing a tranq gun. Had Maya gone down in the same fashion as the Northies kids?

A sharp flash of anger rose in my belly on Maya's behalf. But I kept it on the inside. I had to concentrate on my mission.

My anger disappeared as Scowly put his hand to the night-stick hanging from his belt.

Pulling on the socks, I wriggled my toes and smiled when they didn't poke through. I laced up the boots and then slipped on the jacket. Figg even handed me a brush—and a hair tie. The band had a soft covering, so the hair didn't pull when I wound it into a ponytail. I stared at my reflection—with the jacket over my t-shirt, and my hair up, I could pass for a regular citizen. Hardly a gutter rat anymore. I ignored the gash of orange in my eyes.

"You look presentable." Tenderness tinged Figg's voice, and she almost reluctantly added, "Let's go."

Scowly stepped forward, grabbing me under the armpits, where I was raw from their earlier tugging. Bruises on bruises.

"Okay, I can walk," I said, as Scowly shoved me in the back.

"See ya," I farewelled Maya—this might be the last time she saw me. She tucked into her blanket, rocking, trying to make herself invisible.

The electric sensor locked behind us. Would I ever see Maya again? Was this my last chance? Could I escape and return?

My face was unreadable, but my insides felt like last night's curry disagreed with me. Maybe it was a few days not-quite-fresh, as Maya mentioned. I needed the loo. Perspiration glinted on my forehead despite the chill, and my heart beat double-time. I readied myself to grab the pass and slip away, fade into shadow at the first hesitation from Scowly or Bored. They were comfortable with me. I hadn't been belligerent in their presence—at least not since I'd moved to Maya's cell.

I rubbed at the bruises under my arms; the jacket pulling with the movement. It felt constraining, as did my boots—I'd never worn such heavy footwear before, and I clumped along, my footfalls echoing on the linoleum floor. I was as clumsy as if walking in the moon boots the astronauts wore on television. My footwear rubbed blisters on my heels by the time we'd reached the elevator at the end of the hall.

I stood behind Figg, inching closer as we waited for the lift. The orderlies flanked me but weren't paying close attention. I reached to Figg's hip. Shifted her lab coat to one side, revealing the laminated pass. With one hand holding open her coat, I reached the other to the waistband of her trousers.

Just as the lift arrived, Figg swivelled to check on me, and I snatched my hand back, unable to unclip the lanyard in time.

Scowly noticed me reaching for Figg.

The doors opened, and before I could react, Scowly wrenched both arms behind my back, and clipped steel hand-cuffs to both wrists.

How could I grab her pass now? And I couldn't enact the shield whenever I needed. I wriggled, hurting my wrists as I twisted every way possible. The snug handcuffs didn't give.

My face grew hot and sweat slipped down my temple. This was not going well.

We rode the elevator to the top. My mind flashed to my escape in the courtyard. This was the secretive level, with the white-blocked windows. What lurked inside?

The lift halted and Scowly pushed me into the hall. The orderlies hung a few paces away. Figg gripped my elbow, as if crossing the road with a small child. She'd be easier to overpower than the orderlies, especially since she mustn't know how my powers worked, or she wouldn't have left me to break out of my cell.

Two men in military uniforms rounded the corner. One held a file, and the other rested his hand on his holstered gun.

At least they hadn't blindfolded me, and I still had a chance of repelling gunfire if he became trigger-happy. Then again, bullets were fast. Were my reflexes up to the challenge?

Figg flashed her security badge, and the men saluted, running suspicious eyes over me.

We were in a high-tech section. Navy-blue-uniformed guards passed. Each one wore a security pass with photo ID. The grunts were vigilant of anyone who didn't belong.

Nobody wore face masks up here. It was chillier than my basement cell, and I shivered as the hairs on my arms stood to attention. Just like the men with wired earpieces.

"Yes, ma'am?" One saluted.

"Would you inform Doctor Wood that we have arrived?" Figg said, her voice respectful, but also commanding. I had to assume she out-ranked them.

This was the floor of state secret missions. The men's bearing suggested it was so. Surely that wasn't where they were taking little old me?

The first guard spoke into his wrist comm link, and his eyes flitted to the ceiling as the reply came through the wired earpiece he wore. The other guard drilled holes through my eye sockets with his glare. He could have shorn sheep with his sharp buzz cut.

The two men stood aside and Figg scanned through two more security gates, using the pass she had clipped to her hip. I could only watch. Even if I swivelled backwards, my hands were on an awkward angle, and I couldn't line them up with

Figg's hip. At least not at the speed I needed to be undetected.

We halted outside a door leading off the corridor. Figg swiped her pass and beckoned me through first.

I pushed into a monitoring station with a large bank of control switches and computers. Two uniformed men sat at the control panel, eyeing me with interest, stiff caps resting on their laps. Both of them had multiple stripes on their jacket arms, their manner formal. They must be high ranking.

Glass panelling led into an observation room. Two padded medical chairs sat inside, with thick velcro wrist and ankle straps. There was a curtained divider between the chairs, and electronic equipment positioned behind both.

Figg greeted the men and sat behind the monitors, facing the glass. The orderlies roughhoused me into the observation room. Scowly pushed me into the nearest chair.

"Hey, lay off guys!" I huffed, sounding tough but with a terrified, hammering heart.

The one-way glass reflected my own petrified expression, rather than Figg or the uniformed men scrutinising my every move. The bank of electronics behind my chair bleeped, and the electrical hum was low, almost inaudible. Latent heat from the machines emanated into the frigid cubicle. Scowly twisted my body, and I struggled until I realised he was removing the handcuffs. Feeling returned to my wrists as I sat in the chair.

There was no other exit. I'd have to escape through the same door I'd just entered. I regretted not escaping sooner, squandering my chances before we entered the lift. But I hadn't expected to be cuffed. Maybe this was it; panic twined up my throat like a writhing bird seeking the sky.

A mirthless technician appeared, dressed in military garb, and hooked me to the electrical machines, with wires ending in round pads stuck to my skin.

They pulled a blindfold over my eyes.

Was it just me, or did those machines whirr more sinisterly now that I was blindfolded? I tried not to freak out. How would I enact my force field if I couldn't see the missiles?

This machine, whatever it was, was my last test. Trix had been right, and I'd been so stupid, thinking I could escape.

What use was I dead?

The technician's stiff cuff brushed my hand as he secured restraints on my wrists and ankles, and velcroed them shut. I couldn't move, and I couldn't see. Something invasive was about to happen. The velcro ripped free and was patted down on the other person in the second chair.

Then the orderly whipped off my blindfold, and I squinted against the fluorescent lighting, my vision blurry, blinking back the focus.

The dividing curtain blocked my view of the rest of the room. A trail of swirling liquid led to the divider, as if someone had dragged a wet mop over the linoleum.

Who was behind the curtain? This test was creepy as heck. I'd do anything to have my blood taken instead.

I struggled against my restraints. They were tight and cut into my skin. My flight instincts took over, adrenalin coursing from my belly to the rear of my throat. I swallowed the saliva. What would they do? My chest constricted until I could only pant shallow breath.

"Ofelia," Figg spoke through a speaker. "We're hoping you can help us with our testing. It's very important."

"Why would I help you?" I spat, finding more courage in my words than I felt. It was easier to allow anger than to succumb to terror. The technician strapped an electrical cap—for electrocution?—to my head. The cap had wires that stuck the tips of tiny needles into my scalp. They executed murderers in electric chairs, in the Before. Was that my fate?

"Because you don't have a choice," Figg said. "If you cooperate, the test will be over sooner."

"Yeah, while you fry my brains to butter."

"We only want to chat."

"A freaking conversation?" I wrenched at the restraints, which were pulled tight. "So untie me."

"We can't do that, I'm afraid. It's for your own safety."

"How about I stuff your safety right down your throat?"

"We think you have a special connection to one of our test subjects."

My heart jumped into my throat, and it was difficult to breathe. Did she mean Demi?

"Which test subject?" I asked.

"We can't tell you, or that could compromise the test."

"So, what's the connection?"

"You share DNA."

That had to mean Demi! We shared our mother's DNA. I'd finally reunited with my sister.

"Release her," I said. "Right now."

The microphone reverb shut off. There was a pause. A fresh voice came over the speaker.

"Ofelia, my name is Doctor Wood." The voice was male, and pleasant enough. "But call me Sebastian, if you prefer."

Wait—the same Dr Wood who had wondered at my disappearing scales—that he'd *cut out with a scalpel*? He was worse than Figg—or maybe he'd play good cop?

"What do you want with us?" I asked, less combatively.

"This machine won't hurt you. We don't want to hurt you. I should make that clear."

"So, why are you keeping us in prison?"

After another pause, Dr Wood sounded less sure.

"I don't know about a prison. But we think you're special, you could make a significant difference. A real game-changer."

"What are you saying?"

"Ofelia, if you could be so kind as to humour me." He sounded jovial, colleague-to-colleague over the operating table, passing the scalpel while the patient was out cold. A scalpel with my scales incised from my skin, disappearing into ash...

"Humour you?" I asked, with a hint of hope, my voice inflecting upwards.

"Just one thing we want to try. Please. It won't take long, and then you can leave."

"As in, we can both go home?"

"Ah... sure."

I thought about that. He was my best chance to see my family, but this guy had hurt me before. Why wouldn't he again? Plus, Figg could have told him lies. If they trusted me, why the firm restraints, the blindfold, the sinister wire-riddled cap?

"I need you to make a promise," I said.

"We can arrange anything you'd like."

"I'd prefer not to say in front of Doctor Figg."

"We'll talk privately afterwards," Wood said. "Whatever you wish, Ofelia."

Could I trust him? Maybe he didn't know about the kiddy prison? And he could let them all go.

"What do I have to do?" I asked.

CHAPTER 17

STRAPPED to the chair-of-doom in that creepy, freezing observation room, my skin stung with chilled fear. The sinister electronic equipment pinged, and the sticky pads attaching wires to my arms and legs sent pinpricks of dread through my body.

I tugged at my restraints—a wishful attempt to escape my predicament. Scowly shifted behind me, paying extra attention.

Figg's voice returned over the speaker.

"Thank you for assisting us, Ofelia."

As much as I didn't want to give Figg any advantage, Dr Wood—Sebastian—had promised to help.

I used them, they used me; symbiotic creatures. Limpets, like Imogen. Pretending to cooperate might allow Demi and me to go home. Sebastian seemed more reasonable, surprised at the mention of prison. I'm sure Figg hadn't told him the full story, or else he was playing with me.

Sebastian—the word was soft, expansive. I thought back to the name plaque at Figg's office—her first name was Melina. Somehow it seemed too friendly, too likeable for the person who'd throw my death switch.

I struggled against the restraints. Scowly attached something heavy to my cap, straining my neck muscles. I twisted, feeling the long, thick wire that stretched from the base of my cap into the machine bank.

What happened now? I shivered beneath the warm jacket. Nerves fluttered in my stomach as the machines powered up the electric chair.

Trix said that nobody survived this—we had gone beyond mere testing and fallen deep into my reckoning.

"Sit still for us, while we get a baseline," Sebastian said. His tone indicated that we were pals. Look at me, racking up those allies in hell.

I shifted my head towards the curtain next to me, but the person there was silent. It had to be Demi, right? Maybe they had her sedated.

Dials clicked on both of our machines. Bored's shadow moved into position, on sentry duty behind the other chair.

I flexed my toes inside my boots, not used to having my feet so constrained. I rubbed my little toe against the sock, feeling it slide against the leather. An unfamiliar feeling, this small toe captured.

A few minutes passed. My anxiety grew as the hum increased in frequency, the tone lifting higher. More juice flowing through the machines? My anxiety flourished from general unease to imagining my brain fried, the stench of my cooked grey matter as Figg came to feast.

"Take the restraints off!" I pulled my wrists, but they didn't budge.

"Please keep still, and don't speak," Figg shot through the speaker.

I closed my eyes and counted in my mind, backwards from a hundred. I waited until Figg spoke again, calmer this time.

"How do you feel?" she asked.

"I don't know what you mean," I replied.

"Are you different from this morning?"

"Well, I'm strapped to a chair against my will, with some-thing weird attached to my skull. So... yeah. A little different."

"Anything specific? A tingling, perhaps?"

"No."

"How is your rash?" she asked.

"It itches and I can't scratch it."

"Good."

"No, it's annoying as hell. Now it's all I can focus on. Big guy..." I turned to Scowly, standing over my right shoulder, "do us a favour?"

"Face the front, Ofelia."

I did as commanded, wearing Scowly's frown.

"Think of your home," Figg said.

No way, not with Figg so close. Who knew if this cap on my scalp could read minds as it melted my brain?

"Can you tell me where you live?" Figg prompted.

"No," I said.

"You're from Northies. But where exactly?"

"Why, so you can kidnap everyone else?"

"Who else? Who else is there, Ofelia?"

"Nobody. Just the other orphans."

"And why are they orphans?"

"Because the plague killed their parents," I spat. I didn't know how much she'd researched, but I sure as heck wouldn't tell her about my family, especially Imogen...

This hooked pain caught the rear of my throat when I thought of her. I couldn't let Figg in. I imagined Figg's face, back-lit by the monitors of whatever information they were gathering.

"You're doing very well, Ofelia," Figg said, as if she'd discovered the winning ticket for a prize that rich people valued. A truckload of new jackets, like the one I wore now?

"Who is sitting in the chair next to you?" Figg asked.

"I don't know," I replied. "I can't see."

"Don't see, think."

"You're being ridiculous," I said. "I can't tell who's there with the curtain drawn."

"Try for us, okay?"

I turned my eye-line to the curtain dividing the room. Demi had to be on the other side. But I couldn't tell Figg. Had she connected me with my remaining family? Roland, Mum, Imogen? Were they still hidden in Northies, or were they sitting beside me, too?

At least it wasn't Imogen—the body who'd sat earlier sounded heavier. Their shadowy outline wasn't visible. I could only hear the hum of the machines. If it was Demi, she was most likely connected to the machines, as I was. I didn't understand what Figg wanted from me.

A few minutes passed, until I said, "I don't know, okay?"

"Yes, you do!" Figg said.

"Maybe the guy on TV?"

"What guy?" Figg asked.

"It's a guess."

Figg maintained radio silence. Faint voices floated through the thick walls, but I couldn't make out the conversation. A muffled argument between Figg and Sebastian?

Figg strode through from the control suite. By the crisp clip of her high heels, I could tell I had riled her, but she kept her voice steady.

"Please, Ofelia," Figg said. "It's important that you cooperate."

"Sebastian said—" I began.

"You can talk to Dr Wood after we finish the tests."

"That's not fair! I need to speak with him now!"

"Ofelia, we won't hurt you as long as you help us. Can you

do that for me? You don't realise that I'm your friend. We both want the same thing."

"You have a warped idea of friendship."

"Ofelia, I made you. You're here because of me, and that makes you like my daughter..."

"You're no mother," I said. "Mothers protect their children, not kill them!"

Figg stepped back, nodding at Scowly, who shoved the blindfold on me.

"I'm sorry we have to do this to you, Ofelia. I hate to see you hurting. Please, just follow our instructions."

Panic rose as my sight dimmed to the outline of the stitching, reminding me of the rancid hood when they first brought me here. I was no closer to breaking free. It was my one chance.

"Dr Wood!" I yelled. "Sebastian, please!"

"Be still," a voice commanded inside my skull. Louder than before. It was Trix!

"What the heck—" I said. Trix was nearby. I collected my thoughts, turned them inwards.

What? What's happening? I thought.

"It will be fine," Trix said.

"Ah... Doctor Figg? You need to see this!" Wood shouted from the control area.

"Do not struggle," Trix said. "Cooperate with them, or they will hurt you."

Are you here? I whipped around, but I could only see the line of light where the blindfold met my cheek.

"Yes," Trix said.

Figg's heels dug into the polished floor as she strode towards the control chamber.

"Keep on her," Figg said to Scowly before shutting the connecting door.

"Please be calm," Trix said, and I relaxed, no longer struggling. My shoulders sank. I let my spine curve. As my body relaxed, I felt a wave of energy surge. The machines hummed with my power source.

"That's better," said Trix.

Disappointment hit as I realised the other person wasn't Demi. How could I have been so stupid? But then, was this a good thing? Trix had helped with my powers, and maybe she had powers as well.

What's going on? Why are you here? I thought.

"They want you to talk to me."

I'll shut up then...

"It might be the only way."

How do we get out of here?

"Not yet. Soon."

I sat limp, resisting speaking with Trix.

Not here. Not in this place.

"Remove my blindfold," I said. "Or I won't cooperate."

"Do it," Figg said through the speaker.

Scowly ripped off the blindfold, and I squinted against the glare of light. My eyes adjusted, and the shadow of Bored through the curtain moved closer to Trix.

"And the restraints," I said.

Figg hesitated, so I said, "I mean it, Figg. I won't help otherwise."

"Okay," she said.

The orderly ripped me loose, and I rubbed at my tender, blossoming red wrists. The clasp on the sensor cap was at an odd angle, biting into my chin, and I fumbled to loosen the strap, then gave up.

I'm coming over, I thought, waiting for the response.

"Slowly," Trix said.

I stood, shrugging off Scowly's hand from my shoulder. The wire from the cap extended behind me as I traversed the room.

"Get back," I said, and Scowly held up his hands in mock-surrender.

I stepped towards the curtain. Each footfall took forever, but I wasn't rushing this. My heartbeat pumped in my ears, and my tongue eased moisture around my dry mouth. It hurt to swallow. I hesitated. Reached for the screen hung like a veil on a hidden bride.

Was I ready for this? This moment would change my world. It was physical proof of this voice in my skull.

I dragged the fabric curtain to the side, each clasped loop scraping against the metal frame.

She was not a human adult, but a bipedal creature, the weight of a late-career wrestler, covered top-to-toe in brownish-orange scales that overlapped like a lizard's. Her pointed head had a curled droop at the apex, like a soft-serve ice cream. Three elongated fingers curled on each hand. Her entire being pulsed beneath her scales, her insides throbbing and pushing against the bark-coloured skin. Orange veins flowed beneath the intersection of each hexagonal scale, rivers of molten lava rushing beneath the crust of a volcano. A pattern of flaming lace.

Trix's eyes were a piercing, glowing orange, with a dark centre deep enough to know the complete universe.

The aliens were already here. Studying her eyes and scales, it was clear. I was part alien too.

My mouth gaped, and every word I'd ever known evaporated from my mind—I morphed into a newborn baby, before language formed thoughts. I existed as an emotion, somewhere between wonder and fear.

I mean, everyone fantasised about this moment. What

would you do when you met an alien? I'd hoped I would say something insightful. A small step for humankind, the first bridge to a complete universe of knowledge. Oh, and sorry for incarcerating you and running invasive tests and keeping you a secret. I felt the need to apologise for Figg's crimes.

But I hadn't believed that the voice was an actual alien. It could have been a hoax, or Figg's test. There was no fabricating this being, though. She was achingly, pulsatingly real.

A random voice couldn't compete with seeing Trix glowing, no longer a part of my imagination. Someone not of Earth, sitting velcroed to a chair, peering with those orange, cavernous eyes.

I hugged my arms where my scales hid underneath the jacket. What did this mean? I had similar scales and orange-flecked eyes to Trix. But I was human.

Who was I?

My mouth was dry again from sagging open, so I closed it.

Hey, I thought.

"Hey," Trix replied. Her facial expression didn't change, since she didn't have to form physical words. "I am glad to meet you."

Me too, this is weird.

"For me as well. It is my first glimpse of someone not fully evolved."

I smiled, remembering our earlier conversation. *I'm evolved enough.*

Trix gazed into my eyes, finding a truth there. I could tell her feelings, just as she knew mine.

As I stepped closer, the heat radiated off her. I stretched out my fingers to touch her reptilian scales.

"Careful," she said.

I pulled my hand back, glancing at the reflective glass.

Can they hear us?

"Not our words."

Let's get out of here.

What was this alien capable of? Her bulk was intimidating, she was immense, crammed into the chair dwarfed by her. Could I trust those emotionless, luminous eyes? Should I let her go?

Are you with me? I thought again, flicking my attention behind her chair. Scowly moved closer to me, but Bored kept his distance.

"Yes," she said.

I leaped forward as if a starting gun had fired at the Olympics. Grabbed Trix's restraints and ripped the velcro off in smooth movements. Both arms. Both legs.

The alien rose as if fighting gravity itself. But when she stood at full height, her frame towered over Scowly and Bored.

Bored's mouth fell agape, and his hand fumbled at his belt, trying to pull his nightstick free. At least he was finally doing his job.

Figg and Wood raced into the observation room. The orderlies circled. Scowly stood a few steps away, whipping his nightstick from his belt and throwing it at the alien. Before impact, the green force field shot up and disappeared just as swiftly, the nightstick clattering to the floor.

Trix could create a force field, too! Her shield was more effective than my clumsy attempts. No wonder she'd been able to coach me.

Bored grappled with his walkie-talkie, but Wood leaped onto the creature's back, his arms grabbing her neck. Trix flicked Wood away with the back of her arm. Figg raised a tranquilliser gun and aimed it at Trix's head.

Trix grabbed my arm, and energy coursed through me, like a battery starting. Sparks of electricity fizzed through each cell of my body, branching out from her touch.

Figg fired the gun.

Trix threw up a force field that covered me in her flank. Time stopped. The dart hung in mid-air, grazing the shield.

"Let's go," she said, snapping the strap off my electrode cap.

The force field disappeared, the dart clattered on the linoleum, and I threw off the cap. Trix and I scrambled past Figg, who had less time to react.

As we passed, I wrenched the security card from her belt.

Our momentum sent her sprawling against the chair, as Trix and I hot-footed it to the control chamber.

Sebastian found his feet and lunged, but Trix was too strong. She swiped with her massive arms and flung him sprawling to the ground. He threw his hand out to trip me. I kicked his arm aside, and Trix and I stumbled into the control room. Both uniformed men scrambled backwards. I locked the connecting door with Figg's card.

We watched through the one-way glass. Wood pulled himself up, stunned, from the floor. Figg grabbed Bored's night-stick. Scowly screamed into his walkie-talkie.

We ignored the officials and sprinted from the control area, locking the door behind us. The shouts inside were inaudible from the corridor.

The first part of my plan—grabbing Figg's pass—was over. Now, I just had to snatch the cure, free the kids and escape a high-security facility with a 7-foot alien sidekick.

CHAPTER 18

WE DIDN'T STOP for autographs in the high-security wing. The sanitised hallway stretched in either direction, with uniforms hovering just out of sight—identifiable by their conversation, their efficient, rubber-soled boots squeaking on the floor. Nobody noticed us exit the control room, which was sound-proof. I'm sure they were raising hell inside.

I snuck a glance at Figg's security pass, cradled in my hand, and wiped the sweat from my forehead. To blend in, I straight-ened my jacket, as if that could keep our cover. My eyes found Trix's—lava orange, the pitted black of her irises like the depths of outer space itself—but her expression didn't change. Was she scared, or was it impossible for her to move her features?

"I am not scared, Ofelia, but we have to remain alert," she said to my mind.

Sludgy, translucent goo trailed out of Trix's suction-capped feet. The suction lifted and rolled like the underside of a slug, the soft edges rippling like waves. At least our conversation was stealthy, even if our path was obvious. Just follow the goo.

Trix was the colour of the trunk of a thick oak tree, without the green branches, except her 'bark' was more orange than brown, and smooth rather than rough. Comparing my own scales, they were more brown than orange. There was no mistaking the similarities. My mind reeled at the implications. Who was I?

A shadow fell over the corner of the wing. My heart jumped as if it was trying to escape out of my mouth. This was it—our first showdown. The owner of the shadow had the light step of dress shoes, not military. More of a scuff than a squeak.

A doctor in a blue personal protective coat and plastic face shield rounded the corner. He checked his phone, maybe making plans for the end of his shift. Savouring his messages, he slipped his phone into his pants pocket, a satisfied smile creeping over his face. He wasn't expecting what came next— an anxious almost-sixteen-year-old and a 7-foot alien rooted to the spot.

His smile stiffened, his hand halfway out of his pocket. His expression read like Trix would vaporise him, and for a split second, I wondered if she could.

"Unfortunately not," Trix said to my mind.

"It's okay," I said to the doc.

His eye twitched, and his jaw clenched. But he wasn't as startled at seeing Trix as he should be—she was familiar to him.

"He has not seen me out of restraints," Trix explained.

"Don't go anywhere..." He showed the palms of his hands in surrender. His lips jerked as he formed a smile, but it was a Figg smile. It didn't reach his eyes—just one more adult trying to play us.

My eyes flicked to the corner of the corridor branching off, and in my momentary distraction, the doctor reacted. He scooped his stethoscope from around his neck and threw it at Trix, but she brushed it off with her force field, which she held open, and I basked in the stopped time with her.

She protected me with her glass-like defence, which stretched to capture me at her side, as tall as the ceiling. It was taller and stronger than my efforts had been, and a deeper, less-translucent green. A left and right flank held us snug. Our own solid green waterfall.

I wished for a shield as impressive as Trix's.

Trix waited, holding the shield open. When I turned to her, she nodded. Confirmation that we had this, even if our first test was only deflecting a harmless, rubbery medical device.

"Ready yourself, Ofelia," Trix said.

Time started again. The stethoscope clattered to the floor, and Trix lunged forward, clearing a path. The doctor flattened himself against the wall to let us pass, his hands surrendering above his head, his eyes squeezed shut. If our situation wasn't so dire, I would have found him hilarious.

We pushed past.

The military post at the end of the corridor noticed the commotion.

"Hey!" He poked his head over the desk, and his next reaction was to slap an emergency button like it was a quick-draw game show. An alarm shrilled from speakers set into the wall. Plexiglass rose upwards from the counter to reach the ceiling, the man locked into a force field space of his own. He shouted into the radio clipped to his shoulder.

Great, so now we had a guard commentating our every move.

From behind us, four guards sprang out of the fire stairwell, one reaching for his handgun. Our escape was big news as the siren whined, shooting adrenalin through my body.

"On the floor!" the bear-chested, frazzled guard yelled, raising his gun. "Do it! Get on the floor now!"

He screamed like a drill sergeant subduing fresh recruits.

Three military guards flanked him, raising small handguns.

"Get on the ground!" a second guard shouted, banging

through from the side corridor, standing between us and the door to the next wing. I recognised his sharp buzz cut.

Buzz Cut moved in front of us, and the four guards behind, led by Drill Sergeant.

They closed in, shuffling forward.

These guys were well-trained, hyped and trigger-happy, and trepidation spread out into my body. This was a tall ask, fighting several people. But neither Trix nor I would drop to the floor, as the Drill Sergeant commanded. Where would be the fun in that? It was do or die time, our one chance to escape.

Buzz Cut pulled a taser from his pocket and held it up so we could see.

I flicked my head at Trix. *I'll take the front. You take care of the stairwell scum.*

"We warned you, you failed to comply," Buzz Cut yelled. He pressed his taser, and an electrified dart flew at me, connected to the unit with long, quivering wires.

The taser hit my force field just as Trix reacted. She caught us in identical suspended time. A guard from the stairwell had thrown his baton. The baton pressed its tip into the front of Trix's force field.

She protected us from behind, me from in front.

These bozos underestimated us, I thought to Trix. *They'll have to do better than a taser and baton toss.*

"We are not free yet," Trix replied.

Her force field was stronger, but I had better reflexes, and could activate mine faster. But unless Trix was standing right behind me, I couldn't protect her with my shield, which was only as wide as my body. Her girth was thicker than me by a metre or more. They might maim her with shrapnel if I wasn't agile.

In the frozen time, I positioned myself behind Trix, moving my shield with me to the left.

I raised my eyebrows at Trix. Although she was expression-less, her nod was one of respect. She held up her three-fingered hands, the fingers drooping at the ends, like bent twigs with pointed brown nails.

I turned back, concentrated, and rammed the force field right into Buzz Cut's body. Before time started again, I settled him next to his spent taser on the floor.

Trix pushed her shield into the guards from the stairwell and then un-stopped time with a flourish. The guards flailed on the floor like upended turtles, scrambling to right themselves.

Both groups of guards recovered, getting to their knees, and then their feet.

A third stairwell guard with a mono brow raised his handgun—this fight had gotten real, fast. Another tried to tackle Trix.

Trix slopped to the side to avoid the tackle. The guard scrambled behind his own defensive line.

"Don't harm them!" Buzz Cut yelled. "Lower your weapons."

The men advanced, penning us in. We inched our way towards the connecting doors, past the hapless doctor, who still had his eyes squeezed shut in panic.

Mono Brow proved to have the least brains of the lot of them. He fiddled with something in his pocket—something black, fist-sized and egg-shaped.

Was that a grenade?

Watch out! I thought, and Trix clocked Mono Brow. She hadn't encountered a grenade. But she knew from my expression that it wasn't friendly.

Get that guy, I thought, nodding to the guard handling the grenade like a broken bird.

Trix and I pressed our backs to each other.

Her surge of power shimmied through my back, fizzing in

my tummy as if someone had released the cap of a shaken soda bottle.

I'll use Figg's pass, I thought to Trix.

The guard dropped his grenade and it fell to the floor, rolling along the hallway towards us... the pin was missing.

We've gotta go! I thought, leaping over the grenade, past Buzz Cut. He realised they were in as much trouble as we were.

I swiped Figg's pass at the door to the next wing, pushing Trix through the door. The guards were slow to react, transfixed by the metal egg glinting as it settled on the floor.

I couldn't kill anyone—even men who wanted us dead.

"Come on, idiots!" I shouted.

Buzz Cut and the doctor commando rolled through the door with Trix and I. The other contingent retreated into the fire stairwell.

The grenade exploded.

Heat flashed into our corridor, and we dropped and rolled. A spurt of fire. Deadened sound. And then the shock left us.

I felt for injuries—I was fine, apart from ringing ears. At least I could hear Trix, as her voice was in my head.

"Got to go," she said.

The doctor had rolled to one side, and Buzz Cut was also unhurt. He got up, unsteady. Now that I'd just saved him, he seemed confused.

Would he still try to kill us?

He dithered and checked for injuries, as if he'd forgotten about Trix and I. He shook his head, and reached for his ankle gun. But it was a muscle memory reaction. He was too stunned. Trix and I continued along the hallway before the guards recovered their bravado.

My gigantic alien struggled to keep up with my pace, and the exertion was taking its toll. She wasn't as nimble as I was.

She struggled with Earth's gravity—her home planet might be more forgiving.

The fire sprinkler system enacted, showering us with water, making our way slippery. At least that would wash away Trix's trail.

We swiped through into the next wing, leaving Buzz Cut confused on the other side of the door.

This wing was full of civilians, fearful faces searching for the explosion that had rocked the building. They milled about, reacting to the alarm, the sprinklers adding to the confusion. None were prepared to see me and Trix.

The nurses ushered patients to the fire stairs in the pattering indoor rain. One horror-stricken girl with an electronic tablet noticed Trix, and a nurse threw a protective arm against her charge.

"It's okay!" I shouted. "We won't hurt you, just let us through!"

Trix and I barged through the ward unopposed. People screamed and hit the floor. We were a cascading tsunami, parting citizens as we went.

We arrived at the set of lifts. Because of the alarm, the lifts froze on the floor below us.

Red lights flashed in the hallway and the alarm was shrill, like a piercing wire scraping my eardrum. It was so loud I could hardly hear Trix in my head.

"We cannot go this way," she said.

"Dammit." I scanned the hallway for our escape route. I spotted the fire stairs a few metres away and grabbed the alien's hand. *This way—*

As our skin touched, the energy jolted again, and this time, neither of us was ready for it. I jumped back with the zap, which was enhanced by the water. I felt charged and powerful. Trix seemed revitalised as well. We were like a car battery for each other, and with our proximity, our powers grew.

I took two stairs at a time. Trix was slower, having to duck her head in the compact stairwell. She was clumsy on stairs—and in general. It was like her body was heavier than she was used to carrying. We made way for the patients as we passed them in the stairwell. One nurse had made it to the level below, abandoning her charges and co-workers.

What a fine specimen of a human, I thought as we clattered down the stairs.

At least the water from the sprinklers masked our progress.

We need the first floor, I thought to Trix.

"Why?"

That's Figg's lab. Come on!

"They will apprehend us."

We have to try.

"I can see our most likely future, Ofelia. This does not end well."

I make my own future.

Trix sensed I wouldn't budge, and I felt her mind switch gears. She said, "Take us to the lab."

We banged into the corridor with the offices.

This way.

The corridor was empty of people. Scattered files littered the ground; evacuation had occurred swiftly.

We approached Figg's lab, pausing at the glass door to the inner sanctum.

I held Figg's pass above the sensor, which beeped. Then I entered the code I'd memorised on the keypad. The light switched to green, the glass door hissed open.

I snuck a victory glance at Trix, but her expression didn't change. We entered the decontamination chamber, and the lab door closed. Jets of steam burst out in a spritz reeking of disinfectant. The steam dissipated and the door into the lab itself opened. We sidled into the lab.

The yellow test tube beckoned inside its locked container. I swiped Figg's pass and the container sprung open. I grabbed the test tube, placing it into my jeans pocket. My pockets were deep. It would be snug there.

I've got you, Imogen. Hold on.

"She cannot hear you," Trix said.

We have to free the kids.

"There's no time."

We have to. I stepped back into the decontamination chamber.

"Why?" Trix asked as the foggy cloud blasted us.

We just do.

I couldn't read Trix's expression—it never changed—but she followed me into the corridor, the lab door locking behind us.

We used the fire stairs to head to the basement.

I swiped Figg's pass through to my old cell block. The alarm followed, and the red emergency lights flashed an eerie gloom to the usual antiseptic lighting. Like a mist-shrouded dock at night.

We approached the nurses' station. A panicked orderly held a phone to her ear, spying us straight away.

"Hey!" she shouted at us, then into the phone, "They're down here!"

She slammed the phone and reached under the desk for a large red cylinder with a hose attached to a nozzle.

She started towards us. It looked like a fire extinguisher. What would she do with that?

This way! I grabbed Trix's hand—our power surging through our touch—and I flicked Figg's pass at each cell door, unlocking them as we went. Kids of all ages and appearance emerged from their cells, those who were thin and worn-down, others who were newer recruits, who hadn't lost their bravado yet. The activity excited some, others held back. We'd buzzed all the doors open on this floor.

The orderly bolted after us, brandishing her fire extinguisher. She hobbled on her arthritic knee.

"You're free!" I yelled to the kids. "Get out of here!"

At first, the kids were cautious, wondering why their doors were unlocked.

"Hurry!" I yelled.

The kids noticed Trix, and the crazed orderly charging with a red-painted cylindrical weapon.

"It's okay, don't be scared," I yelled, but the kids couldn't hear us over the din of the alarm.

The nearest girl would have been about Imogen's age, slightly built, sobbing in fear. One kid with pigtails hid back in her cell, holding the door closed behind her. Two more kids retreated.

"She's on our side!" I said to the terrified, unbelieving kids. I remembered the moment—only minutes ago—when I'd first seen Trix. I had been terrified, and I already knew her.

Everything seemed worse with the flashing alarms. The piercing sound dominated and the red-strobing light lent a sinister flash to the whites of everyone's eyes.

"Stay where you are or you get the foam!" the orderly screamed, her face uncontrolled panic. Her eyes never left Trix.

A timid girl left her cell, gathering her long black hair into a ponytail, standing between the orderly and our rabble. Her attention trained on the orderly, then on Trix. But instead of retreating, she noticed me standing next to Trix. It was Maya.

She figured out what was happening, because I wasn't freaking out in Trix's presence.

"It's okay, guys," she said, giving the 'thumbs up' signal and pointing to Trix. "The alien is friendly."

The kids emerged more confidently from their cells, bunching behind Trix, Maya and I.

"Everyone inside!" the orderly yelled, moving closer to Trix and I. Her finger hovered over the trigger.

"Take her down!" I shouted, grabbing Maya's hand. We linked arms and sprinted, our feet lighter than they'd ever been. We were free, and we were full of rage.

The kids knew about safety in numbers. It's why they'd kept us apart.

Trix, Maya and I led the whooping band of miscreants forward, creating a human cascade.

The orderly's eyes widened as she pushed her thumb on the canister.

Foam spewed in an upward swoop into the air, then floated to the ground. The kids weren't sure if it was toxic—either was I. We didn't have fire-fighting equipment back home. But I hoped we'd be okay.

"Keep going forward!" I sounded the battle cry, curling an arm in front. They didn't have to hear my words, they understood my meaning.

As a scrum, we bolted straight at the orderly. Our bodies smashed her to the floor.

She sprawled in the foam, falling onto her back, hitting the ground hard, with the wind knocked out of her and the fire extinguisher sprouting foam into the air.

The kids were free! Their faces and bodies smeared with foam, and they were ecstatic.

Just as we passed the orderly's station, I noticed something on the desk. Something that Scowly had forgotten. The rubber ball!

I shoved the ball deep into my jeans pocket, next to

Imogen's cure, and whipped around to survey the situation. The orderly still struggled in the foam-bath she'd made for herself, sliding on the slick concrete, unsteady on her bad knee.

I swiped through the door to the fire stairs. We waited while the kids wiped foam from their eyes, excited and in awe of Trix. It was amazing how they accepted her. Maybe they trusted me and Maya.

I sent a silent 'thank you', and Maya grinned.

The other adults would descend soon. We had to break out of here.

Two familiar faces stood beside me. One had reached into their pocket and donned their familiar pirate patch, roaring a defiant battle cry. The other had the unmistakable stiff, dread-locked hair. Aze and Mouse Run!

We lifted our chins in recognition, fresh reinforcements.

Our rabble of thirty kids clattered up the stairs, hovering on the ground floor. They waited for instructions.

The alarm wasn't as shrill here. The kids could hear if I shouted.

"Okay, the fun part," I said, as Trix joined us. "Head through the archway. Split up. Run as fast as you can!"

Our horde hollered and burst through the door, scattering like an air force squadron into the yard.

Trix, Maya, Mousie and Aze followed me into the cool, fresh air.

But the orderlies and security personnel were ready.

They hemmed us in, blocking the exit through the archway to the road leading away from the facility. Several ambulances and a security car were parked on the ground level outside the stairs, manned by security men. They crouched behind the cars, their tranq guns poking out.

We tried to broach the vehicles, but they boxed us from freedom through the archway.

Figg and Sebastian burst out of a stairwell behind the cars. Figg grabbed her tranq gun, her face frantic until she spotted me and Trix. She composed herself and took shelter behind an ambulance. Sebastian hesitated, then followed her behind the vehicle.

"Quick, fall in close!" I yelled, and the kids retreated.

"Don't hurt them!" Figg yelled, popping up from behind the car and shooting a tranq dart, headed straight for us. One idiot threw a canister of gas.

Trix was in front and enacted her force field. It unfurled several metres to protect every single kid beside her.

The force field caught each new kid in our time-stop. Each one protected, glancing at the frozen security force. We had discovered a way out.

I marvelled at this huge shield—Trix was a master! She protected every one of us. I grinned at Mousie and Aze.

The darts scraped the force field, suspended in mid-air. I kicked the gas canister, and it boomeranged back.

I thought, *Can you hold the shield open?*

"Yes," Trix said.

I scanned the courtyard in our stopped time, noticing a hole in their defence.

"Okay, people? This is the plan."

The kids gathered closer.

"Ever played bullrush?"

Most of them nodded.

"There's a gap over there." I pointed to the kid-sized hole between the bonnets of two security cars. "Let's charge at the same time. Then scatter on the other side. They can't catch us if we run in different directions. Are you ready?"

The kids nodded, adrenalin keeping their fear manageable. Trix's superpowers impressed in a big way, adding to our confidence.

I gave the Northies signal—the thumb of one hand, held at the side—every kid for themselves. I lifted my chin to Trix, and she let the shield drop.

The gas canister arced towards the security guards standing by the cars. It dropped into a group of men. They swatted the air as the gas engulfed them.

Kids sprinted to the gap between the cars. Maya led the way, her fawn-like face stern with determination.

The kids crawled through. Security tried to nab them, but the wily kids evaded capture. They sprinted through the archway, ending their incarceration. Mousie ducked under a guard's arm. Aze stuck her tongue out at an orderly as she slipped by.

I leap-frogged the car bonnet, and Trix just waded straight through, shoving the cars with the strength of her thick torso. We flicked our shields as Figg fired more darts. Trix and I moved backwards, keeping our rabble covered by the shields. We moved slower than the kids, as fast as Trix was able. But we took the fire as they dispersed past the yard, into the open areas and woods, thirty rubber balls bouncing every which way on Trash Mountain. Mousie and Aze made it past the tree line, and then I lost sight of them. Maya must have made it, too. Trix and I were through the archway. We were free!

I couldn't help one last look for Demi, although I was sure she was no longer here.

I imagined Demi, fleeing with us, over by the—

Sfft!

The bullet grazed my shoulder as it passed. The nick broke through my jacket.

Searing pain overwhelmed my awareness. I stumbled, clutching my shoulder.

My hand was thick with blood as I pulled it away. My legs jellied from adrenalin.

A second gas canister landed to our left. I waved to ward off the tear gas erupting from the cylinder. I tried to kick the canister away, but couldn't see through the smoke. My eyes ran with intense pain, burning as if acid ate into my eyelids. I stumbled, blinded and overcome, forgetting about the pain in my shoulder. Now I struggled to breathe.

"It's over," Figg screeched. "Come inside now! We have work to do."

Trix was unaffected by the gas.

"I've got you," she said, picking me up with her three-fingered, twiggy hands, and tossing me in a firefighter's carry over her rough-skinned shoulder.

Energy surged through my stomach as it contacted her scaly skin. I caught glimpses of the pebbled road through excruciating, running-like-a-waterfall vision. She carried me through the yard, away from the hellish experiments. Away from Figg.

Men leaped into cars, scrambling to follow, sirens blaring. More noise! But the cars created a traffic jam, heading to the archway at once. And by that time, Trix had carried me beyond that sinister place.

We approached the sound of rushing water, a huge electrical charge dispelling as she sloshed into the river that ran beside the buildings. She waded up to her armpits in the water until we swept away in the current. As she dipped me into the water, I panicked.

I can't swim, I thought.

"Just hold on to me." Trix placed her arm under me.

At first I tensed, gripping Trix until my muscles ached, not used to floating. After a while, the fear faded, and I loosened my grip. She dipped me deeper into the water while I used her as my flotation device.

The river washed my eyes as we drifted, and soon I could open my lids and see. They still hurt, as if someone had poked my eye sockets with the simmering ends of burning sticks, but the water helped.

A tendril of blood from the bullet graze splayed out in the water. I inspected the wound as we floated, relieved to see that it was just a nick.

"That's what happens when you're not concentrating," Trix said, placing her hand over the graze. The bleeding seeped in between her slender, scaly fingers; her skin soaked up the blood itself. My shoulder didn't hurt as much, but it still smarted.

I had to say goodbye... I thought, laying my head back into the river.

"But she was not there."

It doesn't matter.

"I will never understand human attachment," Trix said.

I didn't have an answer, so I starfished, floating on the water, Trix's body keeping me afloat, my ears underwater. The world hummed to a different frequency. My eyes were recovering, my vision was less blurry. I stared at the tiny loop on the top of Trix's head, which drooped less. Her expression was as unmovable as slate, her lace-like veins glowing beneath the water, lighting our way. Tiny fish followed, curious about this bright light source.

I hoped the kids weren't rounded up again. They had to make it home.

Another kid bobbed up ahead, carried by the current, but I lost sight of her at the bend. She was too far off to recognise.

The river swelled, peppered by boulders peeking out, and then whitewater swirled, gathering speed.

This did not look good.

The river surged and took Trix and me with it. Trix gripped harder, struggling against the force of the water. It tossed us like sticks between the boulders, the dangerous white water rushing, propelling us forward.

I clung to Trix as the water threw around her massive weight. We sped towards an enormous boulder, looming like a mountain. I closed my eyes.

The river dashed us against the boulder. The impact shocked Trix. Her grip loosened. My hand was crushed between Trix and the boulder, and I wriggled my fingers. I felt her pain where she'd hit her shoulder. I panicked as Trix grabbed me, before I floated away in the wash of whitewater speeding us away from that boulder, right into the path of another.

Smash! We tossed into another rock, sluicing down the flow. My head went under water. I flailed, not knowing up from down. The surge carried me like a broken thing. I held my breath until it felt like I would burst. My head breached the water, and I gasped for breath. The force took me under again.

I opened my eyes under the murky water, carried against my will in all directions. Trix's leg was a way off, and my mind panicked. This was it. This was why Trix said we didn't make it.

My lungs burned as I tried to hold my breath, but it was like I was inside a giant monster, tumbling me about. I had to get air or I would drown.

The last air pushed from my lungs, my eyes open wide in panic, resisting the urge...

I gasped and inhaled water. My body convulsed as I resisted the water, willing it to be air. I was drowning.

Trix's slender hand splashed beside me, lifting me by my hair, her other arm grabbing me under my shoulders.

I coughed, spluttering water out of my lungs, gasping for breath. The air was sweet, my life force returning. After my choking stopped, the gasps turned into breaths, and the river slowed.

Trix floated on her back, and I nestled under her arms. She held me, and we floated by. The danger had passed, for now.

"At least this was a rapid escape method," Trix said.

At least we're not dead, I thought, relief bathing me like the river itself.

The river thinned about a kilometre away; banks hemmed each side. The swift current swirled and deposited us on a bend by a cluster of pine tree branches. We waded to shore, finding a farm with a field dotted with scraggly sheep.

My first thought was to reach into my pocket to check on the cure—miraculously, the test tube was intact and the plastic seal had held.

I reckon they'd overcome us with laughing gas instead of tear gas. I couldn't stop giggling at the expression on Figg's face when Trix carried me to safety.

Her reason for living had left the building, her subjects were free.

CHAPTER 19

FOLLOWING THE RIVER SEEMED LOGICAL. Trix and I wove through farmlands, the parched fields sowed with thinning crops poking from infertile dirt. Sheep pulled at brittle weeds growing around a corner fence post. Black spots plagued the wilted, yellowing shoots of the rows of crops in the next field. Even Pocks' garden, which grew vegetables for the elite Northies residents, was better maintained.

Home. I had to get back, pronto. But first, we needed our bearings.

We didn't talk as we made our way beside the riverbank; we sensed each other's feelings, and our footfalls synced. Her snail-trail clumped onto the dried grass and gravel of the river's edge as we passed. At least it was damper here on the riverbank than further inland, hiding her trail.

I hung back to check Trix out. Her head was shaped like a Brazil nut, with the point at the top curling over on itself, a melted question mark. Whenever we travelled in full sunlight, her scales glowed from within, at the bright orange joining points. Her bulk moved heavily—limbs sluggish, torso a struggle. But she moved as if the air was water. She sloped along in slow-motion. With each step she took, she seemed ready to fall flat from gravity itself. She became more familiar to me as we travelled.

The land spread out in each direction, our line of sight broken by a wind barrier of trees. The few houses had dusty driveways, and fences to keep in the livestock.

These farmhouses felt forgotten. Their inhabitants were on their own, trying to feed themselves and their pitiful animals. This was not the place I'd imagined; green fields, endless food and trivial concerns in houses populated by clean-clothed people. The farms had an ineffective whiff, on the brink of collapse. I could relate to that. My home was just as desperate, although less spaced out and with more people. Without a crowd to hide our presence, the isolation hemmed us in. At least in Northies, we were in it together; we endured as one.

My thoughts returned to home, the cacophony of banging tin sheet doors as residents left for their day of foraging. The burning, prickled scent of smoke from each hearth, cooking what little we had. The sharp sun reflecting off a shack, the stench of so many unwashed residents.

I had no experience of surviving here, on a farm, miles from anywhere. There was no safety in abandonment.

"Where should we go?" Trix asked.

Home, I thought.

My fingers found the ball in my jacket pocket, and I ran it around my hand. It focussed my thoughts, eased the terrified queasiness in my stomach. It connected me to the hearth, to the people waiting for me there. The test tube cure was deep in my pocket, safe after the rigours of our escape.

Would we make it in time to save Imogen?

I pushed my worries aside as Trix and I approached a tall hedge fence on the boundary of a property. My eyes still smarted, but my vision was back to normal, and my bullet wound hurt less. Underneath the hole in my jacket, the nick was bruising, but Trix had stopped the bleeding.

We can't stay here, I thought. What was our next move... or did I already know?

"You want to find your sister?"

Demi wasn't there.

"Your other sister."

I didn't want this alien inside of my head when I wasn't aware of it.

Those were private thoughts.

"My kind doesn't keep secrets. All knowledge is known to everyone."

Well, you're talking about me, and it's not allowed.

"Why not?"

It's called privacy. Understand? You can only hear me when we're talking.

"If you wish."

So, I had to be careful. Sure, she'd helped me and thirty-odd other kids escape from a high-security research facility, where they experimented on kids until they killed them. But I didn't know what Trix's plan was. Was she regrouping with the mother ship to wipe out humans? Would she start a war? Would she ditch me here in the great unknown, to fend for myself?

"None of those things," she said.

I said get out of my head unless I'm talking to you!

"I was joking—another thing our kind does not do," she said. "You only want me to listen when I have your permission. I do not understand, but if they are your rules, I will comply."

She held up one hand, bending one of her three twiggy fingers into a thumbs up. And the corners of her mouth curled, a darkened slit forming.

"Wait—is that a smile?" I said out loud. I guess Trix could hear me, and there was nobody else to eavesdrop.

"You smiled when you wanted someone to do what you wanted." Her head bobbed, like brown ice cream at a jaunty angle, the peak folding over on itself at the top.

"Yes," I continued, "or it's a sign that you aren't serious. Or you agree. Or that you're happy, or that—"

"You humans have a variety of complex emotions that make little sense to me."

"Or... you said something so downright boring that it ends up being funny."

"Did I make a joke?"

"Yes." I grinned despite myself. This alien was growing on me. Not like a third ear or something. Like folds of my own skin.

But chit-chat was over. A police car headed towards the road leading to the farmhouse, kicking up clouds of dust behind its wheels. It did not look friendly. Crunching tyres drove closer, heading our way.

The nearest farmhouse settled into a slight depression, sinking into a crevice. The front porch dipped in the centre and the tiled roof bent at the top, as if tired of carrying its own weight.

We crouched as the car skidded to a stop next to the farmhouse.

They cut the engine and two police officers emerged, scoping the area. They hadn't seen us.

The police officers wore flak jackets and seemed young and uncertain. The radio of one crackled to life, and he pressed his thumb to reply.

"Car 385, no activity," he said.

The officers fanned out from the edge of the farmhouse and the bottom flank spread towards the very hedge where we hid...

It was then I noticed a thinning in the middle of our shrubbery, right where Trix was standing.

One young police officer approached, his hand resting on the holster of his gun, searching the bushes.

He spotted us.

He grabbed his gun from his holster and yelled, "Over here!"

The other police officer transformed into kill mode, sprinting forward, training his weapon on our position. We should have chosen cover with more substance than branches and leaves.

I turned to Trix, and thought, *I want you to hear me. I need to go home to my family*.

The alien turned to me, her pitted eyes twitching the merest change in her expression.

"I understand," she said, and stepped through the bushes, busting a massive 7-foot hole into the leaves and branches. She stood in plain view of the officers and the road with the police car, the blue and red lights reflecting against the orange scales of her skin.

"Stop right there!" the nearest police officer shouted, a slight screech at the end signalling his panic. This was first contact. His expression held frantic wonder at what Trix could do, unsure if this would be his last encounter.

Trix trailed her sludge through the hedge, towards the officer, whose gun wobbled as he struggled to keep his shaking hands still.

The radio on the second officer's shoulder crackled to life. "Unit 385, please report."

"Hey, we've got them," the second policeman said. "Send backup, as in, right now!"

"Confirm request backup," the radio voice replied.

"Most definitely. Send everyone!" the second policeman yelled, keeping his own gun raised at Trix.

"Look, I don't want to assume you're bad…" the first officer said to Trix, taking a breath for bravado. He steadied his hand towards the ground, as if settling a spooked horse. "Are you bad? Do you want to hurt us?"

Trix stared, deadpan, at the officer, who lost a smidgen of his nerve.

"Only if you hurt her first," I said.

"You can hear that thing?" he asked.

"Most definitely," I said.

The policemen glanced at each other, way out of their comfort zone.

"Get on the ground, now!"

"I have another idea," I said. "Why don't we sit on that riverbank until your backup arrives?"

I pointed to the path beside the road leading to the river.

Trix moved forward, reaching her hand to the first officer. He retreated until he stood beside his partner.

"What are you doing?" the first officer asked.

Trix stopped an arm's length away and held out her hand, palm upwards. She curled her three fingers. The officers continued to train their handguns on Trix, watching her pointed nails.

"I think she wants you to hand them over," I said.

The policemen glanced at each other, fear deep in their eyes, and the first policeman raised his eyebrows in defeat. They handed Trix their guns.

"Thank you," I said, as Trix rolled back to me. I threw their handguns into the overgrown, scraggly grass in the field next door.

Trix and I sauntered beside the path to the river.

The cops retreated to their car, finding replacement handguns on the front seats. They scrambled into the car, rolling down the window and taking aim.

"Stop where you are!" one of the police officers yelled, aiming his gun through the open window.

"Last warning," the other yelled. He waited half a breath, then opened fire.

It happened in a millisecond, but Trix had her force field up before the bullets could hit her, and she beckoned me to follow in her time-stopped trail.

I hovered behind Trix. I wanted to do that, too. To protect others, and not just when they were standing behind me. Could I protect all the kids? Maybe every Northies resident? We'd be an unstoppable rabble, instead of an oppressed underclass.

When I was in position, I winked at Trix. She tried to return the wink. Since she didn't have eyelids, the best she could manage was to push her darkened eyeball further out of her head. It was kind of funny.

Can you hold the shield open? I thought.

They'd left an opening to the rear, by the river. I guess they expected us to take the main road. Yeah right, with a massive alien as the least-inconspicuous sidekick ever invented.

I felt Trix's amusement—I *told* her not to get inside my head again without my permission—but her emotion lessons were progressing. She picked things up fast.

I pointed to the gap between the road and the bend in the river.

"Understood," Trix said, and we bolted to the rapid-flowing water. We slipped into the tree line by the river bank. Trix grunted and her shield disappeared. It was an effort, I could tell by her slow progress to the trees. Then we were by the river itself.

The clocks resumed, and the policemen were stunned—checking themselves for injuries.

"Where did they go?" the first yelled.

"They must have an invisible ray..." the second speculated. He peered in every direction as if we'd backstab him at close range.

"Don't be an idiot. Spread out and look for them!"

The men exited their vehicle, scanning the area.

They didn't see Trix or me pass the shore, splashing through the cool waters.

We waded out of sight, keeping low, obscured by the scrub on the river's edge. We kept our footing in the shallows. My boots sloshed through the sandy riverbank and the water washed the sweat from my legs. I tried swishing instead of stomping to splash less. My boots became heavy and water-logged. Trix waded through the water, the edges of her suctioned feet wavering like some sort of sea slug. I guess her feet were happier in liquids than on solids.

We made ground faster than the cops, who had fanned out from the farmhouse. One policeman poked at the hedge, examining the path. Had he seen Trix's trail?

I didn't like my chances in the whitewater, so we fought the deeper downstream current and waded across the river to the other side, slipping into a thick forest. We had a head start from the officers. They shouted in the distance. A few minutes later, a police helicopter scanned the spot where we'd 'disappeared.' The blades cut the air with a sinister intensity. The far-off buzzing shifted to an insistent threat as the chopper approached.

We had to keep moving.

The trees gave us excellent cover. I was in awe of their tall trunks, their comforting green canopy protecting us from above. I felt held by nature, protected by the ancient trees, but police backup would arrive soon. We scrambled through the under-brush, Trix collecting leaf litter in her sludgy trail, struggling in this terrain. The shade from the trees gave me a second burst of energy.

I almost lost Trix amongst the forest—she blended into the trunks of the thick oak trees. But the trees didn't have iridescent orange veins, and her eyes found mine. There was no mistaking her gaze, which dipped into my chest and dislodged a feeling of knowing everything, all at once. I didn't enjoy the sensation; it was overwhelming. So, I pushed it away.

We came to a barbed wire fence, revealing a concrete spillway underneath a highway. We left the forest, following a large open drain beneath the road bridge. Trix stooped to fit. We climbed inside and put our backs against the curved concrete, resting up in the shade.

We paused there for a while, but the novelty of my powers was waning. Here I was, a fugitive, being hunted, and with every chance of getting caught. The sirens and emergency vehi-cles sped along the surrounding roads. We ducked further into the drain, out of sight. My muscles ached, my eyes stung, and I felt ready for a twelve-hour nap. Trix also showed signs of fatigue, going by her less-than-perky curl atop her head.

The spillway sat on a hill, the forest and river spread out below. From our vantage point, we watched the scouting police chopper. The air from its thumping blades flattened the tall grass lining the river.

We'd have to wait until dark and be exceptionally lucky.

The helicopter gave up and its mechanical whine moved further downriver. The immediate danger had passed, but as fugitives, our options were dire.

"What is the plan?" Trix asked me.

I don't know, but I can't go home.

"Was that not what you wanted?"

We have to stay hidden for a while, or we'll lead them straight there.

"They will find us."

It won't be hard, I thought, my eyebrows twitching north. *Have you seen yourself?*

"I stand out," she said.

One of a kind. I let that hang for a moment. *So tell me, what makes you tick?*

She shifted from the shadow of the tunnel.

"I am not sure about ticking, but you may be wondering how I feed?" she asked. My stomach growled at the mention of food. Using my powers gave me a wicked hunger.

"In a word—radiation," Trix answered her own question. "I am like a solar panel, and your sun is weak within your thick atmosphere. I have to replenish my powers."

She moved from the concrete hole into full sunlight and spread out on the ground of the spillway. She settled to the side of the water, caught in the dent. Her pulsing veins lit up. Her irises brightened into a deeper orange, and her pupils renewed their dark depths.

I watched her skin expand as she absorbed what little radiation our sun could give her. Her interlocking scales glowed less brown and more orange, like aged rust. She was magnificent.

Why did you come here? I asked.

"Are you asking about me, or those you call aliens?"

Both.

"I came to make contact," she said.

That's gone well.

Trix's eyes crinkled.

Is that another smile? I leaned forward into the sunlight to see better.

"The mission has developed as expected," Trix said. "They warned me. I refused to listen."

What do you mean?

"They said the humans would not accept me, that they would fear me. They said they tried, but I reasoned with the elders. I thought you had evolved since then."

Wow. Harsh. We're pretty evolved.

"Not as much as I had expected."

That was sarcasm. As in, something that wasn't true, that proved your point completely.

Trix tried to smile, but her mouth merely twitched.

Why is your kind—the Kaseath—here?

"To observe, to protect Earth. Your planet is unique—there are so many life forms, such variation of species. You don't value what you have. We have been here thousands of years."

How long since you landed on Earth?

"In your Earth years—over twenty years. I have lost count exactly."

Have you been captive for that long?

"Most of it, yes."

I'm sorry.

"Our mission is important. It's for the greater balance of the galaxy. That is the only thing that matters. If this planet is saved because humans become extinct, then it's better to trust the natural cycle of nature and space."

Wait—you're saying we might not make it?

"All things die, eventually."

We have to stop it!

"I am trying, Ofelia, but some things are beyond even us."

How can we ensure humans survive?

"You can change your future if you work together. I had hoped that humans had moved beyond fear. That your emotions were more in check. That you were less prone to acts of irrationality and violence. But that is what I have seen since I arrived. At least—until I met you."

I'm more on the defensive these days.

"Yes, because you are one of us."

I stared at Trix. What did that mean? Confusion took my thought hostage. This was too much information.

I'm not human, but I'm not alien either, I began. *I don't know what I am.*

"Does it matter?" Trix said, forcing me to contemplate an uncomfortable truth.

Yes. It really matters.

I felt Trix's discord as she processed that information. She lifted her face to the sun, moving to catch the light. I switched to speaking out loud. The effort of concentrating my thoughts was exhausting.

"So I guess that's why I can make the force field. How does it work?" I asked.

"You make a defence, like the Kaseath. You can stop hurt. But you cannot inflict pain."

"Have you always had this power?"

"Yes," she said.

"Your power is stronger than mine. How do I develop this skill?"

Trix paused, considering. "We teach this power to our young. It is part of becoming the Kaseath. Your powers will grow the more you use them. You may even meld with the power of others."

"Wait—we can combine our powers?"

"If you practise, yes."

"Cool, so I can protect others, like you can." I wanted to protect the people I loved. More than anything else.

"I do not understand why you are sad for Imogen."

"What do you mean?" Harshness caught my reply.

"Humans die," Trix said, gazing straight into my core.

I felt exposed, as if she had encountered me half dressed.

"So?"

"Imogen may not reach the average lifespan of a female human. But everyone dies. Why are you sad, if it is an inevitability?"

"Because I can stop it," I said, a lump forming. I averted my eyes. "And losing someone is always sad."

Before Trix could respond, a helicopter approached, rotor blades chopping the wind, wavering in our direction. The sound intensified. The grey underbelly of the helicopter broached the tree line by the river. It headed to our spillway. The pilot had spotted us.

I waved Trix back under the shade of the tunnel.

Speaking of defensive, I thought, *You ready for this?*

Trix sloped into the cover of the underpass. She had to duck through the opening, but could then stand at full height.

The helicopter descended to face the tunnel, hovering a metre above the ground. Its rotors whipped the hair across my face, the noise deafening. A menacing bird of prey. An enemy to dispatch.

I scooted further into the shadow as a guy in black leaned out of the open door and shot his rifle.

For a moment, my concentration lapsed. Did Demi die with a bullet? Or a botched experiment? My shoulder stung.

I turned a fraction too late—my attention lagged. Saw the bullet fire. Enacted my shield as the bullet whizzed by my cheek.

I fell to the floor. Had he shot me?

"He missed," Trix said, eyeing the lip of the tunnel. "Stop thinking about your family and concentrate!"

I stood up and bolted along the concrete tunnel, hoping like heck that Trix followed. The circle of light at the other end beckoned. My hair blew every which way, obstructing my vision. I sprinted as fast as I could, my feet splashing in the run-off. Trix's suction feet squelched in the watery puddles, struggling against our gravity.

We were prime mincemeat in here. I concentrated on the light at the end, on the daylight streaming through. I felt Trix sloping along behind me. The rotor blades' echo dominated all sounds.

We were a few metres away from the end, my feet pounding the slippery floor. My head hurt like I had sprouted another noggin.

I tripped over a discarded branch, landing on all fours. Pushing myself to standing, I kept going. Before I reached safety, the 'sffft!' of another bullet sang by.

I reached the edge of the underpass. The circle of light expanded, and I was in the open. The helicopter was visible through the tunnel. It tried to take off. Trix rolled into me and knocked me off balance.

"Argh—" I yelled. Trix tried to grab me with her elongated, slender fingers, but she was too slow. I tumbled down the dirt embankment, towards a highway full of speeding cars. I grazed my knees, then my palms, then my face skidded into the dirt. Trix grunted as her body hit the dirt in my wake. We dislodged parts of the embankment as we went. It was an out-of-body experience, as if we were blunt boxes, instead of bruising bodies. I landed with one final 'oomph' at the base of the embankment. I rolled to the side as Trix landed, almost crushing me.

My ankle had jarred, but I wasn't hurt. I scanned our new position.

We'd lost the helicopter but found a public freeway. We crouched in the shoulder, in full view of three lanes of speeding cars. It was too steep to clamber back up the hill, the dirt too unstable.

As soon as Trix stood up, the nearest driver noticed her,

and swerved off the road. The car in the lane beside course-corrected to miss the first car. Both cars braked suddenly. The goods truck behind was heavier and tailgating. The driver blasted the horn. Smashed into the two cars in front. Dove-tailed the semi he was towing. Glass shattered around us as the metal semi heaved on its side, crunching the road. Sparks flew, and I threw my hands around my head to ward off possible injury.

Several cars behind the semi screeched to a stop, crushing into the semi-trailer like bent dominos. People burst from cars, shouting, swearing in shock.

The accident bunched directly in front. The cars stopped to avoid the wreckage.

A man stumbled from the car nearest to us. Then he spied Trix, and everything fell apart.

CHAPTER 20

TRIX and I stood knee-deep in traffic as people emerged from their cars in shock. A kid filmed us on his phone, his eyes locked on Trix. Two men argued beside a rear-ended car, thinking that the crash was deliberate. The bearded man who'd noticed us ushered his distraught wife behind the safety of his car, and she screamed as she saw Trix. Bystanders followed her gaze, and mayhem ensued. The crowd panicked and bolted from their cars, leaving them parked at odd angles with doors wide open, like birds airing wings. The boy remained filming, oblivious to any danger he may have been in.

A balding man returned to the scene of the crash, pulling the filming boy away by the shoulder of his t-shirt.

It was then we noticed the injured.

Trix moved towards the semi-trailer, sagging on its side on the road. The driver struggled to push his door open. The crushed cab was flipped on its side, the door facing the sky with the driver wedged inside. Trix reached up and lifted the bent door clean off its hinges.

"Hey thanks, buddy..." the driver said, before noticing his saviour was a 7-foot alien being. He froze, putting his hand to his head in confusion. "I've got one hell of a concussion..."

Trix held her hand for him to take, and in his stupor, he took it. His body didn't react to her touch, and he allowed her to guide him out of the cab. She sat him on the ground on the edge of the freeway emergency lane. The injured man was bleeding from a gash in his forehead, and Trix reached forward, placing her three-fingered, twiggy hand over the wound. She concentrated. I felt her energy focussing, and then as she pulled her hand away, the gash stopped bleeding.

The man was in shock, taking everything in his stride, and a hoarse "Thank you" escaped his lips.

Moaning erupted from the vehicle in front of the semi. The truck had swerved to avoid a collision. Trix took a step forward, just as the emergency sirens closed in on our location. The vehicles sped along the unblocked emergency lane. They were gaining on the pile-up, and fast.

"There's no time," I said, motioning for Trix to follow me. She turned from the crash site.

I pointed to the bottom of the hill, to a crop of industrial buildings laid out in rows. Trix and I vaulted a concrete lane barrier and kept moving towards the industrial buildings flanking the freeway.

I snuck a backwards glance. Police cars converged on the crash site. Two ambulances followed, slowing to navigate around a jutting parked sedan in the service lane. Uniformed police exited their vehicles and fanned out to search for us— they weren't interested in the crash, leaving the injured to the ambulance personnel. Before the police could follow our trail, Trix and I ducked into a cavernous, dark warehouse containing pallets of grain. Forklifts shifted the goods. The workers didn't notice us.

There was enough food to feed Northies ten times over. The heaped pallets of grains and rice mesmerised me until I felt the electrical jolt of Trix pushing me through the loading dock into the sunlight.

"I have to recharge," she said.

Shouts of police urged us onward.

We sought the sunniest route through the walkways to the next building and used the next as a stepping-stone further into the built-up area. Workers drove forklifts or packaged crates, and didn't notice us slipping from warehouse to warehouse. The stench of starchy potatoes filled the next storage building, a familiar smell, but an unfamiliar sight, to see so much food in one place.

We exited that warehouse, back into sunlight, and rounded a corner. Straight into a group of men in overalls, smoking on the rear steps.

"What the hell?" One man dropped his cigarette onto the front of his shirt.

"Stuff this!" Another man abandoned his packed lunch, his sandwich falling to the asphalt as they fled inside the building.

I was tempted by the discarded sandwich. The meat had fallen bread-side down.

"Come on!" Trix urged me through the open doors of the next warehouse.

Workers packed the area with fuel drums of grey steel. Strips of plastic hung like teeth from the top of the door. Trix sloped through, returning into full sunshine.

We came to the end of the warehouses, finding ourselves on a dock. Shipping containers lay on wide slabs while workers in plastic aprons and rubber boots unloaded buckets of jellyfish from a nearby boat.

The familiar sound of swooping seagulls replaced the banging forklifts.

We'd arrived at a dead end. The harbour stretched in front of us, and I couldn't swim.

As we stood contemplating our escape, workers cottoned on to our presence. Someone hit the evacuation alarm, and a piercing tone overtook the docks. Workers abandoned equipment mid-load and ran off to the rally point, well away from the warehouses.

Just as we thought to return the way we came, five police vehicles skidded through the connecting roadway, screeching to a stop metres away from Trix and I. The leader of the police leaned out of his window, talking into a loudspeaker.

"Lie on the ground. We are authorised to use deadly force."

They'd trapped Trix and me in the V-shaped dock. To the right were stacked shipping containers. On the left, the harbour's fishing boats. In front was the warehouse we'd exited and the police cars angling in from the road.

I didn't know how to captain a fishing boat. It wasn't the fastest escape vehicle, either.

What do we do now? I asked, quelling the rising panic.

"We need to evade those cars."

You think?

"No, I know."

It's an expression.

"There must be another way."

As Trix said that, a barge sounded its horn a few lengths beyond the dock. An idea occurred to me as police exited their vehicles, scrambling to defensive positions behind their cars.

"Lay on the ground, now!" the policeman shouted through his megaphone.

The engine of the barge puttered closer, and I thought to Trix, *Trust me.*

One policeman, in a full flak jacket and visored helmet, ducked beside the car and set his rifle sights on us. One of his mates joined him on the other flank.

"You are now resisting arrest!" The megaphone stated the

bloomin' obvious, while I grabbed Trix's hand, resisting the urge to let go at the now-familiar electrical charge. I pushed her with all the strength I had, and we fell off the edge of the dock, landing on the passing barge, just as a volley of bullets whizzed over our heads.

I landed softly on the sacks lining the barge. Trix was less graceful and landed with her head slipping off the edge. I grabbed her and pulled her to safety.

Two policemen roared as they sprinted after us. They both launched themselves at the barge.

One mis-timed his jump and landed in the water, missing his target. The other landed on the sacks, knocking the wind out of him.

He was almost as tall as Trix. The fall busted the face guard of his helmet. He sneered and wrenched it free, scrambling to his knees amongst the sacks lining the barge.

Trix recovered her balance and stood up, the two of them eyeing each other. The captain of the barge checked over his shoulder, alarm in his expression.

"Keep going!" I yelled. "And she won't ray-gun you to death."

The skipper nodded, yanking the wheel at the last moment, avoiding our slide into the dock. He headed downriver, towards a low-lying bridge.

The barge puttered along, and the other policemen raced to the edge of the dock, training their weapons on us. But the large policeman prevented a clear shot, our human shield.

He reached for his gun, but I grabbed it. He had forgotten about me and concentrated on Trix. I turned the gun on him, but he swiped it from me, and it splashed into the water.

I grabbed the policeman's arm, but my scrawny grip was a mere annoyance. He shrugged me off and pushed me with the flat of his other hand.

"Stay down, kid," he growled, and hurled himself at Trix in a forward rugby tackle.

Trix had trouble keeping her suctioned feet sturdy on the uneven, rounded sacks, and she faltered backwards. The man landed on her torso, and he sent a punch to her face.

Before the blow hit, Trix yanked her head to the side, and the policeman's fist found the hard sack. Its contents weren't as soft as he was hoping, and he grimaced, grabbing his hurt fist.

Trix threw him off with her forearm and braced herself to standing with the barge's side window.

The policeman took time to assess his opponent.

A contingent of police had followed the barge on foot, and waved guns from the shore. But the scattered buildings cut off their progress.

"Aaaargh!" our policeman roared, both arms outstretched as he tried to shove Trix off-balance with his body. Trix wrenched to the side, fighting the gravity that made her so sluggish. Her assailant landed under the captain's steering wheel. The policeman flipped to his back and was on his feet.

The cop approached Trix, punching with a left hook, a right jab. Trix took the blows head-on, and I felt them connect with her, felt her pain receptors respond.

"Hey, leave her alone!" I yelled, landing my own blows on the policeman. But he was as strong as Trix. This could be a long battle.

I scouted up ahead, wondering at our destination. That's when I spotted the bridge, almost upon us. There wasn't much clearance between the barge and the arched bridge. An ancient stone structure from Before. A thought occurred to me.

Hey Trix, I thought, *get up onto the sacks again.*

Trix did as I asked, struggling with the policeman. Neither one winning, as if they were two perfectly matched opponents in a wrestling contest. They both landed blows as the bridge drew closer.

Get ready. Then, just as the bricks of the bridge passed overhead, I thought, *Duck!*

Trix found the deck. The policeman bashed his head on the underside of the bridge. His eyes unfocussed, and he toppled off the barge, splashing into the water.

I checked to make sure he wasn't out cold. He wasn't—instead, he was flailing around in the water, swearing at us, throwing off his flak jacket that threatened to pull him under.

Our barge puttered onwards, under the bridge.

I approached the captain. "Thank you, sir. Would you mind dropping us off at the next dock?"

Maybe my impeccable manners convinced him as he made first contact with an alien being. He steered towards a small ferry dock, holding the barge steady while Trix and I disembarked.

Police cars swooped along the roads flanking the river, but the indirect way twisted about. They had to navigate out onto each dock, then around the clumped buildings blocking access to the river. But we couldn't keep this up. Eventually, they would outrun us.

We spotted a side laneway and slipped from the commotion, pressing our backs to a stack of barrels for a moment to catch our breath, before heading clear of the docks area.

We approached a road leading beyond the industrial district. The road was empty. The police had massed at our barge, questioning the captain.

This way, I thought, leading us via the sunniest route, towards the road.

We exited the industrial complex and headed towards a more commercial part of town, with large buildings sporting neon signs for clothing, household items and food. The buildings bulked up, crammed closer together. We traversed a long-deserted walkway, with an awning covering the footpath. I didn't have to watch my feet to avoid the ruts in the pavement. It was smooth as a sheet of paper, the slope gentle. I almost didn't realise we were headed uphill, and not checking for ankle-twisting conditions felt awkward. It threw off my balance, and I was heavy-footed for the first few steps until I grew used to the smooth ground.

I tried not to gawk at the scenery, which was ordered and intact. No derelict shacks here. Trix inclined her head to fit underneath the walkway. She had to avoid the shade, or her powers would weaken.

How could we hide in full sunlight?

I touched my bullet-grazed shoulder. My palms were rubbed raw from skidding on the embankment rubble and my eyes were dry from the tear gas. I was amassing a list of injuries.

Trix noticed me pressing my fingertips into my palms.

"Are you hurt?" she asked.

Not much, I replied.

"Here, let me help you."

We stopped in the walkway, and Trix put both hands into mine. I felt the surge jolt my thinking. I had instant concentration, and the skin healed. She removed her hands.

"Better?" she asked.

They smarted less—Trix had seriously useful healing powers.

Thanks, Trix.

The walkway would lead somewhere.

We halted before a crowded street up ahead. We scoped the scene from our deserted walkway.

People carried bright shopping bags, dressed in casual wear, without the burden of purpose. They crammed into stores and hung around benches in the arcade, dressed in clothes so clean.

Landscaped trees dotted the sidewalk, with their own mulched square in the concrete at even intervals, leading to the entrance of a massive mall. It was so ordered, so perfect.

I hadn't seen a landscaped garden before—the vegetable patch my mother worked on was for practical reasons, not for show, and had a hefty fence around it to keep out thieves. Here, the plants were just for decoration, each assigned to neat rectangles by the path leading to the exquisite building. Smooth glass arches met at the apex of the front entrance. This mall was not just for selling goods, but for selling a dream. The dream of opulence and excess, relegating us Northies folks to nothing. None of these pristine people had squabbled over blackened carrot ends, or had Pocks' heavies visit when they failed to pay rent. These people had a carefree attitude and respect for other people's personal space.

Not one element seemed out of place. I didn't belong in this world. I was the only human who hadn't showered that morning. They could smell me coming.

I checked the walkway behind. It led back to the industrial warehouses and the police cars scouting the area. The sirens still circled the docks area. We had to keep pressing forward, but where to next?

A lady on the opposite road stared at Trix, mouth open as a guppy. She screeched, as if warding off impending death. Confused shoppers turned to locate the unexpected sound and clocked Trix.

That set the entire street off, and the crowd scattered, grabbing children's hands. A frantic woman dropped shopping in the street and ran into traffic. An approaching station wagon swerved to avoid hitting her.

We were drawing way too much attention.

The mammoth shopping complex across the road trans-fixed Trix. The building was eight storeys high, a winding, white beacon of prosperity. I noticed what had caught her attention—a massive glass atrium in the middle of the building.

"In there," she said.

We dodged across the highway, slipping between two cars. Their drivers saw Trix and rear-ended each other. They'd braked at the last second, so neither one was injured. One car's crushed rear bumper matched the other's smoking bonnet.

I guess none of the drivers had encountered a 7-foot lizard-like alien prowling the streets.

We headed towards the most populated section in the whole suburb, the giant shopping mall. I hadn't known something as massive before. There was nothing larger than Pocks' double storey shack in Northies.

Bodies scattered as we sluiced through the automatic doors. We stood in the foyer, curved walkways of marble and glass beckoning to stores containing luxury goods.

A burly guy with a shadow of a beard tackled Trix. But she brushed him off, and he lost his trucker's cap as he stumbled backwards. He didn't stop to retrieve his cap as he scuttled away.

Small stores lined both sides of the walkway, holding gleaming electrical goods, summer clothes, or food. There was a particular store entirely for shoes. A whole store! Gleaming goods inside the other stores were so foreign I couldn't identify them. The echoed screams of shoppers overwhelmed me in the enclosed space.

The wares were brand new. How could people afford this stuff? We had to save for the scratched-up pots and pans for sale in Northies territory. We'd have to save for a lifetime to afford these pristine electronic gadgets.

A mall cop spotted Trix and reached for his walkie-talkie.

"That thing's in here! Send everyone!" he shouted, struggling to pull a nightstick from his utility belt.

Shoppers of every shape and age screamed and scattered. A teenager hid in the nearest store, trapped as we passed. Others hoofed it right out into the street. Several captured Trix on their camera phones. I imagined their panicked footage later on the breaking news. Would my family see it and worry?

The bodies in here smelt unfamiliar, of soaps and perfumes. The artificial fragrance was off-putting, starting a stress headache, adding to the tension from my near-death experience.

Trix and I found the centre of the complex, towards the glass atrium. She was a wave machine, parting fleeing shoppers.

A fresh emergency alarm pierced the air, echoing around the cavernous space. A recorded voice commanded, "Please evacuate the building. This is not a drill."

We passed a kid, about Imogen's age, but dressed way nicer, in a denim dress with fancy studs. Her hair was caught in two ponytails, and she observed Trix with unafraid disbelief. Merely curious. I waved, and she waved back. But we didn't have time to chat, so I led Trix towards the atrium.

We approached a set of moving stairs leading to the bottom of the atrium, and hesitated, timing my steps to each new stair appearing. This was my first escalator ride, and I gripped the handrail so I didn't fall.

The 7-foot alien and I rode the escalators, while positive musak piped through the speakers, amid screams and retreating footsteps. The mall unfolded beneath us.

Trix and I negotiated the bottom of the escalator as it evened out. It felt as if I was moving until I realised I stood still. My first ride on an escalator was enjoyable. We didn't have time to savour the sights.

We wandered through a food court with multiple outlets offering a different cuisine on their photo menus. Exotic food I hadn't even imagined.

These people were well fed.

We arrived at the central atrium, which was cylindrical, several storeys high. The decor was like a jungle, with deep green leaves dripping in opulent displays. A waterfall spilled from the ceiling into a pond, like a tropical holiday destination. The bright flowers were intoxicating, alluring as a humid climate, rather than our dry heat. If London was tropical, it would exist in this mall.

I was thirsty as heck, so I cupped the pond water in my hands, slurping. Big mistake. Although the water appeared clean, it tasted of chemicals, and I spat it back into the pond.

Trix handed me a disposable drink container abandoned on a nearby bench. I opened the lid and sniffed at the brown liquid. I took a cautious sip. The sickly sweet mouthful had an aftertaste of bitter tea. But it pepped my energy. I found a discarded burger in a wrapper—it tasted of fat and salt, but I needed the energy. I finished my feast and placed the container on the bench.

The shoppers had fled, leaving Trix and me alone in the mall.

Trix sloshed into the pond, to the base of the waterfall. She lifted her head to the sunlight streaming through the glass ceiling. Her veins pulsed while she recharged. She was at peace, enjoying rec time after the excitement.

As I checked our surroundings, I noticed my reflection in the glass frontage of a nearby electronics store. The TVs were massive. One displayed a new show I hadn't encountered before, featuring a couple on a beach. They wore skimpy swimwear and held hands. Did they stream different shows outside Northies? Pollins had crafted shows to keep us ill-informed and easier to control. Northies would riot if they saw the real world. They would want to live here, too.

I moved closer to my reflection and checked my wounds,

first my grazed hands. They smarted less after Trix healed them. The dried blood on my shoulder held firm and the wound hadn't opened with fresh movement. A bump had formed on the rear of my skull. The skin around my eyes was red and swollen. But, considering our predicament, I was lucky to be in one piece.

Now that I'd eaten, my skin prickled with renewed energy. My head throbbed with a massive headache. But our adventures had barely begun.

Two mall cops approached Trix from the rear. She hadn't seen them. They sat inside a white golf cart, like they were hunting wild game, handguns drawn. The first mall cop must have been feeling extra bold, as he commanded, "Surrender, alien intruder!"

CHAPTER 21

THE TWO MALL cops faced Trix in their golf cart, parked behind the fountain, where she stood in the pool, veins pulsing. The cart looked comical to me, with the tiny driver's seat and dinky wheels. I doubted these mall cops had fought a proper villain.

But Trix was still in trouble. If the cops fired from behind, she wouldn't be able to enact her shield. She turned at the man's threat. The men eyed her as they exited the golf cart, easing onto the floor so as not to spook her, their grey handguns trained on Trix.

Nobody saw little old me move towards the electronics store and flatten against the wall.

Trix had recharged. Her skin beat with pulsing bright liquid underneath her brown scales. The pits of her eyes receded deep as midnight, surrounded by iridescent orange. I felt her alertness, her concentration wrapped around my mind. The little curl at the top of her head seemed more perky, less droopy.

The mall cops aimed their guns at Trix. She eyed the fuzz.

"Step out of the fountain," one man yelled.

"Slowly," added the other, circling back behind Trix.

"We are Special Police Officers, trained to use non-lethal force," said the first.

"So just come with us, and we won't have cause to hurt you," said the second, pausing beside a fake plant to take aim at her back.

Trix stood there, waiting for them to become trigger-happy. Although recharged, she couldn't repel an attack from both angles. I had to get in there.

"Hey, losers!" I yelled, and ran into the fountain, leaping over a decorative garden and heading deeper into the pool.

"Get away, kid!" the first mall cop yelled.

I splashed into the pool. My boots had only just dried. Now they clogged up again, weighted with water.

Hi, I thought.

"Hello," she replied, nodding at the man behind her. "Thank you, Ofelia."

Our skin fizzled as I pressed my back to hers. We were ready. Trix lifted her head to the sunlight and then returned her attention to the attack.

"Careful—there's a kid in there!" shouted the brainiac of the year. His friend hesitated.

"You've got to be kidding me..." the first mall cop said, and he boomed, "Get them!"

The rubber bullets fired, one from each man.

Trix and I stopped time. Our force fields shot up.

Mine pointed in the first rent-a-cop's direction, hers to the second—and we observed the menacing men through our green-tinged shields.

It wasn't the best idea to come here, I thought.

"I agree—but where to now?"

We'll figure something out. We have to be more subtle.

"I find it very difficult to be subtle on this planet."

We un-stopped time, and the two bullets fell to the floor at our feet. The cops paused their useless assault. Like any well-trained grunt, they fired again. And again. On each occasion, we repelled the attack.

Once their ammunition was depleted, they clicked empty triggers. We just had to out-wait them.

The first cop grabbed pepper spray from his belt, and the other a billy club, flicking it to extend by about a metre. It was like the nightsticks they'd used at the research facility, except these were straight, without a right-angled handle.

The first mall cop stood up, clenching his fists, his face red with rage. He pointed his finger at Trix.

"Get that... thing!" he roared as he charged.

His mate followed, sprinting for our pool. They rushed with their billy clubs, trying to bludgeon through. Trix swiped them with her extended, far stronger arms, and they dropped to the ground, stunned. She was ready for anything a puny human could throw at her.

"Let's go," Trix said.

We side-stepped between the fallen grunts and I made eye contact with the bull-rushing special police officer. His expression had turned from rage to fear, and he cowered as we stepped over his prone body.

Trix and I headed out as our attackers found their feet, splashing in the pond.

I caught up with Trix and kept pace in front of her, protected by her taller and wider bulk. Her veins pulsed with a dimmer orange glow—she was using a heap of energy in here, and couldn't recharge as we moved away from the natural light.

The fuzz clattered in pursuit, then retrieved their golf cart. The whine of the electric engine shot up a few octaves, speeding after us full tilt.

We reached the doors.

They'd locked the centre down, and the door didn't budge. I smacked the glass with my hand in frustration.

What now? I thought.

Trix copied me, smacking the plate glass. It wobbled, but held. She shoulder-charged the door. It reverberated with the shock, but she wasn't strong enough to karate chop a plate glass door.

I searched either side for another escape route.

The men faced us with their golf cart, aiming straight at us. We stood stock still, waiting for them to make a move.

"I instructed you to follow us," the first man said.

"Please cooperate with the law," said the second.

Grab them! I thought.

"Where are you going?" Trix asked.

You'll see.

Trix strode right up to the golf cart. The men lost their bravado and scrambled from their seats. Trix helped them, lifting one clean from the cab, and flinging him into the decorative pebbled garden. The other's face was terrified as he backed away and surrendered.

"Thanks, fellas," I said, jumping into the now-vacated golf cart.

I rammed my foot on the pedal, and the cart jumped forward. It stopped when I removed the pressure. My ride wobbled in a wavy line as I jammed my foot down again.

Driving was not like the mech cars Pocks ran in Northies. My thoughts reverted to holding the rubber ball aloft on Trash Mountain with Imogen.

"Concentrate," Trix said as the mall cop in the pebbles regained his feet.

I shook my head to turn my thoughts to the present.

This golf cart handled like an unyielding, slow boulder, so I sped up. Now the steering was too touchy.

The cart mounted a kerb around the sloping entrance. The vehicle leaned to one side, threatening to capsize, my body counterbalancing the cart. Spinning wheels thwacked hard on the even floor. I aimed towards the door beside Trix.

The cart wobbled as I wrenched at the wheel. I lost control and Trix coiled to one side, while the cop commando rolled to safety. As the cart righted, I nearly slipped out. I wiped my brow of sweat and idled some distance away.

The other cop had regained his courage and ran after me, brandishing his baton, but I was away before he could catch me. Once I had a wide turning circle of floor, I performed a U-turn and faced the men. Trix and the first cop moved beside the exit.

A thought occurred to me. I rammed my foot on the accelerator. Flogged at speed towards the doors. Straight between the men and Trix.

"Out of the way!" I shouted.

"What are you doing?" Trix asked.

I shoved the accelerator flat on the floor and grimaced as I headed for the glass doors. This had to work. If it didn't, I was a dead woman with plate glass through my skull.

The cart sped towards the doors.

The bumper bar hit first, shattering the glass. Then the body of the cart followed, with me in it. The glass shredded my skin as I rode through, demolishing the massive doors.

The cart's wheels blew, and the steering locked. It limped to a stop a few metres past the doors. I'd busted out!

Let's go!

"Right behind you." Trix stepped over the jagged glass to join me in the car park.

The mall cops peered through the mess of glass I'd created. I guess we were beyond their jurisdiction now, and they both seemed happier for it, grabbing walkie-talkies to report back.

Sticky blood streamed out of several cuts and lacerations on my face and body. But there was no time to stop. Police sirens circled the streets, growing closer in pursuit. But at least we were outside, in the recharging sunlight.

Trix and I snuck through the car park, bent low so the cars obscured our progress. I hadn't imagined this many cars in the entire world. Waiting for their owners to drive wherever they desired—no gated checkpoints here.

Trix's snail trail wound through the park, but she must be getting used to our gravity. She squelched faster.

We lost sight of the mall behind a retaining wall outside the car park, and went off-road, ducking into an alleyway filled with dumpsters and foul smells. It kinda reminded me of home.

I put my finger to my lips, and Trix understood. We pressed our backs against the alley's wall and waited.

Several police cars shot by on the connecting road, sirens blaring, lights flashing. Their sirens snaked up the road and into the car park we'd just exited.

We rested for a moment. The alleyway was only a couple of metres wide, too narrow for cars. The other end branched onto a larger street. Maybe we'd found a way out.

Over there. That way.

We edged down the alley—the discarded rubbish was fresh, held together by black plastic bags, and dumped outside the back doors leading into the buildings on each side.

We reached the end of the alley. In front, a paved street curved away. A set of traffic lights dominated an intersection to our right. In front, a row of monumental buildings. I felt giddy trying to see the top floor, as if I stood on the highest trash spire. Vertigo overcame me as I looked up, where I imagined they'd placed snipers, ready to pick us off. I felt as if I was spinning and falling into the pavement itself; the buildings crushing me, swallowing me up—an intense form of claustrophobia from the buildings themselves. I concentrated on the ground until the sensation passed.

We were far from the peaks of Trash Mountain. Here, the peaks were tall buildings and bridges, highways for cars we could never dream of owning. Here, it took a hundred flights of stairs to reach the top, to hold the high ground. Our powers had a time limit, and we had to see our enemies to resist their attack. Snipers could face any direction on those tall buildings. We were easy targets; we had to find cover.

My lacerated skin stung, and I pulled a larger shard of glass from my cheek, although none of the cuts were too deep. Exhaustion overtook me, draining my muscles of energy. We couldn't keep running forever. We had to find somewhere safe.

And that's when I heard feet scuffing along the alleyway. Three pairs of feet scooted behind a skip bin against the wall at the end of our alley.

Had the fuzz found us?

CHAPTER 22

I CREPT TOWARDS THE DUMPSTER, careful not to scuff my heavy boots, navigating around a soggy plastic bag lying in a puddle. Positioning myself behind the skip bin amongst the familiar waft of discarded garbage, I wondered, were they waiting in ambush?

Stay where you are, I thought.

"Understood," Trix replied.

My skin prickled with goosebumps from the temperature change in the alley. One small foot stuck out from the underside of the bin. Those sandshoes were familiar. A brown sockless toe pushed through the canvas.

I hesitated, waiting for the feet to spring to standing, but they tucked in, as if someone had chased them.

We had the element of surprise as I leaped into view.

"Gotcha!" I said.

Three girls screamed.

"I know kung fu!" one of them yelled.

One's hair was so dreadlocked that it resembled a hat, and the other flipped up her scarlet red pirate patch, revealing two working eyes.

Mouse Run and Aze! The familiar toe escaping its sand-shoe had been Aze's. And the third girl was my former cellmate Maya!

But my friends hadn't realised who I was. Aze squeezed her eyes shut. Mouse Run stared straight up, as if that would make her invisible. Maya squished onto the rancid, trash-strewn pavement.

"There is no way you know kung fu," I said, stepping closer.

Maya peeked at me. Her face morphed from terrified to ballistic.

"What—" Aze said, flipping down her eye patch. "I forgot you dress nice now. I didn't recognise you."

"Yeah..." Mousie said, "what happened to you?"

"You scared me!" Maya found her feet, dusting trash juice from her backside. A stain covered the butt cheek of her jeans, in the pattern of a wonky fish.

"Your bouquet is more Northies than swanky now," I said, grinning, putting my arm around her shoulders for a sister-to-sister hug. "Don't worry, we'll take you to our place. You'll fit right in."

I winked at Mousie and Aze.

"We saw you on the news and I recognised the mall. We tried to find you, but the whole suburb is crawling with police officers. This was the closest we could get."

They noticed Trix observing our encounter with her expressionless gaze. Her hulking form stood taller and wider than the largest bodybuilder at a world-class gym. She was intimidating, but my friends were not afraid.

For a moment, they transformed back into little girls, pondering the wonders of an alien race as they met one in person. They were a little starstruck.

"Tell them hello," Trix said.

"Trix says 'hi'," I said. "You can't hear her, right?"

My three friends shook their heads.

"Can I touch her?" Maya asked.

I didn't have the answer. What would happen? I raised my eyebrows at Trix, and she shrugged her massive shoulders.

"Go on," I said.

Trix unfurled her pointed fingernail towards Maya's index finger. Maya hesitated, waiting for her bravado to return.

Trix turned her hand sideways so that the point of their fingertips met—

Nothing. No electrical jolt, no sizzle, not even a shiver of something passed between them. I guess Trix and I were one of a kind.

"I thought she'd feel squidgy," Maya said, rubbing her fingertip and thumb at the grain of sensation.

"Now that introductions are over, what now?" I asked. "There are cops everywhere."

"There might be a way," Maya said. "I was waiting until they left..."

"They'll find us if we stay put," I said.

"Let's go then," Aze said.

"Trix is kinda conspicuous, though," I said. "We've been attracting too much attention."

"I have an idea." Mousie upended a milk crate and used it as a step into the dumpster. She landed easily, her head just poking above.

"Eww..." Maya's face screwed up in disgust.

Mousie flung a large, tattered blanket from the dumpster. I caught it before it hit the ground. It had been lime green in a former life, but it would be passable. Mousie sifted between the boxes and plastic bags, and then she hoisted herself back out of the dumpster, jumping to the ground. She pulled something from her pocket—a pair of sunglasses with a hairline crack snaking up the left lens.

"I wish pickings were always this good," she said.

Trix took the blanket. We helped her drape it over her pointed head, like a headscarf, and the blanket covered her head, shoulders, and most of her torso. Sure, if someone observed closely, they'd see her suction-capped feet and scaley face peeking out. Mousie handed her the sunglasses, which Trix donned. She passed as someone hiding their Halloween costume, waiting for the big reveal. It wasn't perfect, but it would stop people from recognising her from a distance. We just had to avoid close encounters.

"I'm sorry it stinks," I said, brushing a stain on the blanket.

"I do not breathe, remember? That means I can't smell."

"You'd fit right in at home."

Maya put a shushing finger to her lips and jogged to the end of the alleyway we'd entered. She stuck her head out, glancing at each side.

A beeping sounded—insistent and rapid fire. A warning?

Maya waved us closer. We crouched, prepared for our next foray into danger.

"Is this your best idea?" I whispered.

"Ready? Go!" she replied.

We bolted out of the alleyway and into the busy street. Except, the cars had stopped, queued at a pedestrian crossing. The flashing green indicator and beeping urged on a mother with a pram, crossing in our direction.

"Don't stop!" Maya grunted.

We sprinted across the road, towards the opposite alleyway.

The mother reached down in a practiced move, replacing the pacifier in her baby's mouth. She didn't see our group. The distracted driver of the front car tapped the steering wheel, and didn't notice us. The pedestrian lights turned red and the traffic lights for the cars turned green.

We made it to the other side.

"This way." We followed Maya to the end of the new alleyway.

In front, massive parklands rolled downhill, curving around a fenced pond. Beyond the greenery sat a sea of grey-tiled roofs; single-storey mansions, laid out in neat rows.

"Woah!" Aze said.

Mousie whistled through her teeth in awe.

"What's that?" I pointed to the grey roofs.

"The swanky suburbs," Maya said with a grin. "Let's go home."

"Home?" I said, bewildered. Could that really be the suburbs? I had almost believed they didn't exist, that the houses were fake, just a rumour. But Maya lived here? We would stick out like a gangrenous thumb in the pristine, gleaming suburbs.

The sound of police sirens massing at the shopping centre behind us kept us moving. One squad car raced along the street we'd just passed. My heartbeat sped up to match the wailing sirens.

"Come on." Maya brought us to a smooth pathway that wrapped around the park.

Between the treed circular pathway sat a manicured lawn leading up to a children's play area. The park had greenery as decoration, like icing on a perfect suburban cake. The kids rumbled with each other and sometimes cut in front—I guess self-preservation was a human trait, no matter where you came from. Parents would gently scold their child, pretending to be embarrassed, maybe even apologising.

I was in awe of the people I'd seen so far—their overpowering scents, their makeup and styled hair, their perfectly accessorised outfits. They looked just as alien to me as Trix. I didn't recognise my own kind. Or, perhaps I didn't recognise myself in these people. What did they know of hardship? What did they know of hunger?

Pulling my focus away from the playground, I noticed the fence dividing a rugged, uneven area that fell away to a pond. The fence stopped the residents from losing their footing and going for a swim.

Maya headed away from the families at the play equipment, and we ducked below the fence line, which led towards the houses at the end. Mousie, Aze, Maya and I bent low—we were lacking in height. Trix struggled on the uneven terrain, holding her blanket underneath her chin with one hand. Although she was moving faster than before, she slowed our progress.

The kids were engrossed in their play, not noticing us, and the parents were too deep in their gossip. Our group of five fugitives edged around the tree line of the park into a copse of trees. We hid behind a massive bush rock boulder, catching our breath.

A lizard summited the peak of the bush rock, sunning itself in the heat of day. I glanced over to Trix, who had shrugged off her blanket, wrapping it around her shoulders. She also sunned herself, her expression matching the lizard's. It was hilarious to compare the two. Like the lizard was a less-evolved version of Trix.

This whole situation was so surreal. How in heck's name did I fall into this position? Trix noticed my expression and flipped the blanket back over her head.

"I am not a lizard," she said.

I blushed in reply, then my stomach dropped deep into the earth below me as two cars screeched to a stop on the road above. A fresh police officer scoped the park, approaching the playground on foot. Then two more. They drew their guns, pointed to the ground with a locked grip.

We moved into the cover of thinning trees as the uniforms reached the playground.

The mothers glanced up, confused, and a kid cried as he landed smack on his butt on the rubber flooring.

More police fanned out, shouting at the mothers to keep clear. Uniforms moved to keep the kids safe. But the kids cried, and the mothers rushed to comfort them. The kids weren't scared of Trix—none of them even noticed her. They were terrified of the scary men carrying guns.

"They can't get too close," I said, "or they'll recognise Trix."

We had to move. The chatter from their walkie-talkies burst into static, moving closer.

The uniforms gave ridiculous hand signals to each other as they approached. We had to find safety, and the fuzz was in our path.

Maya flicked her head and Trix and the other kids nodded. We slid to the side of our boulder, keeping to the bushes. We reached a clearing and scooted down a grassy hill heading to the back fence of a swathe of residences.

The entire estate spread out below, from our vantage point halfway down the slope. A massive brick fence topped with coiled barbed wire surrounded a hundred-odd houses, spread to the horizon in a flattening slope. More fences to keep out the riff-raff. The homes had a similar design—painted white, with grey-tiled roofs. I wondered how many generations could fit into each home? Each featured clipped lawns and a letterbox.

The oddest feature was the letterbox. We didn't receive mail back home, not everyone could read. Pocks and his boys hand-delivered messages, and they were less than subtle.

I forgot about Pocks as we slipped towards the brick wall surrounding the estate. Aze limped on her right ankle—maybe she'd twisted it? And Mousie wheezed, catching her breath. I guess they had their own story of escape to tell.

We kept low as we searched for a way in. Maya pointed to a metal gate in the fence, with a touch pad beside it.

She pressed her thumb to the sensor, and the gate pinged, swinging open.

I itched to see a proper house.

I dove through, holding the gate open with my body. Maya rolled her eyes but stepped in after me, and Mousie and Aze followed. Trix lagged, just making it. Her suction feet left a slippery trail on the fancy sandstone pavement.

The gate snapped to.

Maybe the police wouldn't be keen to disturb the elite residents in here.

"I've always wanted to hang out in suburbia," I said.

We edged into the deserted streets of the housing estate, the residents tucked up inside.

We stepped onto the footpath connecting the front of the houses.

A sprinkler head sat on the grass, connected to a hose. It shot pristine water onto the green lawn. The rotating water danced, the liquid launching into the air in a delicate, rotating curved pattern. Like the watery arms of a ballet dancer. It was the most elegant thing I had seen.

I picked the sprinkler up and drank the delicious, clear nectar, refreshing with a sweet aftertaste. How could it just lay here, wasting good water on the ground? At home, it was a half-hour walk to the well, and we'd bring our allotment back in a bucket. We sieved the muddied sediment through a cloth.

The suburbs confused me something wicked.

I washed my face clean of caked blood. Mousie grabbed the sprinkler after me, gulping the water, her matted hair bending as she tilted her head. She handed the sprinkler to Aze, who had her fill, then handed it to Maya, who looked like we were handing her a fistful of dog poo.

"You not thirsty?" Aze asked.

"I'll wait for a glass," Maya said.

"Oooh, fancy..." Aze replied.

Maya gave her a dirty look, but didn't reply.

The water soaked our clothes through, but at least we weren't so hot.

My cuts and scrapes weren't deep and had stopped bleeding. Even the deeper cut in my cheek wasn't oozing blood anymore. My bruised shoulder still smarted, and I rubbed at the graze, scoping out the roads in front.

Every house resembled those next to it, except for subtle differences in design or layout. Each house had a different shaped driveway, or its entrance sat on the opposite side.

"Where are we going?" I turned to Maya. "You know this area."

"My house is close," she said.

"But won't your folks, like, freak out?" Mousie said.

"They're both at work, but my grandmother will be home," Maya said.

"We can't take Trix with us then."

"It's okay. My grandmother stays in her room until dinner."

"Beats staying out here waiting to be caught," Aze said.

We couldn't argue that point, so Maya led our crew into a cul-de-sac. I felt Trix hadn't moved, though—I didn't hear her usual squelching. When I checked, she hadn't followed.

"I can't come with you," Trix said inside my head.

What do you mean? I thought.

"You keep getting found because of me."

We've got to stay together.

"Why?"

That took me by surprise.

Because we have to, we're friends now.

Trix had this weird expression, as if sifting through an entire world of knowledge. She shuffled to the other suctioned foot.

"What is a friend?" she asked.

Someone you like.

"I don't like or dislike you. You are just strange."

What do you mean you don't like or dislike me? That's a crappy thing to say!

"You are angry now."

Yes.

I turned my face away so she couldn't see how upset I was. Was she kidding? Could I trust her now? Maya noticed we weren't following.

"Hurry, you two!" she stage-whispered.

"Why are you angry?" Trix said. "Because I'm not your friend?"

Why are you hanging out with me? What's the point in breaking out of the research facility?

"I cannot tolerate the tests."

Well, me either. But it's different now. So many people have seen you. You're no longer their secret.

"There will always be more tests."

I wanted to be offended. But as her huge scaled frame expanded and deflated with her regenerating powers, my anger dissipated.

I guess you're right.

"Guys, seriously!" Maya whispered, loud and insistent. My friends stopped by the driveway of a nearby house.

Trix shook her head at me.

"Sorry, Ofelia," she said.

Trix pointed with a steady, elongated finger to the trail she had left on the road.

244

"The police will discover me," she said.

I don't care.

I clasped her hand, revelling in the electrical current sparking through our bodies, charging each other. We felt our powers growing.

We can do this together. I let go, waiting for her response.

Trix hesitated, and her indecision dug into my mind. She didn't form words. It felt like—an emotion—welling up inside her. This was new.

"Ofelia, get that thing moving," Mousie said.

Trix's hesitation fell away in our mind-meld.

She followed, and we caught up with my friends, who waited at the end of a driveway. Distant static floated from nearby, followed by a high-pitched blip on a policeman's two-way radio. They were closing in; we still weren't out of trouble.

A ten-year-old kid strolled from the nearest front door. She headed towards the mailbox, distracted by a game on her phone.

She reminded me of a smaller version of Maya—healthy and well-dressed. Her childish round face was well-nourished and her straight, long black hair looked like it was used to shampoo from the commercials. I smiled, remembering my shower at the research facility. The kid was about to walk past—there was no way she wouldn't notice four scrappy teenagers and a massive, disguised alien standing on her lawn.

The kid's attention moved from her phone to Trix. She inner screamed, the kind that sighs out as a whimper.

"It's okay," Maya said. "She won't hurt you."

The kid's eyes were wider than our pan on the hearth at home. Then she noticed the rest of our crew.

"Maya!" The kid's face broke into jubilation. "You're home?"

The girl wrapped her arms around Maya's middle. I waited a discreet moment, allowing for their reunion.

"Hi, I'm Ofelia, and this is Mouse Run and Aze," I said.

I turned to Trix, "And this is—"

"The alien!" the kid finished and sucked in a hiccup.

"Yes," I said. "Her name is Trix."

"She's all over the news." The kid calmed down. The alien was less intimidating once named. She stared at Trix. "Does she talk?"

"Not so much," I replied.

"Can she hear us?"

"Yes." I turned to Maya. "You know each other?"

"Yeah, it's my house," Maya said. "Meet my sister, Sumati."

Sumati wore a fresh summer dress. She didn't have to worry about the origins of her next hot meal. It would be prepared for her tonight, as always. Her terracotta complexion was free of the stress of survival. I could see the family resemblance. She was a more innocent and shorter version of Maya.

Sumati screwed up her face in indecision. Then her expression relaxed, morphing into curiosity. It was clear she trusted the alien and her human companions.

"I got your bedroom," Sumati said to Maya.

"We're commandeering your bedroom then," Maya said, smirking.

"How do you know them?" Sumati asked, inclining her head towards us.

"They saved my skin," Maya said. "But *not* from the United Nations."

Sumati forgot about the mail. "Would you like to see inside?"

CHAPTER 23

I WON'T LIE—I've always wanted to see inside a house, to prove my imagination was real; backyards packed with socialites reclining in lawn chairs, their children dive-bombing the swimming pool. Surely people don't live that way?

Maya's sister, Sumati, stood there, calm as, on her front lawn, waiting for our answer. I glanced to her house, then to Trix.

What do you think? I asked.

"I have led them straight here."

Trix waved her hand at her sludge on the road leading to the driveway where we now stood, its trail mirroring each swirling, suctioned step.

I scanned the yard, pointing to the sprinkler.

"Do you have one of those things?" I asked Maya.

"Yep?"

"How far does it reach?"

"Let's see..." Maya hurried to the bed of flowers growing at the base of her porch and pulled on a hose attached to the wall.

"Keep going," I said until Maya could pull no further.

I grabbed the sprinkler and washed the pavement where

Trix's trail ran into the street. But the sprinkler was inefficient, meant for incremental watering, not snail trail obfuscation.

Maya tugged the sprinkler head free, turning it into a regular hose.

I pressed my thumb to the end of the hose, creating a thick spray, washing Trix's trail clean from the road, across the pavement, and then up the driveway.

Maya turned the hose off and coiled it onto its hook on the wall. Then Sumati pushed the door ajar, and we let Trix enter.

Trix stepped through onto the landing, and I scuffed her slimy trail on the large tiles with my boots as I followed. Once she was inside, I could relax. Trix relaxed too, by shrugging off her blanket and placing her cracked sunglasses on the table by the door.

I took in my first impression of the interior of a real, swanky suburbs, true-life house.

We had stepped into a large tiled living room, with a flat-screen television, a kids' cartoon playing. The colours in the program were bright and clear, authentic enough to jump out of the frame and sing their silly song. A spotless cream couch faced the television. An open-plan kitchen beckoned, with an island bench and a stove built into the wall.

Every surface was clean and free of dust. The black digital displays of electronic devices glinted around the room. The open-plan design was large enough to fit at least ten Northies shacks. That wasn't even counting whatever was through those doors—more rooms?

Trix spotted a skylight to the left of the island bench. She stood underneath, lighting up as she did.

"Where is Aajee?" Maya asked her sister.

"She's in her room."

"Won't that be a problem?" I asked, concern crinkling my forehead as I glanced at Trix.

"Don't worry, it's just our grandmother, and she naps around now while she watches her shows."

"Wait—she has a television in her room too?"

"Sure, we all do."

Mousie let an impressive 'pfft' escape her lips.

"Maya," Sumati began, her eyes misting. "I wore this every day since you gave it to me."

She reached to a clasp holding a golden leaf pendant around her neck.

"You remembered," Maya said, taking the pendant by its soft ribbon from her sister.

"What is it?" Mousie asked, and I nudged her and shook my head. We were intruding on a moment here.

"They presented it to me when I was accepted into the United Nations," Maya replied.

"You were right, it brought me luck," Sumati said. "You came back."

Maya hugged her sister, and I felt a pang at the reunion. Would I see Imogen again soon? We waited until the sisters pulled free, their faces flushed with elation.

My gaze landed on a large, silver, smooth-surfaced box in the corner. I thought I knew what it held.

Maya noticed me eyeing the fridge.

"You guys hungry?" she asked.

"Famished." Mousie licked her lips.

"I sure worked up an appetite during our alien-hunt throughout the city," I said.

Sumati opened the fridge. Food illuminated inside, in the pristine, white-gleaming light of heaven. She pulled glass containers of cooked chicken thighs in a thick green sauce, and a brown curry with the whites of a fish fillet poking through. A third container was filled to the brim with rice.

The Northies rats peeked with bright eyes and salivating

tongues. The more I used my powers, the hungrier I became. I needed refuelling, like Trix, but with food, not sunlight.

Sumati retrieved bowls from the cupboard and stacked them in front of my friends, placing spoons in the glass containers.

Sumati nodded. "Help yourselves."

We forgot our manners and dug into the haul. I grabbed the container of rice at the same time as Mousie. We tugged until I almost dropped the dish on the floor.

"There's enough for all of you," Maya said, shaking her head at us.

"I'm the eldest," I huffed, reasoning with myself that we may require my powers at any moment. Mousie let go.

We didn't need a second invitation, grabbing bowls and scooping everything we could inside. Aze and Mousie had a brief tussle over the fish curry until Mousie conceded and waited her turn.

Once we had filled our bowls, we wolfed the food, chewing around the fish bones. The curries were delicious, spiced and nuanced. The taste exceeded my earlier meals by a thousand per cent. And that included the chocolate bars from the barrel.

Sumati stared at us devouring the spread.

"You're weird," she said. "The food should be microwaved."

"What is this? It's the best thing I've ever tasted!" Aze enthused, wide-eyed.

"The brown one is Goan Fish Curry. The green one is Chicken Cafreal. My grandmother made it."

"Compliments to the chef," I said, and this time I meant every word.

Mousie, Aze and I made quick work of our curry, but Maya didn't seem to be hungry. She poured herself a glass of juice from a bottle in the fridge, and scooted to sit on a stool at the island bench, sipping, watching us.

"When did you last eat?" Sumati asked.

"This morning," I said around a mouthful of juicy chicken thigh.

"They're um..." Maya began, "not from around here."

I grinned at Maya. At least she got it now. I wasn't the only kid licking sauce from my chin and chasing every grain of rice around the bowl.

My stomach ached from eating too fast, but the food helped. Strength returned and my senses sharpened. We lounged and digested our meal.

I nodded at Trix's slime trail across the tiles. "Sorry about that."

Maya threw a small kitchen towel at me, and I wiped Trix's tracks. I lifted off the actual slime—leaving the towel slippery with goo—but there was still a wet sheen pattern to the tiles.

"I'll get some floor cleaner," Maya said, heading into the garage. She banged things about, locating her magical suburban cleaning items.

Sumati stepped up to examine the alien, tracing an outline on Trix's arm, her fingertip pausing on a pulsing vein. She peered at the light coming from within Trix, the orange tinge. Like a glowing net cast into muddy water. Sumati wondered at this new thing. Trix was pretty weird.

A news story flicked onto the television, interrupting the cartoon. It showed footage from several hand-held cameras, capturing Trix and me rampaging at the car crash site and inside the mall. I washed my sticky hands and face in the kitchen sink, and drank in fistfuls of water straight from the tap, just as Sumati handed me a gleaming glass from the cupboard. I shrugged a 'sorry', wiping my hands on my jeans—Sumati held out a rectangular piece of cloth. A solution to every problem.

The couch was soft as I sank into its leathery cushions, and Mousie and Aze joined me. My butt felt as if I had placed it on a fluffy cloud. I could live on this couch. Perhaps I would, although I couldn't remain here without Imogen. She may never sit on a comfy couch, her worries evaporating.

What was Imogen doing right now?

The news footage captured the screams of people running away from Trix and I. The newscaster's words worried me—they got it so wrong.

"We have breaking news of an alien rampaging through the city today," the newscaster began. "A rogue alien caused a major pile-up, with several cars and an overturned semi-trailer involved in a major crash. Then the alien infiltrated the warehouse district, and assaulted a police officer as it escaped on a barge, before breaking into a shopping mall, terrorising shoppers and causing thousands of dollars worth of damage. Authorities locked the centre down, but the alien crashed a golf cart through the glass of a locked entrance, making its escape into the city streets."

"I don't even get credit for the golf cart?" I said.

"Wait—you did that?" Aze asked, whistling through her teeth.

Trix raised the place where her eyebrows should have been in reply. The newscaster continued.

"One eyewitness account said the alien being was over 8 feet tall, brownish-orange in appearance, and glowing from the inside. The being caused several injuries, although there were no fatalities."

"She's not that tall," I mused. One of many embellishments in the story.

The three of us watched the footage of our rampage of destruction. We looked scary from this angle, although I didn't feature, except for one blurry shot as Trix helped the driver from the truck cab. The footage centred on Trix—fair enough too—nobody had seen an alien on Earth before.

But we didn't cause the violence. We were just repelling it. The reporter neglected to report on the cops firing guns at us.

He continued. "Authorities urge residents to stay indoors. They consider the alien very dangerous, so please do not approach, but call the police."

"Woah!" Mouse Run said. "You guys are fierce!"

"Proper criminals, too," Aze said, honouring me with her best pirate salute.

Maya returned with a steaming bucket of liquid and a mop. She'd caught the last part of the news, and she eyed her sister with a grim expression.

"We're not that dangerous," I said. "They shot first."

"Yeah, looked like it from the news..." Mousie said with a wink.

"They got it all wrong..." I tried to explain.

Sumati seemed to decide.

"I know you won't hurt us." She glanced at her sister.

"Yeah, Trix is harmless, right?" Maya asked, her voice wavering. It was a lot to process. But her smile was more curious than afraid. They had to trust Trix. We needed our allies.

Maya leaned the soapy bucket and mop on the floor, but before I could reply, the newscaster continued, and I placed a finger to my lips. The report might help solve our predicament.

"In related news, the latest alien rampage has not cooled the mission most pressing on our minds. Final preparations are in progress for the diplomatic mission to the alien spacecraft. It may be our only hope of finding a cure for the world-wide pandemic. Pre-eminent virologist Dr Figg, who is advising the scientific teams, made a statement today..."

A thrill of anger shot into the bottom of my stomach, seeing that traitor to humanity, Figg, respected by the newscaster.

Sumati sat next to me on the lounge. She grabbed a rectangular black device with colourful buttons. She aimed it at the television and it switched off.

"Hey!" I said. "Turn it back on."

I tried to snatch the remote device, but Sumati leaped to her feet and held it above her head. Refusing to engage in the childish behaviour, I extended my hand, palm-up.

Sumati rolled her eyes at me, but flicked the remote. The story continued.

"And that rounds up the breaking news. We will keep up with the broadcast of the alien pursuit, stay alert for more updates as this unfolding crisis continues..."

"Great, thanks for that," I said, shaking my head.

We can't stay here forever, I thought.

Trix lowered her face from her sunny spot to meet my gaze. "You saw the news report. I am a threat to your kind."

So you just turn yourself in?

Sumati studied Trix like an object from the mall we'd razed to rubble. An intriguing curiosity, an item on sale. Weighing her worth.

"Can you hear her?" Sumati asked me.

"Yep," I said. "Although she's *not helping* right now."

"Can I ask her something?"

"Knock yourself for six."

"Huh?"

"It means go for it," I said.

"Oh, right? Well, alien-person?"

"Trix," I prompted. "That's her name."

"Okay, Trix," she continued. "What's your home like?"

I translated Trix's thoughts as she spoke to me.

"Hotter," I said. "Infinitely hotter. We would fry within a few minutes."

Sumati's eyes were wide again. "Are you from the alien ship, the one on TV?"

"Yes, she is," I said.

Sumati frowned, considering her next question. "How did you get here?"

"She was travelling in the diplomatic emissary."

"Oh, like Maya going to the United Nations?" Sumati asked.

"I didn't make it to the UN..." Maya replied.

"Have other aliens visited Earth?" Sumati asked.

"She says yes—others have come here before her. None have returned to her ship, though." I studied Trix's face. She wore her normal, neutral expression.

Was she lying? She'd said that her kind couldn't lie, that everyone knew everything. She had no reason to deceive me unless she was protecting others of her kind. I would do the same if someone threatened to hurt my family.

"So, where are the other aliens who arrived on Earth?" Sumati asked.

"Most likely dead," I said, feeling no remorse, no sadness in her response. It was a simple fact.

"How can she tell?"

"Because they haven't spoken to her. And because she's told her ship not to come to Earth. She's concluded that it's a one-way ticket."

"We have other items of concern," Trix said to me.

"You're right," I said out loud. "We need a plan."

But before we could think, the door across from the television opened and Maya's grandmother emerged, squinting beneath thick-lensed glasses. Her shoulders stooped, and she wore a chequered sari, as elegant as if she was about to step into a family celebration.

She rubbed fatigue from her eyes and hadn't noticed Trix.

Maya leaped forward, grabbing her grandmother in a hug, twisting her back around to face the bedroom. Maya flicked her eyes at Trix, and I took the hint.

"Oh my little naath," the grandmother said. Her croaky voice held the weight of eighty-odd years. Her hands crinkled like paper as she gripped Maya's shoulders.

"Hi, Aajee," Maya said, waiting for me to react.

I pushed Trix through a connecting door.

Quick, hide, I thought, scuffing her trail with the hand towel.

I followed her into the room, shutting the door behind us. A single bed sat in the corner, with a pink and purple doona covered in shooting stars of every colour. Several soft toys lay on the bed, and next to that, a desk and chair. Posters were stuck to the walls—pop stars holding microphones, and girls on horses, mid-air as they jumped through rainbows.

Maya hadn't lied—a small television sat on the top of a chest of drawers beside the desk.

A second set of doors led into a closet larger than our whole shack.

In here, I thought.

Trix bent around clothes on hangers—more clothes than I'd ever owned in my almost-sixteen years on earth. She fell back onto the hangers and clothes, forming an alien-clothing piece of art.

I wondered how we'd explain her sludge on the pristine bedroom carpet, but we had no time to worry. I slipped out into the living room, sitting next to Aze and Mousie. We remained inconspicuous while Maya and her grandmother reunited. Her grandmother spoke in accented English, peppered with words in another language. Maya was glad to see her grandmother. There was genuine affection in their reunion.

"So why are you home?" the grandmother asked.

"It's a long story," Maya said. "Come meet some friends I made."

The grandmother registered surprise as she noticed the three of us sitting on the couch.

"Hello, welcome to our home," the grandmother said, hospitable despite our dishevelled appearance. Her bright sari dipped as she waved her arm at the island bench. "You have eaten?"

"Oh yes, it was delicious, thank you!" I blurted, nudging Mousie's ribcage with my elbow.

"Thank you. It was the best food I've ever tasted."

At least our words were true, but I felt embarrassed at the mess we'd left—sauces dribbled over the bench top, discarded bowls and container lids and food left out of the fridge. I moved to clean up, but the grandmother waved me away.

"You are our guests," she said. "Let me do that."

She moved in a stooped but graceful way as she cleaned our dinner debris.

"You're a fabulous cook," I said. "What is your secret?"

"My mother," the grandmother said. "She taught me everything she knew."

I wanted to learn where Maya's grandmother had come from. But it seemed impolite to push. Before I could ask more, a car door slammed. A bird chirped in a nearby tree, and then my heart skipped around before finding its beat again.

Outside, adult voices approached.

"It's Mum and Dad," Sumati said, as if this was normal information.

Except I could tell, from Maya's horrified expression, that

Mum and Dad might not appreciate finding our crew in their living room at 5 o'clock on a Monday evening.

Two adults in smart business attire—Maya and Sumati's parents—breezed into the house.

The mother appeared much younger than my own, with soft skin, and makeup picking out her dark eyes. Her life hadn't been as hard as my mother's. Maya's dad was tall, with a paunch and slicked-back hair. They epitomised the couples I'd imagined—poised and confident, as if life had never challenged them. The perfect couple, gleaming like their surroundings.

"Sumati, are you home?" the male voice said, deep and personable.

Neither adult noticed us kids sitting on the couch.

"Hi, honey," her dad said, kissing Sumati on the head.

"What have you tracked in?" her mum said, inspecting the snail-trailed floor. "Were you playing with the neighbour's dog again?"

Sumati smiled with guilty innocence. "He ran inside, by himself."

"A wet dog unlocked the front door and cartwheeled over our tiles?"

I held my breath, hoping she didn't examine the sludge. It was doubtful wet doggy paws created that swirling pattern.

Maya stepped out from the kitchen.

"Dhoo, you're back!" her dad said, rushing in for a hug.

"You're so thin!" her mum said, wrapping her arms around the three of them.

"Were you thrown out of the program?" her dad asked, holding Maya at arm's length, taking in her dishevelled appearance. "How did you get here?"

And that's when the adults noticed three kids sitting on the lounge with ridiculous grins, uncomfortable in the delightful home. We were a sight—my cuts and bloodstained clothes and a bullet hole nicked into my jacket, Aze's pirate patch respectfully flipped up, and Mousie's matted hair folding in half against the side of the couch.

"What the heck is going on here?" Maya's dad demanded, as his house guests stood in a ragged mob.

"I made new friends," Sumati said.

Her mum held onto Maya's shoulders, as if to protect from the miscreants in her living room.

Her dad's foot scraped at Trix's snail trail with the toe of his expensive, shined shoe.

"Family meeting, right now," he said.

Maya and her sister, grandmother and parents took seats at the dining room table, while Mousie, Aze and I pretended to watch their magnificent TV. But we weren't watching the show. We eavesdropped on Maya's conversation.

It wasn't progressing well.

Maya explained what had happened after they recruited her to the 'United Nations', being taken in a black van to the research facility, being locked in a cell, the tests, the violent orderlies, the awful food, Figg.

My mind flashed back to my cell. The desperation and loss of control.

Trix was back in my head.

"Concentrate on where you are," she said.

If Maya's family were taking her return badly, how would they react when they discovered an alien hiding in the bedroom closet?

The family said little, their faces stern as Maya spilled her story.

"So, you weren't in Geneva?" the mother said.

"Keep up, Mum," Maya said, weariness in her tone. "The government isn't recruiting for the United Nations. Did you ever wonder why parents never hear from their kids again?"

"But they give you a better life... it's the sacrifice we make to keep the remaining countries safe," Maya's dad said, as if he'd repeated this in the past, convincing himself.

"It's an honour," Maya's mother finished. "We were so proud."

"Well, instead of making you proud, I was being experimented on and kept in prison."

Maya's grandmother said nothing, but reached out to hold Maya's hand.

"I can't believe it," her dad said, his eyes on the ground in a flash of anger.

"It's true," I said, approaching the table. "I was Maya's cellmate."

"We let them take you..." her mum said, chewing her lower lip, her eyes brimming with tears.

"No, I volunteered," Maya said.

"We didn't volunteer," Mousie said.

"They took us, too," I said. "Although the vetting process back home is different."

Maya's parents abandoned their seats and grabbed their daughter in a bear hug.

"I'm so sorry," the mother repeated, over and over. Her father held on, visibly shaking. Her grandmother didn't let go of Maya's hand. Sumati crouched somewhere in between the group hug.

They'd just been told that their daughter wasn't excelling at international diplomacy as part of the remaining United Nations. That she wasn't keeping humanity safe in the way they believed. Instead, their daughter was a lab rat and would have died if we hadn't broken free.

"I'm okay, thanks to my friends," Maya said, pulling out of the group hug, her eyes shiny with emotion. "With their help, we broke out of the research facility. I'd found Mouse Run and Aze early on, and led us to the suburbs, so I could bust this whole kid torture sham wide open."

The family wiped dripping noses with tissues and the father couldn't stop going back for a longer hug.

"Well, that's what we'll do. We'll alert the authorities," her mum said. "The other parents have to know. Their kids have to be returned, too."

"I failed you as a father," her dad said, dabbing his nose with a tissue. "It's my job to keep you safe. I'm so sorry, Dhoo, I'm so sorry!"

"We won't stand here and do nothing." Her mother's voice caught. I knew how she felt and couldn't keep my own eyes dry, either. Mousie and Aze teared up as well.

I watched Maya's family reunion with a pang of fear—what if I'd said goodbye to my family, possibly forever—even if it was for the good of humankind? Could I make that sacrifice?

I was more selfish than Maya. Nothing could convince me to part with Imogen, to never see her again. Maya's strength of character exceeded mine.

As her family reunited, the fear turned into a pang I hated to admit—it was jealousy, at Maya returning to her family. Would I ever see my own? All I could think about was Imogen, lying in her bedroll, alone and frightened in the night, without her big sister to chase away her nightmares. My fingers sought the familiar test tube in my pocket, twisting about the circular plastic.

Maya gave her mother a proper hug—this time they clung tight, an apology of sorts.

"I'm sorry, I'm so ashamed," Maya sniffed.

"Don't be, little one," her grandmother said. "You have no reason to be ashamed."

The father stood up, wiping his cheeks with the backs of his hands, straightening his perfect hair.

A car engine approached the house, then cut the ignition.

Footsteps from steel-capped boots approached the front door.

"Um, I think we have to go," I said to Mousie and Aze.

They backed into the rear of the open-plan area. Nobody noticed as they slipped out the patio door. At least they had a chance. Trix was more diversional than a couple of Northies kids trapped in the suburbs.

A forceful fist pounded on the front door, and my heart shot into my throat.

Maya's dad opened the door, revealing two police officers, their hands resting casually on their holsters. I had to get Trix out.

I thought to Trix, *Stay where you are*.

"Oh good timing, I'd like to report a crime," Maya's dad began.

I inched closer to the bedroom, but my way was visible from the open front door. One officer recognised me, and all hell unleashed its authoritative force.

"Backup to our location!" the second police officer yelled into his radio.

"Hands up, all of you!" the first police officer demanded, whipping out his gun and pointing it at the family, then me.

Or at the place I'd been seconds ago. I slipped into Sumati's bedroom, with the soft toys and horses jumping rainbows, and Trix hiding in the closet. I nudged the closet door a crack and peered into the gloom. Staring back were two luminescent orange eyes.

We've got to go, I thought.

"I have come to the same conclusion," Trix said, emerging from the wardrobe.

They've seen me, they will search the house.

"I dislike the police."

But so far, their behaviour's been exemplary, I thought, smirking.

A distant siren grew louder out the window, then another joined in. We were running out of time.

"You have no plan," Trix said.

Private thoughts are private thoughts, I replied.

Blue and red flashing lights pierced the window and landed on the opposite wall, and we had a fresh flight to endure.

CHAPTER 24

TRIX FOLLOWED me out of the bedroom as the police corralled the family to one side, near the kitchen.

"We've done nothing wrong!" the father yelled, although none of them struggled. They didn't have an unpleasant experience to harden their stance.

"Please protect my children!" the mother wailed.

Trix and I held back as a police officer pushed the parents against the wall, snapping handcuffs around their wrists. They were gentler with the grandmother.

Trix and I stepped into view of the family, with Trix magnificent and intimidating, hovering behind. The police were too busy handcuffing the family to see Trix or me.

Two fresh police officers grabbed Maya and Sumati, wrenching them into handcuffs.

"STAY AWAY from my kids!" the dad yelled, his face tinged with purple. The police ignored his demands. Sumati's lip trembled and Maya was even more terrified than the first time I'd seen her in the research facility.

Guess Trix didn't look so frightening now.

The police escorted Maya and her family to the waiting

cars, and more uniforms appeared, sweeping the house and noticing Trix step from the hallway behind me.

Trix moved further into the light.

"Holy mother of—" The officer in front shoved his partner behind him.

"It's okay," I pleaded. "She won't hurt you."

His eyes flicked my way before returning to the alien.

Trix brought her hands up in a gesture of surrender, keeping her distance. The two men fumbled backwards, joining their buddies outside. They were too scared to take Trix on one-to-one.

You ready? I asked Trix.

"Knock yourself for six," she said, surprising me. Was this alien getting a sense of humour?

We strolled out into the dusk.

Waiting in the driveway were several black cars with flashing emergency lights attached to their roofs, and two police cars angled towards the driveway.

"Hands up!" a male voice shouted.

We exited Maya's house just as the sun set. That did not bode well for Trix's regenerative powers. She couldn't recharge hiding out in the closet. Would her powers work?

We're screwed, I thought, shielding my eyes against the glare of the headlights.

"It's up to you, Ofelia," Trix said.

Did the uniformed men know how our powers worked?

We would be okay—right? I'd eaten vast amounts of quality food, and I didn't mind the low light, unlike Trix. Maybe we'd survive this attack?

Red dots danced on my torso as the uniforms took aim. I

told Trix to stay well behind me. She had to stand in the shadow of my force field made for one.

Police officers herded Maya's family into the back seat of three waiting cars. Maya turned towards me, tears streaking her face. In the flash of red and blue lights, her expression was terrified. She mouthed 'good luck' as the car passed—her face picked out in high relief by the headlights.

Maya believed in me. She trusted Trix. Was there hope for humans to understand the aliens?

Maya and her family were in trouble, too. We'd have to return for them. First, we had to escape this pickle.

At least Aze and Mousie had slipped away and Trix and I had the house at our backs.

Three men clambered forward on the roof of Maya's house, training more red dots on the backs of our heads.

Crap. They'd surrounded us.

We can't fight them this time, I thought.

"And I cannot help you," Trix replied.

I could try to make a stand. Firing off force fields front and back would be near impossible, even for Trix—and her powers outstripped mine. With my buddy out of action, we had no other choice.

I held my hands in the air, surrendering, and Trix did the same. A man in a fancy uniform poked his head above the car bonnet. The captain? At first, he seemed confused, not expecting us to surrender.

He flicked his arm, and his men sprang forward. If it was a fight at closer quarters, we might have a chance.

Trix came between the men and me. She swiped at the first uniform. He landed on the flower bed. A second and third tried to tackle her. One had her by her leg—she kicked him and he slammed against the garage door, leaving a torso-sized dent. The other grabbed her shoulders and wrapped his legs around her middle. He looked tiny against her. I punched his arm too, but he clung on tight.

The snipers on the roof searched for a clean shot. The guy wrestling Trix was a human shield.

Two more men leaped into the battle. One bellowed a war cry to give himself courage. But they bounced off Trix like early summer flies, weak and inexperienced.

The man wrapped around Trix and wedged his arms around her throat. I was sure Trix didn't breathe air, but he had to go.

She grabbed his arms, and I pulled his ankle, dislodging his boot.

His weight toppled Trix to the ground. She rolled to the side; the man wedged under her stupendous body. As Trix rolled away, the man flattened into the soggy lawn, too stunned to fight, wearing one boot, his uniform sodden. I threw his boot into the neighbouring yard. It felt totally satisfying.

Grab that one, I thought, pointing to the captain. He crouched beneath the hood of his car, within reach.

Trix sprang forward. The snipers had a clean shot.

Watch out!

Trix watched the flash of the bullet leave the sniper's gun.

I leaped forward, in between them, but my reaction was too slow. The bullet had travelled past me before Trix's weak shield enacted.

Instead of time stopping cleanly, the corners of her force field wavered, not solid. The translucent shield held the bullet in place.

Trix grimaced, something she hadn't done before.

It was then that I noticed a junior police officer at our front, stopped in time. His eyes shut against the pop of the trigger he'd just fired at Trix. With our front unprotected, he'd shot the bullet into the front of her shoulder!

She let the shield fall, and the bullet fired from the roof bounced off.

She let out a grunt and dropped to one knee. The slug blasted straight into her flesh, opening a wound in her pulsating skin. The brown protective scales folded outwards, like the unfurling petals of a flower, revealing the orange gash in the centre. Her veins grew brighter still and her body convulsed. Her orange eyes dimmed.

The other snipers lined up their shots. The captain stepped from the cover of his vehicle, sensing their advantage.

"It's hurt!" he yelled, but his men hesitated.

The captain approached, his pistol trained on Trix's forehead. Fear left his expression; his hand no longer shook. "Don't shoot, we need it alive."

Trix rested on her knee, her head bowed. I sensed her pain, the gaping hole in her shoulder pulsating within my own veins. The pain was unbearable for her, and so I grabbed her uninjured arm and let my power flow through my fingers. The orange in her eyes flashed, then dimmed.

I can't do this alone. Grab him! I thought, pointing to the captain within reach.

Trix grunted again and pushed herself to standing, nursing her damaged shoulder. She took a step forward, and the captain shuffled back, aware she was too close. His pistol trained on her, his hands trembling. She reached out and grabbed the pistol from him, her eyes so menacing that I felt myself go cold.

Trix handed his pistol to me.

She wound her good arm across his stomach. A human hostage.

Her three-fingered hand looped around his neck, her long fingers like slender vines. Her grip was loose enough that he could breathe. His men didn't know she didn't want to hurt anyone.

"Hold your fire!" the captain yelled, and his men pointed their gun barrels in the air.

Trix angled her body to the car. Now nobody had a clean shot.

"Tell your team to stand down," I said, shrugging a uniform's grip off my arm.

"Stand down!" the captain said. His eyes shone with primal fear. The hunter had become the prey.

"Give me your keys." I stepped towards the captain and Trix.

He reached into his pocket and thrust the keys into my hand. I took them and glanced at the cars.

"Which one's yours?" I asked.

He nodded at the one on the end and grimaced as Trix squeezed him tighter.

I held the barrel against his temple.

"Okay, sit in the back seat," I said, noticing the steering wheel. Then I saw the dashboard, a vast collection of dials, levers and buttons. I'd never seen the inside of a car from up close.

"Second thoughts, you drive," I said, tossing him the keys, but he was too frazzled to catch them, and the keys dropped to the ground. Trix loosened her grip so he could bend to pick them up off the asphalt.

"Move it!" I was careful to keep behind his body. I didn't want someone on the roof playing sniper and picking me off.

Get in, I thought.

Trix stuffed herself in the passenger side back seat. Her knees squished, her body folded in to fit. I swung into the seat behind the driver's seat, with my gun resting on the back of the captain's neck as he settled in the front. I kept the pistol trained on him the whole time. The captain's men didn't realise that I wouldn't fire the gun. We were toast if they tested that thought.

"Now, drive," I said, surprised at how calm I sounded. My heart strobed and my mouth felt dry with the adrenalin. But at least my voice was sturdy.

The captain started the car, spinning the vehicle in a tight circle, away from his men, the house, and the flashing lights. We drove away.

The captain's men leaped into the remaining cars and screeched in pursuit.

"Where are we going?" the captain asked.

"Speed up," I said. He did so. "Follow the route to Northies."

"Okay."

I rested the gun on the seat beside me. "Turn on the siren."

He flicked a switch on the panel in front of him. The siren shot more adrenalin into my body, the noise insistent and dangerous. The car swerved at speed and my familiar motion sickness rose in my throat.

I checked on Trix.

Are you in pain? I thought.

"Yes."

I'm sorry. What can I do?

"Just drive somewhere safe."

I checked out her wound—the skin pulsated over the entry point. The scaled skin tissue around was trying to close over, but each time it did, it sprang open. The bullet prevented her from healing herself.

Will you be okay?

"We need to remove the bullet."

I'm on it.

This was beyond my expertise—we'd need a doctor with surgical instruments. The research facility wasn't an option.

We sped through the suburban streets, passing hundreds of

rows of houses, like Maya's house, lit by the streetlights. We cleared an automatic checkpoint at the edge of the suburbs. The captain swiped his security badge at a sensor and the massive gates opened, leading out of Cookham East, into the wastelands beyond.

The houses thinned out, the streetlights dimmed, and small shops sprang up. Broken glass peppered the buildings and rubbish blew through the streets. Stray dogs padded along, their ribs showing. Kids who didn't look any healthier played beside the highway.

Then the houses gave way to dim apartment blocks, three or four storeys high. Then the apartment complexes grew taller, the streets were busier and better-lit. The police cars followed, but at a distance, their sirens blaring, lights flashing. We cleared the traffic ahead as the remaining vehicles pulled to the side to let us pass.

And then I saw it—Northies, spread like a gaping rash in the gully below, dissected by the dirty, winding river. It was endless—the browns of the rusting sheet metal and blue tarps poking through, the smoke rising from the hearth of each residence. The stench of things gone bad rose from Trash Mountain, flanking the side closest to the launch site's junkyard. And, beyond Northies, at the launch site—the rocket, on the launch pad, a tiny glowing dot from this perspective.

The smell wafted through the air-conditioning. The sweet scent of decay and untreated sewage. Like orange peel left in the sun.

"You got a radio on this thing?" I asked.

He nodded.

"Get on the blower. Tell your men to back off."

The captain reached for a radio in the car's console.

"Boys, we need you to hang back, please."

The static replied until a voice crackled.

"Roger that, Captain." The cars slowed, maintaining a distance. "Are you okay, Captain?"

I picked up the gun from the seat and shook my head at him. He watched my reflection in the rear-view mirror and replaced the radio.

"Repeat, are you okay, Captain?" the voice said again.

"Turn it off," I said.

He flicked a switch and the radio cut out. He glanced at me in the mirror, then checked out Trix.

"That... thing... is hurt," he said.

"No kidding," I replied.

"I'm trained in first aid."

"We need a safe place to help her," I said. "Know anywhere like that?"

"There's a field hospital on base."

"That is a terrible idea," Trix said to me. "It is too well-guarded."

"We need somewhere more neutral," I said.

"Like where?" he asked.

I gazed out of the window as we passed my home. My heart went out to my family, to Imogen. We were so close, but I couldn't help her like this. The smarting graze on my shoulder was a pain that was becoming too familiar. I had to help Trix first.

The captain read my expression.

"You realise they won't let you go home," he said.

"Just shut up and drive the car," I snapped.

He stayed silent for a while. Trix pressed her hand over her wound. Could we trust this man? I didn't know our next move.

"Take us to a hospital—not the research facility—a civilian hospital," I said.

"Roger that," he replied, and the tyres squealed as he turned a sharp right at the next intersection.

CHAPTER 25

THE CAPTAIN FLICKED off the siren and drove into a circular driveway leading to the emergency dock of the public hospital. He slowed before the entrance, halting next to a parked ambulance.

The captain had kept his word—it was a civilian hospital—I'd read the sign at the entrance. We couldn't demand to see a doctor in the emergency department, however. We would cause a repeat of the shopping centre fiasco. Everyone thought Trix was dangerous and out to kill humans on sight.

I lowered the pistol barrel to the back of his seat.

"What are you thinking?" he asked.

I peered through the glass doors into the emergency room, at the masked nurses tending to patients, at the sterile lighting, the broken people slumped in chairs.

"We can't walk in the front door," I said.

"I'll drive us to the car park."

We sluiced past the entrance to a multi-storey car park. The captain took a ticket from the gate and the arm rose. That was cool—a robotic arm. I was glad the captain was driving. I might not have figured that out.

The car slid up the ramp, through cool concrete. We wound up a few floors until the parked cars thinned out.

He eased into a parking space and cut the ignition.

"Now what?" he asked.

It was a good question. Could I leave Trix here alone with the captain? Would he cooperate? It was risky, but it was our best chance of remaining inconspicuous.

"I'll find a doctor." I eased out of the car, keeping the pistol pointed at the captain.

"And me?" Trix said.

Wait with him, I thought.

"My friend here has twisted human heads right out of their sockets," I said.

"It's cool. I'm cool," the captain said, facing the front.

Are you okay?

"Please get help," Trix replied, settling back further into the seat, an imprint of pain on her face.

I stepped into the car park, the light dingy, the shadows thrown from the cars in elongated fingers. Reaching out to grab me as I passed.

Two adults moved from behind a pylon, caught in shadow.

First Pocks entered the light, an ugly sneer lifting half of his face. A shot of heat travelled to my neck as his fingers sought his greasy ponytail.

"Glad to see you, Lizard Freak," he said, his voice jagged and cruel.

"I'm sure you are," I said, my voice low and full of hatred.

The second adult stepped into the light. Someone who I had hoped to never meet again.

It was Figg!

"What the actual hell?" I yelled as Pocks grabbed both my arms. I struggled against him, but he was strong, and his fingers dug deep into my upper arms. He held me so that it hurt when I wriggled.

"What's this?" Figg's face contorted into grudging respect and she took the pistol from my waistband.

Pocks tutted, his face so close that I could smell his foul breath and old sweat. I wondered if I'd ever add to the bullet holes in his jacket and hoped for a clean shot.

Figg turned the pistol in her hands. Once she'd examined it, she held it limply by her side, not used to being armed.

"You've created quite the chase for us," Figg said. "You didn't know that there's a tracking device on every police vehicle in the city."

"Leave Trix alone!" I demanded.

"Is that what you call the alien?" A smile flickered over Figg's face. "She'll be safe, don't worry."

"She's only safe if she's not with you!" I spat back.

"You got her shot," Figg said.

"They hunted us like animals."

"You're far from animals," she said. "We are concerned about your welfare. Our best doctors will see her. Wasn't it her medical care that brought you to this hospital?"

"Don't you dare hurt her!"

"You don't get it, Ofelia," Figg said, appearing sincere. "We don't want to harm either of you. We want to learn from you both. It's always been that. You can aid humanity."

"I don't know what you're talking about."

"A cure," Figg said. "That's what you want, right? A cure for your sister."

"I don't have it."

"Of course you do."

I stomped—hard—on Pocks' foot. He sucked in a painful

breath and I pushed him away. As I did, my leg dipped to the side, and the test tube with the bright yellow cure slipped into view, edging out of my jeans pocket. I grappled with Pocks, who near twisted my arm off, spinning me. The test tube poked further, aiming downwards. Pocks pinned both arms. There was nothing I could do but watch as the test tube slipped free of my pocket, hurtling to the cement floor of the car park. The tube cracked, and Pocks lost his balance, his thick boots smashing the tube to pieces.

"No!" I yelled, thrashing from Pocks' grip. Figg nodded her command and Pocks let go. I squatted beside the broken plastic, the bright yellow liquid within contaminated, a yellow puddle on the ground. Crystals of plastic shards glinted from within the liquid. I ran my fingers through, trying to scoop it into my palm, but there was nothing I could do. It was unsalvageable.

I'd destroyed Imogen's cure.

Pocks reached out, but I sprang forward, finding my feet, and grabbed the gun from Figg. I pointed it at her, and then at Pocks.

"Stay back," I said, trying to keep my voice from shaking. "Get over there."

I pointed the gun barrel where I wanted them to stand. Figg followed my instructions, but Pocks wandered casually to the side, a manic grin on his face.

"She's good," he said to Figg.

"Shut up!" I yelled, then faced Figg. "Let us go."

"I can't do that," Figg said. "It's not part of the plan."

"So what's the plan?"

"Getting you to cooperate. We need you, Ofelia. You're the key. You always have been."

"What makes me so special?"

"Your DNA is unique, Ofelia. It has the expected strings,

but there's alien DNA mixed in. Because I put it there. It makes you a unique individual. One of a kind."

"Alien DNA? What do you mean, you put it there?"

"Please, Ofelia, we're running out of time. Will you help us?"

I took a deep breath and tried to calm my racing heart. "Let us leave, and I'll cooperate."

"You don't believe that, Ofelia. You won't help us." She appeared to think. "Unless..."

"Unless what?"

I swung the gun on Pocks. His cautionary look chilled me more than his threats. His movements were slow, trying not to spook me.

He held a bunch of metal glinting in the dull light.

"Did you lose something?" he said. What was he holding?

He flicked his thumb to reveal the lucky four-leaf clover on the ring, scratched and no longer green. They were Roland's keys! I'd dropped them back in the launch pad yard.

Pocks jangled the keys and the jarring, terrifying echo went right through the car park.

My heart fell on a trajectory that plummeted several floors. Did that mean—no, surely not. Had they made the connection?

"I haven't seen them before," I said, swinging the gun from Pocks to Figg.

"See, I believe you have," Figg said, reaching into her pocket. I lifted the gun higher and she paused, raising her other hand in surrender.

"My phone," she said.

"Slowly," I said.

She pulled her phone from her pocket and pressed a button on the touchpad. Then she held up the screen. A video played —a news segment. It was Figg, with public-facing smooth hair and impeccable makeup. Doctor Wood lent credibility over her right shoulder, with his white coat and severe expression.

"Earlier today we enlisted a new batch of very brave volunteers to help with the search for the plague cure," Figg said into the camera.

"That's wonderful. And what is the latest development?" someone asked off-camera.

Figg's face was one of innocence, one of discovery.

"It's the first of our human trials."

The camera panned to behind the doctor. Faces I'd hoped not to see like this. It was two adults and a child, in nice clothes. They had showered and were cleaner than they'd ever been.

Staring back at the camera, pure terror on their faces, were Mum, Roland and Imogen.

"I realise this looks drastic," Figg began, putting her phone back in her pocket.

"You're a monster," I said.

"I'm honestly not, Ofelia. I hate using these tactics. But we are desperate for your cooperation. Nobody else has to suffer, and your family could be safe."

Figg held her hand out for the gun, and I pulled away. I had to ensure my family was okay. They were alive only as long as they were bargaining chips. What had Figg said she wanted? For me to cooperate? Would she keep testing on me until she killed me?

Figg said, "I didn't want this. It's more your friend Pocks' style than mine."

I glared as Pocks smirked at the compliment.

"What do you want?" I asked Figg, chin lifted, hoping like

heck I'd be able to do what she asked of me, for the sake of my family.

"I want us to be a team, Ofelia," Figg said. "You don't believe it, but I do. You, me, your friend Trix, we have a higher purpose."

"What's that?" I asked the delusional doctor.

Figg regarded me, and I lifted my chin a little higher, to show that she didn't own me.

"You're the saviour of all humanity," she said.

My instinct was to laugh at this lady, but she was serious. There was no room for insolence, and I needed her onside.

"I'll do my best to help you, if I can," I said, hating myself while saying those words. But Figg brightened.

"That's wonderful, Ofelia. Thank you on behalf of us all."

"Do something for me first," I said.

"What do you want?"

"Take me to my sister."

A flash of unease passed over Figg's face, but then she smiled. "Of course."

———

Pocks lifted the gun from my limp grip and walked me to a nearby white van. I peered through the tinted windows. There was no dividing wall between the driver's cab and the back seats.

Someone sat in the backseat, with a sheet pulled over the face and body. Trix's glowing veins pulsated through the cotton sheet. She didn't move when my body weight indented the shared seat.

Pocks pushed me in beside Trix.

Hey, wake up, I thought.

No reply.

A drip hung from the handle on the roof, feeding below the sheet. They must have sedated her. The shape of her pointed head lolled to one side.

Are you okay?

Crickets.

Pocks slammed his door, and the lock clicked. He settled himself into the driver's seat. Figg rode shotgun. Pocks finger-saluted the captain, who drove his squad car in front, siren blaring and lights flashing. Our point guard.

Pocks started the car and tyres squealed as we wound to the bottom floor of the car park. A mechanical beep sounded as we eased over the speed bumps and turned into the streets.

Our wheels hummed on the highway. The captain's siren parted traffic like the cars were ants avoiding sudden rain down a drainpipe. I expected the occupants of the other cars to see Trix, but we didn't slow enough for people to notice a weird, glowing sheeted shape.

We headed out on a highway, driving at speed, leaving civilisation, until the darkness enveloped our vehicle.

The captain turned off his siren and Pocks sped up, drawing level with the captain's window.

"Thank you, we'll be right from here," Figg said through the open window. "We appreciate the escort."

The captain nodded and hung back. He headed towards the bowl-like glow of city lights on the rear horizon.

I faced the darkness ahead, hoping I'd find answers, that things would become clear. I had accepted that I was part alien. It made sense. But how could Figg have 'made me'? All I wanted was to be reunited with Imogen and be one step closer to healing my family. The rest was too confusing.

We turned from the deserted highway onto a badly main-tained trail, past paddocks full of weeds and dusty earth. Maybe, long ago, this had been farmland.

How did my family get here? Maybe in the windowless black van?

Pocks pulled up beside a stone archway on the side of the road, cutting the ignition, leaving the headlights slivering the night. The archway led to darkness, the terrain just visible by the moonlight.

"How do I know you won't leave me?" I asked.

"I'll come with you," Figg said, slipping from the passenger seat.

Approaching the archway, my heart thumped until it hurt. I swallowed around my dry mouth, pushing Figg out of mind.

Past the stone archway was a poorly lit dirt trail. The gravel crunched underfoot. My eyes adjusted to the thin beams from the moon, revealing shapes as I moved away from the van's headlights. I eased each foot, but the loose stones jangled percussion in my ears.

A small caretaker's house sat in the gloom, next to the gravel road, single-storey and made of old, rough-cut stones. The cottage was built several hundred years ago, in the time Before. Scraggly bushes scratched the stone with the breeze.

Caw! Caw! Caw!

A black bird shifted in the bushes. Its wings flapped air on my face as it launched into the deep sky.

My heart hammered double-time and my nose itched from the bird's feathers. Nobody stirred in the cottage—it had an abandoned feeling. After I'd calmed myself, I scanned my surroundings.

Beyond the cottage, I tasted old grass in the cool night air, the crawling things, the must of rotting fence posts eaten by termites. Water trickled its undercurrent in the dark, the flow large and swift. The stirrings were devoid of life.

The moonlight picked out an iron gate twice my height,

standing in a fenced field that stretched so far into the darkness that I couldn't see its end.

I knew where I was before my thoughts began. My throat clenched. It hurt to swallow as I felt prickles of discomforting rust on the iron gate.

I pushed through the gate, my hand trailing over the peaks of individual slabs of grey stone poking from the ground in gap-toothed rows in front of me. Their pale curves picked out in the moonlight, stretching out to the edge of perception. Flowing into the river itself, submerged underneath the dark water. My eyes absorbed the moon's light, willing the dull ground to show another way.

Desperation nudged at my mind as I accepted the truth.

I was in a graveyard.

CHAPTER 26

FIGG HAD TAKEN me to see my sister—but not Imogen, as I had hoped. The graves weren't fresh, these were old casualties. Did the girl in the research facility mean Demi was one of the lucky ones... because she died?

Of course that's what she had meant. Demi had escaped, just not in the way I'd imagined. If I looked inside myself, into the places I didn't acknowledge, the inevitability had wrapped its cruel fingers around me long ago. I had lost her the moment the snatchers descended on Trash Mountain.

I shook my head and heard myself muttering, "No, no, no. It can't be you!"

But I knew she was here. The first gravestone sat in the grass, carved with the unfortunate victim's name. The letters weren't my sister's. I didn't stop to read the full inscription, scanning for her resting place. I had to see her to understand. Because if I didn't prove she was here, I would deny it forever. I wouldn't survive that.

The letters on the tombstones were just legible in the weak moonlight. I searched each row, pleading with myself. If she wasn't here, I'd return to the van. Let them do whatever they wanted. I didn't believe my wager, though. Hope slipped further from reach with each stone.

I heaved from tombstone to tombstone, processed each name, rejected them. Kids and ages—so young.

Was it wrong that I felt a tug of relief when they weren't Demi's?

But then I found her in weathered lettering.

Demi Stykes, 16 years old.

She'd died a year older than I was now. I willed the letters to form somebody else's name. But it was impossible. The words branded fear into my soul. I don't remember standing there, but I must have repeated her name. The familiar curves of the letters were both damning and comforting. My sister.

She had perished in the facility.

By Figg's hand.

A jolt shot up my neck at that realisation.

I was alert in every way, except I was also numb. My heart beat faster and my breath echoed in my ears—the only sound in the world. The night stopped turning. Trees were still, the entire world mourned with me.

If I stuck with Figg, I'd die too.

I wanted to run until my lungs gave way and my skin melted and I turned into slippery goo decaying into the earth, just like Demi. My rotting bones, my flesh intertwining with hers. That was a comforting thought. No worries, an end to suffering. Our family, growing smaller, finding peace.

My body felt tipped on the side, dipped into deathly, icy waters. My mouth went dry. If I moved, it would make it real, force me to think of Demi dying in that place. How did she die? It wasn't the plague—she recovered, as did I. So Figg had done something to her.

What had Figg done?

I scanned the endless rows of tombstones. Figg's altar of failure—she had killed every one of these kids.

Hot tears poured from my eyes. I heard myself wailing. I didn't realise that the sounds emanated from deep inside, not recognising my voice.

Keening, I lay in the dirt, clinging to the rough tombstone, holding my sister.

———————

There was no escaping reality. My body hurt to move, to think, to breathe.

It was an old pain, a familiar sinking feeling. It began when they snatched Demi, the day I first saw Figg.

When I next noticed my surroundings, Figg was beside me. I hadn't heard her approach. My grief morphed into anger. Anger at Figg, at that place. That she could use people—innocent kids—until they died.

I'd never hug Demi again. It could happen to me, too, and I wouldn't see Imogen, or Mum, or Roland. Figg would never let us leave.

Figg had to die, too. And I'd be the one to end her.

She stroked my hair. I sat, she stroked, as I floated above my body. The strokes felt like someone else's hair, a favourite doll's, perhaps.

I wanted to reach around and strangle her evil throat until she choked to death.

"I'm sorry about your sister," Figg said.

"What?" I asked, confused.

"Your sister, Demi. I'm sorry. She was a fighter, that's for sure, but she wasn't strong enough."

"What the hell did you just say?"

Figg seemed relieved that I was talking.

"We know that Demi was your sister. Your results came back, you shared DNA." Figg let this register.

Rather than replying, I sent my worst stare-dagger right through Figg's skull. Figg nodded, pretending to understand.

"You killed her," I said, my voice low and dangerous as snake venom. Crueller than death.

Figg's eyebrows shot into her fringe. "I didn't kill her. The plague killed her."

"That's crap," I said. "She survived the plague."

Figg's expression softened, which was worse than her condescending tone.

"You're calling me a liar?" I spat, my hatred for her dialled up. My clenched fingernails bit into my skin as I formed a fist. Pain focussed my anger.

"Do you know what we're trying to do?" Figg asked.

"I don't care."

"You should care, because it's the most important thing anyone's tried to do, ever."

"Oh, and I suppose you're doing this important work, snatching kids from their families, killing them and burying them in a freakin' graveyard!" The last part escaped as a sob. I turned away, denying my aching sadness, forming anger again. Struggling to keep it together in front of this monster of a human being.

"I don't want to kill anyone," Figg said, her voice catching with emotion. "You can save us all."

"I couldn't save Demi."

"I'm very sorry about Demi."

"You don't give a crap about her!"

"I care for all of my patients. I'm a doctor. Curing people is my life."

"You're not a doctor. You murder innocent kids!"

"I know it's difficult to understand," Figg said. "The sooner

I can find the cure, the sooner the suffering can stop. Billions of lives are at stake. Without me, the work would take ten times longer. Think about it—ten times as many years, with many more casualties."

Figg waved at the tombstones, then rested her hand on my shoulder. Her imprint sizzled my skin, and I flinched backwards, away from the heat of her body, her corrupted mind.

What did she want from me? I wasn't special. She said that to everyone—she'd said that to Demi.

"Let them go," I said. "Every single child needs to go home."

"You have that power, Ofelia. We're close now. Closer than we've ever been."

My rage burned at this sorry excuse for a human. Fury filled my whole being until it burst.

I sprang to my feet and leaned into my shoulder. I charged at Figg. She couldn't avoid the collision; she hadn't expected it.

My shoulder hit her side and sent both of us flying. Her skull hit the nearest gravestone and her neck snapped back, hard as a bird flying into a glass window.

A gash on her temple trickled blood. She put her hand there, and it bloomed red, a painted flower pattern.

I threw myself at her, and she had no time to bring up her arms. Hitting and scratching, I clawed her arms away from her face. Pummelled with focussed hatred. Overheating with anger.

She fell to the ground, and I kicked out. Her body bent as my foot found her stomach, and in my mania, I was avenged.

Pocks pulled me off her, her face marred with a bloody gash. Her eyes held the same fear we had.

The kids had the same expression when the orderlies beat them.

Pocks ripped a corner loose from the sheet covering Trix and handed it to Figg. She held the fabric to the gash I'd gouged into her cheek. I found her bloodied skin underneath my fingernails, feeling powerful for the first time.

Pocks hovered, ready to subdue any more trouble from me.

"There were so many," Figg said, defeated. "So many children, over the years. It wore me down. I won't lie. I conducted those experiments for the greater good. But it destroyed me. Each child judging at the end."

I didn't reply, just stared at a rock lying at my feet, as if it bent time itself. Reversing time's direction could stop the suffering.

"I am sorry about Demi, Ofelia."

I risked glancing at Figg, and saw her eyes, glazed with tears, staring into the distance. She turned her face from mine and flicked a tear away with her fingernail.

"I'm not made of stone," she continued, "and I'm not a fool. If there was another way, believe me, we would have taken it. This is my life's work."

Figg waved her hand at the graveyard.

"Yes, your altar of failure," I said, seething sarcasm. "It gives me so much confidence for the future."

"It's why I bury them, Ofelia. Every single child that dies, I give them a proper burial. To respect their life, to respect their sacrifice. Each child haunts me at night."

I couldn't give in to rage, I had to defuse my fury to outplay this woman.

Closing my eyelids, I pictured Imogen at home with Mum, staring at the blanket on the wall, those two white eyes in a sea of blue. They would no longer watch over her, lost to the folk left behind.

It was time to forget Demi, if I could. I had to return to my living family, focus my thoughts only on Imogen—the two of us curled up in the decrepit bookstore rubble as I handed her the postcard that said 'Wish you were here.'

To my ears, I sounded genuine. "I'm sorry I hurt you."

I *was* legit remorseful.

Figg regarded me, and I averted my eyes. Thoughts of Imogen helped disperse my resentment. I tried to keep that image of the bookstore in my mind instead, the afternoon sun creating light and shadow over the rubble. Snug in our hidey-hole, under cover of the eaves.

"I should have told you of the connection with your sister earlier," Figg said, removing the bloodied sheet and repositioning it to better staunch the flow. "But the tests had to confirm."

"Did you... did you do tests on Demi, too?"

"Yes." At least she respected me enough to tell the truth.

"Did you test all the kids?"

"It's the quickest way to find the cure—actual human trials. We had several promising leads. We were close."

"Why kids?" I asked.

"Because there were rumours. I heard you survived."

"You only met me a week ago."

"Before I studied the plague cure, before there even was a plague—I worked in gene-splicing, on my personal research."

"So?"

"I knew your mother." She let that hang for a while. "And my research was unsanctioned."

"What are you saying? Did you experiment on my mother?"

"The research wasn't successful. The other foetuses died. They closed my lab, and they let her go. I caught rumours—I didn't know where she was—but I heard she came to full term."

"Foetuses—as in, babies? You experimented on babies?" My voice raised, echoing in the flat terrain, and Pocks swivelled in the driver's seat, letting one leg hang from the cab, ready to subdue me again.

"Everything okay?" he asked Figg. She nodded.

"It was you, Ofelia," Figg whispered. "I made you. You're a miracle—*my* miracle. That makes you like my daughter, and I've been looking for you ever since."

"What do you mean, you made me?" I demanded.

"Has your mother spoken of your father?"

"How is Roland involved?"

"No, your real father."

"I don't know who he is."

"I do."

"Who is he?" I demanded.

"I didn't know my mother, and my father wasn't what you could call affectionate," Figg began, her eyes landing on the graveyard in the distance. "He was the opposite, he was strict, and I don't remember him ever praising me. I've always wanted a different family, one of my own. You, me, your mother, Trix—we are all part of the same cocktail. We're all deeply connected to you, Ofelia. I used Trix's DNA to bring forth my version of family. It's not the same as being your biological mother, but it's the closest I will get. Will you let me help you? Will you let me protect you, as a mother should?"

I was confused. Was my entire family involved? What did she know about my real dad?

Figg's expression was tender, as if I really was her child, as if her love was genuine. How could she love me and hurt me at the same time?

"So who is my father?" I asked, my voice croaky with emotion.

"You've recently met him. It's Doctor Wood, who was assisting my research."

"Are you kidding me? That sadistic doctor is my father?"

"He's a well-respected physician who has advanced our understanding of alien DNA. He's a brilliant man."

"And he seems not to care about hurting children either—you're alike that way."

"Actually, we're both decent people who've been forced into questionable ethical areas for some time. We did the best we could within the timelines. There was no time to wait for ethics boards and committees. Your father understands this, too," Figg replied.

"He's not my father," I spat.

I had no words. I just shook my head, channelling my rage inwards. Figg stepped closer, and I averted my eyes. I couldn't look at her without giving away my anger.

"You have the power, Ofelia. You choose how this ends."

"But I lost the cure, the test tube, back in the car park," I said.

"We have more stored nearby," she said. "We've been running simultaneous testing."

Figg seemed sincere, but I was dubious about trusting her.

"Where?" I asked.

"In a secure facility, controlled by the Prime Minister."

I thought about my next move. Maybe this could work.

"So take me to the Prime Minister," I said. "If I'm that important, he'll want to hear from me. And then I'm taking that cure to my sister."

Figg considered this, glancing back over the headstones, her eyes landing on Demi's resting place. Pocks stepped closer, his boots scraping the gravel.

"That thing is waking up," he growled.

Figg regarded me, and then brightened. "If you wish, Ofelia, we'll take you to see the Prime Minister."

CHAPTER 27

AFTER ALL THE EMOTION, I felt drained, and dozed in the van, my head bouncing on the headrest. When I woke, the blue LED of the clock reflected in the van's window—it was now 9:52 pm. We slowed and climbed a steep incline on a narrow arterial road, snaking around as if driving up a mountain. The city was a thin scattering of twinkling lights on the far horizon as I shook off the residue of my nap. Time to stay alert again.

I checked on Trix, who still hadn't moved.

Hey, wake up, I thought.

But there was no response. Figg had given her another shot, and she was out cold.

This is important. I need you now!

Trix remained oblivious to my thoughts, and I didn't hear any of hers, although I felt the hum of her veins, the pulse of her mind coming to.

"We need to help Trix," I said. "The bullet needs to be removed."

"There's a hospital wing in the facility," Figg replied sluggishly, as if she'd been napping as well. "We'll make sure she's cared for. She has an important part to play, too."

The van struggled with the hill. Pocks cut the engine and yanked the handbrake. Our ride was over.

He wrenched the door open, and Figg pulled on the crook of my arm, her eyes reflecting the internal light in the van.

Pocks wrestled a collapsed wheelchair from the back and set it on the gravel road. He yanked off the sheet, twisting handcuffs around Trix's wrists and ankles.

"Hey, get off her!" I said.

"Behave, please Ofelia," Figg whispered. "It's just a show for the guards."

I nodded, keeping my eyes on the ground. There would be a time to fight. Not now.

Pocks unhooked the bag of fluid from the van and dropped it in Trix's lap. Figg flicked her head in my direction, and I helped ease Trix into the wheelchair. She was heavy, so we didn't lift her, but guided her weight. Pocks wound chains through her handcuffs and attached them with a padlock. She was restrained, and still unconscious, her bent form stacked like thick logs of a felled tree.

Pocks heaved his back into wheeling her up the road, and Figg gripped her hand tight around my elbow. We trudged up the hill. What could be out here? I hadn't imagined a place so desolate, so untouched by human civilisation. The stars hid behind clouds, the moon obscured, a subtle glow in the expansive, lonely sky. Maybe graves wouldn't be noticed out here... mine, and Trix's... and my family's?

I removed the thought from my mind.

What would Trix do?

She wouldn't give up.

We reached the peak of the hill, with a smooth flat area large enough to park a few vehicles. In front, a jagged stone wall sprouted a single bare light bulb. Puffed from the uphill climb, I placed my hands on my hips while we caught our breath.

We approached the light set into a sheer stone cliff face. It was blinding in the surrounding pitch darkness, and I blinked away white orbs that moved with my vision.

A steel door was set into the stone wall. Two men in military uniforms exited the door and marched towards us, pushing past me and Figg.

Pocks stopped, heaving like a smoker, his arms rested on the wheelchair handles. He had this smirk on his face. He tapped one of the bullet holes in his jacket. Like I was next.

I froze at his threat.

A military man took over from pushing Trix, grunting at a weight he hadn't expected.

We approached the steel door set into the walls of the mountain itself. Figg flashed her badge to a security camera set high into the craggy wall, and the door buzzed open.

Pocks smirked, but stayed outside, the new watch. I'd prefer never to see him again. My new mission—to negotiate with the world's most powerful man. It seemed strange for a leader to live here. Was Figg taking me on yet another detour?

She pushed me into the chamber, and our footsteps clanged and echoed—reinforced steel on all sides. The two military men wheeled Trix into the cubicle, and the door banged shut. We plunged into darkness, as the echoes of steel settled into quiet again.

A light flicked on above us, humming with soft electricity. Figg swiped her card at the inner security door. Four cameras pointed from each corner of the ceiling—they weren't mucking around here. It was tighter security than the research facility.

The door buzzed open. We headed down a metal ramp, our boots clanging and echoing in the lengthy tunnel at the bottom. There was an elevator at the end. Figg swiped her card, and we stepped inside. A man wearing a military cap appeared on a small television screen.

"Please identify yourself," the man said.

"Doctor Figg with precious cargo for the Prime Minister."

"Project password?" he asked.

"Humanity."

"Thank you, Dr Figg." The military man reached up to press a button on his end, the lift doors closed and the television screen blanked out. We hurtled downwards, too many floors to count.

As we slowed, my head dipped with the familiar motion-sickness spurting saliva into my mouth, but I held the unpleasant sensation back.

The doors opened out into a war bunker.

Military personnel manned huge computer consoles, moving with urgency about the bunker. A floor-to-ceiling television screen dominated one wall, displaying a map of the world. It highlighted the northern countries in red, with blinking lights in what I assumed were the major cities. The southern hemisphere was in darkness, countries south of the equator filled with black.

What was I looking at?

Everyone wore a military uniform, in a heightened state. Whatever they worked on seemed serious.

Before I could take anything else in, a grey-mustachioed man in his sixties with a gleaming bald head approached and addressed Figg, handing her two medical masks.

"Get them to the interrogation rooms."

Figg handed a mask to me, and I donned it. Then Figg wrapped another mask around Trix's mouth.

One security man wheeled Trix away, and the other led me in the opposite direction, along several hallways. The walls were reinforced mountain rock, the light dull. The world's last defences may be here.

We passed one room, a huge schematic drawing on the table.

"Wait here," the mustachioed man escorting us said. We stopped in the hallway, and I had time to peek at the schematics. It was a massive ship, like an ocean cruise liner, although aerodynamic. A spacecraft? But it was larger than anything I'd seen lift off from the launch pad. It resembled a picture I'd seen long ago, at the bookstore, in a children's book full of long-extinct animals.

The ship looked like an ark.

Before I could process that thought, my escort shoved me down another hallway with stone walls roughly hewn and closer together. He pushed me into an interrogation room with a mirror along one wall—more of that one-way glass. As they locked me in, Figg caught my eye.

"We'll be back soon," she said.

I shrugged, as if it didn't matter, and waited until she'd gone, before sitting on the uncomfortable chair in front of the steel desk.

My skin broke out in goosebumps from the cold. The minutes dragged on, and I used the time to gather more strength. Time elongated as it had in my cell, to a warped reality of hyper-vigilance. I had to check on my friend.

Trix, where the blazes are you? I thought. She must still be unconscious, or they'd killed her already. What about the cure that Figg promised?

I ran my fingers around the rubber ball in my pocket, and my thoughts flashed to Imogen. I considered attempting to short out the lock of the interrogation room, as I'd done in the research facility. But this time I had bargaining power. They needed me. This time they'd listen.

I left the ball in my jacket pocket and tapped my legs, trying to keep warm in the air conditioning. My mind reached out to Trix. She was somewhere here, right? And our powers were better combined. But there was one problem—we were so deep into the mountain that even the strongest solar radiation couldn't touch us. She needed to recharge. Maybe it was enough to kill her. Her sunlight was our water—without it, she would die.

Or not. Maybe her species didn't die? Her bullet wound had tried to heal over, like my bullet graze, and the lacerations from the shattered window, and the scalpel incision...

I shut my eyes and concentrated, clearing my mind, reaching my thoughts to her.

Are you there?

I listened only to the clanking of the air-conditioning vent. It was rhythmic, a pump. Air going in, air going out. Just like breath.

If you're there, please let me know.

"I am here," Trix said, her voice loud in my head.

Are you okay? Relief rushed through me.

"They removed the bullet. I will heal."

Did the Prime Minister see you?

"Yes."

I bet that was a one-sided conversation.

"Especially without what you humans use the most—body language and facial expressions. I am still learning those."

You're doing okay.

"I think I failed. He grew angry and yelled at me."

He might not be pleased with me, either.

"At least he can hear what you say."

I pictured Gill Pollins' cheeks flushing to his temples, his complexion growing red as Trix played the strong, silent type.

We're far from sunlight, I thought.

"I will manage. They have placed me near their power generator."

How can you tell?

"Because I am not dead."

Well, thank goodness for that.

Footsteps scuffed the smooth, concreted floor outside.

I've got to go, I thought.

"Good luck," Trix said, our connection severing like removing a warm handprint.

Two uniformed men flanked the door. And a third appeared—with a pasty, plump face and a sharp-cut suit and tie. His lips were too rosy, his skin too pale, like cooked fish flesh. His cheeks blushed a patchy pink, as if he'd been exerting himself.

It was someone that I saw on the television, giving talks about policy and funding and sending troops where they were needed most. I didn't believe there was much truth in those reports. The most powerful man in the world stood outside my interrogation cell. And he was intimidating.

It was Gill Pollins, the Prime Minister of the remaining countries north of the equator. The countries that survived after our climate went to hell, before the plague spread from the melted permafrost. Pollins' theory was that the aliens buried the plague where it would be exposed to humans.

I had my own theories. Trix wasn't out to hurt me or any other human. She had saved my life a bunch of times. If her alien species wanted to destroy humanity, why had she almost died protecting me?

I also knew that I couldn't trust the Prime Minister. The media had caught him on camera, saying one thing one minute, and the opposite the next. You can't trust a politician, my mother would say. And Roland would grunt that you shouldn't voice such thoughts.

Did Pollins know what was best? Could I trust him to do the right thing by me and my family?

Should I tell him about Figg? As if on cue, Figg appeared over his shoulder, smiling benevolently as she donned her face mask.

Pollins also erupted into a public-facing grin. He slipped a medical mask over his pasty face and wound the ends around his ears. His pudgy fingers brushed through thick, silver hair and his eyes narrowed, studying me.

He moved towards the facing chair. "Hello, Ofelia," he said, in a pleasant, bassy voice. Weird. He sounded younger on television.

"Hi," I said, standing.

"How are you feeling today?" he asked, as if he was logging a field journal at a zoo.

"I don't have the plague, if that's what you're asking," I replied politely.

His lip flinched underneath the mask; his eyes remained steady.

"I'm glad to be working with you, Ofelia. If Doctor Figg speaks the truth, then you're a very special person of interest."

"That's right," I said, hoping my tone implied confidence.

"If it's true, Ofelia, I think you can help us." Pollins moved to sit opposite me, steepling his fingertips together on the desk in front. Figg sat in the chair next to Pollins. I eased into my seat. Figg rubbed the gash on her face, now covered with a white sticking plaster.

I was impatient to see my family, to free Trix. But I also had to be smart—if they had my family, they would be close.

Did Figg have the Prime Minister's ear? Which of them had the power?

"So, Ofelia," Figg began, "tell the Prime Minister who you are."

"And who am I?"

"You're a human-alien hybrid with defensive powers that defy the laws of physics, space and time. And you're the only one capable of communicating with our captive alien."

"Is it true?" Pollins stepped forward, his head cocked to the side. "Can you talk to the alien? Do you have these powers that defy science?"

"Depends which scientist you ask." I glanced at Figg.

He traced my gaze.

"I'm asking you," he said, shifting his weight to the other foot.

"What would you do for me, if you believed?"

"That would be up to you, Ofelia," he said, his eyes gleaming.

I shook my head, wondering if I should play my hand.

"I want you to give me the cure, and let my family go," I said.

He touched the mask over his rosy cheeks, and doubt flashed in his eyes.

"I can understand that," he said.

"Is that a 'yes'?"

"I can't promise anything yet. But..." He played the good cop again. "We'll think seriously about it."

"Then I'm not helping you."

I crossed my legs, swinging my foot, and then snuck a glance to see if he was watching.

Yes, Gill Pollins observed my teenage insolence, and I couldn't tell if he was annoyed or thinking. His attention flitted to a crease in his shirt pocket, smoothing it with his hands. He turned back to me.

"Ofelia, I can be reasonable. I can help you," he began. He stopped stroking his shirt. "I could make you a rich person, offer you a thousand Tins. You know what Tins are?"

"Of course." There might be an alternative yet.

"I have that power," he continued. "We'd release your family and they wouldn't have to work another day. You would be rich and could even buy a cure for your sister. Set yourself up for life. You wouldn't be Garbage Rats anymore."

"Northies rats," I said to myself. "We're called Northies rats."

"I could have a word to your mother's employer. Mr Pocks, was it?" he said. "We only want to run more tests on you and your alien friend. It would be easy."

I thought about his offer. It could be life changing for my family. We could be the rulers of Northies, we could oust Pocks. Run things as we wanted, and buy that black market cure. Hadn't I worked towards this? To save Imogen? Heck, we could buy the cure for everyone, save the entire city.

I was conflicted—he'd offered me the biggest lottery prize I would ever see. We'd be rich beyond anything I'd ever hoped for. Imogen could be well. But maybe KitKat's mother was a fraud? Maybe there was no cure. And I didn't trust Figg, or her ability not to kill me with her experiments.

"I don't think so," I said, feeling the disappointment in my words. For a fleeting moment, I'd been wealthy, but it wasn't enough. My family's safety came first, so I said, "Give me the cure and release my family. That's non-negotiable."

Pollins pressed his lips together underneath his mask.

"That might be difficult without your cooperation."

"I'm not going back to the research facility."

"We can accommodate the tests right here."

"No more testing," I said, folding my arms.

Pollins leaned back and stroked his hair, a thought just occurring to him. I could see his excitement as he put on a nonchalant air. "They say you can communicate with the alien. Is it true?"

"Yes," I said.

"So I have another idea. Instead of subjecting you to more of those tests, you could help us communicate with the alien instead. As a translator. Would that be amenable?"

"So I work for you, and you'll release my family, and give Imogen the cure. I only have to translate?"

"That's right."

I sat back, trying not to let my glee shine through. Surely he couldn't honour his promise of no more tests. Could I trust this man, the weaver of lies? He was just another deceitful politician.

Hiding my enthusiasm, I turned my face away from his. I held the cards now and could bend the most powerful man north of the equator to my will. If they believed I was that valuable, maybe I wouldn't stop at the cure and releasing my family. I could take revenge on Figg, too, and help the friends I'd left behind. And Trix had to be set free.

My smile widened.

"Mr Prime Minister, I know you have the alien," I said. "Take me to her. Let me prove to you who I am."

CHAPTER 28

THE PRIME MINISTER and Figg led us from the interrogation room. Two military grunts formed a rear escort, their semi-automatic guns clasped at their sides, their index fingers rested on the triggers.

We continued past, our feet clattering in the enclosed space, the ceiling too low, exposed pipes snaking ahead. The overpowering smell was like old rust, despite the healthy condition of the steel reinforced beams in the ceiling.

The further into the mountain we went, the warmer it felt. So we must be near Trix—she'd said she was next to their power generator. The Prime Minister was, so far, true to his word. Figg halted at the entrance to a room, glancing at Pollins. She averted her gaze and waited for him to respond. I sensed the time was right, and said, "Um, Mr Pollins? You should know things about Doctor Figg. Before I go in there."

He sighed. "What things?"

"She's been kidnapping children and conducting secret experiments on them. And then she murders them."

"She took you," he said, his eyes darting to the door. "And you look fine."

Wait—he didn't look surprised. And he believed me.

"You knew about the experiments!" I said.

He turned towards me, resignation in his eyes.

"I didn't have a choice. Believe me, if there was another way, we would have taken it."

"You allowed... her... to take my sister. To do God knows what to her. My sister is lying in a graveyard now. All that's left is a *tombstone!*"

He looked guilty, to his credit.

"I am sorry for your loss, it's deeply regrettable..."

"That's putting it lightly!"

"Prime Minister?" Figg interrupted. "Please, let her show you."

I pushed my hatred inside, taking deep breaths. Stakes were high, with no space for emotions. I had to be smart to overcome these awful excuses for human beings, to pretend to give them what they wanted.

Pollins flicked his head at the door. I pushed through, stepping into a cavernous holding room. The chamber had gunmetal grey walls and a window set into one wall, the blinds drawn.

Trix slumped in the main room, leaning into herself. They'd cuffed her feet and hands. At least she was conscious. The bullet wound had closed over, her scales disjointed around the entry point, like mislaid sheets on a tin shack. Her eyes were dull, far from their usual vibrant orange. She needed proper radiation, but she put on her facial expression of happiness just for me.

"Hi," she said inside of my head.

What did they ask? I thought.

"They want a cure we don't have."

Figg and Pollins observed us like a curious revelation in a

circus act. We were exotic animals to be studied and pored over. I'm sure that Trix didn't enjoy it any more than I did.

The Prime Minister stepped forward, trying to hide his enthusiasm.

"So, Ofelia," he began. "I want you to interpret for me. Can you do that?"

"I'm not cooperating until you give me the cure and release my family."

Pollins' smile faded until it was a mere imprint on impassive features. He took a few paces, thinking.

"Of course, Ofelia. Prove to me first that you can communicate with the alien. Then we can discuss your terms."

Pollins' attention flicked from me to Trix, his expression hungry. He didn't know genuine hunger like we did.

"Ask it why it's here."

I waited for Trix's reply, calming myself again, and then relayed her words.

"She says she's an emissary, sent to Earth to negotiate with humans."

Pollins scrutinised me, trying to tell if I was lying. He seemed satisfied.

"Thank you, Ofelia. Ask it what is to be negotiated."

Trix told me. I was surprised, but said it anyway.

"They don't want humans to leave Earth."

"Why not?"

"Because we will upset the balance of the universe." I crooked my eyebrow at Trix. Pollins would never buy that.

"Let's take a different approach," he said. "Why won't they leave?"

I repeated Trix's reply.

"Because they are our guardians. They are to contain us."

"Contain us?" he said, a dangerous inflection in his voice. "What does that mean?"

"It means we shouldn't contaminate the worlds beyond Earth."

He threw his hands up in frustration. "What gives you aliens that right?"

"Billions of years of evolution, and a mandate from the Alliance of Galaxies, Sector 5,201," I translated.

"Billions of years of... are you calling me dense?"

"We are not yet fully evolved." I couldn't help smirking at the rage clouding the Prime Minister's face.

"You're making this up," he growled. "It's a joke. You can't communicate with this thing."

"Trix just wants to go home. She's been very patient, but she says she can't wait any longer. She has to return to her ship."

He tapped his finger on his thigh, reached a decision, and waved to his men.

"That's enough for today. Lock them up."

"I don't think you're hearing her," I said, stepping forward. "She will not tolerate being held prisoner anymore."

I glanced at Trix, and she inclined her head so that only I would notice.

"Men!" Pollins said, taking a hasty step backwards.

"And I won't tolerate it either," I said, springing forward at Trix's side.

"Careful!" the lead military grunt yelled to me. "Don't get too close."

I ignored him, shuffling until Trix and I stood side by side, facing the irritated Prime Minister, Figg, who was furious at my insolence, and the trigger-twitching military men.

"I mean it, Mr Pollins. Produce the cure, and my family, and we'll be on our way."

Pollins' face hardened, as if it would crack, but he held his anger in check. Would he call my bluff? First, I had to confirm my family was safe.

"Wait, we can give you what you want, Ofelia," Figg said.

Pollins' eyebrows twitched downwards for the briefest of seconds. He didn't like her revealing that little titbit.

Figg snapped her fingers, as if that would magically present the cure at our feet. Then she gave a greasy to the military grunt behind her, who stood to attention.

"There's a crate in the storage vault," Figg said. "Fetch it."

The military aide hesitated, glancing at his Prime Minister for permission. He gave it with the slightest of nods, looking sideways at Figg. I observed Pollins. A rage vein pulsed in his forehead, but he kept his expression neutral.

The man returned with a metre-wide slatted wooden box. He set it down at Figg's feet, glass clinking.

"Take it to her," Figg prompted, and the man picked the box up, shuffling towards us, flinching as if he expected Trix to death-ray him to cinders. He rested the box a couple of metres away and shifted the crate forward with the toe of his boot. He was afraid of Trix and his eyes trained on her as he retreated, not game to turn his back.

I glanced at the box—there was a finger-width gap in between each wooden slat. The vials were packed in cardboard boxes, and I couldn't see through. They had nailed the lid shut.

"Enough for your sister, and all your friends back home," Figg said, opening her arms in a magnanimous gesture. Pollins forced a smile I'd seen on television many times before, right when his political opponents had him back-tracking. He resented sharing the cure.

"Now my family," I demanded.

Figg nodded to a military man. He approached the window set into the chamber. He lifted the blinds, revealing a holding room. Inside, shaking and fearful, were my mother, Roland and Imogen!

I rushed to the window, emotion overcoming me, pressing my hands to the glass—my family did the same. Our palm prints met on the barrier that divided us. An overwhelming gush of relief passed through me—they looked unharmed. Scared to heck, but better dressed than they'd ever been, and safe.

"Are you okay?" I called out.

The room was soundproof, muffling their reply. My mother saw Trix and pointed, as if to warn me. I checked behind and gave a thumbs up to say it was okay, and then I lifted my shirt, revealing my scaly stomach. I pointed to my scales and then to Trix.

Mum flicked her glance from me to the alien. I don't know what it was—disgust? No, not for her own daughter. The fear left her eyes. A long-held question was answered. She understood. The alien wouldn't hurt me. She was part of me.

"So, Ofelia, will you help us?" Figg said.

I didn't want to tear myself away from this window. As I rested my forehead on the glass, my family hugged in close. But I had to confront Pollins and Figg. My hand lingered, imprinted with Imogen's on the other side. As I lifted my hand free, our palm prints remained, the swirls and loops of our skin indelible. Imogen still held me in a way. She was so, so frightened. Tears ran down her pale face mask, staining the paper with trails of wet navy blue.

"Yes." I turned to Figg. "I'll help you. But first, let my family go."

"Of course," she said, but she didn't give anyone any orders, and her attention was on me and Trix. My family didn't exist for Pollins or Figg, except as bargaining chips, a way to make me cooperate.

I had the cure at my feet, and my family by my side, but Figg still held the power. She commanded the Prime Minister, along with the men with guns. I was so close to achieving everything I'd ever wanted for my family and myself. It was my responsibility to bring an end to the wildfire of plague that had ravaged my family and my neighbourhood.

But I couldn't leave Trix.

Will you be okay? I thought.

"Yes, Ofelia, we will find a way."

I felt Trix's exhaustion as if it was my own, and so I shuffled back to stand beside her, reaching my hand to hers. It may be a goodbye. I might not bring her with us.

"Careful of that thing!" the lead military man yelled.

Trix lifted her cuffed wrists, the merest of movements. The military man raised his weapon in response.

"Don't hurt them!" Figg yelled, rushing forward and shooting off a tranq dart gun, hoping to surprise us.

Pop—pop.

One dart for each.

But before the sedating darts hit, I enacted my shield, which was just wide enough to capture Trix, too.

Behind my shield, time solidified into a solid stretch of suspension. Everyone else was stuck in the moment. My first instinct was to check on my family. Roland held my mother's shoulders, trying to find the courage for what came next. Mum's eyes squeezed shut, not wanting to watch her daughter injured. Imogen's eyes were wide open, capturing every second, saving every moment for later. Because later, I could be gone.

My reflection wavered in the glass, half mine, half Imogen's. Our faces melded as one, and for a moment my eyes were pure brown, Imogen's eyes settling in my face. I felt more human than I'd ever been. My mission was clear—keep the crate safe and free my family. Negotiations had broken down.

Figg had misjudged her attack. She had fired from our line of vision, so we had time to react. And she had launched missiles, which was the reason our shields could deploy.

Figg's fear had spilled over as she had thrown her weight forward, firing her dart. I caught her mid-air in our stopped time.

Trix brought her hands up—still handcuffed—and angled them into my shield. The metal frizzed with electric jolts. Trix leaned into the shield, so that the jolts fired up her very skin. Sparks of green and yellow fissioned to the side like fireworks. She was charging herself like a battery! She reached out a scaly fingertip and brushed my forearm, the jolt invigorating.

Trix pulled away, and her voice had renewed strength, echoing around my eardrum.

"Let's save your family," she said.

I couldn't argue with that, and even Trix mirrored my grin. I almost lost concentration and my shield wavered.

Ready? I thought.

"Always," Trix replied.

We let our shields drop, and I shifted to the side. Trix shuffled her shackled feet. The darts fell to the ground. Figg landed beside them, her face twisted with fear—first at Trix, then me. She hit her temple on the wall, shaking her head like a dog running into a glass door.

"Hey, stop that thing!" the military leader shouted, bringing his rifle up, pumping the trigger.

Trix's attention was on me, not the bullets. She didn't have time to react, so I threw up my shield first, catching her in the right flank. The poorly aimed bullets bit into the floor in front, tearing holes in the concrete. Only one bullet grazed the very bottom of my shield, where it met the floor.

The trajectory of the bullets worried me. They had just

missed the precious crate of cures, the line of bullets in the ground skirting close.

The other grunts were lifting their weapons to join their leader. I hadn't repelled automatic weapons before, let alone a whole gang of them. Could I do this—withstand their simultaneous fire? Something told me they had perfected their aim through many hours of training.

A moment of realisation hit me—that metallic smell. It wasn't rust; it was the stench of dried blood. Whose blood had they spilt here before mine? Was this Pollins' personal execution ground?

I faced the squadron's muzzles, aimed at my heart. Waited until Trix was ready, and dropped my shield, restarting time.

The automatic guns spat the second round of bullets in a blast of deafening sound.

This time, Trix and I enacted our simultaneous force fields. Time stopped. The only sound was my breathing, ragged and sharp in my chest.

Had my shield held? I didn't feel pain. That was a good sign. A quick check noted the bullets suspended, kissing the shield. But my force field was pale. It was my weakest attempt yet, since I'd first enacted it on purpose.

While my green shield protected me, I had time to observe Figg. Her expression was ecstatic, thinking of what this would do to her career. The Prime Minister's eyes were half open—I hoped he watched this experiment, because I might not withstand the next attack. He deserved to be haunted by whatever happened.

The military grunts locked into firing mode, training their sights, their actions as automatic and unthinking as their weapons.

I had to secure Imogen's cure. My best chance was to push my energy forward, to grab the box in my time-stop, and to contain it behind the shield. Otherwise, it was in danger of being shredded by the bullets aimed at Trix.

I swung my attention to our shields. Trix held the bullets at bay.

One of the round's silver bullet tips pierced through my shield. This was worrying. I stepped to the side in case I couldn't repel it. The third round of bullets were already in mid-air, on their way. We'd have to stagger the shield to capture them. This was some test we'd volunteered for.

My breathing slowed, catching less on the way out, and I concentrated energy and thought on the green force field, willing power into it. Feeling it as an extension of my arms, surging through my fingertips.

I took a step forward, closer to the box, inching my shield ahead. Would my reaction time cover both the bullets and the box?

We restarted time.

The second round bounced off. Before they fell, I advanced another step and clenched my jaw. We pushed our next shields up as the third round hit.

Time froze.

The third round caught to the front of our force fields. I had inched my way to just behind the box; my toe nudged the wood. I was almost there!

Beside me, Trix grunted with the effort of keeping her shield open. The heat of our shields burned my face.

Concentrating on the trajectory of the next volley of bullets, I shoved the energy forwards, towards the military men. I roared with one last push, with half a second between the bullets dropping, and the next time-stop. I leaped over the crate and ground my teeth as I threw up the next shield.

We've got this, I thought, and Trix suctioned her way forward, keeping her cuffed hands in front, to stand next to me, the crate between us. We started time, preparing for the next onslaught.

Just before I enacted my shield, Figg yelled above the noise and smell of exploding gunpowder.

"Stop!" she commanded.

I guess Figg wasn't so keen on being, literally, in the firing line. She inched further away to avoid being hit with shrapnel or a misfire.

I raised the shield again, while the reaction time of the grunts caught up. The last round was easy to repel, and as the bullets reached me, the soldiers were lowering their weapons, looking to Pollins for their next order.

My shield flickered at the edges, losing its solid state and shrinking my safe zone.

I flung the bullets back as my shield disappeared, and the shell casings clattered on the concrete floor.

"Get out of there, Figg!" Pollins yelled. His expression was frantic. I guess she was important to his plans, too.

Five military personnel sprang forward, trying to tackle Trix. She pushed protectively in front, using her strength to shove them off, swiping her handcuffed arms. One banged her neck with the butt of his rifle.

I felt Trix's injury, as if I was injured, too. She clapped both of his ears, stunning him. He dropped to the floor, shaking like a struck animal.

One down, four to go.

Just as I was thinking our job was easy, more military men poured into the room.

They swarmed from the connecting corridor, a dozen strong.

"Contain those two!" Pollins yelled. The control panel for the door blinked beside him.

An idea occurred to me. I stuffed a hand into my pocket,

searching for the rubber ball. Finding it, I yanked my arm back, aimed my throw.

The ball arced over the Prime Minister, towards the blinking panel.

Trix was busy with the tackling men trying to stop her with their weight.

A sharp pain shattered my forearm.

I hadn't seen the military man stab me with his knife.

The knife embedded into soft muscle in my forearm. This was more than a graze. The intense shock was instant. I couldn't think. My breath caught painfully.

The ball struck the panel. The light flashed red, and the door sluiced shut.

"Knocked for six!" Trix said, watching the ball, and not the furnace ignited in my forearm.

At least I'd locked the rest of the grunts outside. Pollins jabbed at the control panel, but he didn't have the code.

"I said don't hurt her!" Figg yelled, yanking the knife from my arm.

I cradled my wound, bringing away my hand thick with blood, then pressing down to staunch the trickling flow.

The new grunts panicked, not as well-trained as Pollins' personal guards. They fired more bullets, smashing the window separating me from my family. The line of bullets cracked the glass in a zagged splinter. Had any of the rounds busted through and hurt my family?

I glanced in Trix's time-stop to check on my family, grouped in the other corner closest to me. The window caved in the time-stop, like a cresting ocean wave.

Trix restarted time and the glass shattered, collapsing onto the floor, leaving a jagged frame in its place.

"Ofelia, watch out!" my mother yelled.

The box of cures was outside Trix's shield, right in the way!

Bullets shattered the box and everything in it. The box itself splintered, as if an axeman had taken to firewood. Yellow liquid oozed from it.

Imogen's destroyed cure trickled onto the concrete floor, staining it a dirty yellow. I sprang forward, breaking the wooden slats free, sorting through the broken glass and liquid.

The vials were destroyed.

CHAPTER 29

DROPLETS OF BLOOD trickled from my arm as I rushed to the window, helping my family climb through. Roland picked Imogen up and handed her to me, her body light as a toddler, rather than an eight-year-old. Then Roland clambered through, careful not to cut himself on the jagged glass framing the bottom of the window. Mum followed, and we group-hugged like passengers disembarking from a year-long cruise.

"Stop the attack!" Figg said. One grunt edged closer to me, his gun held at his side, ready to pounce. "Let's take a moment. Nobody else has to get hurt."

"You can take a moment." I grabbed the rifle from the nearby grunt. He hadn't thought of me as a threat. I tossed the gun to Mum. She caught it deftly, pointing it at Figg's head. Figg raised her hands in surrender.

"Everyone, just calm down," Pollins said as Mum flicked her sights at the Prime Minister.

The rubber ball dribbled towards me, kicked by an unsuspecting grunt. I retrieved it, shoving it deep into my pocket.

My stab wound twinged, and I grimaced. Roland took off his face mask and handed it to me. I wrapped it around my wound and Roland tied it off with the ear loops.

It seemed impossible that the contents of the shattered box of cures had survived. But maybe one had—I only needed one. I grabbed the splintered crate with my good hand, holding it under one arm as the yellow liquid ran down my arm and stained my jeans.

"If you wouldn't mind, Mum." I flicked my eyes at the door panel. She aimed and squeezed the trigger of her rifle, and the control panel burst into flames. Pollins flinched as if she had shot him. The unarmed door slid open. Mum trained her rifle on Pollins as my family shuffled outside, Trix squelching to join our group. We stood safely in the corridor.

"Don't follow us!" I commanded, as the grunts lowered their weapons.

Trix reached forward and yanked the sliding door shut, then crumpled it inwards with her fist. It wedged our attackers on the other side.

Nice one, Trix. I grinned.

Then our group of fugitives bolted.

I pushed Imogen in behind Roland and Mum, up front with the gun, and me and Trix followed, forming a rear guard. Imogen's face grew determined, no longer terrified. But I didn't want to run into any surprise personnel along the way. We were escaped convicts and they would treat us as such.

Mum studied Trix, but Imogen's entire face beamed at my friend. My family had to trust my judgement for my alien compadre.

We arrived at the first room. Trix kicked in the door, leaving a sludge-mark with her squidgy foot. We found a janitor's closet, complete with mop and bucket. I grabbed the plunger and threw it to Imogen, who grinned and held it by the rubber end, stabbing at the air. Now she had a weapon, too. Roland snapped the handle of the mop over his thigh and brandished the splintered, sharp end of an improvised spear.

The next room led to a high-ceilinged vault. There were rows of shelving, stretching too high to reach, stacked with crates just like the one I carried!

At least enough cures to save the city. Maybe Figg had made her breakthrough. Could she save us, after all?

I rattled the nearest crate, and glass tinkled, vials jangling against each other. Mum ran her finger over the lowest shelf. Roland glanced at Imogen, his eyes glistening with emotion.

I dumped my busted crate on the floor. We'd found an upgrade.

"We'll need to haul this out somehow," Mum said.

I tested the weight of the nearest heavy crate. Roland, Trix, Mum and I could carry one crate each, but we'd be compromised in a fight. We weren't out of danger yet.

Roland tugged at the wooden slats of the nearest box, but they held firm. The slats were nailed in place.

Muffled whispering approached the storage room. Soon they'd surround us, with one way in and out of the vault.

"We need to lie low for a bit," I said, leaving the boxes of cures, our party exiting the storage room before the grunts caught up.

Roland lurched ahead, busting doors open. We ducked into a connecting corridor to throw our pursuers off our scent, but it was a maze down here. I hoped someone kept track of the way back to the storeroom. The corridors snaked ahead, with window-panelled doors branching off. Most had a secure pad for entry.

We needed to return for the crates.

It seemed important to grab as many cures as we could. Yes, I wanted to save Imogen. But as much as it hurt, Figg was correct. This was bigger than me, or Imogen, or my family. This was our chance for change.

We motored so fast that we collided into a closed door at

the end of the shorter-than-expected corridor. A startled scientist in a lab coat turned from his blinking control panel, glancing through the porthole window for the source of impact.

Through the window, video footage played on the control panel—the screen flipped to an impossible view—a view from space. Mechanical arms were constructing something, attaching poles and securing rivets and putting larger-than-life model pieces together. They were building something massive. I realised that the small white dot was a man in a full space suit, complete with air-filled backpacks. The scale of the structure he was assembling was unprecedented.

What was Pollins building up there?

Back in our bunker, the scientist twisted to face us.

Imogen was flush up against the door, and I guess she panicked. She stuck the plunger's rubber end against the window, hoping to obscure Trix and the rest of our fugitive group.

"Sorry, wrong door!" She waited until Trix and my family had scooted out of sight. Then she broke the suction of the plunger and pulled it free. A residual ring of moisture remained on the window, and Imogen gave a cheery wave and backed out of sight.

The scientist stepped flush up to the porthole glass, scanning every direction. But he mustn't have seen us, because he shrugged and seated himself back at the blinking control panel, donning his headphones.

"Well done, Limpet!" I whispered, rubbing Imogen's shoulder. She looked as proud as if she'd taken on the whole bunker. Mum flicked her head to Imogen to scout out the hall ahead. Imogen was the stealthiest of us all, light on her feet, an innocent if caught. Who would fear a skinny kid?

We waited for her to return, and I breathed deeply to calm

my racing heart, remaining alert but focussed. This was a high-stakes game we played.

Imogen returned, lowering her voice, and we crowded in to hear better.

"Two guards back the way we came," she whispered. "Another two in the hall ahead. We could slip past in either direction—they are facing away from us—into the connecting hallway."

"Let's go then." I urged Trix to lead. My family was in the middle, and I took the rear position. We crept on, trying to be stealthy, but Trix's suction feet squelched.

A guard ahead inclined his ear to hear better. He turned and spotted our group, mid-step, trying to approach.

"What the hell is that?" his mate shrieked, pointing a shaking finger at Trix.

"That's my alien friend," I said, motioning to my family to keep moving. "If you let us pass, she won't disintegrate you both where you stand."

We advanced on the men, slowing our movements, as if passing prey.

"Don't... don't hurt us," one man said, and the other followed his lead and held his gun in the air, letting us advance.

"Don't call this in, and we'll leave you be," I said.

The first man nodded, while the other struggled to shut his gaping mouth.

I guess Trix was still a secret and the whole bunker hadn't been briefed. Our party snuck into the hallway branching off, while the two men hid behind the dividing wall, whisper-arguing whether to call it in.

"We have to call it in. Do it."

We kept moving along the hall.

Trix's sludge trail was as obvious as a road sign to the capital, and I heard those four sets of boots behind closing in. I grabbed Imogen's hand and dragged us through a doorway, hoping the rest of my gang would follow. We could hide out until our pursuers left.

The room featured open cubicles. Facing each cubicle were rows of silhouetted people drawn onto paper targets. Many rounds had pock-marked the wall behind, where the bullets had bitten.

We'd walked into a firing range.

CHAPTER 30

Two MILITARY PERSONNEL stood poised at the far end of the range, facing the targets. They donned bright yellow protection earmuffs, as if from a construction yard.

The familiar smell of iron-rusted, old blood filled my nostrils. This firing range wasn't just for practice, either.

The two men at the range drew their handguns to begin their session. They hadn't heard us enter because of the earmuffs. Little explosive puffs shot from the barrels of their handguns, puncturing the paper targets at the end. Their aim was impeccable, all head shots between the eyes. They emptied their clips and paused to reload.

I leaped over the barrier, continuing to the end of the range, my family and Trix following. We'd made a monumental mistake—they trapped us in the room. I placed a finger over my lips. Our pursuers may run past.

Nope, our firing range buddies had noticed us.

"In here!" one of them yelled, nudging his buddy. They whipped off their ear protection. "Stay where you are!"

Four military men flocked into the room, leading with drawn weapons. They trained their sights on Trix, yelling for her to stop.

"Drop the alien. Don't let it get away!"

I halted in front of one of the paper targets hanging from the ceiling. The two men already in the range struggled to reload their clips.

"When I say, run to the door!" I grunted, as the two hand-guns shot a round towards us.

Trix and I were ready. We enacted the shields, keeping my family within each flank of our curved barriers. My family checked out the frozen scene in front of them, Roland whistling through his teeth.

"Woah..." Imogen's awe broke my concentration.

Our shields also caught my family in our time-stop. They marvelled at the force field, and the suspended men, and the half-exploded rounds heading our way.

"Wait, you're doing this?" Mum asked, wonder softening her face.

"Yep," I said, taking a small bow, my eyes still fixed on the shield. Imogen giggled.

"Unbelievable...." Roland marvelled, stepping back from the heat of the shield.

Imogen joined my side, her eyes glowing in the electric jolts dancing along the surface like green and yellow fish, her own light show.

"We have to move," I said. "Keep behind the shield."

Trix and I covered us as the men fired off their weapons. My family headed for the door. I moved with them, protecting them on each side. We encountered four men by the door.

"Stop here," I yelled, and we bunched together in front of the paper target closest to the door. I concentrated on the shield, which matched Trix's, holding time open, freezing the moment as long as I could.

I inched forward, moving the shield, until the guns poked through, along with our attacker's hands. Their bodies and minds froze in time, but the guns poked onto our side. My theory was, if they didn't have consciousness in our version of stopped time, they couldn't fire the guns. If I wasn't right, we were exposed, being fired on point-blank.

I hesitated, waiting for their hands to move, but their triggers had already fired.

"Would you relieve the men of their weapons?" I asked my parents.

Mum and Roland pulled the guns free, disarming the men, stacking the rifles back behind the force field to our rear. I moved us forward, away from the men.

"Ready, gang?" I asked, to focussed nods. I let a puff of breath escape as Trix and I reacted as the already-fired bullets caught up.

Then the men glanced at their empty hands—relieved of their weapons—and panicked as they noticed the guns stacked at our feet. Roland picked up a rifle, aiming it at our attackers. Mum tossed hers aside and picked up an upgrade—a semi-automatic weapon. Imogen reached for her own rifle but Mum shook her head.

The men had shredded the paper targets, except for the one behind us. It was still intact, hanging comically by the tip of its head. I found that funny, and a giggling fit overtook me.

"You missed, fellas," I said.

They raised their hands in surrender as my family trained their own weapons back at them. We exited the room. The men scurried to the weapons pile to re-arm.

We slipped on ahead, twisting through the corridors as the men followed at a discreet distance.

They argued as they followed.

"Who knows what that thing can do?"

"Let's just wait for backup," one said, peering as my family, Trix and I kept going.

We arrived at a disused, dim area, wondering if we'd backed ourselves into another corner.

Loud footsteps approached—one from either side of us.

Two squadrons, dozens strong.

Backup had arrived. The bolstered men from the firing range advanced and took aim at our backs.

I glanced at my family for answers, but their fearful expressions weren't helping. The left and right hand squadrons approached our corridor.

Roland brandished his acquired rifle in one hand, his mop handle spear in the other. Imogen waved her plunger. Mum shifted the safety of her own gun off with her thumb.

Stay there, I commanded Trix, and I waded to be the forward guard for my family.

We stood in the intersection of connecting corridors, in a cross shape. My family, Trix and I were trapped in the middle as the sound approached from either side.

Two panicked squadrons marched into view. They raised their weapons and screamed at us to get on the ground. At least this bunch didn't shoot first and confirm targets afterwards.

Roland brought his arm back and heaved his whole body into stabbing the nearest soldier with his wooden spear. The tip of the spear crumbled against the man's shoulder armour, as ineffective as mashing wet paper onto a rock. Roland observed the shattered spear, stuck in a moment of panic. Then he launched the spear like a javelin, as a diversion tactic.

The spooked firing range contingent ducked, unsure of the origins of the missile.

As the mop handle clattered to the floor, the squadrons yelled commands, regrouping.

Roland misfired in panic, leaving a couple of holes in the wall.

Mum squeezed her trigger, and the squadron ducked.

The grunt with the splattered spear on his armour punched Roland's arm with the flat of his hand, and Roland screamed in pain and dropped to one knee.

"Hey, leave my dad alone!" I yelled. The grunt smirked as another grabbed a fistful of my mother's hair.

"Lay on the floor, now!" a commanding officer yelled, stepping forward.

I launched myself at the officer attacking Mum, pummelling his face.

The grunts raised their weapons.

"Get off, you big bullies!" Imogen pleaded as the first grunt kicked the heel of his boot into Roland's Achilles. Roland fell to the floor, clutching his leg.

The man holding my mother's hair banged the side of her head on the ground. She stopped struggling. The man rolled away after I punched him. Roland struck the man on his chest armour and then grabbed his little finger in pain. The man ignored Roland and stomped on my mother's back with his thick soles. I leaped onto him and he slapped the side of my head for my trouble. He twisted to grab Imogen in a headlock, and Imogen struggled for breath. I shook my head to dislodge the pain and pummelled my fists on the man attacking Imogen. Roland moved to help, but a second man punched him in the face, and he stepped back, stunned.

The two squadrons took their aim at Trix. We stood in the crossfire.

"Quick, together," I said, and Trix and I stood back-to-back, charging each other.

We positioned ourselves at a diagonal to the three attacking sides. I stood directly in the line of fire from the left and rear. Trix also had the rear guard, and the second squadron to our right.

The man close to me threw a punch directed at my head.

Before it landed, one man with a sniper rifle fired at Trix, aiming to miss his own men.

"Wrong move, buddy." I swivelled and helped Trix repel the attack.

The man's punch connected with my shield. The time-stop captured the impact as his hand bones shattered.

I caught three men behind our shield, forcing close combat.

"A little help, Trix?" I asked.

My alien friend lowered her head in concentration and slammed both hands onto the arm holding Imogen in a head-lock. The man released his hold. Trix grabbed him by the ankle and flung him clear out into the rear hallway. As his body hit the floor, he bowled over three soldiers.

Another man dug his boot into my mother's back. Trix wiped off his satisfied smirk with the flat of her hand. There was a cracking sound as he landed on his back.

Roland's attacker was trapped half through the shield—his arms and torso were on our side, while his legs were on the other, immobilised in our time-stop. He clawed at Imogen, who squealed in panic. He had her by the knee in a crushing grip. Imogen fell to the ground and kicked out with her other foot, connecting with his eye socket. He loosened his grip, and I shuffled us back until the shield had him on the other side. He couldn't use his frozen legs, and so lay on his stomach, clawing the air.

"Are you okay?" I asked Imogen. Her eyes were wide, but she nodded a brave 'yes'. She stood up and rubbed at her knee with her hands, limping.

My arm stung, and a drop of blood oozed from the gash through the improvised mask-bandage. The droplet smacked the floor in the otherwise frozen sound. I slowed my breathing, inviting a more solid state to the shield. The squadron on the other side curled their lips in battle cries, fists pumped, guns trained.

"Ofelia, there are too many," Trix said.

I glanced through the shield, to the warped firing range men who were ready to 'stacks-on' my family and a 7-foot alien. Checking to the right, I realised that the squadron approaching from that angle were battle-hardened soldiers, too. A different experience to the two green grunts we'd passed before, emboldened by reinforcements. Both squadrons were used to aggressive domination.

"I've got an idea," I said, waving my family and Trix to our left. We were bullet fodder in this intersection, but if we slipped into the north corridor...

"Slowly," I said, grinding my teeth with the effort of keeping the shield open. I shuffled a tiny footstep at a time, moving sideways like a crab holding a boulder many times my size. Sweat formed on my forehead from the heat of my shield. I brought up my hands to concentrate my effort.

My family followed each strenuous step. We moved into the north corridor, away from both frozen scrums poised to tackle each other.

I let the force field drop.

The man who had punched my shield roared with pain at his broken fist.

As predicted, one squadron attacked the other, without their prey in the middle. One fired and struck another in the leg, slumping to the floor. A bullet whizzed past another's ear, and he ducked, too. Then the squadrons collided like opposing football teams tackling each other. They trapped the firing squad contingent in the ruckus. Confusion broke out.

We continued along the corridor, leaving the shouting soldiers to gather themselves. Roland and Imogen limped and Mum held her thumb to a gash in her forehead, where it had struck the floor. Trix sloped slower than her usual laboured gait.

I risked looking back, and one grunt slipped on Trix's wet sludge, his boot squeaking on the floor.

We kept going, the shouts and running soldiers pursuing us. Eventually, we would exhaust the places to run.

Fatigue slowed me and Trix down. The squadrons were regrouping behind us, one voice dominating the confusion, taking control.

"Bravo Company, follow the sludge. Alpha Company, form a rear guard. Careful, men, keep my pace. Let's go!"

We were outnumbered, and running out of luck. Our energy would soon give out. We pushed up a sloping area and found a dead-end mail room.

Now we were cornered by the office and the pursuing squadron. Could we hide in the mailroom? It contained several desks with papers in manila folders, and further back, scattered like abandoned go-karts, was a collection of office trolleys. A thrill of excitement struck my tummy as I planned our next move.

"It might not work," Trix said, sensing my thoughts.

"Just like bowling balls," I said, grinning at Trix.

I grabbed onto the nearest trolley handle, put my feet on the bottom rung and swooshed on down the hall, like it was a scooter. The cart handled poorly, and I jumped free before skidding into the wall. The cart spun to one side, easing to a stop to face me.

Mum frowned, but didn't criticise.

"Grab these," I said, pushing an empty trolley towards Mum and Roland and grabbing a third. I waved to Imogen. "Here, hop on."

Imogen folded into the bottom of Mum's cart, leaning her back against the handle. She winced as she settled her sore knee. Trix clambered onto my trolley, and we stacked the rifles into the bottom of Roland's ride.

I lined up my cart in front—Trix was heavy, but her weight stabilised the cart. We'd have to protect with our shields facing the soldiers.

"Ready?" I asked as we aimed the trolleys sloping down the hallway, back towards the pursuing squadrons. The trolleys were wonky and difficult to aim, but that made us unpredictable targets.

"Go!" I commanded. We pushed the trolleys forward, resting our feet at the base so we swooshed on towards the approaching squadrons.

The soldiers rounded the corner, weapons drawn.

The wheels jolted beneath us, skidding on the slope, as one soldier pumped off a round.

Trix fired off her first shield in response. It reached from floor to ceiling and was almost as wide as the corridor. Our carts kept going while Trix retained her shield, and my forward cart jumped and clipped the shin of the first soldier. He was knocked aside like a newspaper. Another soldier was flung into the air, about to land on his friend standing behind. A splatter of blood sprayed on the wall as our cart dislodged another soldier. The remaining soldiers were further back, and we scattered them on our way through.

Trix and I hurtled at speed, bowling a wonky line straight through the frozen soldiers, with Roland and Mum's carts riding our slipstream. We dislodged men and pushed them to the side with Trix's force field. Toppled like bowling pins in an alley.

We made it through! My cart sluiced a clean line for us, but Roland's wasn't as weighted, and he struggled to slow his trolley before it capsized. But we cleared the squadrons and the rear guard. Roland kicked a time-stopped guard out of the way while I slowed our cart by skidding both boots on the floor. Mum had the best-handling cart and ground to a halt beside me, with Imogen beaming with the thrill of the ride.

Once we gathered, Trix stopped her shield and climbed out of the cart. But the effort had consumed her energy. She could hardly stand, let alone create more shields.

We rumbled the carts back towards the storeroom. Roland limped on his injured leg, and Imogen's knee still smarted, so she rode on the trolley. A spatter of blood wet Mum's hairline as she held a protective arm around Imogen.

"We're almost there," Imogen said, her face lit with fever. A blue-black droplet of plague sweat oozed from her temple, reminding me what was at stake.

There was no more time. Could we survive?

Radio chatter erupted to our left—only metres away— echoing in the maze of corridors. We halted wheeling the trolleys, and I put a finger to my lips. Confused arguing wafted in the background—call signs and commands and project code names. None of it made much sense, but the reply held a panicked tone.

"All of them!" the voice crackled. "They took all of our weapons! Consider them very dangerous. And very much at large!"

We couldn't move discreetly. The trolley wheels squeaked, and we had to make it to the storeroom.

"Over here, I've found them!" the radio owner shouted, as he rounded our corner.

Trix hung back, waving us ahead. She stood as tall as she could, waving her hands in the air and baring her toothless grin.

"Woah! I'm outta here!" The radio owner scuttled away.

"This way," Trix said, heading to the front of our group.

We had looped back up with one of Trix's earlier snail trails. We might just pull this off. Trix led the way, and our bruised and bloodied family followed. But the grunts approached.

"Don't fire, we do this bar-room style," the leader of the squadron said, turning his rifle in his hands and leading with the hardened buttstock. "Fists ready."

One man leaped forward, grabbing Imogen's dress before grappling onto Roland's back. The man threw Roland at the wall, but Roland tightened a grip around his neck. Another grabbed Imogen's arm, and she struggled, but he wouldn't let go. Mum trained her gun on him.

"You're not taking my daughter," she said, then fired the bullet into the soft part of his calf. He cried out and grabbed his leg. Another clawed at Mum. She thwacked him with the butt of her rifle until he let go. The man closest to me thrust with his forearm, catching me in the teeth. For a moment my mouth was numb, and I tasted blood. I realised I'd fallen over, and scooted backwards on my bum as the man advanced. He reached up and struck me again—this time I brought my arm up to protect my face. But his blow landed on my stab wound, opening it further. I grabbed it in pain.

Another man picked Imogen up and flung her in a fireman's carry over his shoulder. That was too much. I roared with sudden energy and grasped his arm. He let go of Imogen, who scurried behind Mum's defiant bulk. The man landed a heavy blow across my cheek. The side of my face flushed into tear-jerking pain.

Trix was in my head again.

"Found it," she said.

The storage room door was ajar, the stacked shelving visible from the corridor.

Mum, Imogen and I inched towards the storeroom and slipped inside. Trix followed, barricading the door with her powerful bulk, but Roland was still outside. He didn't make it.

"Help him," I said to Trix.

She cracked the door, and Roland wrenched himself through the gap. First his arm, then one side of his chest. His shirt tore on a nail in the doorjamb as he reached through. The grunts pummelled and Roland yelled in frustration and pain. I grabbed his arm and yanked, and Trix grunted as she held the door a fraction wider. Roland threw the soldiers off him, his arm slick with blood, and landed in the storeroom. He wiped blood from his eyes with the front of his torn shirt. I hoped it was someone else's blood.

"Are you okay?" I asked, and Mum bent to his broken form on the floor. But he waved us away.

"I think I scared them off!" he joked, regaining his breath.

We regrouped in the storage room, the cures within sight. My forearm throbbed as if my bones and muscles were trying to escape my skin. My face stung.

We'd only delayed the danger zone. We'd have to overcome both squadrons to leave the storage room.

Trix barricaded the door behind us. The grunts bashed the door with their fists. Boots shuffled and then they took turns firing bullets at the door. The bullets didn't penetrate the reinforced steel, but round dents pocked the door each time. They fired at the dents, and one bullet shot through as the men cheered.

"Here—use the trolleys," I said, and we jammed the trolleys together to wedge the door shut. Trix stepped back, out of energy, unable to enact her shield at the bullets coming through the door. We ducked as fresh light filtered through each new bullet hole. Soon the door would be a colander, more holes than steel.

I'd backed us into another corner. There was no way out.

We checked our wounds—Imogen's red knee swelled, probably sprained. She sat in the trolley, her knee stretched out so it didn't hurt so much. Mum took off her cardigan and wrapped it around her head to stop the bleeding from her head wound. Roland wiped the blood clean. The broken pinkie of his right hand was bent at an unnatural angle. His Achilles smarted, going by his limp. I examined my forearm, which oozed blood. I tightened the bandage until it seeped less.

If we stood to one side, we were safe from the bullets. But, with enough ammunition, they would reduce the door to holey cheese. And Trix was out of energy. I didn't feel so good myself, and I needed my alien friend. I couldn't do this alone.

Our attention turned to the shelves.

Roland pulled cure crates from the shelves, stacking them away from the door. I grunted as my stab wound smarted under the weight of a crate as I guided it to the floor. The softly tinkling glass of the vials inside was the sweetest sound—a healing balm. But we couldn't escape this storeroom. The facility was well protected. Our escape with the cure was an as-yet unformulated plan in my head.

The soldiers' voices grew more aggressive as their efforts failed to draw us out. But Trix was so tired, I felt her weakened state, willing it not to overcome me, too.

The nearest crate had a busted slat, and I broke it apart. I squeezed my hand through, massaging the cardboard boxes beneath, ripping one apart. And from inside the crate, I pulled one test tube free, one vial of yellow liquid. Maybe I couldn't save us all. Maybe I just had to save Imogen. I slipped a few test tubes into my jeans pocket.

The bullets ceased firing, replaced by scuffing at the door. Then, a familiar voice.

"Ofelia, it's over!" Pollins yelled.

One grunt kicked the door. It collapsed, the bullet holes meeting like a connect-the-dots picture.

Pollins' nostrils flared like a spent racehorse, flanked by the two military squadrons. Mum pulled her rifle to aim at Pollins' head, and Roland covered the grunts amassing at the door behind them. Figg hovered behind the men, trying to push her way through.

"Careful!" she said, her voice wavering.

Just as I was thinking of our final stand-off, black-uniformed men stepped from behind the last row of shelving in the storeroom, pushing handguns into the soft part of our backs. They'd been hiding back there, waiting for the moment to surround us.

How could I have been stupid enough to walk straight into Pollins' trap?

My arm smarted as Figg inched into the storeroom, the grunts covering every angle in either direction. Red dots danced on our torsos, and this time, our faces. I flinched as one of the targeting lights blinded my eye, blinking away the residual red-haloed circles that remained.

"Now you will cooperate," Figg pleaded. "It's bigger than just you, than just your family."

"You leave my daughter alone," Mum said, clicking the safety off her gun and pointing it at Figg. "Or I'll protect her to my last breath."

I smiled reassurance at Imogen, shaking my head at my parents. I had to try, even if I failed, without Trix's help.

"Mum," I said, looking at her earnestly. "Shoot me."

"What?"

My eyes flicked to the gun. I wish she could hear my thoughts at this moment. I would tell her I could protect us, that we weren't dying today. She had to shoot me so that I could enact my shield.

How could I make her understand? I guessed she would never fire a gun at her own daughter. Not until she understood what I was doing.

336

I winked at Imogen, edging closer to Trix, so that we stood a metre apart, back-to-back. I faced the door, and Trix faced the men behind the stacks. Imogen, Roland and Mum stood between the two of us.

"Shoot me," I whispered to Mum. She still didn't get it. Imogen was close enough to grab her gun and pull the trigger. Trix moved, and a panicked soldier reacted. Figg leaped towards him, trying to wrestle the gun from his grip, but in the confusion, he fired.

BLAM!

The sound came before the bullet. Had my reaction time been fast enough?

But then I realised the bullet hadn't come for me. It was heading towards Imogen! The soldier had misfired on my sister. Instinct took over. I leaped into the air. There was no time for my shield. I was too panicked to concentrate on enacting my powers.

The bullet meant for Imogen rocketed towards her. I threw my body forward, focussing only on the missile.

I took the bullet meant for my sister.

It punctured my side, below my ribcage. My very breath caught fire with pain. Blood seeped through my jacket; the stain bloomed over my printed t-shirt, seeping in a pattern like two fists.

My eyes closed against the wrenching pain as I slumped against the nearest rack.

With a last push, I swung to my sister. In case I didn't make it, I outstretched the thumb of one hand at my side, signalling Imogen—it was every kid for themselves.

CHAPTER 31

My side was aflame, aching with intense pain. How could I concentrate now? The blood was dark. I felt as if sharp, rotating blades shredded my inner organs. The sensation pulled at my skin as my body scales formed over the wound, but sprang back, hampered by the bullet stuck deep in my side.

Mum ran to me, pressing her hand to the wound to staunch the blood.

Cold nestled over me, an icy veil draped across my scalp, then covering my body. My life-force drained out, pooling with the blood puddle on the floor. The thick blood oozed from below my ribcage.

I'd depleted my energy on the shields, and the shrapnel had wedged too deep for me to heal myself. As I tried to sit up, my head felt light, as if I floated upwards.

"Come on, Ofelia," Trix said.

The corners of her mouth-slit turned up in her attempt at a smile. She held out her hand. I grabbed her pointed, slender fingers, her skin coarse and slippery at the same time.

Her energy jolted through my fingertips, into my arms, through my racing heart. The power surged through my body, reducing the pain. I concentrated on the energy funnelling into my wound.

It might be enough to heal me. Could I do this with Trix's help?

"I'm okay, Mum," I said.

"No, you're not. Stay still, honey." It had been a long time since she'd called me that. She placed her hand on my shoulder.

I shrugged off her gesture and left a bloodied, smudged palm-print on a crate on the shelf beside me as I pushed myself to standing, crouching around my injury. The pain was too stark. I couldn't stand up straight, so I bent around my wound. I had to do this.

"Together, are you ready?" Trix asked.

I stepped beside her, panting, doubled over. I am bigger than my pain.

The soldiers aimed their guns at us, waiting for Pollins' order.

Figg joined Pollins at the door, out of breath. Two military men approached, one with a long, sinister tube over one shoulder.

Wait—was that a rocket launcher? Surely they wouldn't launch that thing in here?

"They just might," Trix said, as the military men were downing their weapons, and the other men set the rocket launcher onto the floor beside Pollins. The grunts with hand-guns in our backs withdrew from the room.

"We tried to negotiate," Pollins said, his lips curled back. "Don't think you're not expendable. You were plan A, Ofelia, but we still have the mission to the aliens. You're too dangerous to keep alive. We do not negotiate with terrorists."

"You can't do this, please don't do this!" Figg pleaded, holding onto the Prime Minister's arm.

A grunt slipped the rocket into the tube. It fell snug into the hole with a slight sucking sound.

Automatic rifles were one thing. Could Trix and I repel a freakin' rocket? And while I was gravely injured? I couldn't concentrate with the pain searing through my side.

I drank in my family, possibly for the last time. Had I done my very best to protect them? Mum stood back and linked arms with Roland and Imogen. Her gaze landed on me, an apology. I knew she understood, that she loved me.

I checked my wound. My hand pulled away wet, as if I'd dipped it in red paint. These might be my last moments alive. And I'd failed my family—that would haunt my afterlife. But I was also calm. If this was how it ended, I was ready.

"Get behind me," I said. They knew this was it. But they did as instructed.

I turned to the men in front. The black rocket tube took all of my focus. The grunt aimed the barrel towards me and Trix. Figg turned away, not keen on seeing cannon fodder. Now she would have someone she cared about to grieve for, too. Trix's calm voice intoned inside my head, "Together."

Agreed, I thought, and took perhaps the last deep breath of my life.

The rocket made a 'sfft' sound as it fired.

It was fast and angry. My eyes blinked at the launch. I almost missed the moment.

"Now!" Trix grunted, and we pushed with every effort.

The heat washed over our shields as we forced them up—melding into one massive defence, fissioning and sparking as they joined. The shield stretched upwards in our time-stop, branching out from the point of impact of the rocket. Crackling as it grew, reaching the ceiling. The shield fanned out to touch the wall where my family stood, the shelves disappearing from view. The shield grew the thickest yet, about an arm-width wide.

"Concentrate," Trix commanded, and I cleared my mind of all thought, even clear of marvelling at our combined shield.

The pain in my side intensified.

Sweat dripped from my temple as I moved away from the point of impact. The rocket tip made a saucer-sized dent in the front of our shield, poised behind with the force of a speeding train. The impact point was dazzling to look at, blurring iridescent yellow at the edges.

Trix grunted, and I grabbed her hand, reaching out to the shield itself. I brushed our hands against the solid structure, drawing lines of deeper greens, catching the yellow sparks and making them solid. Once I had swept our palms over the formation in front of the rocket, I stood back. I linked my arm through Trix's.

This has to work, I thought.

"We cannot hold it longer. It will grow weak."

I nodded, glancing back at my family, who stood tucked into our time-stop. Their grim faces tried to convey bravery, but they were just as terrified as I was.

"You can do this, Ofelia," Imogen whispered.

The image of Demi's tombstone flashed through my mind. The graveyard wasn't in darkness. Green grass shot up beside the grey stones, softening their pallor. The sky was a brilliant, stark blue. A white dove brooded in the branches of an overhanging tree, its leaves touched by wind, carrying a tune of hope.

I reached into the depths of my mind, the essence of my heart, the strength of my love. It flowed into Imogen, into everything she was. This was my parting gift.

My gaze fell to my sister. If I could protect her, she wouldn't die today.

Reaching down to hug her, I winced at the searing sensation in my side, but I didn't care. Nothing mattered if this failed. We would discover what happened after a body left this Earth, exploded into flesh and bone.

"It's okay," I said. "Just stay close to me. They won't hurt you."

Did I believe my words? It would make it easier for everyone if that were true.

"I love you kids," Mum said.

"Love you too," Imogen and I said in unison.

Roland ruffled our hair. Imogen grabbed my arm, hugging as if she'd never let go.

"I've got you, Limpet," I said, nodding at Trix.

Trix and I restarted time, keeping the force of the explosion at bay.

The fire ran over the top of the shield, washing us with a furious energy that shattered the glass in the crates. Screams ensued—my family's, Figg, the military men, and Pollins. My howl added to the mix.

The shattering glass showered the room and everyone in it. The fireball of the rocket sucked into the shield itself, imploding rather than exploding. Turning the shield's solid green to red, sparking and flailing in the un-stopped time. Pollins and Figg studied the shield. Figg's face was lit with awe; Pollins averted his glance in fear.

Shock waves reverberated across the entire room, sending glass shards flying, shredding through the armed forces around us, flying at Figg and Pollins.

With a huge sucking sound, the explosion and fire and heat folded in on itself. Disappearing with the shield as it caved into nothingness. The energy wavered in its wake. And then time and space resumed its regular status.

Their armour protected the military men. Pollins cowered

behind the rocket launcher. Figg brought her hands down from protecting her face, the skin of her forearms lacerated with glass.

"Yeah, it hurts, doesn't it?" I yelled, clutching my wound. I'd opened it further with my last-ditch energy release. Dark blood seeped underneath my jacket. I slid to the floor, almost losing consciousness.

Pollins leaned in cautiously, surveying the scene. Figg picked glass shrapnel from her arms. The grunts lowered their weapons, none of them game to take on me and Trix.

The surrounding shelving leaned in and collapsed. Glass shards littered the ground as the thick yellow liquid oozed from each mangled crate. Nothing could have survived the force, the cure lost once more.

Mum and Roland crouched over me, closing in, hugging, crying. I felt weak, having pushed myself beyond my physical limits. The blood seeped into my jeans and the surrounding people floated, not real, wisps of solid forms. The light brightened, the shapes of the room obscured.

I closed my eyes.

CHAPTER 32

I LAY IN A HALF-SLEEP, cocooned by a haloed light. The white sheets were starchy and coarse and I shivered with cold, pulling the textured blanket closer. My head was groggy as my eyes flitted open. A disembodied face approached. I was too tired to keep my lids from closing, or respond to their question, only gleaned by the upwards inflection. The words themselves made little sense. I drifted in and out of awareness until the surrounding sounds became familiar—the crinkle of paper-covered shoes, machines pinging my heart rate, nurses gossiping at their station.

A cool sensation entered a vein in my arm, pushing my blood in an unfamiliar way.

I took a deep breath in, realising that a tube was slotted into both nostrils, pulling it free. My face wasn't as cold, my head clearer. Another nurse checked on me and this time I smiled back.

"Feeling better, sweetie?" she asked. She may have been the nurse at the research facility, but her concern was genuine.

"Where am I?" I asked.

"The hospital wing. I'll let the doctor fill you in."

I grimaced at the fire in my side. The nurse helped me

raise the bed and arrange the pillows behind me so I could sit. She checked the various machines I was hooked up to and left.

As I half-dozed, I observed the workings of the hospital—the staff moving back and forth; the orderlies pushing beds or wheelchairs, patients arriving and passing through. This was not a ward of permanence. I would leave soon too.

I poured myself water from a jug on the tray beside my bed. As I sipped, allowing myself to rest, Figg stepped around my curtain into view, and Pollins cut in front. He did something that annoyed me—he rested his hand on my shin, over the blankets, as if I was his buddy, or maybe his niece.

Figg pushed past and grabbed my hand, which surprised us both. I was too drowsy to complain, but I didn't return the squeeze. My feelings were too confused, my head too foggy to process anything.

"I'm so glad you're okay, Ofelia," Figg said. "How did you do that? It was spectacular—you neutralised rocket fire."

"I honestly don't know," I said.

"Must be the genes, hey?" Figg said wryly, pulling away.

"Must be," I replied.

There was mirth in Pollins' eyes. What kind of man would make jokes after his team had tried to exterminate an unarmed teenager and her family? They could have murdered me in the belly of his own personal firing range. Maybe he wouldn't be as useful as I'd hoped. Should he be leading the remaining alliance of countries?

"You're it—you're our weapon!" he said.

"I'm not a weapon, I'm a person," I said.

"Of course, Ofelia. You are a very special person indeed. You're the key that will save us all."

There was no harming me now. My power was too valuable.

"We need to understand how it works. You'll help us do that, won't you?"

"I have some demands," I said, swallowing around my dry mouth.

Pollins leaned back, removing his hand from my leg.

"Go on," he said.

"Imogen gets her cure, from your best doctor—other than Figg—and the best treatment available."

The Prime Minister leaned in, his face serious. "Ofelia, there is no cure."

"What?" I said, pushing the tray away and sitting up in bed.

"He's right," Figg added. "We were close with this batch. But we don't have it."

"I don't believe you," I said, but their expressions were confirmation. The PM's dipped eyebrows were earnest. Figg gazed at the floor, acknowledging her failure.

"Ofelia, I've done many questionable things," Figg said. "But I've never lied to you."

"That's why we need you and your alien friend here," Pollins added. "The aliens have the cure, and we need you to communicate with them. If we had the cure, don't you think we would have already manufactured it for the population?"

"Not even the Phoenix Compound?" I asked.

"How do you know about that?" Pollins asked.

"Didn't my DNA work?" I prodded, ignoring Pollins' question.

"We tried, but the testing failed." Figg said. "We had manufactured more of the Phoenix Compound to be ready, just in case. But the vaccine doesn't work."

"Were those the yellow vials?"

"Yes. But there were adverse effects in the initial testing phase."

"It's simply not safe," Pollins confirmed.

"More blood on your hands," I said in a flash of anger.

"I'm sorry, Ofelia," Figg said. "I know how badly you want to help Imogen."

There was no cure. I had been working towards an impossibility. I couldn't help Imogen any more than I could help Demi. They didn't need to lie, which meant I'd put myself and my family in danger for nothing. The urge to rage, to lash out, was strong. But my energy was spent, seeping from my pores, and I only cared about one thing now.

"I'm not done," I said. Pollins motioned for me to continue. "You'll shut down the research facility, and Figg's research. And release Maya and her family—they've done nothing wrong."

"Well, I agree, the amenity is long past its usefulness, now that we have... other avenues open to us. And, who is Maya?"

"You arrested her in the swanky—I mean, Cookham East," I said.

"If the family is discreet, I don't see a problem."

I hesitated, unsure of what my next move would be. It might be too much.

My concentration must have registered, because he asked, "There's another request?"

"Yes." I took in a breath. "Our family, and my friends' families—we have a place on that ark."

He steepled his fingers, playing for time. His lips pursed, considering.

"That's what you're building, right?" I asked. "An ark for us to leave Earth?"

"Schedules have been determined. It would be an adjustment."

"You're damn right it's an adjustment. That's what we want. No more Northies life."

He paused, rubbed his chin with his thumb. I worried I'd pushed him too far.

When he didn't reply, I leaned back, folding my arms and glaring at him. "It's non-negotiable."

Pollins smiled and put his hand back down on my shin, over the blanket. And this time, I felt the warmth on my leg, and he nodded. He said, "Absolutely, if you come work for me."

Could I work for someone like Pollins?

"What does that mean?" I asked. "No more tests, for starters."

"We need you to communicate with the alien to help with our mission. It's just talking, Ofelia, and then I'll meet all of your demands."

If it was just communicating Trix's thoughts, maybe it was worth it? Imogen could be better. And, when the time came, we could leave Earth and start afresh.

Isn't that what I wanted?

Pollins was untrustworthy, but I held the bargaining position. If he didn't honour his promises, I could go public. The experiments. The deaths. The fact that Trix was already here.

Before I could accept or decline his offer, my family burst into the room, squealing and crowding around my bed. Pollins and Figg made themselves scarce. I hardly noticed them leave as our family reunited.

We embraced, and I kept a brave face, even though the pain dialled up with each movement, especially hugging, but I didn't care if I ripped every one of my stitches loose. We held onto the moment. Mum smoothed my hair and said, "I'm sorry," over and over.

Roland eyed my bandage peeking out from the side of my hospital gown, concerned at the size of the sticking plaster.

When it seemed the natural time to pull away, I sat up in bed, with my family around, staring at me. I couldn't meet their eyes. It would hurt them to hear it. I didn't know how they'd react.

Dreading my next words, I blurted, "Demi—I couldn't—"

I sucked in a breath that pained my lungs. My body felt rigid, like it was brittle and I could shatter into tiny pieces.

"We figured as much," Mum said, and hurt filled Roland's expression. He turned away before composing himself.

"It was a long shot, love," he said, with sadness. He ruffled my hair, as he'd done in the shack.

I couldn't help it—I became a bawling mess and went in for a group hug—we were back together again.

"So, how did you do that?" Roland asked. "How did you create the—what is it, a force field?"

"I just do. You know, it's a reflex thing," I said.

"That's some talent," Mum said, drawing close to my bed and taking my hand in hers. She squeezed my fingers.

I no longer felt awkward, healing more than just my physical body. I had repaired my family.

"Is it a talent or a curse?" I asked.

Mum shook her head, admiration in her eyes. "You saved your family," she said. "That's as special as it gets."

———————————

My family, Trix, and two recruits accompanied us to the war room. They pushed me in the wheelchair. It was still a struggle to walk. We rode the elevators to the surface, emerging into sunlight at the top of the mountain, into a warmth we had forgotten. Trix spread her arms wide, catching every ray.

Two vehicles waited—a black sedan, and a fresh white van, in better nick than the one we'd arrived in.

The guards split—one moved to Trix, the other to me and my family.

Time to say goodbye to my kick-ass, 7-foot alien friend.

We'll see each other soon, I thought.

"Do not worry about me. I have lasted a long time on your Earth."

Not for too much longer.

"Ofelia, you are the most extraordinary human I have met."

I reached out a finger, and we sparked in the middle as my soft skin met her rough, pointed fingertips.

The recruit beside me cleared his throat. "Time to go, ma'am."

Did he just call me ma'am? I giggled, catching sight of Imogen. I removed my touch from Trix, leaving my friend to duck her head and fold into the back seat of the van. It drove down the mountain. We lost sight of it at the first bend.

Our driver held the back door of the sedan for Roland, Imogen and Mum, waiting until they settled. She held the passenger door open for me as I joined them. Our driver was a chatty lady dressed in black with yellow buttons—complete with a black official-looking cap.

The pain medication fogged my thoughts, so I couldn't follow the conversation. But I felt important at this moment. I snuck glances at my family, reclining and enjoying the luxury as we wound back down the mountain pass and to the road with the abandoned dwellings. I even forgot my motion sickness in my dozy state.

The homes had a hopeful glint in the daylight, friendly even. Even if our houses had broken windows, we would carry on. The desperation of my journey to the bunker seemed a lifetime ago.

Commercial buildings rose, then the industrial warehouses, and we passed through the metres-tall security gate, into the suburbs.

My family ogled large, uniform mansions, each with a

green yard. Our car turned deeper into the housing estate. We wound around smooth roads, snaking further up the hill.

The sedan slowed as it entered a cul-de-sac and approached the house highest on the hill, overlooking the rest of the estate. To my family's eyes, it was the ultimate luxury. The car eased up the driveway and stopped in front of the garage.

"Home, sweet home." The driver engaged the handbrake and held the door for us.

Imogen's eyes grew larger than if she'd found an all-you-can-eat buffet. Roland hadn't imagined this opulence. I got the feeling, however, that Mum had. She was happy, but underwhelmed.

The driver handed Mum the key, then touched the tip of her cap and drove away, the car's rear lights twinkling.

Mum unlocked the front door and Imogen shot around the open-plan kitchen, circling the island bench. She took a running dive at the lounge and bounced until a whooping fit overcame her. She removed the mask, and as I comforted her, a knock sounded on the front door. Our first visitor.

"Hello?" a lady in a white doctor's coat—who was not Figg —called. "I'm here to see Imogen."

Mum welcomed her and let her inside. The doctor smiled at Imogen and took a seat beside her on the couch.

"Let's see what we have here," she said, resting a stethoscope on Imogen's chest. She felt around, listening, placing the scope in different areas. She moved the scope to Imogen's back, asking her to breathe in and out. Imogen's breath caught, and she whooped, and the doctor listened. She had a stern but efficient manner.

The physician removed the scope from her ears and draped it around her neck.

"We can give her medication, which will help with the symptoms," she said. "She will be more comfortable."

Mum nodded, trying to keep the tears from her eyes. She smiled at me, mouthing, "Thank you."

The doctor could help Imogen, but it still wasn't a cure.

The doctor pulled a bottle of pills from her medical bag, handing it to Mum, and said, "Make sure she enjoys the fresh air, on warm days. And that she eats well."

"We've got that covered." Roland opened the fridge door. He swallowed, his mouth watering at the gleaming contents, lit by the little lights of heaven.

Mum shook her first pill from the bottle. Held a breath, and handed Imogen the pill and a glass of water. Imogen gulped the medicine.

"Good girl." The doctor squeezed Imogen's arm. "And how are you, Ofelia?"

"I'm fine, thanks."

"You have enough to keep you comfortable? Any questions?"

I shook my head.

She handed a business card to Mum. "Give my surgery a call anytime. No cost."

"Oh, thank you!" Mum gushed, holding the card like it was a million-Tins lottery prize.

She took a deep breath, and glanced over at Imogen, who watched a show on our new, massive flatscreen. The talking bear cartoon was far from the mandated news we were used to. Who knew that television could entertain?

Mum brushed a happy tear from her eye as she held the front door for the doctor to leave. We had a proper house, with more than we'd ever imagined.

"Who's hungry?" Mum moved to the kitchen, chuckling at our choruses of "Me!"

That night, a strange isolation filled me. I lay in a bed, far from the rest of my family. Which was absurd—we were under one roof, but I couldn't bear being apart. I missed the intimacy of our shack bedrolls lined up side by side.

I crept into Imogen's room and scooted into her bed, inhaling her floral-scented soap as we fell asleep. Her breathing rattled in and out of her chest, but it didn't catch as badly as it had yesterday. She didn't wake up fighting for breath; she slept right through. I'd never slept as soundly as I did that night either.

I woke to her warm body, easing out of bed so as not to wake her. Her hair was a mess against the pillow, her face relaxed. Her eyes moved beneath her lids and I wondered what she dreamt of. There were no limits to her future. We were far from Trash Mountain, from the desperation of Northies. We had bellies full of food and soft beds. And today, our new life began.

A snag had formed in my mind, a sliver of unease forming the browns and dirty blues of the shacks. The people stuck in our old life. It was momentary, but I couldn't shut it out. What made us worthy of this house? People were still suffering.

I left Imogen's bed and wandered into the living room. Mum slid something from the oven that smelt of sunshine mixed with honey and rainbows and a talking puppy.

She looked up. "The cookies have to cool."

It was so practiced, so expertly done. She hadn't baked cookies back home—we didn't even have an oven.

"You weren't from Northies, were you Mum?" I mumbled.

She busied herself resting the baking tray on the sink, glancing at my sombre face.

"No, sweetie," she said.

"So, why did you stay there?" I asked.

"It was our best chance."

My chest constricted, and I felt like blubbering, and wrapping my arms around her, never letting go. She'd given up a life out here, to keep us safe?

I was sorry for hating her before this had happened. Since the snatchers. I was so hurt that she let Demi go. Mum knew there was no chance of saving Demi, but she could keep the rest of her family safe.

She gave up this life for us.

She angled away from the stove, leaning into my hug. I breathed in the fabric softener in her shirt—a slight lemon scent —her warm body cradling mine. My bullet wound twinged, and I moved position.

"Thank you for looking out for us," I said. "It must have been hard."

"Less difficult than the alternative," she said.

Imogen joined us, winding in between our hug. I lay my head on Mum's shoulder as she moved the cookies on the plate.

And that was how I wanted to remember my entire teenage years. Hugging my sister and Mum while she held a plate of fresh-baked cookies. The best things wrapped into one.

I couldn't wipe that image of the Northies clean, but then I noticed something different about Imogen.

The film of sweat on her forehead glinted in a way it hadn't before—her skin was healthy and radiant. The bead of perspiration was clear, not plague-blue.

EPILOGUE

THE ORANGE SUN HUNG LOW, near the horizon, as the sky darkened with pinks that touched the roofs of suburbia.

Roland had dug a hole in the grass of our backyard. And sitting next to it, about to find a new home, was an oak sapling resting on the dirt clods surrounding its roots.

We'd thought hard about this memorial, for this last resting place for Demi. We wouldn't move her bones from Figg's altar of failure—there was no use in disturbing the graveyard of the long-dead. This way, Demi's memory would always be near.

Imogen stood beside me, her arm linked with mine. She held me steady, flinched when I moved, was a part of my grief. Mum had her arm over my other shoulder, holding both Imogen and I. And Roland held Mum.

Standing behind us, bowing their heads, were Maya, Sumati, her parents and grandmother. Our two families had grown close.

And next to them stood Mousie and Aze. Mouse Run had cut her hair short, razoring off the dreadlocked mass of hair that once doubled as a hat. Aze had no need for her eye patch here, shoved into her pocket. Aze's mum stood behind her, and

Mouse Run's grandmother—the one who had raised her since her mother died—sat on a lawn chair behind her.

Roland stepped towards the hole in the yard. His back was to the mourners. He turned to give a speech. He ran his eyes over the onlookers, landing last on our family, and then me.

My nerve gave way, gazing back at the man whose daughter I had lost. My nose congested, and I blinked away tears.

"None of you knew Demi as our family did," Roland said. "But thank you for being here. She would be proud to be surrounded by such love."

Roland gazed straight at me with this focussed, grateful expression. I lost it, and our family hugged each other, holding ourselves up with our grief, a pack of emotional beings, releasing the long-pent-up fear and anger.

Roland wiped his face with the back of his hand. He reached to the sapling, inviting our family to do the same. We lifted that new, green-shooted life, positioning it in the hole. Roland handed a small spade to me, and I packed the dirt until the sapling was snug in the earth.

I handed the spade to Imogen, and she patted down the top of the dirt. We stood back, observing our sister, our daughter, and our friend.

The van arrived later that afternoon, as the food at the wake lost its freshness. Kids gathered on our front porch while the adults were saying their farewells.

The driver, dressed in beige coveralls, emerged with an iScreen in hand. He approached us as we sat by the front door.

"Delivery for Imogen Stykes?" he said.

"That's me!" Imogen replied.

He held out the iScreen and Imogen giggled as she drew her wonky name.

The man unpacked things, setting them on the driveway. First, one purple bike, the seat already set to the height of Imogen's hip, with colourful streamers on the ends of the handlebars. Next, three taller bikes, in melding greens and yellows. All the bikes had training wheels attached to the rear wheels.

The driver handed Imogen a small card, smiled, and hopped back into his van, driving away.

Imogen's face was ecstatic as she opened the card.

"What does it say?" Mousie asked.

Imogen screwed up her face in concentration, but she hadn't been back to school yet, and she handed the card to me.

"It says, 'For you and your friends, to honour your sacrifice. Stay well, from Doctor Figg.'"

"What?" Aze said in anger.

"That traitor! We'll send them back!" Mousie countered.

But I watched Imogen's reaction, and her eyes landed sadly on the bike with the coloured streamers on the handlebars. The bike that was exactly her size. She could ride free in the suburban streets. My feelings about Figg were complicated—I wasn't ready to concede forgiveness—but I didn't hate her, either. I almost felt sorry for her. She was trying so darn hard to join our family.

"It's okay, Imogen. Let's try them out," I said, giving her a little push.

Her beam told me it was the right decision, and I shrugged at my friends, who didn't need a nudge to enjoy a little fun.

We grabbed our respective bikes and walked them to the bottom of the hill, where we could practise.

None of us had ridden bikes before, so it was slow progress, but after about an hour we had mastered them so we could ride down one flat section of pavement, and not wobble too badly. Our steering needed practice. We kept veering off the path, but we didn't care. We were being kids. For that hour, the weight of the world lifted clean off my shoulders. I giggled with my friends and was a happy almost-sixteen-year-old like any other suburbs kid.

The light faded, throwing the overhead sky into deep purple, and we walked our bikes back up the hill. Mousie's house was first, so she hugged us all and said her goodbyes, heading with her bike through a gate and into her backyard. Aze lived further up the hill, closer to our house, and she waved, placing her bike underneath the porch in case it rained. She disappeared inside, too.

Imogen and I kept on pacing up the hill to the very top. I opened the garage—we didn't have a car, so it was empty, apart from some shelving holding tools and a half-full paint bucket. I parked the bikes, closed the garage door, and entered the house. Imogen followed.

Mum was cooking something delectable—she called it a roast—and I let out a sigh. As I watched Imogen settle on the couch, I made a decision that worried the edges of my mind, that didn't give me complete peace.

There was no right answer, really.

I could either compromise my integrity and work for the enemy, or risk sending my family back to a life of poverty and ill-health. There was only one choice. This was bigger than my family. I thought of Aze, and Mousie, and their families too. Not to mention our new neighbours—Maya and her family. It wasn't enough just to save the ones I loved. I had the chance to help everyone, and that made my choice for me.

Sitting on the couch, I snuggled up to Imogen and said, "I'm keeping my promise."

I waited alone on the front step of our new house, away from the muffled voices inside. It felt too claustrophobic in there; I preferred the fresh air.

The door squeaked open, and Imogen emerged, grabbing the post on the porch and swinging her foot absent-mindedly.

"Do you have to go?" she asked.

I pulled her in for a hug, then reached into my pocket for the familiar object that had seen me through this entire ordeal.

"Here, have this," I said, holding out the prize rubber ball. I placed it into Imogen's hand, closing over her fingers. "This kept you in my thoughts. It will bring you luck."

Imogen eyed the ball, turning it in her palm. "But I don't need this to remember you," she said.

"It will help me, knowing you have it when I'm gone."

Imogen didn't reply. Her gaze fell to the ball. She nodded.

"If it will make you feel better." She tossed the ball up and caught it again, grinning at me.

"I'm so proud of you, Limpet." I reached out and hugged my little sister, her body stronger, her frame less bony, her return squeeze firmer.

If I could freeze this moment, everything had been worth it. We had made something of our lives, and we wouldn't die, not today.

A black sedan pulled up in the driveway, the headlights throwing harsh light onto the porch. The driver kept the engine running. Imogen and I squinted against the glare, then the lights dimmed. The driver emerged and packed my suitcase into the trunk. Trix sat in the back seat.

Mum and Roland noticed the headlights through the living room blinds. They joined us on the porch.

"Will you be okay?" Mum asked, and I nodded my reply.

"Don't let them push you around," Roland said, with a playful ruffling of my hair one last time.

I didn't want to go, but I couldn't stay. Time to honour my word.

"Look after Mum and Roland, okay?" I said to Imogen.

"I will."

"And finish all of your homework."

I was out of tears, and I didn't want them to worry. So I hugged them all, wincing as I lifted my arms and twinged my injury. The wound didn't hurt as badly as it had before, but there was a larger ache in my chest, and I was worried it would overcome me.

I broke off the hug and climbed into the back seat of the car, sitting next to Trix.

"I am sorry for Demi, Ofelia," Trix said, shifting to give me room to buckle my seat belt.

Me too, I thought, waving to my family as the car pulled out of the driveway. The homes slid by as we left the gated safety of the suburbs. The entrance snapped shut. Another door closed.

The scenery dropped away as we drove into the wastelands. I fought the motion sickness as we turned at a fresh intersection. The car bumped onto the badly maintained road, gravel crunching under the wheels.

Our new journey had begun.

Would you like to continue the adventure?

When survival means rebellion, even the quietest voice can spark a revolution.

They endured the plague. They escaped the labs.

But saving the world will cost Ofelia everything—including her future.

Rebel Conspiracy launches into a desperate space mission with Earth's last survivors. Can Ofelia trust her greatest enemy long enough to protect the ones she loves?

Read *Rebel Conspiracy*, Book 2 in The Kaseath Chronicles, today!

jackiemccarthy.com/books/rebel-conspiracy

Love The Kaseath Chronicles?

As a thank you for reading, I'd love to gift you a free prequel short story!

Maya's United Nations dives deeper into Maya's adventures before she met Ofelia (don't worry—no spoilers!).

You'll meet familiar faces and new ones, and I think you'll really enjoy the extra glimpse into their world. Plus, you'll get early updates on new releases, behind-the-scenes notes, and more.

Grab your FREE short story below:

jackiemccarthy.com/prequel

Enjoyed the book?

If you have a moment, I'd love for you to share your thoughts wherever you prefer to leave reviews.

Your feedback helps new readers find their next favourite story—and it means more to me than you know.

Thank you so much for being part of this journey!

ABOUT THE AUTHOR

Strong female characters and quirky, empowering tales.

Jackie is an award-winning author of Young Adult (YA) & New Adult (NA) fiction, with a speculative twist. If it's dystopian, futuristic or magical, she'll happily take you there. She stuffs as many strong female characters into her books as she possibly can, for your enjoyment.

Her novel "The Hybrid Cure," Book 1 in The Kaseath Chronicles, was runner-up for YA Science Fiction in the 2025 Incipere Awards.

Jackie has worked in publishing and the media for over 20 years, in both London and Sydney. Her debut novel, "The Ghost Mothers," is (very loosely) inspired by her time on "The Australian Women's Weekly Magazine," many moons ago.

Jackie's latest release, *Rebel Conspiracy*, is the rollicking second book in The Kaseath Chronicles, a YA dystopian science fiction series. If you like fierce heroines, powerful bonds of friendship, and unique galactic thrill rides, then you'll enjoy Jackie's high-stakes adventure.

If you would like to be notified of new books as they are released, you can join the readers' group at

jackiemccarthy.com/sign-up/

For more information about Jackie and her upcoming books, feel free to check out her website at jackiemccarthy.com.

Happy reading, and thanks for stopping by!

ALSO BY JACKIE MCCARTHY

Rebel Conspiracy

(The Kaseath Chronicles, Book 2)

jackiemccarthy.com/books/rebel-conspiracy

The Ghost Mothers

(Standalone Novel)

jackiemccarthy.com/books/the-ghost-mothers

Visit the website for all current and upcoming titles at:

jackiemccarthy.com/books

Ebook ISBN: 978-0-6486942-3-6
Paperback ISBN: 978-0-6486942-2-9
Hardcover ISBN: 978-0-6486942-5-0